# DEADLY SECRETS ON MACKINAC ISLAND

A ROMANTIC SUSPENSE NOVEL

CARA PUTMAN

*To my kids—praying you allow God to direct you to the future and the ones He has for you.*

*The greatest adventure is seeking Him and living for Him.*

# ACKNOWLEDGMENTS

Mackinac Island is a wonderful place our family loves to visit.

Several years ago, I had an idea to write a romance mixed with mystery and suspense that would be set on the island. When we returned, my husband went to Fort Mackinac while I went to the police department to talk to the police chief. He spent time answering all of my questions about what would happen if someone was murdered on the island without offering to let me spend time in their cell, for which I will always be grateful.

While writing the book, I also realized that I needed to understand how a gunshot wound would be handled on Mackinac Island. Dr. Jennifer Shockley very patiently answered my questions and did all she could to make sure I understood what would occur on the island and at a mainland hospital. Many thanks to these gracious people. Any mistakes are mine.

Thank you to my agent who let me know there was an opportunity to write a book for Barbour, and Rebecca Germany, who read my proposal and gave me a chance to write this story.

I was also blessed to have several friends read the book and help me. Initially, Colleen Coble, Robin Caroll, and Sabrina

Butcher helped me brainstorm the idea and flesh out a plot. Then as I wrote, Sue Lyzenga read the book not once but three times, while Sabrina and Casey Herringshaw gave input on the manuscript. Lastly, thanks to my stellar editor, April Frazier, who helped me fix the details and make the plot work.

I also want to thank my husband and kids who make Mackinac Island such a great place to escape. I love walking the island, exploring the trails, and riding bikes around the island with you. I love you!

1

D*on't do it. Don't do it. Don't do it.*

The refrain beat a steady tempo through Alanna Stone's mind as she dragged up the gangplank to the ferry where it rocked in the early morning light at the St. Ignace dock. She avoided gazing to her right in the direction of Mackinac Island. A place of beauty and peace to many, it symbolized all the harshness that could shimmer beneath the surface in a small town. She'd sworn never to return and had honored that vow for eleven years.

Now? Now she abandoned her firmly held avoidance to help her parents. A wave rocked the boat, and she bobbled as she struggled to stay steady on more than her feet.

A man in the green polo that bore the Arnold Transport Company logo steadied her with a smile. "You'll find your sea legs in no time."

"Good thing, since the trip's so short."

He laughed and nodded. "About fifteen minutes."

How could she tell him she wished it lasted fifteen months or years? That time would freeze, and she'd stay on this side of the lake?

Seagulls cawed as they took to the air and swooped around the boat.

Fifteen minutes. That's all it took to start a new life.

Diesel fumes rolled around her as the ferry's engines roared into gear. With a grinding stop and jerk, the boat eased away from the dock and powered across the lake. Alanna sucked in a deep breath then coughed as fumes settled in her lungs. She clenched her jaw and pivoted until she faced east as the boat pushed through the water toward the sun. She needed to face her new reality and the hidden embarrassment. All represented by one tiny spot on the map.

Mackinac Island.

In the morning light, it looked like an emerald emerging from the lake with the Victorian cottages and Grand Hotel popping out like embellishments against the forest backdrop.

The wind blew across Alanna's face, misting it with a fine spray as it tangled her hair. The strands whipped around her neck, but she let the wind do its worst. Even then, it couldn't reflect the chaos churning inside her. Tension tightened her body again. It had been her constant companion during the Menendez murder trial. The case had faded from the front page of the newspapers, and the reporters had finally abandoned their posts at her home and the office. Not the first time media had hounded her, but at least this time it involved a client rather than her brother. She'd thought she had shed the constant headache, but now it roared back to full strength in her temples.

Going home did that to her.

The catamaran shifted beneath her, the engines grinding.

When Mother had called begging for help after Daddy's stroke, Alanna had two choices: return to the island to keep her parents' art shop open or let their lives' work close.

Maybe things had changed in the time she'd been away. Memories shortened. Ugly innuendos against her brother faded.

If only the island could transform into an oasis for her. One she needed after the lengthy, brutal civil trial tied to a murder between feuding neighbors. She still felt the fatigue from a hard-fought victory, one that consumed almost as many of her nights as days.

Her jaw clenched as the boat shifted further and the engines reversed direction. The shuttle chugged toward the island, slowing as it approached. The Arnold dock bustled with activity, but it was the kind propelled by men pushing caddies and horses stamping their hooves. Alanna collected her thoughts and softened her knees to rock with the ferry as it slid next to the dock.

At first glance nothing had changed. Bicycles and horse-drawn taxis lined Huron Street at the end of the dock. Men wearing hotel logo-embellished polos wove between groups of tourists. Their intent gazes focused on destinations while the tourists ambled from fudge shops to knickknack stores.

Alanna stumbled against the railing as the boat stopped. Her feet anchored in place. The other passengers disembarked. She needed to move. Tackle whatever waited for her.

*It's just a few weeks, two months at most.* She could do anything for that long. Get the store open again. Find someone to run the shop. Return to Grand Rapids before the partners missed her too much. That's all she had to do. Grabbing her briefcase, Alanna hiked over the short gangplank. A taxi could take her to the cottage first. No, if she did that, she might not make an appearance at the shop today.

She marched to the trolley lined with suitcases, handed over her claim ticket, and took the handle on hers. It was big, but she could maneuver it the few blocks to the store. She slipped into the flow of visitors pouring off the dock. With her suitcase rolling behind her, maybe no one would recognize her. Even with that hope, her sunglasses stayed firmly in place. If any of her opposing counsel spotted her hiding behind the glasses, they'd laugh. Her reputation as a tiger in the courtroom would lay shredded at her feet.

She ducked behind a group and followed them up the street. She crashed off a hard surface—no. . .somebody—and fell.

"Are you okay?" A rich baritone, eerily familiar, spoke the words.

Alanna nodded from her position on the sidewalk but kept her chin tucked. She couldn't let him get a good glimpse at her or her embarrassment. What if he remembered her? Eleven years might not be long enough to make her anonymous to the man who first claimed her heart.

"There are too many people on the sidewalks not to pay attention. Can I help you up?" The man offered her a hand.

Alanna peeked up then tilted her head back farther and saw the man she'd hoped most to avoid on the island. Her pulse picked up speed, a nod to their long-ago high school summer romance. Her gaze slipped to his mouth, and she jerked it back up as heat flashed up her neck at the thought of their twilight kisses on the dock by her parents' home years earlier. In an instant, the memory morphed into the panicked thought Jonathan might recognize her. She longed for something— anything—more substantial than glasses to hide behind.

His face had matured. The jaw squared, the nose bent like he'd broken it, the eyes green with a tinge of blue—matching the calm waters of Lake Huron. He still towered over her a good six inches or more. Her gaze traveled down his fit form, but he waved his hand in front of her face.

"Help you up?" Mischief danced in his sea-green eyes as if he knew she'd stared at him from behind the glasses.

Alanna hesitated a moment then accepted his hand, finding hers dwarfed in his. A shock raced up her arm. He pulled her to her feet, and she two-stepped backward. "Th-thank you."

"Sure you're okay?"

"Yes." She had to get away before he recognized her. Of all the people to run into! She hadn't prepared for the memories and what-ifs to assault her the moment she stepped on Mackinac Island. Her breath hitched, and she tightened her grip on the suitcase. "Thank you again."

Alanna skirted around him and hurried down Huron, gaze fixed in front of her. She knew he must think her ridiculous, but she couldn't look back. If she did, she'd be lost in his gaze, and he'd recognize her in an instant. If Spencer hadn't ended their year-long relationship, she'd have some defense to Jonathan. Instead, she felt vulnerable to the memories.

If the first moments together, when he didn't know her, were any indication, her long-buried attraction to him would chase her right off the island.

SHADOWY MEMORIES CHASED questions through Jonathan Covington's mind as he watched the woman hurry down the street, the suitcase bumping over cracks in the sidewalk. Her willowy form reminded him of someone, only the short blond hair didn't fit the image. He wondered what color her eyes were, but she'd hidden behind the large sunglasses. Her suitcase bobbled on one wheel, but she didn't slow. If he didn't know better, he'd say a wildcat or black bear chased her—only the island didn't have any. No, the only big wildlife was the tourists. Almost as entertaining but not quite.

Her thin form glided around a mother leading a toddler down the street. At least this time she was more attentive to others on the sidewalk. She hopped as the suitcase bounced against her ankles.

He watched her a moment more, a distant memory tugging

at him. Something about her seemed familiar, but he couldn't tell as she hid behind those huge Jackie O sunglasses, useless on a cloudy morning.

"You getting her number, Covington, or getting back to work?" Mr. Morris watched him with a hint of amusement defying his stiff posture as he braced his arms alongside his trim waist.

Jonathan snapped his fingers. "Knew I forgot something." He pulled his attention from the retreating woman and pasted a grin on his face before turning back to his client. The man expected him to work, not daydream. Besides, he had a relationship. . .of sorts. "Ready for the best pancakes in town?"

Edward Morris snorted, his nostrils flaring. "There isn't much competition."

"Part of the island's charm."

"So Bonnie says." Humor lightened Edward's eyes and eased the lines on his tanned face. Didn't look like the man missed many opportunities to walk a golf course. Jonathan filed the detail for easy access as he prepared an itinerary for the Morrises' event. He needed to nail this event and get the referrals that had to come from them. Otherwise Jonathan stood dangerously close to losing his event-planning business and returning to another job working for someone else. "That woman has been intent on a celebration of a lifetime for our fortieth. Says, with the way couples divorce, we have to make a splash. I hope this works for her."

"That's why I'm here." Jonathan opened the door to Mike's and inhaled the rich aroma of roasting coffee. Everyone else could purchase overpriced brew at the chain down the block, but he enjoyed the hearty coffee served here. The small restaurant was a new and welcome addition to the morning offerings. "Right this way."

"Morning, gents." Mike's deep voice bellowed from behind the old-style counter. "What can I get you this morning?"

Jonathan grabbed a stool at the counter. "Coffee and a stack of your blueberry pancakes."

"Black and Michigan maple?"

"Of course."

"And for you?" Mike looked at Edward, who studied the simple menu as if it were the *Wall Street Journal* he usually tucked under his arm.

"A plain stack and doctored coffee."

"Plain, really?" With all the options on the menu, Jonathan couldn't imagine settling for plain. "Try the apple or cherry. Both are great."

"I'll stick with good ole syrup."

Jonathan shook his head and winked at Mike, who'd watched the exchange with his trademark easy grin. "So what do you envision for this party?"

"We'll need somewhere for the kids and grandkids to stay. Then recommendations for friends who make the trip. And someplace that accommodates a moderately sized group. Maybe forty, though if Bonnie has her way, she'll break the bank and invite everyone she's ever greeted."

"Formal or relaxed?"

"Casual. It's easier for everyone that way."

"Hope you brought your appetite today, Jonathan. I don't want to throw food away this time." Mike plopped a plate of steaming pancakes in front of him. A dollop of butter melted in a pool on the top cake with three slices of thick bacon lining the plate's edge.

"I didn't order the bacon."

"I know. Thought you'd need the extra sustenance." He nodded his head toward Edward. "And here's some link sausage for you. You look like that kind of guy."

"Really?" Edward hiked an eyebrow as he examined the tower of pancakes.

"Most definitely. Someone who's only here because his wife told him to come. What I don't get is where's the missus?"

Jonathan winced. There'd been no way to warn Mike, but the sudden pallor in Edward's face made him wish there had been.

"She'll be here later in the season." Edward pushed the bite of pancakes he'd cut through the syrup but didn't shovel it to his mouth.

Mike shrugged, but Jonathan caught his gaze and shook his head, a small movement to keep Mike from inserting his foot deeper in his mouth. As he watched Edward choke down his emotions with a swig of coffee, Jonathan thanked God he'd remained single. The pain that shadowed the man's eyes when he thought about his wife and her battle with cancer left Jonathan determined to avoid that depth of pain.

Love traveled a path that led directly and unavoidably to heartache. The only question was how long the journey took. He had to look no farther than his parents' caustic marriage or his own string of tepid relationships.

Guess that's what happened when the gal you believed was the love of your life walked away without a glance. Showed how much he understood love. Even now he couldn't persuade his heart to engage with the lady he enjoyed. Something was wrong with him, or love wasn't meant to be part of his life.

The only way to evade the issue was to bypass love.

And as the strong, gruff man swiped under his eyes and cleared his throat, Jonathan determined to maintain his present course and dodge that fate.

A passing glance at her parents' art studio left the impression its owners had abandoned it without notice. It languished between a store filled with knick-knacks and a photography studio. Across the street sat a bike shop with an attached Internet cafe. Alanna shook her head as two teens leaned close to monitors. . . . The Internet invaded even this quiet spot.

She looked at the jumbled mass of keys her mother had handed her the night before at the hospital in Grand Rapids. Mom's hands had shaken as she delivered a brief primer on the keys. Here, in the light of day, standing in this place, Alanna's mind refused to remember which key did what. As she stared at the mess of keys, the monstrous suitcase collapsed on its side into her knees.

"Ouch." Alanna jumped away from the case then righted it, balancing it when it teetered again. Finally, it rested against the wooden wall. She rubbed the back of her knees. The morning couldn't get much worse.

She selected a key, tried to cram it into the hole, and then flipped to another. Alanna didn't know whether to be relieved or disappointed Jonathan Covington didn't remember her. Time had passed, but she hadn't changed that much. Tears filled her eyes as the hopes she'd held for them overwhelmed her. She rammed another key into the keyhole.

"Work. Please work." She had to get inside where she could hide her meltdown. Shed known it wouldn't be easy to return to Mackinac, but the flood of emotions so soon caught her off guard.

The key swiveled in the hole followed by the door creaking open. Alanna stumbled into the dim interior. The air hung heavy, tainted by mustiness rather than the soothing lavender that usually saturated the space. Shadows filled the room, the eerie images playing on the walls flung from the modern art statues standing in the middle of the room. She might not be able to do much about the lavender until she got to the cottage, but she could turn on the lights and fill the silence. Mom must have left the jazz CDs that usually piped through the music system somewhere.

"Hey, lady."

Alanna startled at the deep voice. She turned and stopped at the red GRAND HOTEL insignia on the shirt. One of the best nights of her young life had occurred when Jonathan took her to an amazing dinner at the grand lady of the island. She'd dressed up, and he'd looked so handsome in his suit. She shook her head to clear the memory.

"Need help with your bag?" He gestured to the black monolith that languished where she'd left it.

"Thank you. Could you pull it inside the door?"

He did, taking it behind the counter. "Unless it's your latest sculpture, I doubt you want it left by the door. Need me to carry it upstairs?"

"No, I don't live there. Thanks for your assistance." She dug a single out of her wallet and handed it to him. The man left with a smile splitting his ebony face. If only she could generate that kind of response from everyone she encountered. Without the money tied to it.

She considered the back stairway. Mom used to use it as a studio then had converted it to a small apartment. So far, the space was empty for this season. Alanna guessed she could stay there, but she wanted the comfort and familiarity of the house. The privacy, too.

A sigh shuddered through her. If she truly wanted her privacy, she should have stayed in Grand Rapids and continued braving the media. All the regulars here knew her. Knew the past. Knew the pieces she'd kept separate from the life she'd created on the mainland. There people didn't remember Grady Cadieux's death and tie it to her younger brother, Trevor Stone. There may not have been enough evidence to prosecute him, but she'd seen the questions and anger in her neighbors' eyes. The popular mayor's son had captained the basketball team and had dreams the island's residents adopted as their own. Then he died, and their grief transferred to anger that targeted Trevor.

She parted the lace curtains and peeked at the street. Even though it was barely 8:00 a.m., people strolled up and down the sidewalk. If she wanted the opportunity to sell anything today, she needed to open. Mom had relayed what sounded like a never-ending list of tasks she must complete each day before unlocking the door.

A sigh burbled from the depths of her soul. It was Monday morning, and she should be an hour into case reviews. Maybe at the courthouse preparing for a trial or hearings. Instead, she stood on the one place she swore she'd avoid until her dying days. It helped that her parents lived here only during the tourist season and abandoned the island for the holidays. She'd wondered if they did it for her and Trevor. Her brother wanted to return to the island even less than she did.

She shook her head before the thoughts took over. She couldn't afford to descend into the past. Not when tourists— potential buyers—peeked in the windows. If Alanna wanted to ensure there was sufficient money to pay her father's hospital and rehab bills, she had to get the Painted Stone open and sell some art.

After she flipped several switches, light filled the space. Spotlights highlighted paintings at regular intervals, with smaller works featured in between. Lights she hadn't noticed on the floor emphasized the sculptures. And each wall was painted a rich shade— crimson, eggplant, gold, and midnight blue— that served almost as an extra mat to the paintings. Her mothers artistic touch filled the studio. And her father's fingerprints would dot the office.

Walking behind the counter, Alanna flipped the switches to turn on the computer that served as a cash register. It hummed to life, and she crouched and rummaged through a box for CDs. Finding one that looked promising, she popped it into the CD player and hit **PLAY**. Soft notes from a piano filtered through the room. Add some lavender and everything would be perfect.

"Hello?"

Alanna popped up, ramming her head against the counter with a yelp. She rubbed her hand across the back of her scalp, biting her lip to keep from saying the words that rushed to escape.

"Are you open?" A woman's soft voice edged into the studio followed by the sound of heels clicking against the hardwood floors. "The sign isn't flipped, but I saw lights and the open door."

Alanna smiled around the pain and finished standing. "I'm almost ready, but feel free to look around while I finish."

"Thank you, dear." The older woman had soft white curls that wisped around her face. She wore a lavender spangled shirt over linen white capris, the picture of a visitor. She wandered in front of one of Alanna's mother's large oil paintings. She stood in front of it, edged to the right, then the left. She cocked her head like a seagull eyeing a treat someone had dropped. "This scene is quite vibrant. Do you know where it was painted?"

"Let me see." Alanna slipped from behind the counter and joined the woman. The location couldn't be clearer—the Grand Hotel's long white porch lined with rockers, the yellow awnings peeking from the ground level and first level of the porch. The colors were right. The setting appropriate. But somehow the painting felt off.

Different. Not quite like her mom's usual work. The woman turned to her, a question reflected in her gray eyes. "This is the Grand Hotel. I'm sure you'll see it during your stay. It's quite the landmark for the island."

"Of course. How could I miss that?" The woman turned with a soft smile. "I'll just have a look around."

While the woman stopped to admire each painting, Alanna hurried to the supply closet to get the items she needed to finish preparing the store. Even as she dusted the paintings and turned the sign to Open, her gaze wandered back to the painting.

THE PLATES HELD LINGERING puddles of syrup but otherwise stood empty with every last blueberry and crumb consumed. Mike smiled as he whisked the plates behind the counter. "Can I get anything else for you gents?"

Edward shook his head, and Jonathan grabbed the bill before the other man could.

"Ready to explore possible sites?" Jonathan handed Mike a twenty and then pulled out his portfolio. He shook the image of the woman who'd collided with him from his mind again. To accomplish all he'd promised, they'd need to maximize each moment. And that meant ignoring all distractions, especially the ones that made no sense. Mackinac might be small, but it was filled with event and lodging options. "Several bed-and-break-fasts could be perfect for your family and might even have open-ings since it's still early in the season. But we don't want to wait long. Better to check them today and make your decision quickly."

Edward's focus had returned, his eyes clear of the lingering pain that had stained them during breakfast. The athletic man pulled out a smartphone and clicked away.

At times Jonathan wished technology hadn't invaded the island to the degree it had. Now everyone had iPhones, Androids, and Tablets, all the things that invited the world they escaped to assault the protected beauty up at the tip of Michigan.

"What are the names of the B&Bs?"

Jonathan laughed. "You're eager to get to it."

"Time's a wasting, my man." Edward shrugged, that silly light creeping back into his expression. "I promised Bonnie I'd give her a full report tonight. That means pictures, notes, details. She's really the one who should be here with you." He swal-lowed hard. "But I'll do the standing-in part then let her make the decisions."

Jonathan clapped Edward on the shoulder. "No problem. Let's head to my office. Get you oriented and collect some brochures you can take notes on."

As they walked the block west along Huron, Jonathan watched for the woman. He tried to corral his thoughts, but they insisted on returning to the way her head had tilted like a bird trying to decide whether he was a friend or enemy. They turned onto Market, and he picked up the pace. He slowed at the Painted Stone's door. It stood tucked between a photography studio filled with amazing images of the island and a unique flag shop. The art studio had been closed since the owner had a stroke a week earlier, though it looked like someone had opened the store. He'd have to check on Mr. Stone's status later.

Mr. Morris studied the window, his hands shoved in his pockets, an intense gaze on his face. "You think they could commission something?"

Jonathan startled and glanced at the man. "A painting or a sculpture?"

"Naw. It's a crazy idea. Let's get moving."

"All right. We're almost there." He said a quick prayer for Mr. Stone as he led Mr. Morris down the street. Jonathan led Edward to a side door tucked among the storefronts. It opened to the stairs to his second-floor office. Edward took in his office. It was small with one main room, a kitchenette, and a bathroom tucked at the back. The walls reflected the rich green of the evergreens on the top half with white paneling on the bottom. The white kept the green from shrinking the room but showed every ding and bang. Jonathan made a mental note to touch it up.

"Why don't you take a seat?" Jonathan settled at his cherry desk while he grabbed the folder he'd slapped a label on and filled with brochures and maps of the island. "We'll start at Haan's 1830 and explore a few of the other smaller B&Bs. Then we can look at several restaurants. If you think you'll have more than forty people, we should consider an outdoor venue. One far away from sidewalks." As Edward's eyebrows rose, Jonathan hurried on. "Don't worry, there are plenty of great locations. And several of the hotels have meeting space. But depending on the timing, we could create a fun event outdoors. Plenty of space for the kids to run around and more flexibility in setup."

They reviewed the map and plotted the best way to get from place to place. Edward stood, and Jonathan grabbed his keys and cell phone. He ushered Edward toward the stairs and followed him down.

They had one day to find exactly what Edward and Bonnie imagined for their event. He needed to focus on hitting as many spots as possible while helping Edward define exactly what they wanted. If only he could convince the morning's mystery woman not to return to his thoughts.

## 3

The sun sat poised to rise above the pine trees dotting Jonathan's property the next morning. A bird's muted chatter broke the silence surrounding him. He moved around the kitchen as he started a fresh pot of coffee. He rehashed the prior day while he waited for his first cup. Edward had seemed pleased with Jonathan's suggestions as he took copious notes at their many stops.

When the coffeepot beeped, Jonathan grabbed a mug from the rack beside the sink and filled it. He carried it to the front porch and sank onto the rocking chair his grandfather had made. He blew on the steaming coffee as his gaze searched the spindly pines. Maybe this morning he'd catch a glimpse of the elusive Kirtland's warbler.

He'd tried hard to keep the cowbirds away but hadn't seen any activity to suggest the warblers had returned. If Jonathan's ears didn't deceive him, maybe this fellow was one. The only problem was the bird could be anywhere in a quarter-mile radius. If he was right, the bird had found a good home in the jack pine habitat.

*Chip-chip-che-way-o.* That's how the bird guides described

the sound of the yellow-bellied warbler. To Jonathan's ears, its song rang more melodious in the early morning silence.

Jonathan sipped the strong coffee. There wasn't a better way to start the morning than sitting on his cabin's porch surrounded by God's creation, even the hidden ones. He might not see the warbler yet, but he would.

The alarm on his watch shrieked, wrecking the mornings peace. The trees rustled as birds took flight. He jabbed the buttons on the watch, and it fell silent. So much for a calm start to the day. How could he have forgotten to turn it off when he woke before the alarm? Jonathan shifted against the porch railing, the day's demands replacing the fleeting peace. Might as well face reality. It promised to be another busy, stress-filled day. Better tackle it head-on instead of wasting another moment worrying about how to land the Standeford wedding account and keep another couple, the Wenzes, happy with their anniversary plans. All the meetings with local hotels and associations to gain new business. His mind spun with the details and ideas. Business looked ready to pick up, but he needed to clone himself if he wanted to keep up.

At times like this, he wondered if he'd ever find a way to add an employee. Maybe if he pulled everything back to his cabin. He could always meet people at local spots like Mike's. The problem was his cabin was small. It'd be tough to find space for all his supplies. His office might not be huge, but it did provide the extra space and a bit of separation from his home. Still, working with someone as part of a cohesive team sounded great. Then he could work on the events while someone else focused on marketing to prospective clients. Then his business could really grow.

The steady clop of horses' hooves on the packed road running in front of the cabin invaded his thoughts. People rarely traveled the out-of-the-way road, especially this early.

The taxi passed, containing one passenger, a woman whose short hair turned golden when the sun's rays reached through the trees to touch it. Only a couple of homes dotted the road beyond his small place. Where was she headed?

He blew on the coffee again then sipped.

"Morning, Jonathan." The soft words carried across the short distance echoing from his past.

He spewed the coffee. She knew his name? Two words. Yet with them hope and anger spiraled through him.

It couldn't be Alanna. Not after all this time. Surely not. Would her fathers stroke pull her back to the island when he hadn't been enough? The coffee churned in his stomach. He dumped the rest of the brew on the lilac standing by the steps. His grandmother had babied that bush, yet it seemed to do okay with his occasional coffee bath. Though it never flowered like it did under his grandmother's care.

So he didn't have a green thumb.

Jonathan set the mug on the railing and took a step off the porch. The taxi had disappeared down the narrow lane. Unless he wanted to follow it and risk looking the fool, he'd better stay put. His watch beeped again. He didn't have time to hunt down an elusive woman who knew his name. Maybe it had been a lucky guess. He snorted. *Yeah right.*

Jonathan—one of the top three names on the tip of beautiful women's tongues. Especially when they saw him.

Only one woman had said his name with an inflection that felt like a caress.

He jumped down the steps and hurried to the road. Looked down it. Saw the taxi stop at the path leading to the Stones' cottage. With a glimpse of a beautiful woman hiding behind Jackie O sunglasses, it hit him he'd run into Alanna yesterday. If she'd arrived then, why hadn't she come home last night? He hadn't seen lights when he'd checked the house for the Stones.

Maybe that was all the excuse he needed to confirm the woman in the carriage truly was Alanna.

His watch beeped its warning again.

Time to get moving. He'd drop by tonight. See if she had a good explanation for the way she disappeared, cut him out of her life.

He shook his head, trying to free himself of the immediate hold she'd reestablished. What would Jaclyn think? Jaclyn Raeder, the woman who'd worked her way into his life along with that precious little boy. Sure, he'd never felt the flashes of attraction with Jaclyn, but she was a good woman. And she'd been here. Consistently.

He couldn't go there. Not now, and not after two mere words.

His clients didn't care about the overpowering desire he had to abandon the day's agenda and rush to the house, but Jaclyn would. Clients only focused on whether events ran without a hiccup, snag, or noticeable problem. As long as he was the one losing sleep and weight over the details, they'd sign the checks.

The slow *clop-clop* of the taxi echoed in the quiet. Jonathan smiled when he saw the empty passenger seats. She was back. Now he had to run or he'd miss his first appointment.

ALANNA LEANED AGAINST THE DOOR. What had she been thinking? *Hello, Jonathan?* It was bad enough they'd live next door to each other. She'd prayed he'd moved, but the moment she bumped into him yesterday, she knew he still lived in the small cabin. So she'd been a coward and spent the night in an anonymous bed-and-breakfast. Finding an open room had surprised her—even this early in the season—but it gave her the retreat she'd needed as she formed a plan.

From the moment Mom called with her plea, Alanna's

prayers had included the request for Jonathan Covington to be far removed from Mackinac. That he would be anywhere but here. Why couldn't God have answered that prayer? It would have simplified her emotionally complicated return. Enough strands existed on the island to capture her in the spiderweb of the past. She didn't need her heart involved, too.

Not after she'd worked so hard to pretend she never cared for Jonathan. That their relationship had never proceeded past a weak adolescent shadow of love. But as she hid in the B and B, she had to admit she'd fooled herself. It wasn't the pressure of law school and starting a career that kept her from relationships. She couldn't even blame the uninteresting men she ran into. Maybe they'd been uninteresting because they weren't Jonathan.

In the early light of morning, she decided to attack the mess of emotions head-on. After finding a taxi, she headed to the cottage. Home. It hadn't been that for years. Alanna stood on the porch, bag next to her, key in hand. One jab and twist and she'd fall inside. She hesitated, listening for the sound of heavy footsteps across the lawn. A bird jabbered angrily somewhere near her, but she didn't hear the sound she anticipated and feared.

Alanna took a steadying breath and twisted the key, opened the door, and pulled her bag into the small sitting area. Dropping the suitcase's handle, she marched to the kitchen and stood at the window. A dock angled from the backyard into the small pond the house shared with Jonathan's cabin. Heat curled through her at the thought of the nights she and Jonathan had sat at the end, toes dangling inches above the water, shoulders touching.

Before she got lost in more what-ifs and unfulfilled hopes, she spun on her heel and headed to her small bedroom. As soon as she stepped inside, she groaned. Nothing was as she remembered from high school. Every scrap of pink had transformed into the perfect guest bedroom rather than a teenage girl's dream escape.

If she hurried, she could shower, change, and hike to town before the studio opened. Tonight she could wallow in the past. Now she had to survive the present.

By noon she couldn't wait to leave the art studio and join the tourists staring in the fudge shop windows. The four walls had closed in as she answered questions about the island, none leading to sales.

People wanted free tourist advice. Didn't they understand that if she didn't sell art, she couldn't keep the studio open to answer their questions? Maybe she needed to talk to Mom about lower-priced items that were accessible to more checkbooks.

She merged with the melee on Huron. Today several tour groups stood out in the crowds with their matching ball caps or guides wielding umbrellas. She stepped against Doud's Market's tan wall to let a group of smiling senior citizens pass. Their guide steered them to Fort Mackinac. One lady teetered on spiky heels that weren't designed to navigate the steep hill and stairs leading to the fort. Maybe Ste. Anne's Church would be a better destination for her.

The last tour member smiled as she passed. Alanna nodded at her then continued to the Yankee Rebel. The mix of cleanly painted wood buildings smashed against brick storefronts gave the street a touristy, village feel, her favorite part of the island.

She entered the restaurant and waited for the hostess to acknowledge her.

"Alanna Stone. Over here."

Alanna longed to disappear as the boisterous voice bellowed. A man her daddy's age waved at her from the back corner.

"Come join me."

She glanced around and didn't notice anyone she recognized, though after eleven years she wasn't sure she'd recognize many. In fact, the idea he knew who she was after all this time seemed incongruous. Still, the tables had started to fill. Maybe she should join him.

The man stood and headed her way. He took her arm and escorted her to the table. "This way. It's time you returned, young lady. Sorry it took your daddy's stroke to get you here. This may be a good that comes from it. Time to return, face the past, and clear the air, so to speak."

Alanna watched him out of the corner of her eye as they crossed the room.

"Here, let me help you." He pulled out a chair next to his, waited for her to sit, then scooted her to the table. "Remember me?"

"No."

"Not surprised. I've lost a lot of weight. Had the gastric bypass. Worked like a charm." He patted his waist then brushed a lock of salt-and-pepper hair out of his eyes. "Gerald Tomkin."

"Mr. Tomkin?" The principal? No wonder she'd blocked him. The man always acted as if the whole world wanted to hear every word he said, no matter how inconsequential or irrelevant. But swiping the hair out of his face was classic Mr. Tomkin. She'd graduated with his son Brendan, who had seemed destined to follow in his father's pompous footsteps. After the graduation party accident, he'd been even more unbearable, like he had taken Grady's death personally.

"Your mom kept me up-to-date on your progress. Impressive, young lady. But I knew you had it in you to change the world."

Alanna studied her hands, unused to praise from him. "Are you still at the school?"

"No. Retired last year and now working with the island's foundation. You should get involved. Right up your alley as an attorney. In fact, I have a project to discuss with you. One important to the foundation's future."

"I don't think I'll be here long enough for a project."

A waitress stopped by the table.

"We'll talk more after we order. I'd get the pot roast sandwich. You won't be disappointed." He rubbed his stomach.

Still bossy as ever, but it did sound good. "All right."

The waitress collected their drink orders, and Alanna glanced around. The door opened, and sunlight streamed through the opening.

"Doris, where are you hiding?"

Jonathan Covington—here? Alanna slouched in her chair. She picked up a menu and pretended to study it intently, holding it in front of her face. Footsteps clomped across the wooden floor in her direction. She kept her head buried, refusing to look up.

"Gerald Tomkin. Just the man I wanted to see."

Alanna stifled a sigh and glanced up. She forced a smile on her face, one that froze when she noticed the funny way he looked at her. He clutched the chair across from Gerald. "Still rent your flower garden for photos?"

"Another wedding?" Gerald gestured at the table. "Why don't you join us?"

"Of course." Jonathan took a seat then frowned.

"Flower garden?" Alanna jolted as she felt something on her shoulder. Mr. Tomkin had placed his hand there. She started to scoot her chair away, but that would put her closer to Jonathan.

"I rent it out occasionally for the right event." Mr. Tomkin grinned. "When it's in full bloom, it's a spectacular backdrop." He looked at Jonathan. "When would you need it?"

"I'm not sure yet. But would like to add it to a wedding proposal." Jonathan shifted his attention and quirked his head as if trying to decide if it was really her. "Alanna Stone?"

"Hi, Jonathan."

"What brings you back to the island? Your father's stroke?" His eyes searched her face, wariness keeping a safe distance between them.

"Yes." She tried to meet his gaze but couldn't.

"Is he improving?" Genuine concern lined his voice.

She found his gaze, saw the concern mirrored there. "Not much change. That's why Mom asked me to come."

"Aren't you a high-powered attorney? Can't imagine you staying here long." Jonathan played with the napkin-wrapped silverware at his place.

"I can't. Just long enough to find someone to run the store. Shouldn't be too hard." She hoped. Then she'd run to the ferry as fast as she could.

Mr. Tomkin nodded then turned to Jonathan. "So tell me about this wedding."

Alanna tuned the two out as they talked details and locations.

"Then you can help me talk Miss Stone into helping with the foundation. As an attorney, she's exactly what we need to wade through the tangled mess of finances."

Jonathan shrugged, a shuttered look clouding his face. He served on the board? Another reason for her to avoid it if they pressed her to serve. She couldn't get involved, not when a legal dispute here could delay her return to Grand Rapids.

The waitress returned and set waters in front of them, somehow knowing to add a third for Jonathan. "What can I get you today?"

They rattled off orders, and the waitress disappeared in the back.

Alanna took a sip of water, watching Jonathan from underneath her eyelashes. His jaw tightened, and then he took a deep breath and seemed to make a decision.

"Maybe we can catch up tonight."

"Maybe."

Gerald guffawed. "I see you two still have something between you. Good thing Jaclyn's not here." He leaned toward Alanna, like he could get any closer. "That mama wouldn't be happy. And her little boy is latched on to Jonathan. You're a regular daddy figure."

"Gerald." Jonathan's frown should have stopped Gerald.

"Let me warn you. . . . Nature Boy here spends his extra time scouring the trails for the Audubon Society. Don't see the relaxation in that, but to each his own."

Jonathan shrugged, an easy gesture that didn't dislodge the distance in his eyes nor the tightness around his mouth. "Not all of us thrive on conflict."

"Touché." Gerald laughed, but hardness settled in his eyes.

"Maybe I'm tiring of it. The mess with Hoffmeister is enough to wear anyone down. You know what that's like. Lots of conflict." He glanced up, and then a sharp grin twisted his face. "Lookie there. Isn't that Jaclyn, Jonathan?"

Jonathan glanced toward the door and nodded as the red-haired pixie made her way toward their table. "Sure is."

Maybe Alanna should be glad Jonathan didn't bound from his chair to welcome her. Instead, it felt like a load of rocks from the shoreline dropped in Alanna's stomach. The thought of eating anything left her nauseous.

Jonathan leaned toward her. "You okay?"

His sensitivity only made matters worse. Now tears and regret puddled with the debris from the past. "I'm sorry. I don't feel well. If you'll excuse me."

She bolted from her chair and fled before either man could say anything and before Jaclyn arrived at the table. Alanna didn't turn back, didn't glance in the window, didn't stop as she felt the past waiting to pounce.

## 4

Alanna unlocked the door to the Painted Stone, her hands shaking and heart pounding. What was she thinking? The last thing she should do is spend one moment more than necessary with Jonathan Covington. When she abandoned the island, she'd left him behind, too.

What had Gerald meant when he threw out that comment about Jaclyn? It had been years . . . . Jonathan couldn't have waited. It was only normal for someone as good-looking and kind as Jonathan to find a woman to spend his life with.

He couldn't have waited. She knew that. Really.

But a father? She'd glanced, couldn't stop herself. He didn't wear a ring.

If he was a father, then she needed to stay away from him. Keep at least twenty feet between her and the first man to kiss her. The man who still made her pulse gyrate. She'd be crazy to spend one moment with him. . .especially alone at the pond. They shared too much history there. Summers roaming the woods. Stolen kisses on the dock.

"Come on." She twisted the key to the side and pushed the door open. It ricocheted off the wall, and she left the keys hanging from the lock. She hurried to the counter and shoved her purse beneath it before slipping into the tiny bathroom to check her reflection. Her eyes were wide, her cheeks flushed. She tried to pat her hair back into submission, but her hands trembled.

That settled it. She was a fool.

"Anyone here?" A woman's voice lured her back to the shop.

Alanna pasted on a smile and slipped from the bathroom. "Can I help you?"

The woman dangled keys in her hand. "You left these in the door."

Alanna's cheeks flushed hotter, and she stepped forward. "Thank you. I rushed in."

"I'd say. Looked like a woman with the past on her heels."

The woman had no idea. The past squeezed her from all sides. Alanna pulled her thoughts to the customer. "Can I help you find anything?"

"I'm all right." The woman gave the keys to Alanna then turned to the artwork. "Has this studio been here long?"

"My parents opened it twenty years ago, the summer I turned nine."

"Umm. What brought them to the island?" She cocked her head to the side as she studied one of Mother's richly detailed landscapes.

"Mom always wanted to paint but claimed no time and no inspiration. We vacationed here one weekend, and that changed."

"Any of these hers?"

"Only the best." Alanna pointed to the large four-by-five painting the woman stood in front of. "This one was painted from the side of the fort. Knowing Mom, she didn't take the road up— she would have hiked a back trail. She called it getting in the mood. And a walk through the woods always worked. But that's why you see the fort and then the roofs of the buildings around here leading to the lake. Most people would paint looking up at the fort, but not Mom."

"She's very talented."

"Thank you."

"You might think I'm just saying that, but"—the woman reached into her bag and pulled out a slim business card—"I teach art at U of M. Her color use reminds me of a student of mine. It's quite distinctive."

Alanna studied the card. Janine Ross, associate professor. In her coral capris and white shirt, she didn't have the look of an artsy person. She wore no multicolored, dangling earrings or wildly swirled scarf. And with short blond hair missing any teal or purple highlights, Janine looked like a career woman enjoying a weekend escape.

"Not what you expected?"

Alanna chuckled. "I guess not."

"I've spent a lifetime breaking expectations." Janine moved to the next painting, giving it only a cursory glance before working her way along the room. "I like the bold use of color on the walls. They act as an additional mat."

"That's what Mom said, though you should have seen my father's face when she handed out the gallons of paint."

"Have you thought about printing note cards? Tourists would love them."

"True." Alanna moved to the counter to make a note. A customer didn't need to know she hadn't stood in the shop for eleven years. "I'm sure Mom's considered it. . . ."

"Tell her to call me if she needs a printer. I know one who does excellent work."

"Thank you."

Janine stopped when she came back to the first painting. "Are you certain this is your mother's work?"

"Yes." Alanna approached the painting and pointed to the squiggled signature in the lower right-hand corner. "That's her John Hancock."

"The resemblance to my student's work is uncanny. Huh." She stared a moment more then made her way to the door. "What was his name? Trevor?" she muttered as she exited onto the bustling sidewalk.

Trevor? Why would the professor mention Trevor? As far as Alanna knew, her brother hadn't taken any art classes, but really they'd drifted apart. It was possible. And with years watching Mom paint, it couldn't be unusual that he'd picked up her love and technique.

Alanna watched her progress up the street for a minute then turned back to the painting. It was ridiculous to think that the painting could be anyone but Mom's. Most artists approached Fort Mackinac from the front. The stairs were daunting enough from that perspective. Few people had the energy to work their way up the roads and then wind a path through the trees. It seemed too much work for an uncertain reward. Yet Alanna had helped Mom lug her easel, paints, and supplies through all kinds of narrow trails and switchbacks in the hunt for the perfect sunlight.

After Alanna entered high school and had to juggle its heavier course work, Trevor accompanied Mom on her painting hikes. He'd carried a sketchbook with him on those trips. Before she'd left for college, she'd snuck a few peeks at the pages. He had talent, but painting? Could he have taken classes from this professor after he followed Alanna to U of M?

Alanna studied the painting, this time breaking it into grids as she methodically examined it. Little things seemed off, but she hadn't accompanied her mom in so long, maybe she didn't know Mom's style anymore. How would Trevor make such detailed paintings without returning to the island, something

Alanna was certain he hadn't done? Still, the woman's words raised a niggling doubt. It was her mom's signature, but was it her painting? It seemed an absurd thought. Why would Mom ask someone to create paintings for her to sign? Mom came alive when she held a paintbrush in her hand and studied a canvas.

The tinkle of the bell dancing against the door pulled her thoughts from the painting. A group of four women walked into the studio, their loud chatter bouncing off the floor and muting the smooth sounds of jazz. Alanna smiled at them then slid behind the counter, careful to stay out of their way as they wandered the room.

She doubted they would buy anything. And that's what she needed. Customers who had the interests and pocketbooks to make purchases. Daddy's medical bills wouldn't get paid by lookers. Especially if the art they sold wasn't by the artist claimed.

No amount of knickknacks and art by other Upper Peninsula artists could cover that kind of fraud.

JONATHAN REPLACED the phone on the hook. Everything was lined up for Edward and Bonnie's anniversary celebration. The owners of Haan's 1830 would hold its rooms and suites for the family, and he had a couple of other B&Bs on notice that there could be overflow guests. The rest was up to Edward. If he got the word out in a timely fashion, this could become the wonderful event the man had envisioned.

It was after six, and Jonathan felt ready to escape to his cabin. Maybe he'd spend some time fishing at the pond. There wasn't much to catch, but what was there always fried up nice for a quick meal.

And there was something about sitting in the middle of the

woods by the pond that settled him at the end of a busy day. He could commune with God while he waited to see if anything bit on his bait. That led to peace in the midst of the chaos. With event planning, there was an abundance of that—almost too much.

He just had to fish and avoid Alanna and the complications she brought.

The thought tempted him to avoid the dock, but this long holiday weekend would fly by with a wedding and reception, so he'd better grab moments while he could. Jonathan locked up and hustled down the steps as he slipped his messenger bag over his neck then slid the bag to his back. At the side of the building, he unchained his mountain bike and straddled it. As soon as a gap appeared in the tourists on foot and bike, he pushed into the flow of traffic.

Where most tourists continued along Lake View Boulevard, he veered up Cadotte Avenue and then biked steadily up the hill. His legs pumped in a steady rhythm as he worked the bike around a few others. This was what made the island such an ideal place. You worked hard all day then released the day's cares and stress on the bike ride home. He couldn't think of too many other places that allowed the same release.

The yards evolved into thick woods, and still he hiked. His cabin hid on a road that most visitors never discovered. So while the island's population swelled from a few hundred to several thousand during the summers, he still lived on an isolated patch of God's creation.

After fifteen minutes of steady pushing, he reached the turn to Scott's Road and then the cutoff for his cabin and the Stones' home. His house looked like it was constructed with a child's Lincoln Logs compared to the Stones' Victorian. His needed landscaping of some sort. Something to make it look like somebody who cared about the place lived there.

He snorted at the thought. Since when had things like flowers and grass mattered to him?

He parked his bike alongside the house and shook his head. Since a certain Stone had returned. He'd never bothered before because of the extra work it took to get anything onto Mackinac. It was difficult enough getting the groceries up from the dock or Doud's, but plants? He'd never bothered.

That settled it. He needed to get it out of his head that Alanna Stone was anything special. She'd left without a glance back only to return without warning. He stomped into the small living area. He bumped into the lone chair at the tiny table on his way to the refrigerator and growled. He had to evict her from his thoughts before she resumed permanent residence.

The pond beckoned, but he couldn't risk sitting on the dock. Not with his thoughts already filling with Alanna. Been down that road. Not willing to travel it again.

He fiddled with the cans in the pantry until he settled on clam chowder. That should banish any romantic notions if she deigned to wander by. Or maybe he should go by her house.

Stupid. He threw the can opener back in the drawer and dumped the soup in a bowl. While he waited for the microwave to work its magic, he stared out the window. Normally the view of the pond calmed him. Tonight all he could see was the past. Alanna and he laughing on the dock as they sat shoulder to shoulder. What had happened to that? To them?

The clop of horses' hooves and the jangle of harnesses along with the creak of wood reached him through the open window. A taxi bringing Alanna home?

The microwave dinged, and he pulled the steaming bowl out, his attention focused on the road.

"Hot dog." He whistled and placed the bowl on the table before hurrying to stick his burning fingers under the faucet's cold water. Fifteen minutes later, he placed the empty bowl into the sink when someone knocked at the door. Jonathan stared out the window a moment then brushed a hand over his hair.

Sooner or later, they'd have to say hi. It'd be awkward if they didn't.

"Get it over with," he muttered as he squared his shoulders.

"She's only someone you used to know."

Really well.

Which she destroyed when she threw him away along with the island she'd learned to hate.

## 5

Alanna hadn't felt this nervous since taking the bar exam. She tugged the hem of her shirt while she waited at Jonathan's door. As the silence stretched, her ire grew. If he didn't want to talk to her, fine. She wouldn't beg.

She turned from the door at the memory of Grady Cadieux's body being pulled from the frigid water. He'd looked so blue. So dead. The paramedics had labored over him, and she'd prayed he'd make it—especially when she saw Trevor's face as he struggled from the water. Brendan Tomkin's saunter looked forced, but no one else seemed to notice as everyone focused on a too-still Grady. The paramedics loaded him in the ambulance and zipped him to the clinic before boarding the ferry that transported him closer to a hospital, yet all their efforts failed, and he still died.

A stupid stunt by kids who liked to prove who was better than the other. And Trevor got pulled into their ridiculous cock-fights. Then one kid died and another's life was ruined by accusations, spoken and unspoken. Somehow Brendan slipped into the background and avoided attention. She'd never understood how he managed that. Guess it helped when your dad was the principal.

To top off the memories, she'd left her keys at the Painted Stone. She fought the desire to disappear into the night and avoid Jonathan, but he had a spare key. She had no choice but to see him...after her embarrassing departure at lunch.

What a perfect example of the disaster her decision to return was.

Mom and Dad could have found someone else to run the studio. Then she'd be back in Grand Rapids in her well-ordered and controlled life rather than standing on Jonathan's porch.

The door opened, and she spun from the fence dividing the properties. Jonathan leaned against the door frame. Any concern that had been in his eyes at lunchtime was replaced with a studied distance.

"Alanna." He moved from the doorway and took a step toward her. "You're really back."

She nodded, the motion jerky. "For the moment."

"Your mom talk you into this?" There was something hard, almost cruel, in his voice.

"Mom said to see you if I needed help. Sorry to bother you. I'll break a window."

His shoulders slumped. "Look, I'm sorry. It's surreal seeing you. After all this time."

The words felt like an indictment. She didn't need that. Not on top of the memories that flooded her on every corner of this island. "Good night, Jonathan."

"Wait. Do you need the spare key?"

She nodded, wishing she could deny it. At this rate, he'd think she'd fallen apart. "I left mine downtown."

He ran a hand over the five o'clock shadow on his cheeks. "I've got a key in here." He disappeared into the house, but she didn't follow. A minute later, she heard what sounded like a junk drawer being dumped on a table. "Found it." Footsteps hurried toward her. "Here you go."

"Thanks." She stared at him, the weight of the past pressing against her.

His phone rang, and he glanced at the screen. "Sorry, I've got to take this."

"Well, good night."

"Night, Lanna." Before she turned away, he'd opened the phone and said hello to Jaclyn. Her stomach lurched at the idea his girlfriend had interrupted their conversation.

She climbed the fence and like a fool hoped he'd follow anyway. Cut the conversation short and come after her. Instead, muffled conversation followed her as she hurried home. She should be grateful for the thick stand of trees that stood between them. That hid him. Then she might be able to forget the divide. One she'd allowed with her loathing of this place. Trevor didn't deserve the lies and tarring he received after Grady's death. The blame could have been placed on anyone. But the island's residents had thrust it squarely on his thin shoulders.

The muffled conversation ended, and she sighed. Why, now that it was impossible to have Jonathan, did she wonder what they could have had together?

When she entered her parents' home a minute later, she stood in the entryway taking in the living room. She'd return the key later. For now she wanted to relax. It didn't look as if her mom had redecorated any space but Alanna's room. If anything, she had added layers of paintings to the living room. Every square inch of wall was covered with landscapes in brilliant colors.

The paintings looked. . .right. The way she remembered. Her mother had a distinctive flair for putting colors together in a rich, eye-catching manner. The style was that of an Impressionist master, but the colors danced with life and vibrancy. She approached the paintings over the fireplace. They were stacked three deep on the mantel. And the closer she came, the more she knew they were her mother's work.

With that realization came an inkling. Maybe the art professor wasn't crazy to think someone else painted those at the studio. At least a few of them. She pulled a painting down and laid it on the couch. She repeated the process until artwork covered the couch and floor. Dusk filled the room, and Alanna flipped on one of the Tiffany floor lamps. The light splayed through the stained-glass shade, casting rose-colored shadows on the walls. No matter how she studied the paintings, she couldn't find the nebulous something she looked for.

There had to be some clue that indicated her mother and no one else painted them, but Alanna couldn't identify it. Then as she scanned them again, Alanna noticed the red geraniums painted into the art. A potted plant sat next to most of the front doors. Hadn't that been the flower Mom had used at her wedding reception to bring joy to each table?

Her cell rang, a Matthew West song about not wanting to waste life. She fished the phone from her pocket and opened it. "Hello."

"Hey, girl." Samantha Rice's bubbly voice brought a smile to Alanna's face. "Whatcha doing?"

"You wouldn't believe me if I told you."

"That good?"

"Better." Alanna didn't want to stir up all over again the crush of emotions she'd experienced in coming home.

"Aren't you going to tell me?"

"Let's just say I'm settling in."

"Not too well, I hope. This apartment is empty and dull without you." Sam's pout made Alanna laugh, something she hadn't done in too long.

"It's not like I've been around that much."

"Sure, the trial kept you busy, but you at least slept here most of the time." Sam made an oooing sound, like a ghost. "It's creepy here alone. You've never heard so many creaks and groans in one place."

"You could come here." Alanna clapped a hand over her mouth. Returning home must bother her more than she realized.

Sam snorted. "That would require me to have some idea of where you are. Tell me, and I'll get the time off."

She opened her mouth but couldn't do it. She needed the separation between her worlds. "Never mind."

"That's what I figured. Well, glad to know you arrived wherever it is you went. Let me know if you need anything other than forwarding your mail to your mom and feeding your cat."

"Thank you."

"That's what friends are for. Even if you're being overly secretive. I'm ready to believe you're a secret agent or something equally crazy!" As Alanna hung up, she wondered why she couldn't just tell Sam the truth. Most people associated Mackinac Island with a relaxing getaway. Sam would probably think it was the perfect place to recover. Could it feel like a retreat? Maybe it should. The events that caused Alanna to run happened eleven years ago. Maybe it was time to stop hiding.

The next morning, Alanna awoke to light streaming through the eyelet curtains. Her room had transformed from Pepto-Bismol pink to white and pristine. She stretched then burrowed back under the covers. How long would it take her to get down to the Painted Stone? Taking the taxi yesterday was an expense she couldn't afford every day.

A cool breeze fluttered the curtains. Maybe her old bike still rested in the storage shed. If so, she'd ride it down. Otherwise she'd need to find one. The island was too big to walk everywhere.

Alanna got ready then grabbed the storage shed key from the junk drawer and walked out the back door to the storage building. It sat a few yards to the side of the house, surrounded by lilac trees. The paint peeled on the cream-colored building. She worked the key into the padlock then slid the door to the side. The early morning light penetrated the shadows in the small building. Cobwebs hung in strands from the rafters, making Alanna wonder when her parents had last used the building. Without a horse, she couldn't imagine either of them walking into town every day. The walking in wouldn't be a problem since it was primarily downhill, but returning was a doozy.

Back in a corner, she found her old bike with the large basket on the front. She pulled it out and tested the tires. She'd need to find a pump, because those flat inner tubes weren't taking her anywhere. After digging, she found a bicycle pump buried in a corner and got the tires filled. She hopped on and took it for a spin around the yard. The wide tires bounced across the lawn. She'd make it to the studio, no problem. She ran back inside, grabbed her purse, and headed down the road.

As she pedaled to town, the bite in the morning air made her wish she'd grabbed an extra jacket and gloves. By noon the sun would burn off the clouds and warm the air, but late May mornings held on to the cold, with the temperature hanging in the forties. She shivered as she chained the bike behind the Painted Stone and unlocked the door. The downtown area held the calm of a waking town. The tourists remained ensconced in their warm rooms, leaving quiet in their absence.

Alanna took advantage of the stillness to dust the paintings. The work of four or five artists dotted the walls. Everything from modern slashes of paint to her mother's Impressionist leanings.

Alanna considered rearranging the paintings to bring some order to the mismatched styles, but first she'd check the storage room. See if any paintings waited to replace any she sold. Somehow she had to get buying customers in the store while finding an employee.

The bell dinged over the door, and she exited the storage room with a smile. Her steps faltered when she saw who entered. "Mr. Hoffmeister?"

A short, balding man pivoted on his heel. His shoulders were slightly stooped from a lifetime of pushing fudge along marble tabletops. Gray curls ringed his head like a crown. The rich smell of chocolate flavored with mint clung to him. He appraised her with intelligent, chocolate-colored eyes, a cautious smile twitching the corners of his mouth. "Alanna Stone. I'd heard rumors you were back."

"The grapevine in action."

"This is a small place."

Alanna bit back a sharp retort. "Yes, sir."

"You here to help your parents?"

"For a bit."

He nodded. "Is that it?"

Alanna straightened the pens lined up on the counter, avoiding the old man's searching gaze. "Don't worry. I'll leave as soon as I can find someone else to work here."

"No one wants to run you off. I've missed seeing you around."

"Unlike. . ."

"No one ran you off then, Ms. Stone. You did that on your own." It hadn't felt that way. "Everyone assumed we did it."

"No one ordered Grady to jump into the water."

"How do you know?"

"You young fools were down the hill from my house. Besides, Ginger filled me in."

Alanna's mind spun with the possibilities. As an eighteen-year-old, she'd never stopped to think who might have seen the party. They'd all assumed they were too sneaky to have adults notice. "You could see?"

"Of course. And with Ginger there, I kept an eye on things. How do you think the paramedics got there so fast? It would take a deaf and blind fool not to notice the bonfire."

The bell jangled as the door opened again. A couple walked in wearing the resort casual clothes indicative of guests at the Grand Hotel.

The woman, looking like a flamingo in her head-to-toe pink ensemble, approached the wall of Stone originals. "Honey, look at these colors. Can't you see this one over the fireplace?"

"Sure, darling." The man nodded with the bored air of someone who didn't know an original from a paint-by-number kit and would rather hit the links on the hotel's golf course.

If he was that indifferent, Alanna could taste the sale. She glanced at Mr. Hoffmeister and then at the couple.

He waved her off. "Stop by some night. I'll get you some of your favorite fudge, and we can catch up. Maybe Ginger can come over and you can reconnect. She needs more friends." He raised his fingers to his head in a salute. "It's good to see you."

"Thank you." She watched him leave then turned to the couple. Slight unease she couldn't shake tightened her shoulder blades. Ginger had dated Grady, been certain they would have a fairy tale come to life. Then Grady died, and she changed, altering the close friendship Alanna and Ginger had shared throughout school.

Alanna shook free of the thought. Maybe tonight she'd stop by Mr. Hoffmeister's shop. Eat fudge and hear him out.

"Ma'am, I think we'll take this one." The woman smiled broadly while her husband tugged at his back pocket.

Right now she'd sold a painting. A surge of hope pulsed through her.

## 6

J onathan hurried across the street and into the breach. Well, that's what it felt like as he rushed to reach the foundation meeting. Having a four-color, glossy presentation for each member of the foundation's board of directors wouldn't do him a lick of good if he arrived late. He wished his printer had fed the paper without jamming on every other page.

If Jaclyn hadn't called as the printer jammed on the last brochure, he still might have arrived on time. But she'd cried through another crisis, and he'd listened because he couldn't cut her off.

The squat white building with a bright red door and black shutters on each side of the windows sat next to the community building. He sidestepped a tourist and opened the door. He eased his shoulders down and hoped his face didn't reflect evidence he'd run across the business section to arrive late.

"Good morning, Laura."

The mid-forties brunette looked up from her computer monitor at her desk. "There you are. Mr. Tomkins about to go into his late-is-unacceptable dance."

Jonathan sighed. "Guess it's good I arrived."

"You betcha. Go on back." Her fingers clicked against the keyboard as she spoke.

He followed the pine hallway to the conference room. The door stood open to reveal a battered oak table surrounded by eight chairs.

A whiteboard on the wall had a dozen bullet points with various arrows connecting the ideas.

"Jonathan Covington." Mr. Tomkin leaned back in his chair, his arms crossed across his chest.

"I told you he'd get here." Bette Standeford, an older woman with blond highlights trying to cover her gray, leaned back in her chair. She'd been a regular on the island longer than he could remember, making it her year-round residence a couple of years earlier. A few months ago she'd sent her niece his way to plan her wedding. It was good to have her here and on his side. "We're eager to hear your ideas."

Jonathan strode into the room with his chin up and messenger bag at the ready. He might sit on the foundation's board, but the foundation had made it clear he wouldn't get the work without providing a proposal that wowed them. "Thanks for inviting me to share some ideas with you."

"Word's spreading that you've got good ideas." A man in a polo with one of the B&B logos on it studied him. "So what do you have for us?"

"Whatever it is, I hope it's good." Bryce Morris, the event manager at the Grand Hotel, studied Jonathan. "You've brought a few clients our way. I appreciate it, even if it doesn't take much effort . . . ."

Polite laughter circled the table, and Jonathan smiled. Moments like this energized him. Those on the island recognized his work. Now if he could get them to send referrals his way, it would help with his plans to expand.

Jonathan met Mr. Tomkins appraising gaze. "Where would you like me?"

"Right there."

"All right." Jonathan opened his bag and pulled out the file filled with presentations. "I've brought preliminary ideas for a new festival." He handed out the sheets, and the next five minutes disappeared as he spun his vision for a swing event under the stars. "It's popular in other locales. Most important, it would complement the jazz festival without competing."

Gerald shook his head. "I don't see retirees going for it."

"Sure they will. It's music from their childhoods, and the younger crowd has rediscovered it. It's the perfect mix."

"Why not something like country?"

"Mackinac Island isn't exactly a big buckle, ten-gallon hat, and cowboy boots kind of place."

"Are you stereotyping, young man?" Bette grinned as she lobbed the question.

"I like being called a young man, but no. Not any more than fudgies do." She smiled at his use of the local term for tourists. "There might be a day to try an event centered on a country theme. But we'll ease our way there. Think where most people who visit come from—Chicago, Indiana, Michigan. Not exactly cowboy country." The conversation ricocheted, disagreements surfacing only to have Gerald squash dissenting views. The more time Jonathan spent around him, the more Gerald's used-car-salesman persona grated on him. Did Jonathan really want to coordinate an event with that man reviewing his every move —because anything Jonathan did for the foundation ultimately had to please him.

"Bottom line, Mr. Covington." The formal words didn't elicit much hope. "We've got the music festival in August. If you can't give us new ideas, then we'll look elsewhere." Mr. Tomkin leaned back in his chair and crossed his arms. "We need some-thing fresh."

"Remember, something completely new takes time. It has to be branded and launched well. Otherwise you'll lose money on something more time could have saved."

Gerald studied him then looked at the other members. "Well?" Almost an hour later, Jonathan escaped the small building.

While the foundation members liked his ideas, Mr. Tomkin prodded to a point Jonathan didn't expect. Maybe Jonathan hadn't pushed enough. Or he'd been too honest. Still, he hadn't endured a challenge like that in a while.

He inhaled deeply, trying to shake the uncertainty that clouded his mind. Tomkin had made it clear the contract wasn't his— at least not without some major revisions to his proposal. Now Jonathan wasn't sure he wanted to try again. Not when it meant pleasing Tomkin—an impossible task. He needed to refo-cus. Fast. His afternoon calendar overflowed with conference calls for various clients, the kind who actually liked his ideas and paid for them.

When the Painted Stone stood in front of him, he stopped. The lights were on, but the store looked aban-doned. A lingering guilt replaced the blasé feeling from the meeting. He'd been too harsh last night. Maybe their summers together hadn't meant as much to Alanna. He needed to let the past go. Good grief, she disappeared eleven years ago, and he had Jaclyn. The thought didn't bring the satisfaction it did even a week earlier. It didn't matter.

Anyone else would have moved on years ago. It wasn't her fault his attempts had flopped. That he clung to the future he'd imagined for them. He needed to face facts. Real life didn't measure up to the ideal.

He needed to apologize but limit it to that. He straightened his back and walked into the store.

"I'll be with you in a minute." Alanna's alto carried across the room from the back. Didn't her mom have a studio of some sort tucked in there? It had been last season since he'd received an invitation to see Rachelle's latest work.

"There's no hurry."

At the sound of his voice, she popped around the corner. "Jonathan?"

He shrugged. "Bet you didn't expect to see me."

"Not after last night." She crossed her arms over her torso.

"What can I do for you?"

"Look, I wanted to apologize for last night. I was a boar."

She nodded. "You were."

"Were you going to explain why you left without a word? Back then?"

Fire flashed in her eyes as her face paled. "Why do you care now? You could have asked then if it mattered." She glanced around the studio. "It's not like my parents left."

He studied her, pondering the right words to diffuse her anger. Maybe he shouldn't have been so abrupt last night. Now his frustration had transferred to her, and he couldn't really fault her. Maybe they could find a way to reach a truce and survive their time as neighbors.

Look, I'm sorry for how I acted last night. I never expected to see you back on Mackinac after all this time. Guess I was unprepared." He shoved his hands deep in his pockets. "Sorry to bother you. I'll see you tonight."

Some of the stiffness evaporated from her posture. Did he make her feel like she had to protect herself from attack, or did the island do that? He turned toward the door then paused as a painting caught his eye. "You know, there's something about these new paintings of your mom's that's different."

She frowned and came to stand beside him. "What do you mean?"

The question wasn't nearly as hostile as he'd expected. How could he explain to her something indefinable? "I'm not sure."

"You'll have to be more specific. After all, don't you think an artist's style can evolve over time? She's painted for decades."

"Maybe."

"Maybe? You must have missed art appreciation in college. Just look at Van Gogh. His use of color and technique definitely changed."

Jonathan cocked his head to the side as he studied the painting. Mrs. Stone's perspective in her paintings tended to be different from other artists. Maybe because she lived on the island for months each year she saw things others missed. But still, she chose different angles. He studied the painting a moment more. It wasn't the angles that looked off. Was it the colors?

"See, you can't explain it." Alanna seemed happy, almost as if she forced the emotion. "You're hypercritical."

"Maybe, but I don't think so. You might ask her about it."

"And when would I do that? In between the doctor appointments and physical therapy? Or when she's meeting with contractors to try to figure out if they can reconfigure the house so they can return?"

She had no idea how attractive she looked when her eyes flashed like that. The cheeks that had drained of color earlier now had the flush of roses. Her lips parted as if she wanted to launch her next salvo. He placed a finger on top of them, and she froze.

"No need to take out your anger on me, Lanna." The pet name slipped from his mouth.

She sputtered a moment then stepped back. "Nobody calls me that."

"Nobody but me." He leaned closer, his breath catching. What was he doing? He cleared his throat and took a step back. He glanced at his watch. He needed to move or he'd have angry clients to deal with in addition to prickly Gerald Tomkin. "We'll continue this tonight. My place. Six o'clock."

"What? You think I want to spend time with you?"

"Yes."

"What if I have plans?" Something in her expression begged him to keep asking even as her words resisted the idea.

"Change them. We need to talk." He'd pull out the extra chair. "Six o'clock."

"I don't think I can leave here by then." She brushed her lips, as if still feeling his finger there.

He memorized the moment. Maybe they weren't through after all. The thought caught him.

"There's so much to do, and I can't afford to miss any moment that someone might come."

"Most stores close by six. Especially this early in the season." He leaned toward her, closing the space, feeling the pull to get closer to her. "Don't worry—it'll be painless. You don't have to cook, and I promise not to poison the food." He looked at the wall of paintings again. "And I have a client who might want to commission something by your mom."

The door opened, but he kept his gaze locked on Alanna.

"Jonathan. Fancy seeing you here."

He closed his eyes then turned toward Jaclyn. "What brings you here?"

"Need new artwork for the spa." Her words were light, but she studied him. "Introduce me?"

"Alanna, I'd like you to meet my. . ." What? Friend? Girl-friend? Neither word tasted right. ". . .Good friend Jaclyn Raeder. Jaclyn, this is an old friend Alanna Stone. Her family owns the Painted Stone."

"Uh-huh. Surprised I haven't seen you around." Her smile had a bite to it.

Alanna looked between the two of them, an ah-ha moment crossing her face. She covered it with a smile that didn't reach her eyes. "Nice to meet you, Ms. Raeder. I'd be happy to help you find the right art for the spa. Where is it located?"

"The Grand Hotel."

Alanna's eyes brightened, and her smile grew bigger. "Do you want to pick out some artwork now?"

"It's why I'm here."

"Nice to bump into you, Jaclyn. Tell Dylan hi for me." Jonathan turned to Alanna. "See you tonight, Alanna."

A small smile twitched Alanna's cheeks. "All right. If I can get away."

"If..." He backed toward the door. There'd be no "if" about it. If she didn't come home, he'd bring the food to her. A woman had to eat, and he could easily grab some sandwiches and salads at Doud's. She couldn't hide forever.

"Until tonight." He caught Jaclyn's eye and grimaced. He'd have a lot of explaining to do. Something that had to wait until he had a better idea what might develop between him and Alanna. One moment it felt like no time had passed between them, and other times he felt every year of the eleven.

## 7

Traffic on the street never slowed through the afternoon. A steady flow kept her in the studio in case customers wanted to explore the collection. As a result, hunger gnawed in Alanna's stomach, but she didn't think she could leave. Not yet.

And it had nothing to do with Jonathan's invitation. She'd decided not to hide. Not from him.

Okay, maybe she'd look for every excuse she could find to stay away. Once Jonathan left, Jaclyn had straightened her petite frame and turned the full force of her charm on Alanna, but it had felt staged. The woman's auburn curls had bounced each time she tossed her head, and her smile had the edges of a cobra. Like the woman intended to learn everything she could about Alanna without giving much information about herself. Well, other than the fact she and Jonathan were more than friends.

The hour Jaclyn had stayed had passed with lots of awkward moments, times when Alanna looked up to catch Jaclyn studying her. Intently. Alanna had wanted to assure her she had nothing to worry about. But couldn't.

Jaclyn had taken her cute self from the studio without a painting. She'd promised to come back with a purchase order, but Alanna didn't plan on seeing her again. She should have told the twenty-something that she hadn't seen Jonathan in eleven years. That whatever they might have had disappeared a long time ago. But she hadn't. So the thick fog of discomfort remained.

Enough.

She shook free of her unease and pulled up Google on the old computer and waited for the server to chug through cyberspace. Then she pulled up the *Grand Rapids Press.* There had to be a better way to find an employee, but at the moment she couldn't think of one, especially since she didn't want to hire a local. The last thing she needed was to answer the questions, *Where have you been? Why did you leave?*

A woman walked by arm in arm with an older man but pulled him to the window. She pressed her nose to the glass as she looked in. Alanna considered waving, but would that invite or intimidate her?

Instead, she clicked to the classified ad section of the paper and scanned a few for inspiration. She tried to frame an ad in her head. *Studio on beautiful Mackinac Island seeks summer help. E-mail your resume to:*

To where? She entered the studio's general e-mail address then looked up as the bells danced.

So the woman had talked her escort into entering.

Alanna did a double take as the woman gracefully swayed across the floor. Her escort looked familiar. So familiar, Alanna fought the urge to dive into the back room and stay there until the couple left. After all, they wouldn't buy anything. Too bad her mama didn't raise a coward. Alanna raised her chin and squared her shoulders.

It wasn't every day the opposing counsel on the case that had splattered her image across every newspaper in the state for more than a month walked into her parents' studio.

He leaned against the door, his posture indicating he'd rather be anywhere but here. His gaze traveled the room, sliding over her before coming back. He pushed from the wall, a wolfish grin on his face. "Alanna Stone?"

"Hello, Bennett." She tried to hold a pleasant smile but couldn't.

"So this is where you ran. The legal grapevine's gone crazy wondering where the conquering heroine disappeared. Glad to see it's not a nervous breakdown."

Sure he was. "Nothing like relaxing here. Can't get much slower paced."

"Too much so if you ask me, but Tabitha likes it." He shrugged. "After the trial, I owed her."

"You sure did, baby."

Bennett smiled at Tabitha then turned to study Alanna. "Why are you here?"

"Having that nervous breakdown." She winked, even though it killed her to be nice to the man. He'd made her life miserable for the duration of the pretrial and trial. Anytime he could make an argument, he did. The annoying part came in the way the judge allowed him to do it. She'd fought so hard for her clients.

"Really? After that win—which I'm appealing."

Alanna stifled the groan that rose at the thought of more battles with him.

"Ready, Tabitha?"

"Not yet. I think I want this one." The blond, who looked a bit like a poodle with her bouncy, curly hair, pointed at one of her mom's largest paintings. "This would look amazing behind the dining room table, don't you think?"

Bennett rolled his eyes. "If that's what you want..."

"You promised I could have anything. This is it." She pointed a perfectly manicured finger at the explosion of color. "The fall shades are perfect."

"Fine." He turned to Alanna. "So how much is that beauty?"

Alanna forced back a grin. This could be the perfect payback for all the trouble he inflicted. "Let me look it up for you." She clicked a few keys on the keyboard to pull up the database. "Could you tell me the name?"

"Watercolor Sunsets."

"Really?" Interesting title since Mom only used oils.

Tabitha leaned closer to the small block of card stock next to the painting. "Yes."

"All right." Alanna clicked on FIND then entered the name. When the information popped up, she added five hundred dollars to the amount. "Five thousand five hundred dollars."

Bennett flinched. "For that piece of canvas and a bit of paint? I could make that in my sleep."

"You're welcome to try, but this artist's work sells quickly. I wouldn't wait too long, or it might disappear."

He led Tabitha into the corner and chatted for a moment, but by the set of the woman's jaw, Alanna knew the painting would leave with them. Five minutes later, she wrapped the painting like a mummy in bubble wrap before sliding it into an oversized box. "Be careful carrying this. The paintings are always heavier than you expect."

"My wallet's certainly lighter. We'll send a courier. Come on, Tabitha."

The woman sidled up next to him and practically purred. Alanna released the joy that had built inside. A sale—and to a man like that. She couldn't believe it.

"Thank You, Lord!" She breathed the words as she disappeared into the storage room to find a replacement. A few minutes later, she returned lugging a new painting. Jonathan scanned a wall of paintings. A picnic basket sat at his feet.

"Sorry, I didn't hear you come in."

"No problem. I brought the picnic to you." The smell of something sweet yet spicy wafted from the basket.

"It smells great." Alanna drew in a breath and smiled. She wouldn't hide her hunger, but the way she suddenly longed for time with Jonathan surprised her. She couldn't be swayed simply by a great-smelling picnic. "I can't tell you how glad I am I stayed. I just sold my first large painting. Since I was a teen anyway."

"Congratulations. Need help hanging that one?"

"Sure." In an effortless movement, Jonathan hefted it onto the hanger. "Thanks."

Jonathan brushed his hands on his jeans then glanced at the floor. "Do you have anything we can sit on? I forgot to grab a blanket."

Really? He didn't plan to mention Jaclyn? Fine, she'd play along for the moment. "I don't know. Let me check the studio."

The first time Alanna had walked back there, the lack of mess surprised her. It used to overflow with half-painted canvases and piles of sketches and tubes of half-used paint. Now it felt almost sterile with only splatters of paint dotting the cement floor and empty easels. Her mother must have done a deep clean before leaving Mackinac. But Mom never dealt with stress and uncertainty that way before. Instead, the house and back areas of the studio would get more chaotic as her stress increased.

Jonathan would follow her back here in a minute if she didn't find something and get out front. She opened the closet door and pulled out a folded canvas tarp. Bright paint splotches dotted it, making it a colorful swirl. Her low heels clicked against the floor as she hurried back to the front room. She slowed and watched Jonathan stroll the edge of the room. He seemed to carry a burden as he trailed from painting to painting. When she stopped, he turned toward her.

"Will this work?"

"As long as you promise me the paint's dry." He rubbed his thumbs down his jeans.

"I promise I haven't used it."

"Good enough for me." He walked over and took the bundle from her. A shiver slipped up her arms where his hands glanced against her. He stilled and looked deeply into her eyes. Could he read her thoughts? She hoped not as they ricocheted like colliding atoms without any order. He cleared his throat and stepped back. He flicked his wrists, and the tarp ballooned before parachuting to the floor. "How's this?"

"Good." The only good thing about having a picnic in the studio was anybody passing by could see. Alanna could only imagine the electricity that would leap between them if they were secluded in his little cabin. She'd spent years convincing herself there was nothing special between them. Now in minutes he'd eradicated that idea.

Jonathan crouched next to the basket and opened the lid. In a minute, he'd pulled out a tub of fried chicken and the fixings. Her stomach growled as the wonderful aromas filled the space. Then he pulled out a bottle of sparkling cider and a pair of champagne flutes. Her heart thudded as he set them on the tarp.

Rebound. That's all this was. If Spencer hadn't told her a couple of weeks ago he didn't plan to buy a ring, she wouldn't feel so vulnerable. So needy for love. She must stiffen her defenses. Fortify her resolve. Remember Jaclyn's slate eyes as she watched Jonathan.

"Is this okay?" Questions carved lines into the corners of his eyes.

"It's been awhile since I've had fried chicken."

"You used to love it."

"Still do," she assured him as she wondered if they'd keep things so surface.

"You got so quiet, I wondered."

"Just thinking."

"As long as it was good thoughts."

She nodded then sank to the edge of the cloth. "How long have you been on the island?"

"Since Gram and Pops decided the winters were too much for them. I usually abandon this area for the worst months of winter. But I love it here. Always have."

A shiver tickled her spine at the thought of the long, harsh winters. "Nothing like riding snowmobiles to get to school."

"Never did that, but you always said you liked it."

"When I was young and didn't know better." Winters in Grand Rapids might have tempered her. Now she couldn't imagine spending the winter in a place with as much snow as Mackinac Island endured.

Jonathan reached into the basket and pulled out a plastic plate and set of silverware. After a quick prayer, he handed them to her. "Dig in."

Silence settled over them as they filled their plates and ate. Alanna wondered if she should force conversation but didn't feel up to the challenge. Then Jonathan started asking questions. He probed what college had been like, shared some of his crazy college stories, then asked about the churches she'd attended. It seemed his faith had grown as hers had while they were apart.

"So what has God taught you lately?" Jonathan pushed his plate to the side and focused on her as he waited for her answer.

She shifted and picked at a piece of lint on her slacks. "That's a good question. One I'll need to think about. I know He's working but not sure I can articulate how on the spot."

Jonathan nodded. "Fair enough. It's a question one of my

roommates in college still likes to ask. Always makes me think hard." A comfortable silence settled over them.

Could Jonathan become a trusted friend again, or should she keep him at arm's length? If only her parents' home didn't sit next door to his. The island was too small to avoid him anyway.

He wiped his fingers with a napkin and set it on top of his empty plate then leaned back on his hands and studied her. She swiped a strand of hair out of her face and behind her ear, fighting the urge to blush under his scrutiny. "What?"

"Would you have returned if your dad hadn't gotten sick?"

Alanna looked at a point beyond his shoulder, unable to meet his intensity. "Probably not. I got pretty good at avoiding it. Everything I loved died with that stupid party."

"You always talked about coming back after college. You wanted to be part of the future here."

Not anymore. Not after they betrayed her brother. Her posture tightened as she felt the familiar anger return. Someday she needed to move on, but being here on the island brought it all back to stark reality. She clutched it to her like a protective shield.

"Do you see Trevor often?" Jonathan's quiet question jerked her from her thoughts.

"He's my brother."

Jonathan shrugged. "Sure, but I know lots of siblings who never see each other."

"That's not us. Or it shouldn't be. I always imagined that at some point he'd quit being my twerpy brother and become one of my best friends. Then we both left, and it felt like any time we spent together threw us both back to Grady's death. It was less painful to just not see each other." The relaxing, romantic evening spiraled downward with the trend of her thoughts. Romantic? She had no right to think in those terms—not with Jonathan.

"Have him come here."

"Back to Mackinac?" Alanna snorted, not caring what kind of impression that made. "He wants to be here even less than me."

"That night was more than a decade ago. How long will it control you?"

"Control me?" Her voice rose. "You don't know what you're talking about, Jonathan. Believe it or not, everyone brushed me with the same brush they applied to Trevor." Tears clogged the back of her throat, and she launched to her feet. "Thank you for bringing dinner, but I need to lock up and get home." If only that meant her apartment in Grand Rapids. Especially since the reporters probably had abandoned their nightly stakeouts.

Even if they haunted her doorway, anything would be better than staying one more moment on this island with the shadows of the past.

## 8

Jonathan had known the past distorted Alanna's vision, but he hadn't expected her to order him out. The ease of their earlier conversation had surprised him. Now he'd collided with her erected barriers.

She stopped long enough to shove plates and containers filled with remnants of their meal back in the basket. Moisture filled her eyes and threatened to overflow. The oh-so-tough Alanna Stone looked ready to break.

It couldn't be simply what happened to Trevor. There had to be something more adding to the stress. Jaclyn? He wished he could have stuck around for their conversation. He'd explore that later, because now it was abundantly clear she wanted him out. Gone. Disappearing.

He touched her hand, felt it tremble under his. "I'll get this. You do whatever else you need to." As soon as she nodded, he stifled a yawn. He couldn't afford fatigue, not when he had several hours of work waiting when he got home.

In less time than he expected, he followed Alanna out the door and waited as she locked it. "I'll bike home with you."

"I have a stop." Her words were tight, almost strangled.

The island might be safe, but there was no way he was going to leave her to make her way on the roads by herself. It would be dark soon, and in the wooded areas it would already feel like night had fallen. Besides, the tourists had arrived, and with them came the typical round of drunk and disorderlies. In her frame of mind, she might forget how the island could be at night.

"I don't mind waiting." He'd make supercharged coffee in the morning.

She glanced at him a moment then threw her purse strap across her shoulder. "Whatever you like. You always did what you wanted anyway."

The way she said the words had a bite that made him almost change his mind. Yet his mother had drilled into him the need to be a gentleman when it came to ladies. Always. Regardless of how they treat you. He'd extend grace for now. He pulled back at that thought. Grace shouldn't be extended in dribs and drabs.

"Really, Jonathan. Go home. I'm fine." As if to punctuate the comment, Alanna threw a leg over the bike and pedaled into traffic.

The *clop-clop* of dray horses' hooves against the asphalt didn't distract him. He shoved the handles of the picnic basket over the handlebars and pumped to follow Alanna. If she didn't want him, fine. He'd stay behind, still her silent guardian.

Raucous music filtered out the open doors of the Man O' War. A young man stumbled out and right into Alanna's path. She swerved the bike, narrowly missing a woman on foot in her efforts to avoid the drunk. She pulled to the side in front of I'm Not Sharing Fudge Shop.

Jonathan eased to a stop next to her. "Want some dessert?"

Her hair flipped across her face as she turned toward him. "Go away, Jonathan."

"Not happening. Last time you disappeared for eleven years."

"I need to ask Mr. Hoffmeister a question."

"That old guy? He's nice enough . . . ." But why ditch him for Mr. H.?

"Really, Jonathan, go ahead. You've got better things to do than watch my bike. Where's it going?"

Her insistence made him want to demand he tag along. She was up to something, and he wanted to know what. Guess he was ultra-nosy at the moment.

"Come on, Lanna. I'll keep my mouth shut."

"No." She pushed at his handlebars, and he wobbled as the basket slid to the side. "I'll see you *later*."

How much rejection should he endure before he acquiesced? "If you're sure. . ."

"I can find my way home. Good night, Jonathan."

"All right then." No matter what his mom had told him, you couldn't be a gentleman if the woman refused.

ALANNA WATCHED Jonathan pedal down the street. He looked over his shoulder once, and she waved. She didn't need him acting like a burr attached to her side. She turned to I'm Not Sharing Fudge Shop. Maybe Mr. Hoffmeister still worked evenings. He'd always insisted that was his favorite time to man the shop since he could observe everyone pass by.

Maybe he knew something about what happened to Grady. How could she have forgotten his cottage faced the area they'd chosen for the bonfire and festivities? Between that and whatever Ginger knew, she needed to talk to him.

An electronic ding announced her arrival. The old man hunched over a paperback as he sat on a stool behind the cash register. He marked his page and then glanced up. A grin split his face, revealing stained teeth. "Alanna! I wondered when you'd stop by. Need some fudge?"

"Yes, sir. I haven't missed much but your fudge. Someday you'll have to share your special ingredient."

"No can do. If I did, nobody would need me anymore. Can't have that." He grabbed a piece of wax paper and a knife. "Now what would you like to sample?" He pointed at a couple of blocks. "How about the mint chocolate? Or the peanut butter? But if I know you after all these years, I'm thinking the peppermint tickles your taste buds."

"Sounds great." As soon as he handed her a thin slice, she broke off a corner and slipped it in her mouth. The sweetness melted against her tongue, and she moaned. "This is so good. I'd better take a pound and be grateful I bike and walk everywhere."

"I knew you'd like it." He sliced off a bigger chunk and wrapped it in a one-pound box. "What else can I do for you?"

He sidled back to the cash register and rang up her order while she considered how to proceed.

"I wanted to ask what you remember."

"About that day?"

"Yes, sir."

He slipped her money into the cash drawer then sank to the stool. "That was a long time ago, kid. You have to let go."

"You must have talked to Jonathan."

"Jonathan?"

"Covington. He told me the same thing."

"Haven't talked to him, but we're of the same mind. What good comes of stirring up that hornet's nest?"

Alanna clutched the box as if gripping a lifeline. "Because I want the world to know Trevor wasn't involved."

"Everybody there was."

That stung. She'd been there. To this day she wondered if

there was something she could have—should have—done to avert the tragedy.

"Look, you can carry this burden the rest of your life, let it color every day and everything you do. Or you can release it and trust those around here to move on with grace. You might try it yourself." He glanced at his watch and stood. "Time for me to close up."

"What's this about you and Mr. Tomkin?"

He frowned. "Nothing for you to worry about. He just wants to build a monstrosity next to my house. Seems shocked I think he should follow all the building rules."

"Being neighbors can be hard on a friendship."

"It certainly can." He glanced at his watch. "Suppose I should start working on closing duties."

Alanna nodded. She'd be back, but he'd made it clear he didn't want to talk—not now. His words about grace echoed in her mind as she left.

Grace wasn't a new concept, not after all the sermons she'd heard on the topic. But applying it to this situation? That seemed impossible. Not when she had an island's worth of people to forgive. Forgetting and moving on came easier, until her parents needed her to return.

The door clanged shut behind her, and she turned to watch him hit a light switch. She couldn't imagine how many times he'd closed the shop in his lifetime. Through all kinds of events on the island, he stayed. Thought she should have done the same.

It wasn't that easy. Never had been.

Her streak of justice ran too deep to ignore, especially when it involved family. Someday she wanted a family of her own, but not if what happened to Trevor could repeat. She needed to right this. Then she could pursue a family. Maybe she was stubborn, but now that she had returned, she needed to find the truth. See if there was any way to clear her brother.

She straddled her bike and looked up then startled. Talk about stubborn. There stood Jonathan Covington leaning against the wall of Doud's. "What are you doing? I saw you leave."

"Making sure you make it home." A thread of challenge rang through his words. Just like when they were teens and he insisted she let him do something—usually something completely unnecessary.

"Go home, Jonathan."

"That's exactly what I plan to do." He lifted the Coke bottle he held. "Needed something to drink."

She tucked her slab of fudge in the bike basket. "Sure you did. Come on, since I can't shake you."

He chuckled. "That's right. I'm going to watch out for you."

Her back stiffened, and she pushed down on the pedals. "I'm not a young teenager anymore. I am fully capable of taking care of myself. Especially in such a small, *safe* place."

"I'll sleep better knowing I didn't leave you to find your way in the dark."

"I think the Coke'll keep you up." No point mentioning the hundreds of times she'd hiked these same roads and trails. She might have left eleven years ago, but that didn't erase a childhood spent exploring every inch of this island.

Silence fell as they hiked through neighborhoods and into the woods. Alanna felt her lungs burn as she fought to keep up with Jonathan. He didn't break a sweat as she gulped oxygen. She pumped harder, refusing to let him stay ahead. Not after all the times they'd raced up and down the roads. Then he rarely bested her. She couldn't let him start now, no matter how much her body screamed in protest.

The trees acquired shadows as the sun sank beneath them.

The shadows changed the way everything looked. She hadn't noticed the new houses and lanes on her couple of trips to the studio. Without Jonathan, she might have gotten turned around, but she wouldn't give him that gem to use against her the next time he insisted she allow him along.

He stopped at her driveway, and she skidded to a halt next to him. "You all right from here?"

"What? Your mama didn't tell you to walk the girl to her door? Isn't this the equivalent of honking the horn?"

"I didn't think you wanted me any closer." He reached out and caressed her cheek.

"I. . .don't."

He leaned toward her, closing the space between them. "Say it like you mean it."

"I don't need you."

"Don't believe you. I know you better." A strange expression flashed across his face at the words.

"You know the girl I was."

"I see the woman hiding in the shadows."

Her heart stilled as he stared into her eyes. Then his gaze traveled to her lips, his eyes hidden by the shadows. She clutched the handlebars but couldn't move. Years of history zinged between them. She had to break away. He had a girl, possibly a child, though she struggled to reconcile the Jonathan she'd known with a child out-of-wedlock. She couldn't interfere in that. She didn't want a reason to stay on the island one day more than necessary.

She slid her bike back and forced a smile. "Good night, Jonathan."

As she hiked up the lane, it took all her willpower not to look back and see if he still watched her. She didn't need this attraction between them. Not now.

She parked her bike and then slipped inside the front door.

She couldn't trust herself with any man, let alone Jonathan. Not after how easily she'd handed her heart to Spencer. The way he'd callously thrown it back proved she didn't know men and couldn't make a good decision. Not when in a couple of short days she was ready to jump back into Jonathan's arms after an eleven-year absence.

Only a fool relinquished her heart that quickly.

## 9

Jonathan settled at his kitchen table, laptop open and loading spreadsheets while he scanned his calendar. The picnic basket sat unpacked at his feet. Alanna might fight him, but tonight had illustrated how much remained between them. Now to decide if he could retreat to friendship.

His phone rang. He looked at the display and grimaced. Jaclyn. How could he so easily think about Alanna when Jaclyn had remained constant? Would Jaclyn fight to keep up with him as he pumped his bike up the roads? She worked at the Grand Hotel for a reason. She liked things a certain way. A way he couldn't afford. He flicked the phone. "Hey, Jaclyn."

"What're you doing?" Her sweet voice had a sultry edge to it, one that usually made him clear his calendar.

"Work."

"Now?"

"It never goes away."

She sighed. "Don't I know. When can we get together?"

No mention of this morning? Jonathan cleared his throat. He

didn't want to clutter his calendar. Not right now. "Let me check some things tomorrow." Coward. That's what he was.

"Fine. Good night." Jaclyn hung up before he could say anything. He'd smooth things over tomorrow.

Tonight he had to get some work done or he'd have unhappy clients. And while he might look like his professional life was well established, he had bigger plans for his tiny firm. He loved how God always provided, but he'd like to implement some of his ideas for growing. Before he could hire an employee or two, he had to buckle down and find the time to make his current clients' visions reality while finding new clients.

He nursed the half-empty Coke and berated himself. He really hadn't had time for Alanna. Not when she acted as elusive as the Kirtland's warbler.

From the first moment he saw her the summer before his freshman year, he'd known she was special. The girls at his high school on the mainland didn't interest him after a summer exploring Mackinac Island with Alanna. Each summer he returned, and the bond grew. He'd thought she felt the same, but then she'd left. He could have pursued her, but why chase someone who never called or wrote?

Now she'd returned.

And he had Jaclyn. The thought made his shoulders tighten. Until yesterday, he liked the idea of more days with Jaclyn. Now he felt a churning, uprooted sensation.

Maybe it indicated he had a chance to see if he'd imagined everything and expanded on it during the intervening years. Or a chance to shatter a good woman's heart while another woman broke his. Jaclyn was a kind woman, one he should be happy to spend his life with. But now that Alanna had arrived. . . He'd never imagined one day around Alanna after all this time would reignite what they'd had. He couldn't begin to imagine how to explain to Jaclyn. What if she'd walked by the studio, glanced in, and seen the picnic? How could he explain that what looked intimate wasn't? The worst part came from the realization he didn't want to explain it away.

One fact remained uncontradicted: Jaclyn didn't match the standard Alanna set. With her love of life and drive, Alanna had set the bar too high for anyone else to hurdle. And that wasn't because absence made the memories sweeter.

The computer dinged. Guess he had e-mail.

Time to get back to work and get those revised ideas ready for Tomkin.

THE NEXT MORNING, Jonathan took a few minutes on his back patio to listen for the Kirtland's warbler while he inhaled his coffee. No brew existed rich enough and caffeinated enough to get him through the day. He might as well set up an IV drip and drag it behind him.

The morning was pretty quiet. He couldn't hear the warbler, let alone scan for it with the binoculars that rested at his side. Maybe this weekend he could claim the time to stalk the little, impossible-to-find bird.

If he did that, he wouldn't have time between events to sit at home wondering what Alanna was doing next door. Though if she hadn't found an assistant by then, she'd be down at the studio. Her family couldn't afford missed income on what was usually the busiest day of the week.

Add in Memorial Day, and the weekend should hop with tourists taking advantage of package deals at the Grand Hotel and bed-and-breakfasts. Then he had a wedding to coordinate on Monday. Any peace he'd pulled around him evaporated at the thought. For someone who loved event planning, weddings weren't his thing. They paid the bills, but a part of him felt like he stole from the couples when he encouraged their vision of happily ever after.

Having Alanna back on Mackinac didn't change his position. Especially as they struggled to find footing as friends.

His mama had raised him to treasure one woman. The problem came when that woman walked away without a backward glance. Then she returned bearing scars. Oh yeah, he was ready to go plan the final details on someone's forever commitment. Could he pretend? *Help me, Lord.*

This wedding he hadn't prayed about first. Mistake number one.

Then the bride changed her mind every other minute, and he didn't say anything. Mistake number two.

Not answering her call last night? Mistake number three.

He'd have to talk her off the ledge today. An emotional bridezilla.

The sound of the door opening next door filtered across the space, jarring him from his downward-spiraling thoughts. Time to act rather than think. And if he happened to catch Alanna on the trail, all the better.

Five minutes later, water dripped down his neck as he pulled on khakis, a polo, and a fleece pullover. He shoved a couple of protein bars in a pocket and hopped on his bike. He didn't see Alanna or her bike as he headed out. The fact he checked made him chuckle. For a guy who didn't believe in true love, he sure wasted effort keeping tabs on Alanna. He could still catch her. He couldn't imagine her riding hard enough to glisten before she got to work. Coming home was different than getting there.

He steadied his breath, pumping just to the point of raising his heart rate but letting gravity pull him toward Lake Huron. He hadn't gone far when he saw a hot-pink shadow on an old bike. Hot pink? Still her color after all these years, though he supposed she called it something fancy like fuchsia now.

He pedaled harder to help gravity's pull until he reached Alanna's side. A headband pulled her hair back from her face. The wind had pulled a few strands loose, and they framed her face in a way that left his fingers itching to tuck them behind her ears.

She didn't even glance at him. "Don't you have better things to do?"

"Going your way, ma'am." She must have caught his mocking tone, because she turned to him and made a face. "I'll slide around you then."

"You betcha." The way she said it with her mouth tipping up in the corner made him laugh.

"You haven't been gone that long."

"Feels years longer." Then she glanced at him with that same ole mischievous glint.

"Uh-oh."

"You have no idea."

Next thing Jonathan knew, he trailed a hot-pink streak flying down the road. No way would he let her win. Not when he'd invited himself, creating the race.

He pumped up-down, up-down. Alanna seemed to have a sixth sense—or maybe she had developed a mother's second set of eyes— because she knew exactly what he planned and slid into his way each time. He grunted as he braked hard, wheels locking to avoid her latest attempt to cut him off.

"You aren't playing fair." He gritted his teeth and tried again.

"Just trying to win." Her voice wasn't flirtatious or wry, just intense. They reached the point where Scott's Road intersected with Leslie Road and turned right, but then she surprised him by turning right on British Landing Road, extending the time before they reached the busier roads. Maybe she had eleven years of frustration to take out in one bike race.

But as the trees raced past them on British Landing Road, he wondered if she'd remembered where they'd intersect Lake Shore Drive.

ALANNA'S LUNGS strained to provide the oxygen her muscles demanded.

Who's crazy idea was it to make an easy ride to work a race across the island?

At this rate she'd need a shower when she reached the studio, despite the May chill in the air. Guess it was a good thing the upstairs apartment stood empty. Who'd have thought forty-five degrees would fail her along with her Secret? Didn't matter. She was not giving up. If she had any control on the race, she'd win. Plain and simple.

But no matter how many times she swerved or swayed, Jonathan wouldn't back off. It made her think of the way he kept coming around. She'd only been on the island a few days, but already she'd gotten his message: he didn't plan to go anywhere.

She bore down and swerved around a fallen limb. The bike didn't have big enough tires to go over things like that. Not without bumping her off the seat and possibly giving her a flat. More broken branches had her steering in a crazy-eight pattern until she feared losing control. That wouldn't leave the image she wanted in Jonathan's mind. She flipped down a gear and hoped it helped. Next thing she knew, her back tire jolted, and she swayed to keep her balance.

An *oomph* from Jonathan made her want to look over her shoulder, but he bumped into her tire again.

"What are you doing?" Her voice rose, out of her control as adrenaline spiked her system.

"Trying to stay alive," he huffed. "What's with the pell-mell dive down the hills?"

"Just trying to get to work."

"In one piece?"

She snorted. "What other way is there?"

"Slow down, crazy woman." There was something in his voice that made her want to stop, ask for details. But she couldn't. She wouldn't.

"And let you slip past me? I don't think so." She leaned forward, pumping harder still.

"Watch out!"

The command in Jonathan's voice pulled her gaze up in time to see a branch loom in front of her face. It smacked her cheek, knocking her to the side. She fought for balance but couldn't find it as her bike rocked side to side. She inhaled, trying to tighten her core as her Pilates instructor harped.

Next thing she knew, she lay on the ground, her bike wheels spinning over her head. She made a mental note to tell her instructor that advice didn't work on bikes. Stinging erupted across her shins and palms where she'd collided with the ground.

Jonathan skidded to a stop and slid off the bike next to her. "Are you okay?"

Alanna touched her cheek, feeling a lump and knowing the pain would kick in soon. "Does it look as bad as it feels?"

"Better." The concern in his eyes belied his words.

"I'm not sure I believe you."

"Do you think you can get up and bike home?"

"Nothing doing. I've got to work." She touched her cheek again. "I'll stop for ice."

"Let's get you up." He reached down and offered her a hand.

She accepted his help and moaned as he tugged her up.

He stopped instantly. "Did I pull too hard?"

"Nope." She grinned at him. "Just wanted to make you

worry." He looked like he wanted to drop her hand. "Just kidding."

"No you aren't, imp." He searched her gaze. "I don't want anything to hurt you."

She stilled, lost in the intensity of his look. If someone asked her for directions, she knew she wouldn't know the first place to direct them on the small island that had been her home for nine years. And at the moment, she didn't care. Being lost in his green eyes seemed like the best thing she'd done in a long time. She inhaled a shallow breath. Would he kiss her? What would it be like after all this time?

He looked down, breaking their connection. He pulled his left wrist in front and showed her his watch face. "We'd better get moving. We can get you ice and still open in time."

She blinked. Had he caught her staring at his lips? She dragged her gaze to his eyes then over his shoulder to the pine trees towering over the trail. She needed to get away from this. . .thing. . .growing between them. She did not come here to resurrect ancient history.

She wouldn't sign up for that. Not willingly.

"You're right." She pushed her bike upright. "Can't have anyone thinking I'm not working today. The last thing Mom needs is a call from some helpful soul keeping tabs on me."

Alanna wobbled onto the bike. Taking a moment to let her equilibrium stabilize, she started pedaling without waiting for Jonathan. He'd catch up. The bottom of the road loomed. As it did, her heart hiccuped.

How could she have forgotten what lay at the end of this road?

different from

# 10

She skidded to a stop at the side of the road. Her breath hitched, and she couldn't get her lungs to expand. She couldn't breathe, and the realization terrified her.

She had to leave this place. But her legs wouldn't cooperate. She stood paralyzed, straddling the bike with the view of waves crashing against rocks along a rugged beach confronting her.

A woman slowed down, concern on her face. Not Ginger Hoffmeister. Not now. Yet there was no doubt the short, slightly rounded figure belonged to her high school friend.

In an instant, she transported back to that day in May.

*The sun burned hot on her face as she joined the other high school students. Seniors for one more week. The words tasted as sweet as cherry preserves on her tongue.*

*In a couple of months, she'd head to University of Michigan, but before that a glorious summer of freedom stretched in front of her. She could spend every evening at the dock with Jonathan Covington. By Memorial Day weekend, he'd be back at his grandparents' for the first of many stays over the summer. She couldn't wait to see him.*

*But tonight her classmates celebrated. It had never felt so good to dance in the sunlight.*

"Alanna?" Jonathan touched her shoulder. "Are you ready for this?"

"Ready?" She choked on the word. Who could be ready to revisit the place that changed their lives?

"Alanna Stone?" Ginger approached, her auburn hair inches shorter than the long ponytail she'd worn in high school. Her nose still perked up at the end, but her emerald-colored eyes held concern. "You're back?"

Alanna sucked in air, trying to force it into her lungs. Black pricked the edges of her vision. She needed oxygen. Now.

"Lean over." Jonathan pressed against her back until her forehead practically kissed the handlebars. "That better?"

Alanna wanted to scream, "No!" Not while Ginger Hoffmeister stared as she panicked.

"What happened?" Ginger's soft voice conveyed concern, concern she couldn't possibly feel or she would have contacted Alanna after her freshman year of college. Three years on the same campus, and Ginger had ended their friendship with her distance.

"Nothing." She pressed the word past the knot tightening in her throat. Pushing back, she dislodged Jonathan's hand and straightened.

"You're sure you're okay?" Ginger studied her. "I heard you were back. Sorry I haven't stopped by the studio."

"I didn't expect you." Bitterness laced her words even as she gritted her teeth together.

Ginger seemed to absorb Alanna's indifference and shrunk back. "It's good to see you." Ginger pushed off, leaving them behind.

Jonathan studied Alanna. "What was that all about? I

thought you were friends."

"We were." This was too much. The scene of Grady's accident and now Ginger. They'd been inseparable growing up. She missed the history they'd shared.

"Ready to get going? We can be at the Grand Hotel in minutes and by the library before you even notice you've started riding again."

He was right. Before the morass of pain and images sucked her under, she jerked from his touch and pushed the pedals. She hadn't noticed the bicyclers out for a ride in the early morning air, but she'd created a scene. One rider glanced away after making eye contact.

"I have to get away from here." She stepped forward, thrusting the bike into traffic between two cyclists and hurrying into the fray.

This wasn't a day to watch the last rays of the sun rising. No, today was a day to bury her head at the Painted Stone and pray for a quick escape. Nothing good happened to her here.

She never looked back on the ride around the perimeter of the island, yet she sensed Jonathan behind her. She didn't need him shadowing her every move. Discovering every secret she kept hidden. No, she needed to push him away. Keep a safe distance. And get off this island as fast as she could. Tomorrow if possible. The weekend, definitely.

JONATHAN SLOWED DOWN. He should head home and take a shower before slipping into the office. Good thing his first meeting wasn't until ten. He watched Alanna power around a couple out for an early morning ride.

Why did she run from the past? From him? The real Alanna was far different from the one he'd carried in his memories. Her return highlighted that. Much as he didn't like it, maybe he needed to see. How else would he move on?

Thirty loomed around the corner. He didn't want to live alone the rest of his life. He'd always imagined a passel of kids wrestling with him every night after work. Waiting for a mirage wouldn't make that dream a reality. He loved every moment with Jaclyn's little boy, Dylan, but he wanted kids of his own, too.

Until she confronted whatever demons chased her, Alanna wouldn't return to the strong, feisty woman he remembered. She had feisty in spades, but strength eluded her. Instead, she seemed worn down. Weary. Yet drawn to the past like a moth to the bug zapper on his porch.

His legs burned as he pumped home. A quick shower later and he again had dripping hair as he stood in his kitchen. His stomach growled. A protein bar wasn't going to fill him after that ride, but he didn't have time to make breakfast. He grabbed a browning banana and peeled it as he exited the small cabin. The cabin hadn't seemed too small before, but with dreams of Alanna floating in his head, he knew she couldn't be satisfied with a place like his. No room to make it her own.

He shoved the last bite in his mouth and headed down the hill, eventually taking Fort to Market. He avoided looking in the Painted Stone's window as he rolled past. The last thing he needed was another dose of Alanna's poison.

The moment he stepped in the office, the phone rang. He sucked in a deep, steadying breath then picked up the implement. "Mackinac Island Events."

"Jonathan Covington, just the man I wanted to talk to." The gruff voice rang with strength.

"Good morning, Mr. Morris."

"Edward, son. How many times do I have to tell you that?"

"A few more to overcome my mother's training."

The man's rich laugh tickled Jonathan's ear. "This is why I

like you. Polite with a deadly sense of humor." A moment of silence descended, and then Edward cleared his throat. "Bonnie loves all your ideas, like I said the other day, but it's not enough. Any thoughts on how we can make it bigger? She's the love of my life for as long as the good Lord lets me keep her. I want to celebrate her in a big way."

"Well. . ." Jonathan's mind spun, thoughts engaged by the challenge of creating something client worthy on the fly. "She's a special lady."

"That she is."

"What does she like to do?"

"Mentor young moms. You wouldn't believe the number of times I come home even now to find her stretched out on the couch and a young mom and her baby sitting next to her. She's always giving." Edward cleared his throat.

"Do you want to add something to the events or find something she can take home?"

"It needs to be something that's a visual reminder of our love. I'm not the best at saying the words. Too much like my dad in that respect. But I don't want her to ever doubt me."

"Didn't you say she liked art? Maybe a painting from the island?" Edward had broached the idea earlier. Jonathan hoped he still liked it.

"Maybe." Jonathan could imagine the man stroking his chin. "But it needs to be extremely special. She's always loved art though. Before she got sick, she served on the local art council. I know she misses it."

"You liked what you saw at the Painted Stone. How about I talk to a local artist about a commission? I can send photos of her art—they're vibrant pieces, and I bet she could paint something that reflects a love like yours." Did the silence mean Edward didn't like the idea? Jonathan scrambled to come up with anything else. "Or we could. . ."

"I like it. E-mail me examples. Bonnie loves color. The more the better."

Jonathan exhaled. Glad to do it. I'll stop by this afternoon. Hope there's enough time to make this work if you like her style."

"What's the artist's name?"

"Rachelle Stone."

"I'll Google her. See what I can find. Keep thinking in case this doesn't work out."

"Yes, sir."

Edward's rich laugh was back. "It's Edward. Talk to you soon.

Jonathan stared at the phone a minute before replacing it on the cradle. Now he'd done it. He would have to see Alanna. But he'd give it some time. He had a pile of work to tackle on the Lyster wedding first. Beginning with calling the bride. He pulled out the Lyster binder and looked up Theresa's number. He dialed and said a prayer for patience. The woman rode the emotional waves of wedding planning like an awkward first-time surfer.

The phone rang to the point he expected voice mail. At the last moment, he heard it click.

"Hello?"

"Ms. Lyster?"

"Yes?"

"This is Jonathan Covington."

"Well, it's about time. I'm driving to Mackinac right now."

Jonathan glanced at his desk calendar. Yep, there it was in bright red letters: *Theresa Lyster arrives.* "It will be great to have you back here."

"I don't know how we'll get everything done in time. The wedding is in four days, and there's so much to do."

"That's where I come in. Remember you hired me to make this a special event without burdening you."

"It's a nice theory, but it's still my wedding. My parents have invited all their hoity-toity friends, and it doesn't feel like my day anymore." She inhaled so deeply it sounded like she wanted to suck all the air out of her car and might stand on the verge of hyperventilating.

"Is anyone coming with you?"

"Rebecca Simpson, my maid of honor."

Perfect. Someone to help anchor the bride while he did the work. "How about I set up a spa session at the Grand Hotel this afternoon for the two of you? I'll make it right after tea so you can enjoy a relaxing afternoon. I'm checking in with the florist and caterer. Touched base with the party supply company yesterday, and they're set. Everything is coming together great."

"What will an afternoon like that cost?"

Jonathan stifled a chuckle at the thought. One didn't get married on Mackinac Island without a certain disregard for costs. It wasn't an easy place to reach, and everything had a price.

"Wait. Add it to Daddy's tab. After all, he's why I'm stressed." He heard giggling in the background. Must be the maid of honor. "Come by when you get on the island, and I'll take care of the details. You relax. Tomorrow we'll cover what's left."

"All right, Jon. You're a lifesaver. Maybe I'll survive after all."

As soon as Theresa hung up, Jonathan dialed Jaclyn. Instead of looking forward to the excuse to talk, he dreaded hearing her voice. If he'd needed any proof he had let things get out of control with Alanna, he had it. Jaclyn had started as his contact at the Grand Hotel's spa but had grown to be a good friend. More than a friend when he was honest. Then there was Dylan, her two-year-old.

"Grand Hotel Spa." Jaclyn's voice held the professional tone of a busy manager.

"Hey, Jaclyn."

"Jonathan." Warmth crept into the word. Guess she'd forgiven him. "What's up?"

He chitchatted a few moments then got back to business. "I need a couple massages for a bride and her maid of honor. I'd like them to start with tea and then come to you. Assign your best masseuse."

"Sure, Jonathan. When do you need these?"

"Today."

"Today?" She groaned. He heard the rustle of pages in the background. "I'm not sure I can do that. Not even for you."

"This bride needs the special treatment, and I need the time to finish the work on her wedding." He pictured her chewing on the end of her pen as she studied the calendar. How many times had he seen her do that?

The page flipped a few more times. "All right. If you send them up here for the final tea slot, I can squeeze them in with Analise and Nicole. But you'll have to tip well since they'll stay late."

"No problem. It's going on 'Daddy's' account, and he can afford it."

"You owe me dinner, too."

It wouldn't be the first time by a stretch. They always had a good time, but with Alanna back. . . Jonathan considered saying no. "You're right. I've got the wedding Monday . . . ."

"Jonathan, we miss you. I'd almost believe you have someone else."

Her words pierced him. "I'll call later."

"Fine. I'll talk to you then." Jaclyn hung up, and he hoped she didn't take an eraser to the appointments.

One crisis averted. Now to plan the Standeford wedding proposal and then snap photos of Rachelle Stone's art. Which meant seeing Alanna. Again.

## 11

The sun tried to poke through the cloud cover as Jonathan strode up Market Street toward the Painted Stone and Fort Mackinac. Just when he wanted to pull his jacket collar up to protect his neck from the cold, he'd step into a pool of sunshine and feel spring.

He whistled a flat tune as he ambled. He had too much to accomplish to walk slowly, but the thought of seeing Alanna held him back. He sidestepped another tourist as he approached the paned-glass front of the studio. It beckoned him, but he stood a moment checking for Alanna through the windows. The studio stood stark, nobody filling its space. The ridiculousness of his hesitation tensed his shoulders. He needed to get in there, get the information, and leave. If he hadn't promised Edward photos, he'd have called.

Space, he needed space to clear the hold Alanna's return had on him. He needed to get his head straight. Fast. If Rachelle Stone had created that web page like he'd suggested, he wouldn't have to approach Alanna now.

His phone buzzed against his hip. He snagged it and glanced at the caller ID. Since he didn't recognize the number, he let it slide over to voice mail and opened the door. The bells jangled their greeting. He winced. Alanna would round the corner in a minute then freeze when she saw him. Not the kind of reaction he liked to elicit in a woman, especially one he was attracted to. He strode to a painting. Maybe if he stood engrossed in one, he could miss her inevitable reaction.

Jonathan picked a painting that illustrated the view from Fort Mackinac down across Lake Huron to the lighthouses. The artist had painted the field of grass a vibrant green—the color of cucumbers. Roofs poked through the trees until gentle waves rocked the island with a rich blue the color of a blue jay's feathers. Lower, the Round Island Lighthouse peeked from the bottom right-hand corner of the painting, looking like a squat, barn-red ice-cream cone topped with vanilla custard.

The painting held Mrs. Stones scrawled signature in the corner but didn't look right. Jonathan studied it a moment but couldn't peg what bothered him. He snapped a photo with his phone then turned to the next painting. This one was a winter scene, the storefronts bursting with color against the blinding white of snow-covered streets.

The click of heels ricocheted against the hardwood floor. "Jonathan?"

He kept his gaze on the painting as he snapped a photo of it.

"What are you doing?"

"I have a client who wants to commission a painting for his wife in honor of their fortieth anniversary."

"Why take photos?"

He turned to look at her, noting the fine lines straining the edges of her eyes. "He liked your mom's art. Since she doesn't have a website, he asked me to take some photos to e-mail him. Can I have her current contact info?"

Her jaw worked, not the reaction he'd expected. Shouldn't

she show some excitement that he'd made the recommendation?

"I doubt she has time right now with all Dad's problems."

Jonathan slipped his phone in his pocket. "Shouldn't she make that decision? After all, aren't you here to keep the studio running?

And doesn't that mean they need the income a commission like this could provide?"

The lines tightened as she frowned at him. "I don't like it."

"Okay. I don't like these paintings."

"What do you mean?"

"They're missing something."

Alanna fisted her hands against her hips in a tight stance. "Excuse me?"

"They don't quite fit Rachelle's style." The words sounded stupid as he said them.

ALANNA FELT heat flush her neck. It wasn't from his presence. Couldn't be.

Could her mom accept the commission? Even a few thousand dollars would help immensely. She watched Jonathan for a moment. He nosed closer to the painting until his schnoz almost touched the paint-layered canvas. He stepped back and squinted. He looked ridiculous, but she mimicked his motions. As she neared the layers of paint, she stilled.

That's what bothered her.

Mom didn't layer oils like she had in these paintings.

Sure, she liked to add a sense of texture, but these paintings seemed to have the oils caked. Maybe her style had evolved. It wasn't like Alanna had paid tons of attention since she bolted from the island. College then law school and launching a career had absorbed her.

Mom had given her small paintings of her favorite spots on the island for the occasional birthday and Christmas presents. The lighthouses. A favorite cottage. Altogether it formed a nice collage of the area. But she hadn't seen large paintings for a long time other than those at the cottage. Long enough for Mom's technique to change and get heavier?

Alanna didn't know, but she wouldn't admit anything. "You're ridiculous."

He shrugged. "Maybe, but your mom's one of the best artists around. My client has planned an anniversary weekend here for his wife. A painting that commemorates their love and the island is ideal." He squinted at the painting then turned to her. "But I want her to paint. Not some knockoff."

Alanna jolted at his tone. "How can you say that?"

"Because these aren't your mom's paintings. And I have proof." He turned to the winter scene. "See here. . ." He pointed at Ste. Anne's Church. "Rachelle would have ensured the stained-glass windows were accurate."

"Maybe she wanted to do something different." But she knew Jonathan was right. Her mom loved that church, always had. Mom had wanted to renew her vows there but changed her mind when Alanna refused to come. Remorse cloaked Alanna at her selfishness. She should have swallowed her anger and forced herself to return for one ceremony. She could have taken the ferry back as soon as the celebration ended. Instead, she'd claimed a case wouldn't let her escape. She'd let her pride and fear hold her back.

Now that seemed ridiculous. After all, how many locals had hounded her the few days she'd been back?

"You with me?" Jonathan's voice jerked her from her thoughts.

"You're still wrong."

"Nope, and I'll find a way to prove it."

She turned from the painting and felt pulled into his gaze. His eyes reflected his high intelligence. If she wasn't careful, he would identify what was wrong with the painting. "What?"

"You know I'm tenacious."

With everything but chasing her. How many mistaken relationships could she have avoided if he'd asked her to come back? "Most of the time."

His eyebrow arched. "Really. Then I'll show you how much it's woven in the fabric of who I am."

"Why waste your time on something so insignificant?"

"It's not if I suggest a client buy a painting from your mother only to learn he didn't get what he paid for."

She tore her gaze from his and pivoted so her body angled toward the painting and away from him. Heat flushed her cheeks, but she prayed he didn't notice. If he did, he'd know immediately that the possibility bothered her, too.

"What about Jacklyn?"

He looked at her like she'd gone crazy. "What?"

"Don't you have a child with her?"

Color flushed up his neck. "Seriously? You think that?"

The shrill ring of the phone pierced the space between them like a wonderful warning. She hurried toward the desk, her stomach twisting at his expression. "I've got to get that."

Jonathan didn't move. His stillness reminded her of an alert Doberman. Poised and ready to pounce but studying the surroundings first. Exactly what she didn't need.

She had to call Mom and find out what was going on with those paintings.

The phone rang as she picked it up. "The Painted Stone."

"Hello. This is Patience. Is this Alanna?"

Alanna's heart sank at the sound of her mom's best friend.

She shouldn't be surprised that Mrs. Matthews would eventually call.

"A little birdie told me you'd returned." The voice held the warmth of someone welcoming the prodigal home.

Alanna rubbed at a knot of tension at her temple. "Arrived a few days ago."

"And you haven't called?" The woman clucked her tongue. "My dear child, I promised your mother I would keep an eye on you. Can't do that if you never come by."

Alanna couldn't think of the last time she'd been called a child. She'd slipped that title off at least fifteen years earlier.

"Are you there?"

"Yes, ma'am." She sighed. "I've been busy keeping everything going."

"For a successful attorney like you? I doubt the studio is the least challenge."

Jonathan cleared his throat, and Alanna glanced his way. He pointed to his watch then the door. "I'll be back."

"All right." They'd have to finish their conversation. But postponing it until after she talked to Mom provided a needed reprieve. She had to figure out what was going on. Shouldn't be too difficult for someone who pieced together complex disputes.

"Alanna Stone." Mrs. Matthews's tone was tinged with welcome.

She rubbed her temple harder. "I'll stop by soon. It's tricky with the studio's hours."

"Your mother always managed."

Alanna didn't even attempt to hide her sigh. "I'm not Mom."

"That is true." The old woman chuckled. "Your mother's life would have been easier these last years if you'd been more like her in your teens."

The bell jangled, and Alanna turned back around. She

smiled as she watched Mr. Tomkin walk in, a padfolio tucked under his arm. Just the distraction she needed.

"Well, thank you for calling. I've got to assist a customer."

Alanna hung up without waiting for Mrs. Matthews's good-bye. She'd learned in fourth-grade Sunday school that little short of perfection satisfied the woman. She already knew she wasn't perfect.

"Mr. Tomkin. What can I do for you?" Anything he needed couldn't be harder than dealing with Mrs. Matthews and Jonathan.

## 12

The man ignored the art as he approached the counter. He had the intent focus of a man on a mission from which he would not be distracted. By the set of his chin, she wasn't certain she'd like whatever had brought him to the studio. Maybe she should have stayed on the phone.

"Alanna, we need someone talented like you to set up shop in this town. You'll notice there aren't any attorneys."

She took a step back and sank onto the stool her mother used. "We've never needed them when Mackinaw City and St. Ignace have attorneys."

"Not true. We need someone who's involved here."

The thought of practicing law on the island made her skin itch. She fought not to scratch her arms as she stared at him. "I already work in Grand Rapids."

"For someone else. Here you could work for yourself."

"No thanks."

He stared a moment as if formulating his next argument then shrugged. "Think about it. I'm here because I need your help on a foundation matter. Your dad was instrumental as a founding member. Now he's gone, and you can fill his shoes."

He set his padfolio on the counter and pulled out a paper. "Here's the agenda for the next meeting. As you'll see, we have many important items to discuss and vote on."

The bell jingled, but Alanna focused on Gerald. "I'll see what I can do."

"Alanna Stone." She turned with a start. Brendan Tomkin? What was he doing here, with the same baby face and nose-in-the-air look he'd had in high school? "I heard you were back."

He'd changed since high school, bulked up and thickened from the scrawny high schooler. He approached his dad with a strut. "Ready to grab a bite?"

Gerald glanced at his watch and frowned. "I was in the middle of an important conversation."

"Come on, Pops. I'm hungry. Alanna will still be here when we're done."

Alanna bit back a sharp comment but forced her lips to curve. "We can talk after the meeting."

"I suppose. It really is urgent." He turned to his son. "Where are your manners?"

Brendan rolled his eyes before he plastered on a crooked smile. "Like to join us, Alanna?"

"I really can't. Have to stay here."

Brendan made a motion toward her. "See?"

Gerald mouthed, "Sorry." Alanna shrugged. It looked like at the core Brendan hadn't changed since high school. "How are you doing, Brendan?"

"Fine. Selling insurance like crazy on the mainland. Why?"

"I just thought with the anniversary of Grady's death you might be. . .melancholy." Boy, that sounded stupid, and the look he gave her reinforced that.

"Why would that matter?"

"You were friends. Always looked like good friends."

"Not really. The island didn't give me too many options. Our school didn't need two guys jockeying for the girls. He just thought he was in my league. Besides, he was too pompous for my taste. He thought he was better than the rest of us. Too bad he couldn't swim better." Brendan grabbed his dad's arm and tugged him toward the door. "Catch ya later, Alanna."

Not if she could help it. If her class had contained more than eight students, she never would have spent any time with Brendan as a teen. His attitude hadn't changed, and even then it made her want to listen to fingernails on a chalkboard rather than his self-important monologues.

Alanna watched the two round the sidewalk a moment then tried to remember what she'd been doing when Mr. Tomkin showed up. From the brief moment with Brendan, it seemed clear he'd inherited his father's pushy personality. She shook off the moment, shoved the paperwork to the side, and picked up the phone. Maybe she'd catch Mom between doctors' appointments and visiting Dad. She dialed the number and left a quick message at the beep.

"Mom, call me on my cell as soon as you get this. I need to ask you some questions about the studio."

She set the phone back on the hook. She'd never thought of practicing law on Mackinac Island. But then she'd never considered going to law school until the police interviewed Trevor after Grady's death. Dad had found an attorney, but the man hadn't impressed her. She'd determined to treat her clients differently. With respect and full information about what was happening in their matters. Could she find the kind of cases she loved up here? Complex litigation like the murder trial she'd just braved. Cases that required a creative approach to pull the jury and judge into the story.

While the cases drained her, she loved the puzzle of putting together a compelling defense. But the last murder trial had really zapped her energy. The thought of diving into another case that would consume every hour and spare thought exhausted her. Should she consider the slower approach of small-town practice?

Who was she kidding? The last thing she wanted to do was stay here. She shouldn't entertain the idea.

Alanna rolled the mouse back and forth, waking the computer from sleep mode. First, she placed an ad in the *Grand Rapids Press*. It would run online immediately and in the paper after Memorial Day, and she prayed the right person would read and apply. Then she opened a spreadsheet that listed paintings, artists, and if an item had sold. Maybe she could figure out who her parents bought art from. If she could determine that, she could see if a painting had been mislabeled.

Mom used to fill the studio with her own pieces; then, as she built a following that spread across the region thanks to the island's faithful visitors, she slowly added other artists. Usually they were friends from the art community or they had a resonating style. Either way, the studio acquired a more eclectic feel. Maybe with managing others' art, Mom had less time to create her own.

The bell on the front door jangled as a group of tourists entered. Alanna stood and approached the group of middle-aged couples.

"Is there anything I can help you find?"

A woman with bouncing copper curls turned to her with a grin. "A souvenir. I need something that will help me remember this remarkable place."

"It is that." Alanna made a mental note to find smaller pieces to display. Anything less pricey than the big canvasses currently in the showroom. Shouldn't Mom have done that a long time ago? Like the art professor suggested, a rack of postcards and assorted note cards based on Mom's paintings would be a simple improvement. "I'll check the back, but perhaps you'll find something in one of the pieces here. Is there a certain place that is especially meaningful?"

"The Grand Hotel. I'd love a scene that makes me think of *Somewhere in Time.*"

Alanna hid a smile as the woman gushed about the old movie filmed at the landmark hotel starring Christopher Reeve and Jane

Seymour. Surely any of the paintings would satisfy that criteria.

She slipped into the back and rummaged through a stack of smaller canvasses. These didn't have frames and looked unfinished compared to the ones hanging on the walls in the main room. She pulled several of the smaller pieces to the side and inspected them to make sure someone had stretched the canvas tight. She could display several immediately at a lower price point many of the islands tourists could afford. By leaving the framing to the purchaser, they could perfectly match the frame to their decor.

Muffled voices carried to her as she carried the art to the showroom.

"These really are nice pieces." A gentleman in khakis and a polo shirt stood in front of a large watercolor. Alanna bit off a frown when she saw it wasn't one of Mom's pieces. "The artist has a nice eye."

"Only the best at the Painted Stone." Alanna arranged the small canvasses on the countertop. "Here are a few pieces that might interest you as well."

The woman with the curly hair hurried to the counter. "Oh, these are perfect. How much?"

"Two hundred and fifty dollars each." She hoped her mom hadn't agreed to pay the artists more.

Another woman, this one about ten years younger than the others, walked over. "Why aren't they framed?"

Time to test her theory. "To allow you to frame a bit of the island in a way that fits your style."

"Hmmm." The woman tapped a lacquered fingernail against her lip and studied the paintings. "Interesting idea, but I prefer those I don't have to work on."

"Don't worry about her." The redhead leaned across the counter and made a show of lowering her voice. "She likes to think she's an interior designer. We just call her the know-it-all."

The man next to her snorted while Alanna bit her lip to keep from smiling. "What brings you to Mackinac?"

"A niece's wedding, which corresponds to our thirtieth anniversary. I keep telling Ted he's getting twice the bang for his dollars. A wedding trip and a second honeymoon."

Her husband bumped against her side and grinned at her. "That's my Alice—always thinking, even if you aren't always kind."

Confusion furrowed the redhead's brow before a flash of something like indignation replaced it. "Leanna is a know-it-all. She knows it, too, don't you, darling?" Alice put a hand on her hip and a pout on her lips.

"Sure enough. Mark likes me with a bit of contrariness."

"See?"

Her husband leaned down and kissed Alice's pout off. "Find anything you want?"

"I've already got it." She grinned at him with a look that came only after years of marriage.

"You do?" He waggled his eyebrows at her, and Alice laughed.

"Yep, but if you'd like to make me really happy, there's a little painting over here I'd love to take home."

Alanna tried not to let her longing for a love like that mar the moment as Alice led Ted to a medium-sized painting of the porch at the Grand with a beautiful gold frame. The red geraniums that lined the porch provided a pop of color against the white rockers and yellow awnings. Alanna closed her eyes to block the view of the lovebirds considering the painting. She was ridiculous, really. She didn't know what that couple had been through or endured, only that they seemed to reap the reward now.

Would she ever have the same? A lifetime of love to come home to?

The image seemed improbable even as she longed for it. A partner-track attorney at even a medium-sized firm had to give too much time to her job to have an outside life. The partners had only allowed her this time off after realizing she'd fried her last brain cell in the murder trial. It wasn't the fact her family needed her, but the idea she could embarrass the firm as easily as she'd brought it positive media. Though she didn't think working at an art studio qualified as a vacation.

The low ding from the computer let her know she had e-mail waiting. As Ted tugged the painting from the wall, she winced. Maybe the e-mail would be from the perfect person who had found the online listing already. This person could sweep onto the island, take over the studio, and allow her to return to Grand Rapids.

"This is the one." Ted slammed the painting down on the counter, scattering canvasses.

"Be careful, you big lug. I don't want it damaged before we leave the store."

Ted winked at Alanna before he turned to Alice. "Of course not, though then we wouldn't have to haul this monstrosity back."

"Whatcha calling a monstrosity? You'll look at that every day in our dining room."

"That's what I'm afraid of."

If a twinkle hadn't lit his eyes, Alanna might have created a reason he couldn't buy that particular piece. Instead, she gladly swiped his credit card and then swaddled the painting in bubble wrap. "I added an extra layer to protect it from bumping."

Leanna tapped a bubble until it popped. "It'd take another layer to get it through the weekend. You have no idea how rough and tumble these two are."

Her husband walked up and slipped an arm around her shoulders. "You want one?"

"Of these?" She ran a finger around the room. "Not on your life. They aren't our style."

As the couples exited with Ted lugging the painting against his chest, good-natured bickering followed them.

Another ding reminded her to check e-mail. If she didn't get some resumes in pronto, she'd need to place more than one old-fashioned newspaper ad. While part of her wondered if anyone still read the paper, she had to try something, because she couldn't stay on the island indefinitely. Not if she wanted to keep her real job at the firm.

After a few clicks, her in-box filled the screen. One looked like a promising prospect for the job. Then she opened the resume and changed her mind. If a person couldn't spell basic words, she didn't want to trust that person with her parents' livelihood. Guess she'd keep praying and looking.

As she scrolled down the list of e-mail, she didn't see anything worth answering until she reached an e-mail from her brother. Maybe he had an update on Dad's condition. She opened the e-mail.

A groan slipped out as she scanned it.

## 13

Weight pressed against Jonathan throughout the afternoon.

He raced around downtown finalizing the details for the wedding rehearsal and ceremony. The events would run flawlessly, but he couldn't focus on them. Instead, the image of Alanna's blond hair serving as a frame that partly hid her face kept cropping up. He'd drive it from his mind, only to have her image reappear.

He hadn't been this distracted—well, ever.

He strived to be the consummate professional, completely devoted to his work. Then she returned. And his brain didn't comply with his instructions anymore. The more he told himself to focus and get the job done, the more his thoughts strayed. And that didn't mention the chaos she brought to his personal life.

When he finally returned to his office, he sank into his chair. He swiveled away from the computer and rubbed his face. He didn't need the distraction. Not now. Not from her.

His cell phone vibrated against his hip. "Jonathan Covington."

"Hear anything from the artist?" Edward Morris's unmistakable voice telegraphed he had other things on his mind.

"I've talked to her daughter. I should know something soon." Like whether Rachelle still painted. Had her arthritis flared up, causing painting to be too painful?

"All right. There isn't much time. I'm willing to pay for an original."

"I'll feel her out before connecting you. Mrs. Stone is a very good artist."

"You're hesitating."

"Only because her husband has health issues that might require her focus."

"That I understand."

Jonathan nodded. Edward could understand those pressures. "How is Bonnie?"

"Holding up. I think our plans for the anniversary celebration have given her something to focus on. A date to live for."

"I'll do all I can to make it everything she dreams."

A moment of silence, and then Edward sighed. "I'm counting on it."

After he hung up, Jonathan stared out his office window. This was an important event. It was smaller than many he organized, but if he made it memorable for Bonnie Morris, all his effort and time would be worthwhile. Her fight with cancer reminded him too much of his mother's. He stopped to pray for Bonnie.

Tugging the Lyster wedding file in front of him, he double-checked the myriad details involved in the intimate event. Based on the guest list, he could expect new clients from this wedding. If there was one thing he'd learned in event planning, it was that each event generated future leads.

After confirming the setup for the rehearsal dinner, Jonathan pulled out the Standeford file. This couple had differing views on how their wedding should play out, with the groom refusing to bow to the bride. Did he really want to tackle the job of bringing harmony to the event? After a moment of prayer, he dove back into his notes. Ideas began to flow on how to incorporate a movie theme along with the more formal tone the groom and his mother wanted.

He pulled up his planning software and plugged in details. An hour later, he had the outlines of a proposal. He'd expand it later, but for now he needed to check in with Theresa Lyster. Her phone rang to voice mail, and he started a message when she buzzed him.

"Jonathan Covington, if I weren't getting married in a few days, I'd kiss you."

He laughed at her giddy words. "Analise and Nicole did a great job?"

"Phenomenal. I may have to move here just to have them keep me relaxed. What a wonderful idea!"

"You're welcome."

He heard a rustling, then Theresa whispered, "You should take Jaclyn to dinner and add it to Daddy's bill."

Jonathan laughed. "That's not how I do business, but tell Jaclyn I'll meet her at Man O' War at seven."

Theresa repeated his words. "Thanks again for everything."

"My pleasure." He hung up, grinning. If only it were so easy to keep everyone satisfied.

He turned back to his computer and printed the Standeford proposal. Then he spent a few minutes fleshing out thoughts for the Wenzes' anniversary celebration before shoving his files in his bag. After dinner with Jaclyn, he'd work from home.

As he dodged foot traffic on the way to Man O' War, Jonathan whistled a Michael Buble tune—one of Jaclyn's favorites. When he walked through the restaurant's door, he scanned the dining room for Jaclyn. Often she arrived first to claim a great table for them, but he didn't spot her. He approached the hostess.

"How many?" The gal spoke with a slight accent, one he couldn't place, but she blended with the numerous international students who found summer employment on the island.

"Two."

"Yes, sir." Another sign she wasn't a native, or she'd know his name. "It'll be fifteen to twenty minutes."

He gave her his name and accepted a pager. Guess he had a few minutes to wander, though she warned him the pager had a limited range.

He strolled Main Street and watched for Jaclyn. Her tight red curls were the kind that made a man want to tease them with his fingers. Though she'd sent every signal she wouldn't mind, their relationship tended toward friendly but inched toward romance. Her son accepted him with enthusiasm on picnics and bike rides. That had felt like enough.

Before Alanna returned.

He wasn't sure how that impacted Jaclyn.

Jaclyn bounced into him. "Hey there, handsome."

"Jaclyn."

She lifted her cheek for a kiss. He obliged, wondering why their customary greeting felt odd. He couldn't let Alanna get to him. It wasn't fair to Jaclyn or him.

He forced his attention to the beautiful woman in front of him as Jaclyn chattered about her day. When the pager vibrated, he pointed her to the door.

"Sorry I didn't get here earlier." She tossed her curls. "It's a big weekend at the Grand. Everybody wants special treatment. The phone didn't stop ringing all day."

"Thanks for squeezing in Theresa."

"Anything for you, Jonathan. You know that."

The way she said it with stars in her eyes made him feel

small. She gave every indication she'd fallen deep—despite his efforts to proceed cautiously. Where her adoration used to make him feel bigger, stronger, tonight it made him question what kind of man he was. He shouldn't vacillate. A real man committed for the long haul. One glance at Jaclyn showed she thought he had. Leave it to him to lead a great gal along while his heart remained secretly entrenched with another.

Hie hostess led them to a table under the big plate-glass window. Jonathan pulled out the chair for Jaclyn and then angled his away from the window.

"I've filled the air. Your turn. How was your day?" Jaclyn plopped her elbows on the table and then her chin on her hands as she studied him.

"After you helped me with a nervous bride, I worked on her special day and planned another."

"I'll never understand how you find so many concepts."

"Lots of magazine subscriptions."

"Are you serious?"

He straightened the silverware. "That and files. My mom and dad kept everything. That gives me lots to work from."

"They're talking about you at the Grand." Pride showed in her eyes.

That was great news. Prospects from the hotel could fill his calendar.

She frowned, the expression uncommon. "You don't seem excited."

"You didn't see my smile?" He grinned widely. "That's really good news. Tell them thanks."

"You can do it next time you come to see me." She batted her eyelashes.

"Sure." He leaned back and glanced around the restaurant. Where was their server? A young man in a white shirt and black pants caught his eye and threaded tables toward them.

"What can I get y'all to drink?" A southern accent tinged his words as he slid a basket of warm sourdough rolls between them.

After taking their drink orders, he disappeared, and Jonathan found himself looking at Jaclyn. Tightness etched around her eyes.

"Was there somewhere else you needed to be tonight?"

Jonathan shook his head. He adjusted his stance in the chair, leaned toward her, and grabbed a piece of bread from the basket. He tore it into small pieces as he studied her. "Guess I'm distracted."

"You think?"

"Tell me more about your day." The meal flowed quickly with the server sliding salads in front of them, soon followed by sandwiches. They waived off dessert and stood to leave.

Jaclyn waited in front of him, a question in her eyes.

Regret pierced him. "Sorry about tonight."

"At least you paid." While he could tell she meant it as a joke, there was truth to her statement. He hadn't given her the attention she deserved, but he'd paid.

"Promise next time I'll be a better companion."

"All right. I'll give you another chance. Join me for a picnic at Arch Rock on Memorial Day."

"I have a wedding."

"The day before then."

He could squeeze in time then. "I thought it was one of your busiest days."

"Nothing I can't have someone else cover for a couple hours." Her expression wavered as she swayed from side to side, her skirt swirling around her knees in a slow dance. "Please? We miss you."

"All right." The image of her son with eyes the same color as hers confronted him. It had been awhile since he'd seen Dylan. "We'll do something Sunday afternoon."

Jaclyn rolled her eyes, but the smile had returned. "See you then."

She turned to head up the street toward the Grand Hotel. His gaze followed her until it slammed into Alanna's. All of a sudden he felt as if she'd caught him doing something he shouldn't. That was ridiculous. He needed to get her out of his head.

Make that his heart.

He spun on his heel without acknowledging her.

Right now he needed to put distance between them. As quickly as possible. Not an easy feat on the small island with their cottages next door to each other. He stopped when he realized he couldn't get home this way. He had to pass her if he wanted to sleep in his bed. Muttering under his breath that he was a fool, he reversed direction and headed toward her. He'd cut up the street as soon as he could, but he had to get his bike or it would be a long walk home. A long one that provided too much time to berate his foolish, rebellious heart.

## 14

Alanna's thoughts swirled as she strolled Main Street. She should head home, should have hours earlier. Mom's e-mail had informed her Daddy had taken a turn for the worse, and Alanna had to stay longer. Mom simply couldn't return to the island without Dad. Each time she'd tried to reach Mom, voice mail was all she heard. Now her thoughts strayed to that awful graduation party while she wandered the streets.

Without Grady's death, she would have skipped law school. All the years of study she would have invested in something else. Something closer to home. Returning left her wondering whether she had wasted so much time for nothing. She certainly didn't feel fulfilled. The rush of winning a case wore off much too fast.

Someone bumped into her, and she pulled her attention back to the busy sidewalk. "Brendan?"

"Lookie here. It's Miss Alanna. Imagine bumping into you twice in one day."

"How are you? I'm kind of surprised you're still here. All that talk of leaving."

"I'm on the mainland. Just came back for the party week-end." His breath smelled of alcohol as he grinned. He'd had as much to drink as any of the kids at the graduation party. A leer creased his face, one Alanna hoped came from the alcohol. "It'd be great to catch up, but I'm off to see a girl. A pretty one. One you know."

"Who?"

Brendan ignored her as he moved down the street, looking far steadier than she expected. A mumble reached her. "Enjoy the surprise."

Must be the alcohol talking. Certainly made no sense, but in her short interactions with him, Brendan didn't shine in that area. She wondered how he managed to sell any insurance with that surly personality.

She'd forgotten how crazy the island became on long week-ends like Memorial Day. Guess people started the weekend on Thursday. The hum and pulse of activity used to excite her. Now. . .she didn't know what she thought. A little quiet sounded good.

She glanced up and spied Jonathan on the sidewalk a hundred feet or so in front of her, standing very close to a cute twenty-something. Jaclyn?

Electricity fairly crackled in the space between them. As she watched, Alanna remembered the times Jonathan had eyes only for her. She'd left so much behind all because of that tragic graduation party. Why had everyone been so quick to blame Trevor—and by extension her—when most of the island's teens had turned out for the celebration-turned-tragedy?

Her phone vibrated against her hip, but she couldn't pull her gaze from the two. Not as she saw what had been her future play out in front of her.

She turned on her heel and stepped away. Any appetite she'd had disappeared in the vision before her. Who was she kidding? She'd dated other men, one even seriously, since leaving. Jonathan had to do the same.

She'd read too many fairy tales. Too many stories of Prince Charming waiting for the perfect woman. Even hunting for her. Jonathan had certainly never bothered to do that.

One call, that's all she needed then. She brushed moisture from her cheek as she rushed up the sidewalk toward the white clapboard library and narrow beach behind it. The sun had lowered in the sky, and she told herself she'd watch it set behind the lighthouse.

She stumbled when she hit the rough pebbles of the beach, nothing like the sand beaches near the oceans or even at the Dunes in Indiana. She slowed her pace, extending her arms as if walking a tightrope. That's what her life had become. Drained from the trial and media assault, she'd driven to the island, braced against the thought of what waited. Now she could add the pain of Jonathan's nearness to her concerns about the paintings.

What had happened to the simple time in the studio her mother had promised? In and out in a few weeks, a couple of months at most, with no problems. Instead, everywhere she turned she encountered a challenge. She thought she'd prepared for the season, but now she wanted to run as fast as she could, abandoning the island and all it held.

A cool breeze blew off Lake Huron, sending a shiver down her arms and back. She hugged her middle and hunkered down on the beach. Small whitecaps teased the shoreline a few feet away. The last few years had felt quiet, almost docile outside of courtroom tussles. Now she wondered if it only felt that way because she stuffed all her real emotions so far beneath the surface she hadn't recognized them.

Anger over her brother's treatment? Ignored.

Fear over returning to Mackinac? Shoved to the side.

Questions about how her family could remain? Oblivious.

For someone who was known for her strength, she'd lived a deluded life. Sheltered in her Grand Rapids condo, working for a hard-driving firm, she could pretend she had everything she needed. After all, she had a handful of girlfriends and the occasional relationship.

Now it all seemed as shallow as the water lapping the shore. She didn't have a single person she could call to share her concerns. Even her roommate would wonder at the sudden attempt at intimacy. Conversations moving from "It's your turn to clean the kitchen" to "I think my mother is committing art fraud" didn't happen every day.

She pulled her knees up and wrapped her arms around them. She glanced at the sky. Watched as God painted stripes of vibrant color across the clouds. A rich salmon chased magenta, turquoise, and violet. She needed to get up, start moving. If she didn't, she'd have to find her way home in the dark. She could do it, but with the way her thoughts wandered, it wouldn't be a good idea.

Her gaze traveled the length of the vista. Sometimes it was hard to believe the God who created such beauty on a cosmic scale cared about the details of her life, but she prayed He did.

If He didn't, she was lost.

MEMORIAL DAY WEEKEND started with ferry loads of tourists. The population on the island exploded with those who needed a dose of relaxation. Alanna spent Friday ringing up orders and answering questions. By the time she hiked home, she could hardly move. Her body was used to sitting all day, not the up and down of running a retail shop followed by an uphill bike ride.

All she wanted was to sit down on the dock with a good book

until the light got too dim to read. She turned the bike into her drive then slipped off it to park it in the shed. The key dangled in her hand, useless as the shed's door slid open with ease.

Hadn't she locked it that morning? She must have, since it was part of her routine. She might have left the big city behind, but she hadn't abandoned her habits. Even from this remote location, it begged trouble to leave the door unlocked.

She stared into the shadow-encrusted interior. Should she go ahead and push the bike in or run for help?

*Don't overreact.* She'd feel ridiculous if she ran next door only to find nothing wrong. But if she didn't and something was wrong in that dark space. . .

She shook off the thought. "This is ridiculous."

Her words filled the silence but didn't settle the creepy crawlies on her back. A whine that sounded like a cat's screech came from inside.

Alanna dropped the bike and backed away from the shed. She spun on her heel and hurried toward the house. The broken pansies lining the paving stones that connected the house and shed almost stopped her. What had happened? Someone or something had trampled the flowers and unlocked the shed.

After fumbling to unlock the back door, she rushed into the kitchen and called Jonathan.

"Alanna?"

"Do you have a flashlight?"

"Flashlight?"

"Yes." She nodded then felt like a fool. "Something's wrong in my shed." He yawned, and Alanna wished she hadn't called. "Never mind."

"I'm coming. Give me a few minutes."

Alanna hung up and filled the teakettle. It had started to hum a shrill tune when Jonathan walked in the kitchen. He wore khaki shorts that had more holes than fabric and an oversized Michigan State sweatshirt. His hair looked rumpled and his face tired.

"Did I wake you?"

"Don't worry about it. I thought I'd get ahead of the weekend. Won't sleep much between now and the wedding." He hurried to the stove and picked up the kettle. After setting it on a cold burner, Jonathan turned back to her, his green eyes probing. "What's wrong?"

Biting her lower lip, Alanna grabbed a couple of mugs from the cabinet. "The shed was unlocked when I got home."

"Happens."

"I always lock up."

"Always? Even here?"

She nodded. "I've seen the worst in people. And tonight it's confirmed. The plants along the path are broken like someone stepped all over them. And the shed. . ."

"There had to be more than it being unlocked." He studied her like he knew she wouldn't be that kind of woman. The one who panicked at every sound or event.

"It's too dark to see what's in there."

Jonathan hefted the flashlight and flicked it on. She squinted against its light. "Bright enough to penetrate any dark corner and hefty enough to knock out any lurkers." His tone was light, yet he didn't laugh at her concerns. "I'll go check, and you can wait here."

"No way. I want to see."

He shrugged and headed out the door. Alanna flipped on the back-porch light then hurried to catch up. The crickets had started their evening music, filling the night with a sweet melody. Against that backdrop, her earlier fear seemed blown out of proportion. Then a shrieking wail filled the night. She hurried forward and collided with Jonathan. He let out an *uhf* the flashlight fell from his hand, clattered to the ground, then blinked out.

Jonathan's arms slipped around her. "Steady there."

She stilled, a flood of electricity zipping through her. A longing to stay right where she was warred against the need for space—lots of it. Jonathan dropped his hold and stooped to collect the flashlight. He thwumped it against his thigh, and it sputtered to life. "That's better."

She nodded, even though she disagreed. She'd felt safe while he'd shielded her. Now she felt foolish and alone.

Jonathan hurried to the shed and stepped inside, and she watched the light play across the entrance.

"Lanna, stay back." His words pulled her forward even as his command pressed her back.

"What did you find?"

"Nothing I want you to see. Go back inside." She hesitated, and he must have seen. "Go."

"No, this is my home right now. I need to know what's going on." She tried to look around him as he stepped from side to side, anticipating her moves. "Let me see."

"You don't want this in your mind."

She hesitated another moment then pushed around him. A trap of some sort had been slid into a back corner. In its clutches writhed a young rabbit, weakly trying to escape. "Who would do something like this?"

"I don't know. Please go inside."

Alanna glanced at the rabbit once more then spun on her heel and hurried back to the kitchen. She rummaged through the cupboard for tea bags with shaking hands. Her dad never set traps. He might complain about the rabbits and other animals that chomped at his plants, but he'd never use something like that. So how had it ended up in the shed? Someone must have purposefully placed it there. Why?

Did she want to know even if she could find out?

She shuddered and prayed for peace while waiting for Jonathan to rejoin her. Heaviness weighed his face as he came inside. She handed him a mug of tea.

"Thanks." He took a sip without looking in the cup and then spewed his mouthful across the table. He swiped a hand across his mouth. "What is this?"

"Mint tea."

Jonathan set the mug on the table. "No thanks." Concern shadowed his eyes as he looked at her. "I've got a call in to the police. Not sure when they'll get here. I don't like this, Lanna."

"Me neither."

He slipped around the table and sat next to her. As he placed an arm around her shoulders, she sank into his side. For the first time in a long time, she let someone else be strong for her.

Would he prove worthy of that trust?

As she felt him wrap his other arm around her, she prayed he would.

## 15

Saturday passed in a flood of tourists and long hours, made even longer by the late police visit the prior night. When the chief had finally left, Alanna got the distinct impression he didn't like her. "You sure there wasn't a trap in the shed."

Alanna had nodded. "Daddy never trapped or hunted."

"Hmmm. It didn't just crawl in that shed." He studied her as if searching for more.

"I've never seen it before."

"I'll take it back with me." He looked at the trap with the enthusiasm of a condemned man. "Means a trip off the island in the morning." He heaved a sigh. "All for something that will have your daddy's prints on it."

Alanna had wanted to argue, but fatigue won. Now Saturday passed in a collage of images, none distinct, yet all tied together. The image of tourists morphed into customers that melded with the paintings. When her stomach growled a rousing chorus, she locked up and headed for Main Street. The island would have to endure a closed studio long enough for her to find food.

Fifteen minutes later, she waited in line at the deli. A flock of tourists made slow decisions in front of her. She'd have to remember to call ahead. After waiting awhile, Alanna spun and collided with the person behind her.

"I am so sorry." Heat flashed up her cheeks as she took in the perfectly groomed woman. Short black hair stood in gelled spikes that gave the woman a funky edge when combined with her artsy earrings and large necklace.

"Alanna Stone. Some things never change. Still head in the clouds."

Alanna took a step back and tried to smile. "Ginger?"

Ginger Hoffmeister studied her as if waiting for another breakdown. "When I heard you were back, I couldn't believe it. After all this time? Are things that bad for your dad?"

"It's still touch and go." She cocked her head as she studied Ginger. "You've changed your look."

"My daughter dared me to be different. The things a mom will do to make her child happy. I think I let her talk me into something a bit edgier than I should have." Ginger brushed the hair at the nape of her neck. "Auburn to black. Shoulder length to spikes. What do you think? Should I refuse the next time Kaitlyn talks me into mother-daughter bonding?"

Alanna considered her old friend another minute. "I like it. Reminds me of the girl who wanted a dragon tattoo in high school."

"Yeah, I guess. I'm glad my parents threatened the convent over that one. Can you imagine a tail wrapped around my neck?" Ginger mock shuddered.

"Probably wouldn't have liked it long."

Ginger quirked an eyebrow. "You never did anything like that? Even in college?"

"No. Remember I couldn't even get my ears pierced? I'm such a chicken."

"I'll never forget how green you turned simply walking by that store in Cheboygan."

"So how are you?"

"Single and one kid." Ginger's eyes softened with the pride of a mama. "Kaitlyn is my life. We live in St. Ignace, but I'm here most days for work. Will your dad be okay?"

"We don't know yet. Day by day." The line moved forward. Alanna placed a quick order then turned her attention back to Ginger. "Where do you work?"

"The police department. I heard you had some excitement last night."

Alanna grimaced. "I'm sure the chief is telling all kinds of stories."

"Don't worry. He's investigating."

"Who knows if he can find anything." A thought struck her. Could Ginger help Alanna review Grady's file? "How hard is it to get access to old police files?"

"For a case?"

"Yes."

Lines appeared around Ginger's eyes as she studied Alanna. "Why would you want that?"

"No particular reason."

Ginger thought a moment. "The chief doesn't hand out files willy-nilly."

"Aren't there freedom of information requirements?"

"Sure, but do you want to wait that long?"

"No. I just wanted to review Grady's file."

Ginger tapped a perfectly manicured finger against her lips. "Tell you what—I'll see what I can scrounge up. Not making any promises though. But it'll have to wait until after the weekend. The fudgies will keep me hopping in dispatch."

"Okay." Alanna grabbed her sack. "Thank you."

"What do you think you'll find?"

"Maybe nothing, but I want to read it." Alanna slipped from the store and hurried back to the studio. If Ginger came through with the file, that would be easier than explaining her reasons for seeing the file to the police chief.

SUNDAY MORNING ALANNA hurried to reach the island's community church in time for the service. She'd lingered in bed too long worrying about who'd attend that morning and if any of them had heard about the chief coming to the cottage. Add her eleven-year absence, and it could be an awkward morning filled with people who remembered the old her. After fifteen minutes imagining how they'd treat her, she decided Jonathan was right. She needed to move past Grady's death and her assumption that people blamed her, too. She hadn't accepted his challenge and jumped in the water. Neither had she pushed him in and forced him to swim in the bitter water. The thoughts propelled her down the road away from her home.

Half a block from the church, she slowed to a stop and closed her eyes. This morning wasn't about her. It was about stepping back and spending time worshipping her Creator and Lord. *Father, help me pull my focus from me. Forgive me for being so selfish that I can't pull my gaze up. I long to worship You whole-heartedly.*

A whisper floated through the trees, a breeze that kissed her cheek. In that moment, her concerns disappeared, and she walked into the small sanctuary with a smile on her face. Her low-heeled sandals clicked against the oak plank flooring. Sunlight filtered through stained-glass windows lining the pews, the mix of soft colors lending an Impressionist light to her white skirt. She settled on a pew in the middle as the pianist played the opening notes to a hymn. Alanna leaned back and let the music wash over, peace floating through her.

More people filtered in before the pastor took his place at the front and led the small congregation in a few songs. Alanna kept her eyes closed to avoid the distraction of whoever might stand near her. When the sermon started, she opened her Bible and journal, taking notes on the pastor's comments about finding freedom in the Lord.

Freedom was certainly something she needed. Freedom from the painful hold of the past. Freedom from the quandary of her mother's paintings. Freedom from her fears about what others thought of her.

Most important, the freedom to be the woman God had created her to be.

As the congregation stood for the benediction, Alanna glanced back. In an instant, her peace evaporated as she glimpsed Piper Cadieux. Piper's hair was longer and lighter than when she'd watched Grady with the adoring eyes of a girl who thought her older brother could do no wrong.

Alanna turned forward, a heavy cloak of dread flowing over her. Piper tied her directly to the past. The girl's middle-school crush on Trevor had led to her spending every spare moment at the Stones until Grady's death. Alanna would never forget the pained accusations in the girl's eyes after that.

How would Piper respond now?

The service ended, and Alanna sank onto her seat. Maybe if she stayed put until the sanctuary cleared she could avoid Piper. Only cowards acted that way, but she didn't want a confrontation. Not in church.

This was ridiculous. What was the worst that could happen? Piper turned her back on Alanna? After all this time, that shouldn't matter.

Alanna stood and stepped into the walkway. "Piper."

The petite young woman stood in front of her, shoulders back and feet apart. "Alanna. I assumed you'd never slink back."

"Guess everyone did." Alanna swallowed and clasped her hands in front of her. "How are you?"

"Fine. Running Mom and Dad's gift shop while they squeeze in a last vacation. Then I'll take over the B&B when they return. We're shorthanded."

What could she say to that? "I'm having trouble finding a clerk for the studio."

"Tight labor market this year. We'll manage even if I have to run both places. Hard to imagine this little girl can do all that?" A glint matched her words.

Alanna nodded. "Guess I pictured you as you were when I left."

The sanctuary emptied, and they started toward the door.

"Want to grab lunch?"

Pipers words surprised Alanna. Maybe Piper remained the friendly person she'd been when not shadowed by a shocking death. Maybe an agenda lurked beneath her words. Either way, Alanna couldn't walk away.

"I think I'd like that."

Piper led the way down the street to one of the island's many restaurants, only the sound of horses' hooves clomping against the road filling the space between them. Alanna tried to think of something to say, but everything felt forced like she wanted to try too hard.

As the hostess seated them at a table, Piper picked the seat across from Alanna. "Are you settled?"

"As much as I can be when I'll only be here a bit."

"Not staying?"

"No, just helping Mom and Dad."

Piper nodded. "You always had such a great relationship. So much better than the happy little home I had."

"It wasn't perfect."

"From all I saw, it looked that way. I loved spending time at your home. Your mom always treated me so well." Sadness lingered in Piper's eyes. "After Grady died, it just got worse. Only this time it was quiet. Like Mom and Dad retreated into their pain."

"It must have been awful."

Piper shrugged. "Proof life doesn't happen like we expect."

The waitress took their orders, and Piper talked about former classmates. As she rattled on, Alanna imagined the yearbook sitting on the table, Piper telling what each person had done since she graduated. When the waitress returned with salads for the girls, Piper took a breath. "That's everybody. I talk. . .a lot. . .when I'm nervous."

"Nervous? Why?"

"It's been a long time since I've seen you. Why didn't you come back earlier?"

"Guess I worried about what everyone would say."

"And now?"

"It isn't what I imagined. It's almost like that day has disappeared from our history. I'm surprised nobody talks about Grady."

Piper nodded. "It's like they've forgotten."

"Or moved on."

"When he died, everything changed."

Alanna nodded. "In unexpected ways. Coming back makes it like it just happened."

"Maybe. The island is frozen in time to me. To the week Grady died." Piper rolled her napkin into a tight roll.

Alanna reached toward her then pulled back. "I'm so sorry he died."

"That makes two of us. I dream, and he's still here. Sometimes the college basketball star he imagined. Other times he's stocking shelves at some big store. Then I wake up."

"Do you blame anyone?" Alanna studied Piper as she asked the question, looking for any sign that contradicted the young woman's strong words.

"No. Grady didn't have a lot of common sense. He'd take any dare, no matter how foolish. Anybody who grew up here knows swimming to the lighthouse that early in the season is a recipe for disaster." Piper sighed, and then her hazel gaze locked on Alanna's. "I've grieved. Do you think you still question because you ran?"

"Not with the way people blamed Trevor for the race. If I'd heard one more time he's the one who should have died since he took Grady on. . ."

Piper nodded. "A lot of people said that, didn't they? I'm glad two boys didn't die."

Alanna paused, something Piper said catching her attention. "Two?"

"Yes." She tilted her chin and stared at Alanna. "You know. You were there."

Alanna shook her head. "There were more than two people in, the water. At least Brendan went in, too."

"No." Piper pushed against the table. "I'd remember."

"You weren't there. Not then. There were at least three, and at one point four, in the water." Alanna couldn't be wrong. More than Grady and Trevor jumped in the water. If she'd been wrong all this time, it changed everything.

That's why she'd left.

Why she'd abandoned her life on the island, her friends, her families. People had targeted Trevor, and she couldn't watch. Not when others joined in the race.

## 16

A fter lunch Alanna hurried to the studio. If she'd hoped for her swirling thoughts to calm when surrounded by her mother's art, reality disappointed her.

Instead of peace, the longer she looked at the paintings, the more the belief her mom couldn't have painted them confronted her. One more piece of the truth she'd built that threatened to crumble at a touch. If she probed too hard, she didn't know what she'd find.

Life was supposed to be something she controlled. That's why she'd left. But as each day passed, God stripped another layer of the protective veneer she'd applied so carefully. Every illusion she'd created that coming to the island was risky but could be a break disappeared with the idea she had been wrong.

Wrong.

The word stuck in her throat.

Tourists flowed in and out of the shop, but it wasn't enough to still her roller-coaster thoughts. Each time she convinced herself Piper had it wrong, a wave of doubt assaulted her.

At five she had to escape. She turned off the lights and locked the front door.

"Where are you going?"

She stilled at Jonathan's voice as her pulse picked up. "I thought you had a picnic. And rehearsal dinner."

"I do and did. The bride had the rehearsal early. Wanted it in the same light as tomorrows wedding. And I forgot something important. Dylan needs a kite with the wind like this." He held up a narrow package.

"Oh." She fumbled the keys to hide. He couldn't know she'd hoped he'd changed his mind and wanted to spend the evening with her. She couldn't lean on Jonathan. Not when she planned to leave and he had no plans to move. Not when he had Jaclyn and Dylan.

"Are you okay?"

She couldn't face him and his concern. He'd seen too much weakness already. She nodded, eyes on her keys. "Have a great time."

Jonathan stood a moment longer then nodded. As he stepped away, she glanced up. He didn't look back as he hurried toward Fort Mackinac. Why did she want him to so much? She grabbed her bike and pushed through the traffic until she could break free and pedal the rest of the way home.

The balance of the long weekend passed in a flood of tourists and avoidance. She didn't see Jonathan but didn't expect to between his picnic and wedding. Instead, she spent any moments not at the studio alone. After her experience with Piper, she couldn't stomach trying to find people to ask what they remembered about the accident. Not yet. Besides, all the visitors kept residents busy as they made the island memorable. In the tight economy, everyone needed the tourists to come, stay, and return again and again.

She pasted on a smile when at the studio and tried to settle into a book when home. By Monday night, she tired of moping. Patience Matthews had told her to check in, so she would. Alanna shuffled through the junk drawer for Mom's address book. After sifting through discarded keys, enough pens to equip Congress, and a stack of miscellaneous appliance guides, she finally found the thin spiral-bound book. Slipping to the *Ms*, she found Patience's number.

"Mrs. Matthews?"

"Yes?"

"This is Alanna Stone."

"Have plans for tonight?"

Alanna looked at the frozen pizza she'd pulled out. "Not really."

"Good. We're getting ready to grill a few burgers and brats. Come on over."

"Can I bring anything?"

"Just yourself."

Alanna brushed her teeth then grabbed a gallon of lemonade and hopped on her bike. After zigzagging the island on roads most people would never discover, Alanna worked her way along Mackinac to the Matthews's cabin. A dilapidated hotel stood next to it, looking like the perfect setting for a horror movie or ghost. She bumped across the grass to the porch. After leaning her bike against the rail, she climbed the two stairs. She and Trevor had spent many summer days playing along the beach in front of the house with the Matthews kids. Now they'd left, and the rocky beach held a few kids who tripped into the water then screamed and ran out. Alanna shook her head. Crazy kids. The lake wouldn't be warm for at least a month. Even then, *warm* was a relative term.

The screen door bounced against the wall. "Alanna Stone." Alanna turned to see Patience approaching her, arms wide open for a hug. She slid into the older woman's arms and sighed. She felt safe, protected.

"It's about time you got over here."

"I've only been on Mackinac a week."

"That's an eternity, and you know it. How many days did you spend over here growing up? It's practically your other home." Patience pulled back and studied Alanna. "You carry the burdens of the world still."

"Something like that."

"Well, burgers are coming off the grill, so first we eat."

Alanna followed Patience around the house to the backyard where a patio table waited adorned with a bucket of early flowers, platter of corn on the cob, and stacks of buns and condiments. The aroma of cooking meat colliding with early lilacs embraced Alanna. She inhaled and felt her muscles relax.

Earl Matthews pivoted from the grill. "Hey, girl. Still like them medium well?"

"Yes, sir. No mooing please."

He grinned and pulled the last burger off. After a prayer, they settled down and ate. When they finished, Earl scooped up the plates. "I'll leave you to catch up."

"I didn't mean to chase you away."

Patience made a brushing motion. "Don't worry. He has some DVD he wants to watch. One of those macho adventure movies." Patience grabbed the lemonade and refilled their cups. "So tell me what's worrying you."

"Have you seen Mom painting?"

"Lately? No, she's been gone." Patience looked at her with lines between her eyes.

"That's not. . ." Alanna tried again. "Has she done much painting around the island? You know, hauling all her paints and things around like she used to."

"Some, but she also said she didn't need to see it anymore

since she's painted so much. I think her arthritis has bothered her, too. Must make holding a paintbrush challenging."

"Didn't she worry about capturing the light?" Mom had prided herself on following in the Impressionist line of chasing the light and capturing the ways it played.

"I'm no artist. That falls to your mom and brother."

"Right." Alanna took a sip of her lemonade, the tartness puckering her lips even as it cooled her throat. "Does anyone talk about. . ."

"That day?"

Heat climbed Alanna's throat. "Yes."

"Only occasionally. Days like the anniversary. Guess you missed that, huh?" When Alanna nodded, stomach tightening at the thought, Patience slid her chair closer. "You could have stayed. Everyone else did." She sighed. "You aren't the only one that day impacted. We all hurt. You can't have a tight-knit community like this without a death—especially tragic—impacting everyone. We've moved on. Even the Cadieuxs understand it was an accident. Exactly what happens when young men go crazy. They haven't figured out yet that life isn't guaranteed. The stunts I've seen." She shook her head. "Unfortunately, that one didn't end well."

The truth echoed through Patience's words. Running hadn't solved anything. Instead, all the emotions of that day exploded inside with each new turn or person confronted.

As she rode home, she prayed. She needed to find the truth, whether or not it was what she remembered.

It was time to let the truth set her free.

～

ALANNA SPENT Tuesday morning evaluating how many paintings she'd sold during the weekend. If sales continued at this steady pace, the Painted Stone needed more large art.

Alanna hated the idea her mother would ship more paintings while Alanna continued to believe they were frauds. The only alternative was bare walls, and that wouldn't pay her father's medical bills.

Several times she had picked up the phone to call, only to be interrupted by customers. This morning she sat in the shop with her e-mail application open trying to form the words for an e-mail.

Maybe that would make the tough questions easier to ask. At least then she wouldn't have to hear the hurt in Mom's voice when she took it as an accusation.

*Mom, business has picked up. People have bought several paintings since I arrived. Which leads me to a question...*

Alanna stared at the words. They would only make Mom defensive. She rubbed her temples as she considered how to rephrase the note.

The phone rang, and Alanna snatched it up. "The Painted Stone Studio."

"This is Gerald Tomkin."

She sighed and pushed back the thought that she should have let his call go to voice mail. "Good morning."

"Now that the holiday weekend is behind us, I hope you've had a chance to consider joining the foundation board."

The pounding in her temples intensified. "I'm honored. But I'm an attorney. Wouldn't a CPA be more helpful?"

"You understand the island and its history. You'll understand what we're trying to do with the foundation better than some outsider who might have the right piece of paper. After all, you can't get into law school without brain power."

She bit back the urge to correct that fallacy. "I really don't plan to be here long."

"Mackinac will work its magic. I'm betting you stay." His cajoling wore down her defenses. It wasn't like she couldn't continue via e-mail and teleconferencing after she left. If she wanted.

"You're persistent."

"Part of my charm."

This sounded more like the man she remembered from school, convinced he was always right. . .and usually correct in that assumption. "All right. I'm happy to do what I can while I'm here."

As for the rest, she'd wait and see how the meetings went.

"That's all I ask. See you tonight at seven thirty."

"What?"

He hung up before answering.

After the long weekend, the last thing she wanted was to spend the evening sitting at a table with people she barely knew and discuss business she didn't care about. No, she'd imagined a night with quiet music, a bit of candlelight, and a heaping bubble bath—lilac scented to match the flowers emerging across the island.

A ding from her computer pulled her attention from the burgeoning pity party. "Let this be good news." She crossed her fingers and moved the mouse to click on the envelope.

An e-mail from Trevor popped up, subject line reading *Ready for more?*

Increased ability to tell people no? Sure.

Added chances for true love? Certainly.

More peace and hope in her life? Absolutely.

But as she opened the e-mail, Alanna knew Trevor didn't

mean any of those.

> *Hey, sis. Mom mentioned this weekend the studio might be low on paintings. Especially if you've sold more. You have, haven't you? I'll get some up there ASAP. I've got three or four medium-sized canvasses ready to ship as it is. And with a bit of nose to the grindstone this week could have another three ready to go. TTYS. Trevor.*

She read and reread the words, a heavy sensation cloaking her.

The words confirmed in black and white Jonathan's accusations and her fears. What it didn't do was explain why. Dread shrouded her at the thought. Could she fix this?

Alanna looked out the window, wondering when Mom stopped and Trevor started painting. No wonder something felt different. He would have the feel for Mackinac, but his perspective would differ from Mom's. That would also explain the lack of geraniums. A guy wouldn't notice that detail. No matter how much he trained himself to copy her style, he wouldn't achieve perfection.

Jonathan walked by, and Alanna swiveled on her heel, hand to her face, and ducked beneath the counter. Maybe he hadn't seen her. The last thing she could handle at this moment was talking to him. He'd see right through her when he asked how she was. He always could.

After the three-day weekend, she didn't have the reserves to pretend this latest twist didn't upset her. The rest of her family might not follow Christ, but she did—one good thing that came from leaving the island and heading south for college. She'd looked for friendship wherever she could find it, even in campus ministries. She hadn't expected to find Christ at the same time. How could she reconcile what they were doing? Was it even possible? Her gut told her it wasn't, which meant she'd have to confront them and figure out how to get them to understand why it mattered.

Alanna waited another moment. Surely Jonathan had continued on his way. After all, he'd had a busy weekend, too, with that wedding.

For years she'd imagined she'd marry long before her thirtieth birthday. Now she just avoided weddings. That was easier than seeing how close she'd inched to the date without even a boyfriend.

*Boyfriend.*

She puffed hair off her forehead with a breath. What a ridiculous word after a certain age. Namely anytime after college. Really, couldn't someone come up with anything better?

And who said thirty made her an old maid? She needed to get her nose out of a book and into the real world. A world where women married later and later. She deflated. It might work for them, but she'd imagined life with someone to share it with before adding a couple of kids to their union. In fact, that someone had been the man on the other side of the window for too long. But like it or not, he was taken—it was time to slay that vision permanently.

Maybe then she could move on and find her Prince Charming.

And maybe one day he would stop looking like Jonathan Covington each time she pictured him on his white horse.

Alanna's calf muscles tightened, and she groaned. Hiding here all day wouldn't work.

She inched her way up until she could see over the top of the counter. Her gaze locked with Jonathan's, where he stood looking in the window. Heat flooded her cheeks, and she sank back down.

Could things get worse?

## 17

A hint of warmth touched the day as Jonathan headed down Market Street. The clock said it was time for lunch, and his stomach agreed. He ignored the fact he could have reached restaurants faster if he'd taken Main.

His path had nothing to do with passing the Painted Stone. Yeah right. He shook his head but didn't alter course. If he happened to glance in that large window as he passed, it didn't mean anything.

Other than the fact he had a divided heart. He'd spent part of Sunday evening with Jaclyn and Dylan, and when his thoughts hadn't strayed to Alanna, he'd enjoyed it. But his mind wandered more as the picnic wore on.

He sidestepped a bike and frowned at the kid riding it. The sidewalks weren't the place for those. At least the island had emptied at the close of the long weekend. He had a couple of weeks until his next event, giving him plenty of time to plan and dream up business. If he could maintain focus. . .a big "if" right now.

Maybe he should find a replacement for Alanna and usher her to the ferry and off his island home. His peace had abandoned him the morning she showed up at the cottage. He didn't like being poised for any sound from her side of the tree line. Took all the relaxation out of being home. In fact, he might as well move down to a Main Street apartment.

He slowed at the studio, hands in his pockets, and looked inside. A blur of motion by the counter caught his eye. He glanced around but didn't notice anyone in the Painted Stone. Maybe he should make sure Alanna was okay.

"Jonathan. Just the man I wanted to find."

"Hello, Gerald. Headed to lunch?"

The man patted his trim stomach. "In a bit. First, I need a favor." Jonathan eyed him. What would it be this time? "If I can."

"Escort Alanna Stone to tonight's meeting." He eyed Jonathan like an eagle spies its prey. He must have found what he was looking for in Jonathan's expression. "I knew you wouldn't mind."

"There's a meeting tonight?" Jonathan scrambled for any plausible excuse to get out of going. Alanna wouldn't agree to anything Gerald asked. After all, she'd spent hours during the summers bemoaning what an awful teacher and principal he was.

"Got to finalize some plans for the lilac festival if we hope to raise any money. If we want to use your plan for the swing festival, we'll try out the process during the lilac festival."

Sounded like another way to get free services. Too bad he didn't have an out since he sat on the board. "I'll see what I can do."

"I knew you would. See you tonight."

Jonathan bit back the impulse to say, "Yes, sir," and turned back to the window. As he did, Alanna's blond head peeked above the counter. Had she hidden there this whole time?

He bit back a smirk. She must feel something, even if he merely annoyed her. It gave him a place to start.

He set his chin at a cocky angle and sauntered into the studio. All he missed was the fedora to pull off the Humphrey Bogart air she'd always loved in those old black-and-white movies.

As the bell jingled, she stood and brushed the front of her shirt. Now that he looked more closely, she seemed to have adopted the style of one of those classic actresses. Boatneck T-shirt and pedal pushers, or whatever they called those short pants.

"Jonathan, you can't tell me you came here this often when my parents ran the studio." She crossed her arms, and a soft swipe of color lit her cheeks from the inside.

"Gerald asked me to escort you to tonight's foundation meeting."

"You don't need to do that." The color leeched from her cheeks.

"It's no problem." He leaned an elbow on the counter and invaded her personal space.

"Really, I'll be there without someone playing babysitter."

"Doesn't matter. I always keep my promises." He stood. He hadn't meant the jab that accompanied the words, yet by her stiffening, she'd caught it all the same. "I'll come at seven."

"But the studio is open until then."

"Not tonight." He shrugged as he moved toward the door. "You know how it is. Gerald snaps his fingers and gets what he wants."

Jonathan didn't have to look back as he left to feel the heat of her gaze.

After a full afternoon plotting with the manager at a local B&B that couldn't afford its own event planner, he scrubbed his face and then swiped his teeth with a toothbrush. The effort wasn't for Alanna. He needed to look his best if he wanted the foundation to hire him. And as he looked at his calendar, he needed the business to fill out his late summer. Otherwise it had the makings of a slim year. Unless he started working out of his cabin, he didn't have places left to cut back. Like it or not, Alanna had to come with him to the foundation. He couldn't afford annoying Gerald Tomkin.

He hurried down the stairs and onto the street. He needed to get to the studio before she left. Knowing her, she'd try to escape before he arrived.

The studio's lights flashed off as he approached. He waited in front, and a moment later Alanna opened the door and turned to lock it. She spun around then jumped back with a squeak.

"Jonathan!" She pressed a hand over her heart then reached out and smacked him. "Are you trying to scare me?"

He rubbed his chest and frowned. "No."

She sighed, and a bit of the stiffness eased from her shoulders. "Well, you did. I really don't need you to babysit me."

He offered his arm. "I won't bite."

Alanna eyed his arm then decided it would be okay for the short walk. She filled the space with small talk as they walked to the foundation building. A few bikes lined the rack in front.

"How many people serve on the board?" Alanna licked her lips as she examined the bikes.

"Eight. The tried-and-true island lovers."

"So they'll all know me."

He heard the unsaid "and my history" and wanted to throttle her. "Someday you have to shed that, Alanna."

"Sure. As soon as men like Gerald Tomkin don't look at me with knowing in their eyes. You have no idea what that's like. I've decided to find the truth so I can put that day behind me. It's time."

"More than time."

"I've heard you each time you've said that." She removed her hand from his arm and studied the building. "Might as well get this over with. Guess I have 'fool' stamped on my forehead."

"What?"

"There's no other reason I'd do this." She marched up the stairs, her flat slippers echoing against the wood.

"What about your heart to help anytime you can? You always jumped in to causes."

"I guess that hasn't changed." She said it with an eye roll, but he was glad. That was the part of her he'd first fallen in love with. Well, after her long legs and beautiful smile.

THE MOMENT she stepped through the door, Alanna knew she should leave. This wasn't where she wanted to be. Not now. Not with Jonathan next to her. They'd look like a couple to all the people who'd known her as a teen. But some things couldn't begin again, and she couldn't erase the past.

Instead of a reception area, there was a thin desk with a laptop and phone. In front of it sat two folding chairs. A short hallway fed off that room, and a light shone from a doorway.

"It's this way."

"I know." She brushed past Jonathan, only mildly regretting taking out her anxiety on him. He might not deserve it at the moment, but give him a few minutes, and he'd say or do something that would make her forget he could still be sweet.

As she entered the hall, the soft murmur of voices filtered toward her. She closed her eyes and sucked in a breath. *Help me do this, Lord.*

Steps approached the doorway, and a moment later Gerald Tomkin stepped in front of her. "There you are. I was about to call the cavalry."

"No worries. Jonathan ensured I got here."

"Even though she didn't need me." Jonathan stuck out his hand, and Mr. Tomkin gave it a quick pump.

"Come in, come in." He clapped his hands together as soon as they were in the room, and the conversations around the table ceased. "You remember Alanna Stone. She's agreed to fill her dad's spot on the board until he returns."

A few folks had the courtesy to wear pasted-on smiles, but Alanna sensed they wanted her here even less than she wanted to join them. She studied Mr. Tomkins profile. Why would he insist?

She glanced around the table and smiled when she reached Mr. Hoffmeister. "I didn't know you were on the board."

"From time to time." He patted the vacant chair next to him. "I do my part."

Alanna squeezed around the oak table and slid into the chair. "Thanks."

"You need to come back by the shop."

"Maybe now that the weekend's over. Bet you sold lots of fudge."

"Enough." He pointed his chin at Mr. Tomkin standing at the head of the table. "He'll keep us here all night if we aren't vigilant."

"Sounds fun."

The older man snorted then shook his head. "You always did have a sharp way with words."

If he only knew. That's one thing that made her effective in the courtroom, but not so much in the studio.

The meeting started, and Alanna held back her surprise when Jonathan didn't sit at the table. Instead, he leaned against the wall, a position that looked more uncomfortable as the meeting droned on and he stifled a yawn. Alanna shifted against the seat, frowning as the faux leather squeaked. She felt like a kid again, trapped in another of Mr. Tomkins unending classes.

It didn't look like he intended to have any more mercy on her now than he did then.

A yawn stretched her mouth, and she snagged a glance at her watch. Nine o'clock? No wonder it felt like she'd sat there forever and a day. She slumped back against the headrest.

"Are we boring you, Alanna?" Mr. Tomkins pointed words jerked her upright.

"No, sir."

"Good. Is there any other business?" He looked around the room, but everybody shook their heads until he reached Bette Standeford. "Yes?"

"I thought we planned to discuss Mr. Covington's proposal."

"That's at the next meeting."

Jonathan straightened at his words, and a frown tugged his face down. "If we wait, I won't have enough time to get everything implemented."

"Tonight we have to focus on the lilac festival. We've got to raise some money, or there won't be anything left to give."

Mr. Hoffmeister leaned close to Alanna, the rich scent of chocolate making her stomach rumble. "That I don't understand."

"What?"

"I thought there was extra in the account before he took over." Hoffmeister rubbed his eyes. "I've never much liked numbers. But Gerald's comments have me rethinking the books."

Mr. Tomkin cleared his throat. "Anything you'd like to share, Tony?"

Mr. Hoffmeister skewered Mr. Tomkin with a glare before waving his hand. "Not at the moment."

"We'll wait with bated breath."

"I bet you will," Mr. Hoffmeister muttered under his breath then glanced at Alanna. "Sorry about that. We can't seem to have a civil conversation anymore thanks to his stupid house plans. The island has clear requirements for houses. . .but he's above it all." He stopped as if catching himself. "Well, come visit me."

Alanna nodded, keeping her eyes trained on her old teacher. "Not tonight."

"As soon as you can. There are things we should discuss." He stood and edged toward the door. "See you at the next meeting. These old bones have to get home if I'm going to work tomorrow. If you need me, you know where to find me."

The others took that as their opportunity to escape, too. In a few minutes, the room had emptied, but Alanna remained. Where before she thought the meeting would never end, now she wondered what game Mr. Tomkin was up to and why he'd insisted she attend.

18

---

There's something I don't understand."

Mr. Tomkin didn't turn from where he stood at the whiteboard working the eraser back and forth across the smooth surface. Alanna waited a moment. Why ignore her?

"You don't need me." She glanced around the now-empty boardroom. "The brightest people who live here serve on the board. I don't add anything."

"You're wrong." He turned toward her and propped his hands on the table. A furrow lined the top of his nose. "Something strange is going on, and we need someone who can dig.

"Why me? I've been gone years. You're the local stalwart."

"True." Something glinted in his expression as he leaned closer. "It has drawbacks. I've made my share of enemies. People who think I created the problems. You're an outsider, just what we need."

She could see that. The man seemed pricklier under the surface than when she'd known him. "I really don't have time. . .and won't be here long."

"Sure you do. What do you have to do after the studio closes. . .unless you're spending all your time with Covington?" She bristled as his tone scraped over her. He crossed his arms and stared her down. "Even then this doesn't require much. Just the skills lawyers have. Here." He walked to a stack of books. "I just need you to review these."

Alanna looked down at her stenographer's notebook. As he'd talked, she'd doodled a series of interlocking circles. That summed up life on Mackinac. The island was small enough the people and events that tried to remain separate ended up bound together, like the ripples a stone makes in the water circling ever outward.

He must have noticed her distraction. He sighed. "It's late now. I'll stop by tomorrow with these."

"All right." She'd like to stop him, but he'd aroused her curiosity. She wanted to know what those books contained.

A stiff wind blew off the lake as she exited the building. Twilight had melted into darkness, and she wished she'd grabbed her bike rather than walking. Now she'd have to swing by the studio before working her way home. She glanced around, half expecting Jonathan to be waiting near the street-light, but he wasn't. She shook away the disappointment. He hadn't promised he'd wait. She'd hoped though.

She stuck to Main Street where there would be more people and the streetlights cast wide circles of light. Soon the sound of music slipped from the restaurants, and a man stumbled from the first one she passed.

"Hey, gorgeous. Just who I was looking for." He tripped into her path, and she stepped onto the street to avoid him. One of the taxis pulled to a quick stop behind her, and she raised a hand in apology as she continued on her way. She kept her steps quick and her eyes locked in front of her as she stepped back on the sidewalk. Many of the stores were dark, and she wished for a bit more traffic as she heard the man bumbling behind her. His movements didn't sound coordinated enough to be a threat, but she kept her eyes peeled for a police officer on bicycle.

Even though she'd decided to discourage Jonathan, right about now she'd love to have him beside her. His strong presence and broad shoulders would deter many from bothering her.

Now she felt exposed. Vulnerable. Alone.

A shiver skittered up her spine, and she picked up her pace. Light poured from several more restaurants, but still no sign of an officer. As she passed I'm Not Sharing Fudge Shop, she glanced in. Mr. Hoffmeister sat on his stool talking to someone on the phone. She waved, but he didn't notice.

Alanna picked up her pace and crossed the street. She glanced over her shoulder and saw the drunk slouched beneath a light-post. While his posture said inebriated, his gaze had locked on her. She tossed her hair and scurried around the corner out of his line of sight. Once she reached her bike, she could leave him far behind and hurry home. Did he have anything to do with what happened in her storage shed? She shook the thought free.

All she wanted was the sanctuary inside her childhood home.

JONATHAN LET the night embrace him as he sat on the rocking chair. His heavy fleece parka kept him warm in the cool air as long as he buried his hands in its pockets. The house next door looked empty from what he could tell through the trees. Should he have waited?

Maybe he'd misinterpreted her signals that she wanted him to leave her alone.

It rankled, but he'd honor it. Didn't mean he had to relax

before she made it home. He'd feel ridiculous if she'd slipped in and was tucked in her bed sound asleep while he played night watchman. He could think of a few choice things to call himself, including fool.

He rubbed his neck where the breeze snuck under his collar. Kind of like how Alanna had slipped under his guard. Amazing how one could spend eleven years actively forgetting someone, only to have the walls tumble down the moment she reappeared.

The cicadas sang their lullaby, loud and in tune. The faint scent of pine slipped around him as the trees rustled. He glanced at the Indiglo symbols on his watch. He'd give her fifteen more minutes then call to make sure he hadn't missed her.

The evening had wasted his time, plain and simple. He couldn't identify Gerald's game, but it annoyed him. He'd joined the foundation board before Gerald became president. Ever since he could make better use of his time at home. Then to have Gerald delay any decision on his proposal. . . Jonathan had to force his anger back. He wouldn't jump too many more times for the man.

In fact, if he invested more time in working with the island's many bed-and-breakfasts, he'd land plenty of new projects. And it wouldn't mean the silly games the older man threw around in some twisted power play. Come on, this was a small town on a small island. There were much bigger things to invest his time in than a tug-of-war over who had the last say.

Something crunched on the road. He stood and took a step to the edge of the porch. Was that Alanna?

He toyed with acting nonchalant and ignoring the sound, but he needed to know she was okay. Gerald had something on her, but Jonathan didn't think she knew it yet.

He rubbed his hands over his head. Time to get a haircut.

But that would mean stopping by the Grand and seeing Jaclyn. Right now he didn't want the complication. He bit back a yawn. When had she become a complication in his life?

He didn't want to answer, so he walked down the path to the road. His steps crunched through the debris of fallen leaves and branches. He wouldn't sneak up on whoever worked their way up the road. It was too dark to see much, except what the small light on the approaching bike illuminated. The bike turned onto the drive to the Stone home.

Slowly he released a breath. At least now he knew she was home.

He glanced at his watch again and frowned. Alanna shouldn't be this late. What could he do? She didn't want him to be her protector. "Jonathan?" The word carried like a whisper over the stillness. The song of peepers filled the quiet. In the morning, he should get down to the pond, see what changes had occurred as spring reached the island. Sounds crunched his direction, and he waited.

A soft sigh filtered toward him, and Alanna leaned against the split-wood fence lining the road.

"Long night?"

"Long week." Her shoulders were pushed forward as if by unseen forces. "I never should have come back."

Not this old argument. He'd tired of it. "Really? We all face the past."

"But I'm learning things. Things that change what I've always thought." She scrubbed her face with her hands. "I'm not making sense. That's part of the problem. Nothing adds up."

Jonathan considered the faint outline of her profile. Her shoulders slumped in a defeated slant. He stepped closer as he thought about how to respond. "Have you talked to your mom?

"No." She snorted. "Reaching her right now is like calling the president. No one's answering when the number's mine." She pulled straight. "Can I ask you a question?"

He nodded then realized she might not be watching. "Sure."

"What would you do if you caught your family in a lie? One that doesn't necessarily hurt anybody, but it's still a lie?"

"Depends."

She didn't respond at first, but he held his tongue. How much did she want to know what he thought?

"That's the great wisdom you have to offer?"

He turned toward her and brushed his fingers along her jaw, noting the way she shivered. "Alanna, there's a lot about my family I would change. Some days we get along, other days we can hardly stand each other. But we're family. So I put up with some things. Most of what we do impacts nobody else. If my sister did something that hurt others, then I'd have to say something. Or if she hurt herself, I'd speak up. It's part of being family."

"But it's not hurting anyone else." Her words didn't have the fierceness that came with conviction. "And I can't anticipate the consequences."

"What do you mean, consequences?"

"I'm not sure." She sighed and pulled back from his touch. His fingers felt chilled by her absence. "But that's my problem."

"You're an attorney. A good one. You can figure out the consequences. But I think you already know what you need to do."

"It doesn't mean I like it."

He chuckled at the fight in her tone. "True. But aren't families worth fighting for?"

She pushed from the fence and took a step toward home. "Thanks."

"That's what friends are for."

"Yeah, friends." She brushed hair from her face as she

paused a few steps away. "I've meant to ask, did you ever catch Grandpappy?"

Her question surprised him. Grandpappy? "You remember that old fish?"

"The one that always got away?" A smile colored her words. "Of course. I take it you never caught him?"

"I didn't have my good-luck charm."

"I haven't been that for a long time." She leaned forward and kissed his cheek. "Good night, Jonathan."

Jonathan stood there, rooted by the sensation of her quick kiss as she melted into the shadows. How much closeness could he handle?

The sound of her bike moving up to the house followed by the click of her door echoed in the stillness. He leaned against the fence as waves of memories crashed over him. The times they'd sat on the small dock "fishing" as an excuse to spend time together. He'd use worms while she pretended to fish with marshmallows. They'd sit shoulder to shoulder, ready to reel in the fish that lived in the pond, the descendants of the fish he and his grandpa had initially stocked the pond with.

At the time, he'd thought they'd spend the rest of their lives shoulder to shoulder, taking on the world.

Another dynamic duo. Poised to change the world.

Then life happened. The world changed.

And so did they.

## 19

Alanna leaned against the door. What had she been thinking? Kissing Jonathan, even if on the cheek?

She covered her face with her hands and sank to the floor. She felt drained, exhausted. Yet her mind whirled. If she didn't get some rest, the next day would be a nightmare. But all she could think of was her ridiculous question. Grandpappy? The island had muddled her brain. Why else would she ask about a fish? A fish?

That sealed it. If Jonathan hadn't already decided he was better off without her, she'd left no doubts. Who would want to be with a woman who focused on a fish that had probably died years ago when her family overflowed with liars? Especially when she wasn't sure she wanted to confront them and bring the truth to light.

Her mind hurt from the implications. At some point her mom had started selling her brother's art as hers. She must add her signature to the corner after the paintings arrived. Alanna didn't know whether she should hope Trevor knew about it or if she wanted him to be oblivious to the fact the paintings weren't sold as his. But she couldn't imagine her mom doing something like that.

Alanna pulled her knees up and lowered her forehead to rest on top of them. Cold seeped through the floor into her seat, but she didn't move.

Her parents had dragged them to church growing up, but the extent of any faith seemed to end at the church doors. And many cold winter mornings, it had been easier to stay home than trek via snowmobile. It wasn't until she started college and searched for answers to the mess of her life that she found a personal relationship with God.

In the years since, she hadn't probed the depths of her parents' faith. In the short pockets of time she had with them, it hadn't seemed important. Now. . .

Now she wished she'd pushed.

Because as things stood, she couldn't imagine how to start the conversation. *So, Mom, how long have you defrauded the world?* That couldn't end well.

*God, give me wisdom.*

A way to turn the problem around existed. She just needed to think creatively. That's how she handled clients' legal problems. Look at the situation from every possible angle. Examine it until she could finally find one that minimized the potential problems. The one that put them in the best possible position.

That's what she'd do. Pretend her family was her client. For the moment, she'd ignore the fact that if she truly represented them, she'd have to choose, since a conflict existed between her mom and brother. That complicated the matter too much.

A yawn stretched her mouth to the point her jaw popped. Tomorrow she'd research the legal issues. Now she'd sleep.

The next morning when the shop stood quiet, Alanna turned on the computer and prepared to dive into the legal issues. Each time Alanna opened the search engine, her fingers froze, poised over the keys. If she started searching, she'd confirm the problem. She clicked over to LexisNexis and entered a search string. Hundreds of cases pulled up. This could take forever. She glanced around the studio. Guess it was a good thing the shop remained empty.

Alanna pulled up the first case and scanned the facts. Not relevant. She'd worked her way through the first twenty when the door opened.

Police Chief Ryan stopped just inside the door. "Miss Stone."

"Hello, Chief." She swallowed and tried to smile. "Do you know anything?"

"The trap was wiped clean. Without something there, we don't have much to investigate."

"Nobody else have an unpleasant surprise like this?"

"No, ma'am."

Alanna nodded. "Thank you for letting me know."

"Easy enough to do. Wish I had better news." He slipped back out the door before Alanna could say anything else.

She turned back to the cases and read a few more before the door opened again.

"Good morning, sweetheart."

Alanna's head jerked up at her mother's voice. "Mom?"

"Yes, ma'am. In the flesh." Rachelle Stone looked like a radiant rose with her strawberry-blond hair piled in a loose chignon and an evergreen trench coat laced tight around her waist. Only the dark circles under her violet eyes gave any indication of her trials.

"What are you doing here? Why aren't you with Dad?"

"Trevor's with him." A cloud sailed across Mom's face before she painted on another smile. "There's nothing I can do for him, and we're boring each other. The space will do us good. Besides, Trevor said you needed more art. Guess he's tracked sales."

"You can do that?"

"I can't. But he can. He's much savvier about technology." Her mother waved a hand in the air then pulled off her gloves. "The Internet still baffles me."

Alanna pulled in a deep breath. Was this God's answer to her prayers? Sending her mom? "I'm glad you're here."

"I certainly hope so." Mom loosened the floral scarf from around her neck. "I am your mother, and this is my home."

"Yes." Alanna bit her lip. "I have some things I need to talk about."

The door opened again, and Mom spun on the heel of her pointed boot. "Ah, good." She stepped toward the employee of the ferry service. "I trust you were gentle with the paintings?"

"Always am, Mrs. Stone."

"That's why I like you."

Alanna rolled her eyes as her mother practically tweaked the grown man's cheek, and he blushed. When had Mom developed this larger-than-life personality?

The man stacked the boxes against the wall, leaning each carefully next to the others. Alanna couldn't wait to explore the contents even as she dreaded discussing them with her mom. What if Mom hauled them in back and added signatures?

Alanna closed the window on the computer. No need explaining her search to Mom. A few minutes later, Mom pressed a bill into the man's hand, and he tipped his hat as he headed out with a whistle. Mom studied the stack of boxes.

"I really should have asked him to haul these to the back. Shortsighted of me." She brushed a hand across her brow, and Alanna saw a flash of worry. "It's amazing how quickly one loses the routine." Alanna slipped around the counter and hurried to Mom. She hugged her, concerned about how pronounced her shoulder blades felt. "I'm sorry about everything with Dad. How is he?"

"Good as can be expected. That's what the doctors like to say.

'But it's going to be a long recovery.' " She bracketed the words then slumped. "The doctors are saying months. We'll miss the whole season."

"The whole season?"

"Yes, couldn't do it without your help."

Alanna swallowed hard as Mom sank deeper into her hug. I can't stay that long. I'll be lucky to last another week, maybe two, before the partners demand my return."

"We need you here."

"I have a job."

"We're your family." Mom pushed away and studied Alanna. "You've hidden long enough. I wouldn't be surprised if one good that comes from this is you giving up your ridiculous phobia of Mackinac."

"Mom. Maybe Trevor could come. Take care of the studio when I need to leave."

"You know he can't do that." Mom planted her hands on her hips and jutted her chin out. "He can't until everything's cleared up. You, on the other hand, have acted like a child long enough. He had to endure two years of people looking at him like he should have died rather than Grady. You left for college. You weren't involved in the stunt like he was."

"It's not that simple. Besides, I don't think anyone else still thinks about it like we do. Maybe we're fixated."

"Don't muddy the water, young lady. Your experience is not your brother's."

The door opened, and Alanna looked up, hoping for some relief from the intense conversation. Her heart sank as Mr. Tomkin entered.

"Rachelle."

Her mother spun around and stiffened. "Gerald."

"I heard you were back." Alanna didn't like the way he studied her mother.

"I see the grapevine still works."

"You haven't been gone that long."

Alanna leaned forward as her mother muttered, "Not long enough."

"Is there anything we can do for you?" Alanna took a step and slid between the two. The vibes between them were odd. Uncomfortable. She searched her memory for any reason but came up empty.

Mr. Tomkin smiled at her in a manner that looked more like a grimace. "I said I'd come by last night." He tapped the brief-case pinched under his arm. "These are the ledgers."

"Gerald, Alanna's not back to give you legal advice."

"You're the only one she can help?" There was something about the way he said it that worried Alanna. Like he knew about the paintings. "How's your arthritis, Rachelle?"

Alanna pointed at the briefcase. "I can't promise anything, but I'll look."

He strode to the counter, and Alanna joined him.

"I'll carry these back." Mom fluttered a hand at the stack of paintings, a pointed look shooting from Alanna to the paintings and back.

"This won't take long," Alanna emphasized.

Gerald opened the case and spread the papers across the counter then wiped his hands down his shirt. "These spread-sheets tell the story."

The numbers swam in orderly rows across the pages. Alanna stared at them as her eyes glazed over. If she'd wanted to study spreadsheets for hours, she would have taken the CPA exam.

"Don't you see?"

"I see lots of numbers." She moved a hand across the pages. "I need context."

"A few months ago, we held elections, and I became president of the foundation." He held up his hands. "Look, I didn't want the position, but it's a small island. There aren't many people to volunteer for jobs like this."

That made sense.

"First thing, I sat down with the books. I've had to balance budgets at the school for years. If the books aren't good, you're in trouble before you even start. Besides, I needed to know if we had anything to give away. The foundation's still new—about five years old. Enthusiasm's high, but people's dreams are often bigger than their pocketbooks."

"So what did you find?"

"That's the thing. Something's fishy. See here." He picked up a spreadsheet and pointed to a couple of columns. "From what I can see, there's an account here that doesn't match any the board approved. The policy is that after the board approves a grant, the bookkeeper opens an account. Then each time a check is issued, it's entered here." He pointed at another line. "I've identified six accounts totaling about twenty-five thousand dollars that I don't think are valid. I had my bookkeeper look at things, and she can't figure out why those accounts are there."

"Then what do you think I'll find?"

"Not sure, but you're smart and you aren't involved. I need proof that something is wrong before I say anything. Hoffmeister was the president before me, and with the bad feelings between us, I must have solid proof before I say a word." He pulled the pages into a stack and slid them into the folder. "Here you go. Technically, there's still money in the accounts. But I'm nervous about making disbursements until I have a better sense of where that twenty-five thousand went and whether we'll get it back. That's the big reason I keep postponing action on Jonathan's proposal. He's got good ideas. But. . .if we don't have the money, we can't add anything."

Mom came back and grabbed another box. "No need to dramatize everything, Gerald."

"We've got a problem here."

"Maybe, but you're just asking Alanna to confirm suspicions. She can do it if she wants. You always said she was the smartest student you ever had." She dragged the box a few feet down the hall.

Alanna wished she were as certain as Mom. The thought of spending her evenings poring over pages of numbers sounded as much fun as having her wisdom teeth yanked. "I'm not a forensic accountant."

"Who said anything about CSI?" Gerald picked up the folder and shoved it into her stomach. "Just take it. You'll find a way." His gaze followed her mom until she disappeared down the hall.

This really wasn't as complex as any of her cases. She could spend a few evenings on it. "All right. I'll see what I can do." Alanna stared at the papers she really didn't want to accept. Guess she knew how she'd spend her free time for a while.

---

## 20

The day had evolved from one call to a dozen e-mails to a large crisis. By the time five o'clock arrived, Jonathan couldn't wait to lock the door and escape. Tonight he'd pick up a few things at the deli then head home and sit on the dock. Maybe he'd catch Grandpappy this time.

A smile crooked the corner of his mouth at the thought. All the times he'd fished, he'd stopped looking for that old catfish years ago. Guess every fisherman had to have the one that always got away. But Alanna remembered.

If she dredged up that memory, there must be more—important things—she recalled.

When he reached the cabin, he shoved the grocery items in the fridge and strolled to the dock. He collected his fishing gear from the small shed and plopped down on the edge. The shadows from the trees edged along it, playing a cold game of peekaboo with him. Maybe he should wait for a day when he could fish before dusk shadowed the dock.

Still, he sat there a minute.

Had Alanna figured out what was wrong with the paintings?

What would he do if she did? He only had guesses. But based on her intensity, he had a feeling she'd uncovered the fraud.

Now the question was what she would do about it. He was just glad he wasn't in her place. He only had to delay Mr. Morris. She'd been thrust into the family business, tasked to keep it running, and faced with the unknown. All while wrestling the past—alone.

He marveled that Alanna hadn't married yet. Surely through law school and her career she'd met men who shared her goals and ambition. Maybe her experience with love mirrored his. Disappointment that couldn't be overcome. Close but never a fit. He enjoyed Jaclyn, but it wasn't love. He shifted on the dock and fed bait on the hook. Thrust the pole to the side and swung it forward, watching the line spool out.

The dock shook, and he stilled.

A minute later Alanna settled next to him. "Mom's here."

"What brought her back?"

"Other than spending time with her daughter?" Alanna bumped his shoulder with hers. He stilled at her playfulness, wondering if it was forced. She sighed, a sound that seemed to come from her toes. "She brought paintings."

Oh. He chewed his lower lip. "That's good, right? Means you sold some."

"I guess." She ran a hand through her bobbed hair. "I'm not sure what to do with them. How to address the paintings with her."

"Family can be tough."

"You have no idea." Alanna turned her gaze from the water to him. "Why did you move here? You could go anywhere."

*I waited for you.* But he couldn't say that. . .not without scaring her off or sounding like a fool. Instead, he shrugged. "I always liked it. When an opportunity came to buy the event-planning business from Mom and Dad, it made sense. I'd done a bit of that for a small Christian university and was ready for a new challenge."

"Has it lived up to your expectations?"

He tugged the line and watched the bobber dance. "Yeah. It's hard work, but most days I enjoy it. There's something special about bringing someone's vision to life. Speaking of, I need to talk to your mom about that commissioned painting."

Alanna stood and brushed her khakis off. "I don't know."

"She'd appreciate the extra money."

"What if she's not painting?" Alanna sealed her lips and grimaced. Did she want to reclaim the words that hovered in the silence?

"You figured it out?"

She nodded. The sound of birds rustling in the trees drifted around them as he studied her locked jaw. After a minute, she shuddered then looked at him. "But what am I supposed to do with that? I have no idea when it started. I don't know what to do with the paintings she brought today. I can't be a party to lying. . .but how do I fix it?" A tear slipped down her cheek. "I'm not even sure they'll realize it's wrong. And if I don't handle this right, Mom could land in serious trouble."

Jonathan considered his words. Did she want to be heard, or did she want his opinion? "Have you talked to her?"

"Mr. Tomkin arrived with his set of trouble before I broached the topic."

"Start with her. See what she says before you get too worked up."

She swiped at the tear and gave a watery smile. "Too late for that."

"What does it hurt?"

"You're right." Alanna swallowed. "Guess God gave me the perfect opportunity. We'll be face-to-face rather than over the phone or e-mail. He seems to be loading my plate pretty full."

"Deal with your mom first. She's a great lady. I can't imagine it's anything so horrible you can't work it out."

"I hope so. I'll let you get back to catching Grandpappy." She started toward land then turned. "What are you doing for supper?"

"What bachelors do. Making a sandwich or something easy."

"Come over. Mom's making pasta, and she'll make enough for a small army. Say in an hour?"

"As long as you won't use me as an excuse not to talk."

"Are you kidding? You'll be our buffer." She smiled then turned and hurried toward her home.

Jonathan watched her a minute. She might be upset, but she was still the most beautiful woman he knew. And she'd found a strong faith.

An hour later he wandered around the fence separating their yards, holding an island guidebook. He hadn't been sure what to bring, and none of his grandma's flowers bloomed yet, though he'd seen some around the island. Another couple of days and the lilacs would color the world with beautiful fragrance but for now provided nothing for his hostesses. He couldn't wait to see Alanna's face at his offering.

He slipped around the back of the house. Mrs. Stone had told him to use the back door after he showed up one too many times at the front. Mrs. Stone opened the door before he knocked.

"Jonathan. We've missed you. You taking good care of my girl?" A mischievous light glinted in her eyes.

"Trying. ma'am."

She laughed. "That I understand. She's an independent one."

"Mom, I'm right here."

"I'm not saying anything I haven't told you." Rachelle turned back to him. "I'm glad you came. One of Alanna's better ideas."

"Mom. . ."

Jonathan chuckled at Alanna's exasperated tone. In some ways, the clock rolled back to before Grady died. These two always picked at each other in this good-natured manner. At the time, he'd assumed that's what teenage girls and their moms did. Now he decided it must be moms and daughters. He leaned down and kissed Rachelle's cheek. "Thanks for letting me invade."

"I haven't been gone long enough to forget those crazy meals you called real food."

"What can I say? Cooking is not my thing."

"That's an understatement." Rachelle ushered him into the cozy kitchen. "Make yourself at home. We'll be ready to eat in a bit." Alanna turned from her station near the sink where she shredded lettuce into a large bowl. "What do you have?"

Jonathan patted the cover of the book after he placed it on the granite island. "Just a guidebook."

Alanna stepped closer, her nose wrinkling as she read the title. "A guidebook to Mackinac? Don't you think I know everything there is to know? I grew up here."

"Sure. But aren't people notorious for missing the things in their own backyards? Thought you might enjoy flipping through it."

"In all my spare time?"

"Exactly." He matched her grin. Alanna finished the salad while he stood and filled glasses with filtered water from the fridge. Wonderful, tangy aromas filled the room, tomato tinged with Italian seasoning and garlic. Rachelle shoved a pan of garlic bread in the oven and then dumped a pile of pasta in a colander in the sink. "Anything else I can do?"

"Sit down and get out of the way, young man." Rachelle winked at him as she turned back to the oven and checked the toast. "So tell me what's happened while I've been gone."

"Did Alanna tell you about what happened here?"

"No."

Jonathan explained about the shed. "I'm not sure if the police learned anything."

"Alanna, you need to move down to the apartment when I leave. We can't have you out here alone. I've never heard of anything like this happening."

Alanna glared at him. "It's not anything to get upset about, Mom. I talked to the police chief when he stopped by. It looks like a one-time event with nothing for them to follow." She tossed carrots and cheese into the salad with a little more force than necessary and then added a few cherry tomatoes on top. She set it on the table and then sank onto the stool catty-corner from him. Circles darkened the skin beneath her eyes, high-lighting the worry that crowded out the joy he'd seen earlier.

After another minute, Rachelle turned from the stove. "We're ready."

She carried a bowl filled with bow-tie pasta and marinara sauce to the small, round table. After placing it in the center, she took a seat in front of a bank of windows overlooking the pond.

Jonathan loved being in this kitchen, embraced by this family. When his parents' marriage had fallen apart, he'd known he could count on the Stones to love deeply. Now he wanted to be there for them, though he'd leave the instant Alanna asked. The idea she even wanted him there for the conversation surprised him. Miss Independent might not be so sure of herself after all.

Mrs. Stone started passing the bowls of food. "Forgot the salad dressing. Still like ranch, Jonathan?"

"You haven't been gone that long, ma'am."

She smiled at his mirrored words and popped to her feet to retrieve a bottle from the fridge before handing it to him. He poured a generous amount on top of the lettuce.

Alanna snickered. "Like some salad with that dressing?"

"You know it."

"You always have buried the good stuff."

"Only way to eat it." Man, he loved the banter. But he hated how it reinforced the silence that waited at his cabin. Most days it didn't bother him, but now that Alanna had returned, the echoes seemed highlighted.

Easy conversation filled the spaces, but Jonathan could sense Alanna's hesitation. He glanced at her, and her eyes held a slightly panicked edge as she met his gaze. He nudged her under the table, and she took a deep breath.

"Mom, I need to ask you something."

Rachelle looked at her. "Of course."

Stillness cloaked the room until Alanna shifted on her chair. Rachelle placed her napkin on the table and put her hand on Alanna's. "What's going on, honey? You've always been able to talk to me. Is this about you and Jonathan?"

Alanna's eyes widened. "I wish it were that easy."

Jonathan sat back and crossed his arms. "Hey."

"You know what I mean." Alanna frowned at him and then turned to her mom. "I don't know where to start."

"The beginning is usually the best place. As long as you aren't pregnant, this should be simple."

## 21

P regnant?" Heat flashed up Alanna's cheeks as she buried her face in her hands. Leave it to her mother to go to such a ridiculous place. "Mother!"

Jonathan snickered and coughed across the table. She glared at him, longing for nothing more than an opportunity to smack him upside the head. . .after she shook her mother. He cleared his throat and pressed his napkin against his face. "Sorry."

"Sure you are." She turned back to her mom. "Seriously? Pregnant?"

"Well, you are almost thirty. You wouldn't be the first woman to give up on finding the right man. Just tell me it wasn't that last boyfriend of yours. What was his name? Scott?"

"Spencer, Mom." Alanna rolled her eyes. All of a sudden, bringing up the forgeries didn't seem quite so daunting. "This isn't about me. And I'm not pregnant."

"Then what's it about? Good gravy, you acted like it had something to do with a death."

She sucked in a breath and squared her shoulders. Now or never. "Mom, those paintings you brought to the studio today. Did you paint them?"

Her mom's gaze darted from Alanna to Jonathan and back again. "What?"

Jonathan leaned forward, but Alanna stopped him with a stare. "Don't even. . ."

He smirked but put his hands up. "This is all you, Alanna. In fact, I'll leave if you like."

"No, you don't." She pinned his foot under the table and turned back to Mom. "We have to talk about the studio."

"So talk." Confusion flashed across Mom's face and colored her violet eyes. "But why would you question who painted them?"

"Because the paintings aren't right." Alanna's tongue refused to cooperate further.

"I didn't notice anything today. In fact, I like how you pulled out some of the unframed pieces. Setting them at lower price points was a good idea. Makes them more accessible."

"The problem is"—Jonathan interrupted, and Alanna didn't know whether to hug or slug him— "we're not sure who painted some of them." As her mother began to sputter, he held up his hand. "That's a problem, because I'm sending potential clients your way, but they want to buy one of your paintings. Not one with your signature."

As Jonathan explained, Alanna couldn't help wondering if he'd figured it out, how many others had. The damage-control potential numbed her.

Mom looked between the two of them then laughed, a high, shrill noise. "You can't be serious." She paused then frowned. "You are. I can't believe my own daughter and a man who's practically a son would insinuate such things."

"Then tell me they're yours. That you painted each stroke and didn't add your name at the end." Alanna refused to back down even as a bright red flushed her mother's face. "Tell me the canvasses you brought today weren't painted by Trevor."

"Of course I did." Mom tipped her nose in the air as she studied them. "What else would I do?"

Alanna swallowed her disappointment. Her mother had just lied. Without blinking. "Then why did Trevor e-mail asking if I was ready for more of his paintings?"

"We. . .your father and I. . .have discussed for years adding some of his paintings. Maybe Trevor thought he could push you into doing it." Mom rolled her shoulders. "I'm sure that's all. Why would I stop painting? I've always loved it."

"I don't know. Maybe arthritis has made it difficult. Patience mentioned it's flared up. Jonathan, too. And he has clients who want to commission one of your pieces. Trevor's good, but he's not you. Anyone who knows your work can tell. Jonathan figured it out. There could be others."

Her mother turned to Jonathan, ice in her eyes. "Explain what you mean when you say the paintings aren't mine."

"They don't have your passion, your vibrant use of color. The emotion is missing from them."

"Pshaw. That doesn't mean anything."

"But it does when your signature element is missing." He leaned closer to Mom. "Rachelle, Trevor doesn't place the warbler in each painting. I had to look a long time before I identified that. Yours always have the warbler tucked in a tree near the front."

Alanna stared at him, amused he'd found a marker she hadn't. "They also don't have your usual nod to the Grand Hotel."

"My what?"

"The red geraniums." Alanna shrugged. "And I've never seen a winter scene. You love color too much."

"Maybe I decided to try something new."

Jonathan shook his head. "I don't think so."

Alanna watched the exchange, noting the softness in Jonathan's expression as he engaged Mom.

"Well, it's too bad I can't catch the last ferry. You've made me feel quite unwelcome in my own home." Rachelle pushed to her feet. "I'll leave the cleanup for you."

Alanna watched her mother stalk down the hallway. She groaned and covered her face with her hands.

"I'd say that went well."

"What?" Alanna parted her fingers and stared at Jonathan as if he'd gone crazy. "That went well? My mother is furious and ready to leave. That's a rousing success?"

"You don't need to yell."

"Oh, I feel like it." She looked at the ceiling. "That's not how it's supposed to go, God."

Jonathan looked around, a worried crinkle at the corner of his eyes.

"What?"

"Praying I don't get caught in the fire when lightning flashes."

"Har, har." Alanna tried to keep her voice strict but failed. "What will I do?"

"Pray, and knowing you like I do, come up with a brilliant plan to fix everything."

Alanna shook her head. "I don't think enough time has passed. Besides, people made up their minds about us a long time ago."

"No." Jonathan took her hand, and shivers slipped up her arm. "You gave up on them. There's a difference."

Alanna lurched to her feet and pulled her hand free. "That's your theory."

"It's a good one. You'd admit it if you weren't so close to everything."

She grabbed dishes and carried them to the sink where she

turned on the water and plugged the drain. She ran her fingers through the spray, testing the temperature before she added soap. If only she could dunk this situation in warm, soapy water and fix it. Too bad life didn't work that way.

She brushed hair out of her face then dropped the plates in the water. It sloshed onto her blouse, but she didn't care. She ran a dishrag over a plate, rinsed it, and placed it in the drain. The silence pressed against her. Wouldn't he say something? Or had his impression of her plummeted with the confirmation her mom and brother defrauded art collectors?

Jonathan was right. This problem could be solved. If a client came to her with a tangle like this, she'd work through it with them and reach some kind of resolution. When it involved her family, she quit? That didn't seem right. . .at all.

She spun on her heel, flinging suds around her. One landed on Jonathan's cheek, and he didn't crack a smile or make a joke out of it.

"You're right."

"Me?" He placed a hand on his chest. "You're admitting I'm right?"

"Don't get all carried away. . .but we'll fix this."

"All right."

"You're going to plan an amazing event where we will unveil my brother as an artist. It'll be a big homecoming. By the time it's over, everyone will want one of his paintings and consider it an honor to have one of those with Mom's John Hancock."

"Now wait a minute. I'm not sure I can do that."

"Sure you can." She grinned at him. "It's the least you can do."

"Fine. What's your role?"

"I'll clear his name."

JONATHAN LEFT SHORTLY after her bold statement, and the next morning Alanna woke up to the sound of the door slamming. She groaned and rolled over. Her mother had stayed locked in her room the rest of the night, and Alanna didn't have the energy to smooth things over. Mom would find her when she was ready.

At the sound of something scraping through the gravel, Alanna threw back the covers and hurried to her window. The sight startled her.

Her mother yanked her suitcase through the gravel, making tracks down the path to the road. A taxi waited at the edge to collect her. Maybe she would have to track Mom down to make things right. Especially if the woman abandoned the island before seven o'clock.

Alanna pulled on the sweatshirt she'd tossed across the chair. She slid down the hallway and hurried down the stairs. Yanking open the front door, she stopped as the cold air slapped her in the face. She wrapped her arms around her stomach and shivered. "Mom?"

Her mother's back stiffened even more.

Fine. She'd follow the stubborn woman to the cab. The gravel poked through her socks, making her dance on tiptoes down the space between them. "Come on, Mom."

"I have to go." Her jaw was squared in the hard line it took when anger flooded her.

"Don't leave like this."

Mom huffed then turned on her heel, thrusting the suitcase between them. "Alanna, you're doing a nice job with the studio. But do not pretend you have any idea what we've experienced the last few years as we kept everything going."

"Then tell me those paintings are yours." Alanna thrust her hands on her hips.

"I don't need to justify anything to you."

"If they're yours, say so. If not, we have a problem. That's fraud, Mom."

"In whose opinion? Yours? You lost the right to say anything when you left and never came back." Mom's words rose from her whisper before she dragged the volume down.

The words punched through Alanna, stealing her breath. She tried to gather her thoughts, but they fled with the animosity flashing in her mothers eyes.

Mom snorted. "That's what I thought. You left and got your fancy degree that makes you think you know better than the rest of us. Well, wake up. You can think whatever you like. I've done nothing you can censor." She thrust back her shoulders and flipped around. She pasted a smile on her face as she handed her suitcase to the driver. "Thank you, George."

The cab pulled away and was soon nothing more than the steady clop of the horses' hooves. Alanna watched until the wagon disappeared from view over a hill. She rubbed her hands over her arms, trying to dissolve the chill that settled over her with her mother's words.

Was she wrong? Did it really matter that her brother painted the artwork rather than her mother? The angry words cycled around her mind, counter to the soft smell of lilacs carried on the breeze. She stood there, paralyzed until the soft crunch of shoes on gravel interrupted the song of the morning birds.

The musky scent alerted her to Jonathan's presence. "Good morning."

She nodded, unsure she could force any words past the rock sitting in her throat.

"So, Rachelle left."

"Yep."

"Guess she didn't like our questions."

Alanna chuckled. It was that or cry. "That's Mom for you. Passive-aggressive is alive and well."

"Don't see anything passive about walking out like that." Jonathan slid around until he stepped closer and their shoulders nearly touched. "I'm sorry."

At his simple words, the lump in her throat locked into place. How long had it been since someone said such simple and direct words to her? Her emotions collided in a pool of conflict. Part of her wanted to collapse into the strength he offered. Another part resisted the thought of allowing her weakness to show.

---

## 22

While their shoulders might barely touch, Jonathan felt the moment Alanna distanced herself from him. One moment she leaned into the comfort he offered. The next he might as well move to Antarctica for the lack of openness on her face. He sighed and stepped away.

"If you need anything, you know how to find me." He waited a minute, giving her a chance to call him back. In the face of her continued silence, he started back to his cabin but paused to look at her again.

"Thanks." The whispered word reached him as Alanna stared at the trees gathered across the road. Her jaw clenched a moment then released.

Jonathan ran his hands over his head as he hurried home. Alanna didn't make anything easy. He'd volunteered to help, so rather than moon over her, he should start fleshing out the event she wanted.

He didn't like the idea of her waltzing around the island asking questions. She'd been gone a long time. Old wounds had scabbed over. She was bound to irritate others if she refused to leave the past alone. Until she asked for his help though, there wasn't much he could do.

Now that she knew about the paintings, she'd add that to the questions burning through her. If she was determined to clear her brother, she'd bulldog residents about the graduation party. Asking the questions no one wanted to answer. And she didn't have a clue. Well, maybe she did now that her mom had left without a word.

It would benefit everyone to unbury the event people ignored. The wound festered below the surface, and now Alanna would change that.

Jonathan entered his cabin and sped through getting ready. A protein bar served as breakfast as he hiked downtown. Maybe he couldn't ask the questions for her, but he could poke around the edges. If he didn't, she'd only make things worse.

ALANNA FUMED through her morning routine. Between her mother leaving like a spoiled teenager and Jonathan, she felt wrung out before she'd been awake an hour.

The simple solution? Leave.

Head back to her job at the firm. Her apartment in Grand Rapids. Her roommate and cat.

She couldn't do it though. It wasn't in her to slide back into that world before she resolved the questions and problems she'd uncovered. She didn't walk away from a fight. She was a litigator after all. But those battles hadn't revolved around her family.

The coffee perked in the pot while she stared out the window across the pond.

*God, what do I do?*

He was truth. Would He lead her to truth? She wasn't sure how to begin, other than investigate Grady's death. That would be tricky. Everyone seemed to have placed the event firmly in the past. But if she could clear Trevor, he could put his name on the paintings, and her parents could properly display and sell the work. Then only the people who'd already bought the wrongly signed art would need some type of restitution. For now they could wait.

Alanna poured coffee into a traveling mug and doctored it with flavored syrup and milk. Her thoughts gave her a headache, the kind that could pound a drum beat the rest of the day if she didn't tackle it now. She rubbed her temples in an effort to loosen its hold before she opened the studio.

She had to find an employee. Then she could investigate to her hearts content and eventually leave.

When she reached the Painted Stone, Alanna made short work of the opening duties. As soon as she flipped the sign to OPEN, she settled on the stool at the counter. While the computer booted up, she made a short list of people to talk to. . .people who lived on the island all those years ago and who might have memories about what happened.

Then she opened her e-mail. As the messages poured in, she glanced through them for resumes. She sorted through the few, disappointed only a couple lived close enough to interview. Guess she'd need to advertise in closer newspapers if she wanted to find someone quickly rather than spend the season on Mackinac. The partners would love that.

The bells announced a new arrival. She glanced up and smiled when Ginger entered. The woman had a firm set to her posture. A small smile pasted on her face almost looked as if it belonged.

"Good morning, Alanna."

"Hi, Ginger. What can I do for you?"

"I've got what you wanted." Ginger placed a thin file on the counter.

Alanna pivoted it toward her so she could read the label. CADIEUX, GRADY. His case file. She'd almost forgotten about asking for it. "Thank you."

"I hope you enjoy the reading." Ginger's lips tightened. "Some things are better left in the past."

"Some," Alanna agreed. "But not this."

Ginger blinked quickly. "Another example of life not being fair."

Alanna studied her. Why did she care so much about someone who had died so long ago? Had they still been dating when he died? She tried to remember.

Ginger swiped at her eyes then squared her shoulders. "The past is over, right?"

"Is it?"

"Not when my baby never knew her daddy." Ginger spun on her heel and hurried from the studio as her words hovered.

Her baby? Grady's? How come she hadn't heard that? She might have left Mackinac, but Mom had done a good job the first few years of keeping her up-to-date on the lives of her friends. Then she resigned herself to the reality Alanna wouldn't return.

Ginger's daughter was Grady's. Would her search hurt the girl? Bringing to the surface questions Ginger wouldn't want to answer?

A couple wandered in, both looking vaguely familiar, but Alanna couldn't place them. A common occurrence after eleven years away. "Can I help you find anything?"

"Looking for inspiration." The tall woman smiled, but it didn't reach her eyes.

"Enjoy." Alanna watched the two a minute then turned back to the file Ginger had thrown at her, thoughts spinning. She scanned the file but didn't see anything she hadn't expected.

Still, she'd needed to look. Next she'd dig up news articles from Grady's death. See what she could learn there.

The door banged open, the bell jangling an angry song. Alanna looked up and straightened when Mr. Hoffmeister marched in. He nodded to the couple but didn't slow as he approached Alanna.

"Good morning." The lines drawn deep in his face didn't match the words. He wiped his hands on his formerly white apron, smudges of rich chocolate fudge coloring it. The cloud of chocolate following him made Alanna's mouth water.

"Mr. Hoffmeister. You just missed Ginger."

"I know. She's why I'm here." The lines around his eyes tightened, and Alanna could almost feel his pain.

"Are you all right?"

"Fine."

She eyed him, unconvinced. "What are you doing away from the fudge?"

"Needed to clear the air a bit." His words bit between them.

Alanna leaned back, wishing the stool had a backrest and slanting a quick glance at the couple. They seemed focused on the paintings, but the woman had pivoted slightly toward them. Great. "Okay."

"I know you've been away awhile. So you might have forgotten a few things. Like how those who live here take care of their own. Well, we do."

"Yes, sir. I remember." The violation of that code had kept her away.

"We don't like people poking around in matters best left alone. You have to be careful, or you'll get hurt." He placed his palms on the counter as if to steady himself. "Leave the past where it belongs."

"I will if I can, but I need to see if I can uncover what happened. Free Trevor to return."

"There's no 'maybe' about it." He slammed a hand on the counter, and she jumped. What happened to the sweet man she'd always known? "Alanna, I've always liked you and your family. But if you dig into the past too deeply, it will only harm your parents. They still live here. . .try to make a living here. I know you don't mean to jeopardize that. Please stop asking your questions."

What did he mean? She'd barely asked any. Her glance landed on the folder. Did this have something to do with Ginger? "I promise to be careful."

"I don't want to see my daughter or granddaughter hurt. And be careful about Tomkin."

Alanna let that soak in as he studied her intently. She resisted the need to squirm. "I've known him a long time."

"But not the last eleven years. He's changed. Devious." Odd how his words mirrored the ones Mr. Tomkin said of him. Finally, he nodded. "Someone will get hurt if you don't leave the past alone. I've said what I needed."

Alanna's jaw dropped as he spun and marched out of the studio as abruptly as he'd appeared. What had happened to the man who wanted to talk to her? Share secrets from the past with her?

She hurried to the windows and watched him hustle down the sidewalk. Where his posture had always been board straight, he now walked like a man burdened. He'd shoved his hands in the pockets of his navy Dockers and hunched his shoulders. Without much breeze, he didn't fight the elements. No, it looked like he fought a war within himself. A battle she wanted to glimpse. Especially if that shed light on her brother's mess.

The rest of the morning passed with a few people glancing in the windows, but no one ventured inside the store. Once she'd freshly dusted each piece, Alanna sat back down at the computer. She pulled up an article on Grady's death. As she read it, the details leaped into her mind in fresh color.

*It had been a quiet spring day. The kind that still had a chill that bit through clothes whenever the wind kicked in off the lake. That didn't stop the high school seniors from heading to the narrow beach the moment Mr. Tomkin dismissed them. Within an hour, a towering bonfire burned, kicking heat around as the flames danced higher and higher, as if straining to touch the sky.*

*Her classmates had paired off, but Alanna remained alone. If Jonathan had lived on the island, she wouldn't have sat on a log by herself. Grady brought a cooler with him, and when she opened it, longneck bottles waited in a bed of ice. She closed the lid, refusing to join in that part of the celebration. As the alcohol flowed, each person's plans for the future spiraled into crazier and crazier areas. According to them, she'd attended high school with a future president, cancer-eradicating doctor, and next NFL pro-bowl quarterback.*

*The laughter rolled around the fire after Grady made that claim. She still lay awake some nights wondering if they had all backed off, would Grady have stopped there? Instead, the juniors and sophomores had arrived—Trevor with them. Grady scanned the group and launched to his full height.*

*"Who wants to race?" He puffed out his chest and flexed his arms. "I can beat any of you to the round lighthouse."*

*"Don't do it, Grady." Alanna wrapped her arms around her and shivered. "It's too cold to do anything in the water."*

*"Yeah, at least wait until summer to prove you're a man." Alanna had cringed as Brendan Tomkin egged Grady on. Didn't he know that's all it would take to make Grady follow his insane plan? One glance at his face reinforced that Brendan knew exactly what he was doing.*

*From that moment, the afternoon spiraled along its deadly path.*

*First Grady then Trevor had entered the water. She tried to pull
Trevor back, but he wore his goofy grin. "It's no big deal, sis."*
   *Nobody had seen what was coming.*

The door opened, and the bell jarred Alanna from the past.

JONATHAN'S CELL PHONE RANG, and with a glance at the caller
display, he reached for it then pulled back. What did he have to
tell Edward Morris? Not what the man needed to hear. No, he'd
let voice mail get the call then track down Rachelle Stone. He
couldn't wait any longer to let Edward know whether he could
order a painting. She'd need time to create the perfect painting
to honor Edward and

Bonnies marriage. And he needed confirmation Rachelle
would paint it. Trevor might be a capable artist, but without his
name on it, Jonathan wouldn't connect him to Mr. Morris.

As soon as his phone beeped to indicate he had voice mail,
he scrolled through his contacts until he found Rachelle's cell
number. He entered it then waited for an answer.

It rang several times, and he wondered if he'd joined her do-
not-talk-to list.

"Hello?" The voice sounded bone weary, unlike the usual
pep that filled her words.

"Rachelle? This is Jonathan."

"Yes?"

"A client would like to commission a painting."

"Jonathan, stop."

"He likes your work. This fits with commissions you've
painted before."

"Used to. My time isn't my own now."

"Wouldn't the income help?"

She sighed, and he heard her burdens. "You have no idea. I know Alanna is trying, but the studio must make more." She was silent, and he waited. "Trevor could do something."

"Not good enough. This is to honor a client's wife who's fighting cancer. It has to be you or not at all." He pushed back in his chair, gut tightening. Maybe she'd just say no again, and that would be the end. It felt like he'd crossed a line with his pushing. Perhaps she couldn't paint now. Maybe creative types needed more than physical energy to work their magic.

A rustling sound like she'd placed her hand over the phone scratched his ear. Then muffled voices bantered for a moment.

"Jonathan, I'll see what I can do."

"Can he contact you at this number?"

"He can try. It all depends on how Don feels."

"Of course." He couldn't ask her to sacrifice her husband's needs for a client. "You'll hear from him soon." He cleared his throat. "You didn't need to leave this morning."

"I did." An alarm sounded in the background. "I've got to go. Take care of my girl, Jonathan."

"Yes, ma'am." The call disconnected before he was certain she'd heard. Didn't matter. She knew he'd do anything for Alanna.

His e-mail dinged, and he opened the message. Edward. He smiled ruefully. The man knew how to get what he wanted. Jonathan composed a quick message and hit SEND. Then he turned back to his plans for another wedding, this one a fifties theme. He wondered if the bridesmaids would wear poodle skirts. That would create unforgettable images for the photographer and make a fun reception. In fact, he knew the performer to call, an Upper Peninsula singer who specialized in the sounds of the fifties and sixties.

He sketched out some thoughts and then sent an e-mail to the bride and her mother. With any luck, the women would sign off on his ideas and he could get the performer signed for the event.

His phone rang and didn't stop the rest of the afternoon. When he finally reached a break, he stood then stretched. He wandered to the window and looked down on the foot traffic. There weren't many people around. Guess the tourists weren't in the mood for a chilly last day of May on the island. It would pick up; it always did.

Until then he knew the business owners would pray for the day the mainland folks flooded the island. Much as he loved the peace and tranquility, without the chaos of non-locals, the island remained a shell of itself.

Something clomped against the stairs. He glanced at his watch. Company now?

## 23

A s soon as the clock reached six, Alanna bolted. Tomorrow she'd interview prospective employees by phone, but for now she needed to clear her head. Forget about everything.

A trip around the island might clear her mind. At least that's what she hoped as she mounted her bike. At the end of the street, she stopped at the library. Biking around the island could wait, but the search for answers couldn't. She wandered the aisles of the small building until she found the slim section of yearbooks. She flipped through the one from her senior year. So many photos showed a small group of tightly knit teens. When there were only a couple handfuls of students in a class, you got to know each other well.

Alanna stopped flipping when she reached Trevor's picture. He looked so young and full of boyish excitement. He'd been all of a sophomore with the future waiting. A few pages more and she stared into Grady's cocky face. He looked like he ruled the world rather than the small kingdom of the Mackinac Island school. Even her photo conveyed someone with big dreams.

What happened to those? Somehow her vision of her future died along with Grady. She'd fled the island rather than return after college. She'd wanted to make a difference; now she invested herself in a job she was good at but didn't love.

Someone cleared her throat, and Alanna glanced up with a start. An elderly woman with gray hair cut in short layers around her face studied Alanna.

"Sorry, ma'am, but it's time to close." She cocked her head.

"Of course." Alanna closed the yearbook. "I'll get out of here now."

"Don't I know you?"

Alanna shrugged as she pulled the book close like a shield. "Maybe, but it's been years since I've been in the library."

"Hmmm. I could swear you're the image of Rachelle Stone."

"I've heard that before."

"Alanna?" The woman grinned. "Well, it's time you came back, kid. You probably don't remember me. Tricia McCormick. Went to college with your mom and followed her here."

"That's right." Alanna carried the yearbook to the copier and started copying the pages showing the classes. "Sorry I didn't recognize you."

"It's been years." Tricia's look traveled to the bookshelf. "Reminiscing or searching?"

"A bit of both." Alanna returned the yearbook back to its slot.

"Your mom said you could never let it go." The woman sighed. "It was a sad day, but the rest of us moved on. Time for you to do the same."

"I can't."

"Still stubborn I see. I don't know what you'll find here, but feel free to come back as often as you need."

Alanna nodded then hurried to her bike and away from the

woman's gaze. Tricia McCormick knew the old her as well as anyone on the island. Well enough to know she bulldogged questions. And this was one she couldn't walk away from.

Should she continue around the island?

The shadows had lengthened while she read inside. Maybe she'd find Mr. Hoffmeister. See if he was still angry. It seemed so out of character for him to make accusations like he had. Especially when she hadn't really started digging. After all, how would he know about her conversation with her mom? And what did that have to do with him? It wasn't as if she'd done much yet to look into Grady's death. Her presence alone couldn't be enough to get him out of sorts. Could it? Had Ginger run to him after she dropped off the file? That seemed unlikely but possible.

She eased her bike to a stop in front of I'm Not Sharing. The lights warmed the windows and inside of the shop. It looked empty, but she got off anyway. As long as the lights were on, the shop was open.

The door opened easily as she pushed it, the bell announcing her entrance. As soon as she entered, the familiar fudge-laced air flooded around her. She waited inside the door on the mahogany-stained, plank floor. The display cases stood with shelves almost bare of fudge. Looked like the morning would be early and busy or the store wouldn't have fudge to sell.

Muffled voices whispered from the back area, but Alanna couldn't see anyone. She waited a minute, taking in the shop. Whoever worked tonight had worked hard to get things ready for closing.

A couple of empty marble tables sat in the prep area. Counters stood clean and ready for new batches of fudge to be worked and cut into yummy slabs. She waited a few minutes to give the conversation in the back a minute to wrap up, but still no one came out to check on who had entered. Had they missed the bells when the door opened? Must be an intense conversation.

Guess she'd use the little bell resting on top of the glass case on the counter next to the old-fashioned cash register. None of those fancy computers for I'm Not Sharing employees. They still made change the old-fashioned way, one dime at a time.

Alanna hit the bell, the tinny sound not reaching far. She waited a moment then knocked it again, harder this time. "Hello?"

It sounded like a door in the back slammed, and she ran her hands over the smooth, walnut counter. Clearing her throat, she tried again. "Hello? Mr. Hoffmeister?"

Maybe someone else worked tonight.

"Coming." He huffed around the corner, sounding out of breath, then skidded to a stop when he spotted her. "Alanna Stone. You're the last person I expected tonight."

"I know. I was headed home, but decided I needed to check on you."

"Why?"

"This morning was. . .surreal. Have I done anything to offend you?"

He pulled his glasses down and rubbed his eyes. "Just a long few weeks."

That didn't explain why he'd come and publicly scolded her. He must have seen her skepticism.

"I probably got carried away. Between your questions and that monstrosity Tomkin wants to build"—he shuddered at the words— "I'm distracted. But you need to let everything drop between Grady and Trevor. That's done and over."

"Trevor still walks under a cloud of suspicion. Can you say you don't blame him for the accident?"

"Each of you played some part in it."

Alanna winced as his words slammed into her, the edge hard and on target. "Still. . ."

"It's unsolvable, so stop. Find an employee for the shop and go home."

"This is my home." She paused at the word, shocked she'd said it and even more surprised that she meant it.

"Hasn't been for eleven years. A few weeks won't make that much difference. Go back to your job, friends, and new life. Leave us alone."

Alanna stepped back, unsure what to do next. "Why warn me about Tomkin?"

"No reason."

"Not buying it. You don't make accusations unless you have something to back it up."

"Let's not talk about this now. Come back tomorrow. It's been a long day, and I'm ready to head home."

He looked exhausted, strung out, with crow's feet etched into the corners of his eyes. "Just one minute."

"Fine." He looked at the counter then raised worried eyes to hers. "Didn't you ever find it odd the amount of thrashing out there?"

"Out where?"

"In the water. Think about who was there. And what happened. It wasn't an accident. Roughhousing's one thing. This wasn't."

"Then why didn't you say anything?"

"What makes you think I didn't?"

A clang erupted from the back. Mr. Hoffmeister jerked as if he'd been prodded. "Think you want some fudge?"

What had smelled so good when she stepped in now turned her stomach, but as she looked at Mr. Hoffmeister, she nodded. "A slice of the mint chocolate please."

The older man grabbed a piece of wax paper from the box

and then reached into the display case, his hand shaking as he claimed a slice.

"Not that one." Alanna couldn't remember him ever reaching for the wrong kind. Peanut-butter fudge didn't look anything like the mint. "Mint please."

"That's right. Old brain is fuddled at the moment." He chuckled weakly as he grabbed the right kind. He pulled out a bag but seemed to take extra time before he handed it over. He ran her debit card through the machine that looked oddly out of place next to the giant cash register. His movements jerked abnormally as he slid the receipt to her. "Have a good evening."

"You, too, Mr. Hoffmeister." Alanna left the store then turned to watch him from the window. He shuffled across the floor as if he carried the weight of a hundred problems then locked the door and flipped the sign. She waved, and he lifted a hand.

The street was quiet as she shoved off and pedaled home. The white bag glowed like a flag in her bike's basket, waving a surrender to all who passed her. When she got home, she opened the bag. A small piece of paper, like it had been torn from the cash-register tape, fluttered to the table. Mr. Hoffmeister's scrawl had her squinting as she tried to decipher it.

*Alanna, come by my house tomorrow night. I'll explain then. If I don't answer, you'll find the key by the German shepherd. She guards the house for me.*

She stared at the slip. When had he found time to write it? She'd been there the whole time. And why not just tell her when she was in the shop? Why all the secrecy?

The questions bothered her as she tried to go to sleep and woke her during the night.

~

THE NEXT MORNING Alanna got a late start after her restless sleep. She slipped a headband on to hold back damp hair as she hurried to the studio. She slowed when she approached I'm Not Sharing. Police crime-scene tape fluttered around the outside. Dread sank like a weight through her at the image. What happened after she left? A few of the island police officers stood around the perimeter of the tape, their expressions hard and unwelcoming.

She eased to a stop.

"Keep moving, miss." A uniformed officer still wearing his bike helmet gestured her on.

"What happened?"

"Can't say." He waved his arm. "Please keep moving."

She eased back into the bike traffic. After she opened the Painted Stone, she'd call the island grapevine to find out what happened. Until then she had a couple of job interviews to conduct. At the pace her investigation wasn't moving, she needed to leave the island as soon as possible. In fact, yesterday sounded better all the time.

With a last glance at the yellow tape flapping across the shop's door, Alanna finished biking to work, her thoughts shadowed by the unknown. She focused on the interviews, which passed smoothly enough, with only one of the candidates showing enough interest to invite for an in-person interview. It helped that the college student lived in St. Ignace during the summer. After arranging the interview for the following morning, Alanna helped several people who wandered into the store. She sold paintings with mixed emotions.

She vowed to unravel the twisted mire around the art as soon as humanly possible. She munched a sandwich at the counter, counting down until she could take a legitimate lunch break again. Peanut butter and jelly had never been her favorite sandwich, and right now she'd give anything for a pot roast sandwich at the Yankee Rebel. She tried to imagine the nutty aroma of her sandwich was the meaty one the Yankee Rebel served instead, but her imagination couldn't quite make the transition.

She finished the sandwich then placed a want ad in another paper. Eventually one would work. It had to.

Early that afternoon she looked up from the web page she'd opened. Jonathan stormed into the studio, a frown creasing the bridge of his nose.

"Jonathan, what's wrong?"

"Didn't you hear?"

She shook her head. "Hear what?"

"Mr. Hoffmeister was murdered last night."

The blood drained from her face, and she felt an accompanying dizziness. "The tape..."

"The state police detective and crime scene unit have been at I'm Not Sharing since one of the employees discovered him this morning." Jonathan leaned against the counter. "I can't imagine who would kill him."

Alanna sagged against the wall. A weight plunged her stomach to her toes while spots danced in her vision. "He seemed all right." Just distracted. Her thoughts spiraled as she considered what could have happened.

"He seemed all right?"

"Last night. I stopped to get some fudge on the way home." Jonathan didn't need to know what they discussed. Or about Mr. H.'s odd actions when he came to the studio. "That poor man."

Jonathan nodded. "I can't imagine anyone killing him. It must have been a botched robbery. The island's been so quiet, I can't imagine whoever did this got away with much money."

"I hope you're right." The idea that a murderer could be a neighbor chilled her.

"How did he seem when you saw him?"

"Okay. Distracted." What more could she say? She hadn't been Mr. Hoffmeister's closest friend, but she'd always liked the man. He'd been like the uncle you loved to be annoyed at. Soft and gushy sometimes and mildly odd the rest. She hadn't spent enough time with him since returning though. Whatever he might have known about Grady's death had died with him.

Alanna tried to rein in her thoughts, but they returned to what he might have known.

"I hope the police close this soon." Jonathan rubbed his face as if trying to wipe away his grief. "I always liked him. Nobody deserves to die like that."

"How. . .how was he killed?"

"I don't know. Nobody knew at lunch." His face clouded as if listening again.

"I got here and forgot. I assumed it was a robbery." She shivered as a deep chill settled over her and the words of his note waved through her mind. He'd known. Somehow he'd known. "How horrible."

Jonathan nodded. After a minute, he pushed back from the counter. "Be careful. We don't know who did this."

"You, too."

"Promise you'll wait for me to ride home. Your parents won't want you out alone."

Alanna considered protesting but realized he was right. The thought that someone would murder anyone. . .on Mackinac? It didn't compute. She couldn't think of a time someone had been killed. Maybe the island had changed in ways too terrible to contemplate.

The rest of the afternoon evaporated as Alanna searched the online news services for information. As she scanned for anything, she wondered if she should give the note to the police. The lack of details had her nerves bunched. Was it important?

As she considered its cryptic message, she decided to wait until she had time to collect what she knew in an organized manner for the police. As the stream of customers continued, she knew she'd have to wait until she reached the sanctuary of her home.

The shadows had started to lengthen by the time Jonathan returned. She hurried out to meet him, locking the door behind her. The cleaning and prep for tomorrow would wait. Right now she wanted to feel safe within the four walls of her house.

The silent ride up the hills felt rushed. Like they both fled to a place of peace, but Jonathan wouldn't do that. Usually she wouldn't either. What if she'd been the last person other than the killer to see Mr. Hoffmeister alive? After she got home, she'd write down everything she could remember from his rush into the studio to their short conversation and his halting actions at the shop. Then she'd talk to the police. If only she'd caught a glimpse of whoever had been there when she'd arrived.

Her sigh must have reached Jonathan as he pumped up the hill in front of her.

He turned in his seat and glanced at her. "You okay?"

She swallowed. How to answer that? She hadn't been great friends with Mr. Hoffmeister, yet she felt his death.

They reached her driveway and turned down it. Once she parked her bike, he followed her to the door and then walked through the house with her.

"This is silly." A giggle ended the sentence, one she'd love to swallow back. "It's not like whoever did this would come here. Mr. Hoffmeister lived on the opposite side of the island."

Jonathan continued his search, opening the pantry door. "Better safe. . ."

Alanna didn't say anything else until he'd looked in each of the upstairs rooms. "Would you like to stay for supper?"

"The last time I did that, your mom left."

"Tonight will be different." As she studied his serious eyes, she wished she could form the words. *Please stay. Don't leave me alone.* Instead, she prayed he could read it in her gaze. What happened to the independent woman from Grand Rapids?

Murders normally didn't affect her.

Usually she didn't know the victim.

## 24

Alanna moved around the kitchen, her movements stilted and jerky. She must look like Mr. Hoffmeister had the night before—a tad off. Jonathan sat at the island, awkward and out of place like he didn't know how to help and wondered if he should stay. She needed him here. While her mind knew whoever killed Mr. Hoffmeister had no reason to venture this far into the island, she couldn't relax and feel safe.

She opened the refrigerator, scrambling for what to offer as a meal. "Sandwiches okay? It's not glamorous. . ."

"I'm a bachelor." Jonathan cut off her excuses. "Any meal I don't prepare is a good one."

She grabbed meat and cheese. Jonathan stood and selected glasses from the cabinet. "What would you like?"

Alanna pulled back from the fridge, her hands filled with ranch dressing and other condiments she set on the counter next to the ham and Swiss. "Water's fine."

He turned on the faucet and watched the water fill first one glass and then the other. The silence felt awkward yet necessary. Jonathan seemed lost in his thoughts, and she didn't rush to fill the dead air as she sliced a tomato and some lettuce before arranging them in salad bowls. She didn't blame him. Something like this didn't happen on Mackinac.

She bet if she asked the police chief, the man would affirm her gut that no one had been murdered since before she was born. Still, in the age of the Internet, the outside world intruded on Mackinac. In a minute, she had sandwiches prepared and a simple salad for each of them.

"Mind if I grab some chips from the pantry? Your mom always keeps a stash."

"No, but that's Dad's stash." He'd always had a weakness for chips, especially Cheetos. The more fake cheese colored his fingers, the better.

Jonathan pulled back the door and tugged a tube of Pringles from the bottom shelf. "These work?"

"Sure."

They sat at the table, and Jonathan said a quick grace.

"I talked to Rachelle yesterday."

Her gaze collided with Jonathan's. "And?"

"I asked her about commissioning a piece."

"I bet that went well."

He shrugged and shoved another Pringle in his mouth. "Not as bad as I expected. She didn't say yes, but she didn't say no either. I insisted she had to paint, not Trevor, since that's what the client wants."

"She admitted the paintings aren't hers?"

"Not in so many words, but I connected her with the Morrises. We'll see what happens."

Much would be resolved if Mom started painting again. Then Alanna wouldn't have to worry about what to do with new paintings. Mom probably wouldn't deliver any again.

As she took the last bite of her sandwich, someone knocked. She looked at Jonathan, and he shrugged.

"Expecting anyone?"

"No." Who would it be? People hadn't exactly lined up since she'd returned.

Jonathan followed her to the door and peeked out the window before she opened the door.

Police Chief Ryan stood there with a man in a bedraggled suit that identified him as an underpaid detective. They were here? With a murder to investigate? She straightened and quirked an eyebrow. "Can I help you?"

"Alanna, this is Detective Brian Bull from the state police. Do you have a few minutes?"

Jonathan started to push past her, but she shook her head. He frowned but planted himself at her side. "What's this about?"

"Don't get worked up, Covington. This doesn't concern you."

By the way Jonathan's chin hardened, the chief's words were the wrong ones.

Alanna sucked in a breath. There weren't any attorneys to call on the island, so she'd handle this on her own for the moment. Shouldn't be too hard, even if the old saw stated only a fool had himself for an attorney.

"Alanna." Chief Ryan frowned at her, his bushy gray eyebrows meeting in the middle of his face. "Shouldn't take long, assuming you don't have anything to hide."

"I'd like to know the subject matter." She studied him as carefully as he did her, not missing the challenge in his expression.

"Hoffmeister."

Jonathan gaped at the police chief. "You think Alanna knows something?"

"Pretty certain." The police chief studied Alanna coldly. Yet the detective was the one that worried Alanna. He had a slouched appearance, but his eyes moved constantly, taking in everything. What did the man expect to find here of all places?

Alanna sighed as she caught Jonathan's shocked expression. Maybe she should have emphasized her visit. No, she didn't know it would add anything to the investigation, and her plan to contact the police in the morning was sound. He'd have to understand when she explained later.

"I'll answer your questions here on the porch, but first I need to grab something." Alanna slipped inside and grabbed the folder she'd slid Mr. Hoffmeister's note into last night. She also grabbed a pad of paper and pen before returning to the porch and sitting on the nearest white rocking chair. She placed the items in her lap and folded her hands across them. In a moment, her knuckles turned white from her laced fingers, and she tried to relax. She needed to remember all the advice she'd ever given clients when preparing for interviews or depositions. It had seemed easy then. Now she could barely pull the first word into her mind.

Jonathan stood in the doorway, the stiffness in his posture telegraphing he would stick close until she asked him to leave. Right now, that was the last thing she planned. She needed someone with her. A witness who could vouch for her in case things didn't go well.

Detective Bull pulled a slim notepad from his inside breast pocket and flipped it open. He poised a pen over the paper. "When was the last time you saw Mr. Hoffmeister?"

"Yesterday." No reason to hide that piece of information.

He jotted a note. "Where did you see him?"

"First at the studio. Later at the shop."

Jonathan frowned at her. She ignored him. Her focus had to stay locked on the police chief and detective. She only hoped she could remember everything after they left. It seemed like her vision narrowed with gray areas on the outskirts. She wanted to shake it off, but would that look somehow guilty? She should have paid more attention in her criminal law continuing education classes.

"When you say, 'the studio,' where is that?"

"The Painted Stone, the studio my parents own."

"Are they in town?"

"No, my father has a health issue, which is why I'm here." She bit her lower lip to stop elaborating. Stick to the question asked. How many times had she instructed clients that way? But she'd also tell them never to talk to police without an attorney present.

Detective Bull studied her, and she relaxed her posture. He glanced at Chief Ryan, who nodded. "How long have you been on Mackinac?"

"Since the week before Memorial Day."

"Have you spent much time with Mr. Hoffmeister?"

"We've talked a couple times."

"Prior to yesterday?"

"Yes." A trickle of sweat slid down her shoulder blade.

"What were those conversations about?"

Why wasn't he asking her more about yesterday? "Different things. An accident from eleven years ago."

"The one where the teenager died?" the detective asked.

Chief Ryan shook his head. "I warned you to leave it alone."

At his words, Alanna wished she had her digital recorder out and on. He wouldn't have inserted himself like that with a recorder capturing every word.

Detective Bull frowned at the chief then turned back at Alanna. "Why did you see Mr. Hoffmeister yesterday?"

"He came to the studio to tell me to quit looking into that death. It was unusual for him, especially since I haven't done much other than talk to him once. He'd been pretty open then."

"And last night?"

"I stopped by the fudge shop to see if he was all right."

"Why wouldn't he be?"

"I don't know. He seemed out of character at the studio. I needed to know he was okay."

Chief Ryan snorted. "Meaning you needed to harass him and the librarian last night."

He knew she'd stopped at the library? She turned toward him.

"I flipped through an old yearbook. Nothing more. I need to piece together what happened. Since Mr. Hoffmeister lived near the accident location, he suggested he knew something."

Jonathan placed a restraining hand on her arm. Alanna sucked in a breath and vowed not to say another word to the chief. Let him egg her on all he wanted; he wouldn't get another word from her. Not now.

The chief crossed his arms and stared at her. Fine. She'd ignore him. She had bigger concerns with the detective leaning against the porch railing. Her eye was drawn to the peeling paint that had started to flake from the railing. Her dad always kept the house meticulously maintained. How many summers had he made Trevor and her scrape and paint? What had distracted him from the appearance of perfection?

"And last night?"

"I stopped at the shop on my way home. When I entered, nobody was out front. I waited a minute then heard voices in the back. After a minute, I rang the bell, a door closed, and Mr. Hoffmeister came out. He seemed agitated, but I bought a slice of fudge and left."

"Did you see anyone around?"

"No. When I left, I didn't see anyone." *Stick to the question, Alanna.* Jonathan removed his hand and stepped back, and she felt cold and alone in his distance. She shivered and rubbed her hands along her arms. "When I got home and opened my bag of fudge, this fell out." She slid the note from the folder and handed it over.

The detective pulled on a glove and then accepted it. He took a moment to read it before handing it to Chief Ryan. "Why wouldn't he just come out and say he needed to talk to you?"

"I don't know. Maybe he was afraid of the man in the back."

"I thought you said he'd left?"

Had she? Alanna couldn't remember and understood why someone could get rattled in the middle of questioning. "Do you need anything else right now?"

The detective studied her, seeming to test whether he could press her. Whatever he saw in her posture turned him to his notes, difficult to see now in the shadows created by the sinking sun. "Not at the moment." He pinned her with his gaze. "However, I recommend you don't leave the island. Certainly not without letting the chief know first."

"Excuse me?" Indignation flared in her chest at his order.

"Right now you're the last person who saw Mr. Hoffmeister. That either makes you his murderer or a material witness. We'll be in touch."

The two men nodded then faded off the porch and into the shadows. A headache pounded at one temple. Alanna tried to regulate her breathing and force her muscles to relax. She might have sat in numerous interviews, but she'd never been the interviewee. She prayed she didn't repeat the honor.

"Are you going to tell me what that was about?"

Jonathan's voice snapped her head around. "Sorry?"

"You had an exciting day yesterday."

"I had no idea how exciting until you told me about Mr. Hoffmeister." She sighed.

"Alanna, they think you did it."

"No, I wouldn't still be here if they could prove that."

"There's a step between believing and proving."

She shivered again and pushed out of the chair. "I'm going inside." She left it open about whether he'd follow her. Maybe Jonathan didn't want to stay. She wouldn't blame him. It wasn't every day the police interviewed her.

"It's not that simple." Jonathan joined her in the kitchen.

Alanna opened the freezer and pulled out some chocolate-chip cookie dough chunks. After turning on the oven, she plopped the pieces on a cookie tray. Chocolate-chip cookies and milk wouldn't solve everything, but they made a good start on comfort food. It wasn't like she could call her mom for commiseration. She rubbed her temple then slid the pan in the oven.

"Alanna, sit down and explain what happened." Jonathan pulled out a chair, led her to it, and eased her down.

"Somehow the police knew I was at the shop last night." How? It hit her. "The debit card. They must have checked the transactions. Makes sense."

"You don't have anything to hide?" Hope edged his words.

"No. In fact, I planned to sit down tonight and write out what I remembered and call Chief Ryan in the morning. Once you told me he was dead, I knew they needed the note. I couldn't break away or organize my thoughts at work, or I'd have called him earlier. I wish Mr. Hoffmeister hadn't locked the door after I left."

Jonathan frowned at her. "Why?"

"Then someone else could have been the last person to see him alive."

## 25

W hen he got home, Jonathan looked for something to distract him. Instead, he stalked the edges of the small cabin as questions chased him. How could one person get in so much trouble so quickly? He could tick off the problems: Alanna's investigation into Grady's death coupled with the odd things around her house and now becoming a person of interest in Mr. Hoffmeister's death. He didn't like any of them, including the fact there were no suspects involving the break-in at her shed. Could it have been a warning to back off that she'd missed?

That girl knew how to return to town and wreak havoc.

He'd never believe she had anything to do with Mr. Hoffmeister. Someone had. Someone who might still be on the island or left on the last ferry.

Mr. Hoffmeister didn't seem like the kind with enemies. Even his dispute with Gerald only led to silence or heated arguments. Never fists.

Jonathan moved across the backyard and sat on the dock. For once the thought of finding that elusive bird or catching an elusive fish didn't hold his thoughts.

Not since Alanna arrived.

Alanna.

How could he help her? He doubted she'd call her parents. That left her alone since Trevor wouldn't be much help. The kid had enough problems, and he was too selfish to notice others. Jonathan sighed. That wasn't completely fair.

His phone rang, and he tugged it from his pocket. Jaclyn. "Hey."

"What's wrong?"

"Nothing."

"Sorry." He could almost see her forehead wrinkle. "I know you too well."

"Just got back from Alanna's. Long day with what happened to Mr. Hoffmeister."

"You were with Alanna?" Her voice rose to a hysterical pitch.

Jonathan rubbed his jaw. What did he say now? He could understand she wouldn't be thrilled at the news, but Alanna had needed him. He heaved a sigh. "Yeah."

"I knew her being so close to you would be a problem."

"We're just friends."

"Sure you are." She huffed. "Friends with quite the past."

"What did you need?"

"Just wanted to talk to you. Never mind." She clicked off, and Jonathan knew she was upset. He'd have to do something about that. Tomorrow.

A breeze rippled small waves that were barely visible on the surface of the pond. He could almost hear God whispering in it. He needed to release Alanna and the whole mess to the Master. He gritted his teeth. He wanted to fix it. Make a plan like an event. Steps 1 through 144. Step by step, execution by execution, he'd manage her out of the mess.

Too bad that wouldn't work.

If anyone could figure it out, Alanna would. She was the

attorney, after all. She'd know what she needed to do. He was kidding himself to think he could do something she couldn't.

Except she hadn't been on the island for years. He had.

Surely he knew the players better than she did. He couldn't imagine Rachelle keeping her up-to-date on all the gossip from here. Alanna had made it clear when she left that she was done with the island and its residents.

He let his mind wander over the people Hoffmeister spent time with.

Tomkin. Mrs. Washington. Who did he talk with over coffee in the winter? The list wasn't very long.

How could a man have spent a lifetime on the same small patch of earth and not have many friends? Everyone on the island knew him. . .but that was different from someone who would kill him.

If something was taken, then the murder might make sense. Hoffmeister had simply been in the wrong place. It sounded cliche, but nothing else made sense. Not for the man he knew.

He let his thoughts wander as the leaves rustled overhead. The soft scent of lilacs mixed with something sweet like vanilla alerted him to Alanna's presence. She settled down next to him until their shoulders touched.

"Hi." The word was so quiet, he had to lean closer.

They stared across the dark pond, nature providing the only backdrop and music. He lost track of time until he felt her shiver.

"Come here." He tugged her closer and put his arm around her shoulder. "Crazy night."

"Yeah."

"Wanna talk about it?"

"Not really. I'd rather think about something else." She brushed a strand of hair from her face. "I've gone over yesterday a dozen times. I can't think of anything to tell the police that can point them to who killed Mr. Hoffmeister." Another shiver shook her. "I wish I knew who was in the back of the shop. Maybe they didn't leave. Maybe he left the back door unlocked, and the person came back. That's all I have. A bunch of maybes while the police want facts."

"Then we'll give them facts."

"How?"

"Tell me what you remember about the voice. Could you identify the speaker?"

"No, it was too muffled. Probably a man, but I'm not certain. See how helpful that is?"

This didn't look good. She hadn't said anything that would direct the police to someone else. "Anyone loitering when you left?" She sighed and studied her hands. "No. It was a pretty dead night. See why I didn't rush to the police? I don't know anything. There has to be something. I didn't do it."

He held up his hands to protect himself from the vehemence in her words. "Hey, I'm in your corner."

"I know." Alanna rubbed her temple again. "This is so frustrating. How do I tell them anything that will prove I'm innocent? I don't even have an alibi. No one saw me come home or spend the evening alone."

He grimaced. "Sorry I didn't stop by."

"Who knew that would matter?"

A SEEMINGLY SIMPLE DECISION—COME to the island but keep people at arm's length—might now turn her into a prime murder suspect. Anyone who knew her would know she couldn't do something like that—ever. Yet Alanna had done nothing to endear herself to the community and rebuild friendships. As a result, she'd been alone last night, knowing if she'd invited Jonathan over—while it would have relieved her loneliness—it might further ignite the strong attraction between them.

It had been late, and she'd thought the better decision was to remain alone.

Now she wished she had a roommate, a talking parrot, a video system. . .anything that could vouch for her.

"You still with me?" Jonathan's voice tugged her from the quagmire of thoughts.

She looked at him, pulled into the concern she saw etched on his face. He'd always had a face that would make a movie star proud. Part Brad Pitt and part Ethan Hawk. "I'm sorry."

"So what do we do to change this up?"

There was only one thing. Stir up the hornet's nest and see what flew out. "Guess we dig deeper."

"Into what?"

"I want to know what was happening at I'm Not Sharing. Mr. Hoffmeister wasn't alone."

"The police won't like that."

"I don't appreciate being their number one suspect." Alanna stood. "Let's go inside." She stood and walked to the house and grabbed a pad of paper and pen. "I'm going to keep poking at Grady's death. It's unlikely they're connected...but Mr. Hoffmeister was ready to tell me something." She started listing the names of the kids at the bonfire. "I should have done this the moment I got back. With the help of my friend Google, I'll track down my classmates and see what they remember. Maybe Grady's death wasn't an accident."

Jonathan grabbed her hand, and the pen stilled. "You understand what you're saying?"

Alanna nodded around the sudden boulder sitting in her throat. "It might have been murder."

"Why would teenagers do something like that?"

"Maybe it was an accident that got covered up, and now they can't afford to have the facts changed."

Jonathan's eyebrows arched. "That's a stretch. How does Hoffmeister tie in?"

"I don't know yet." That was the problem. She only had suspicions. The kind that got people killed? "I'm checking anyway. There weren't that many people. How long can it take?"

"What about your mom and Trevor?"

"You still have a party to plan." She pointed a finger at his chest. "You have to make it the event of the season. Hold it during the lilac festival."

"Impossible! That's a week away."

"I thought you liked doing the impossible for your clients."

He rubbed his square jaw, a flash of competition in his eyes. "Sure, but they have to give me time."

With her sweetest smile, she leaned across the island toward him. Only a breath separated them, and she felt the tug to lean closer. She licked her lips and tried to break the connection. "If you're as good as you say, a week or two is plenty."

His laughter startled her. "Darling, I'll take your challenge, but that also means you have a deadline. You can't unveil your brother as the artist without clearing the air."

"I know." One more reason to wrap everything up. As if avoiding jail wasn't enough.

Jonathan sobered, seeming to accept she was serious about investigating. That's what attorneys do. Track down facts. And she'd check in to Mr. Tomkins accusations. Maybe they tied into Mr. Hoffmeister's woes. All of a sudden she felt exhausted.

"So what's next?"

Alanna smiled. "How good are you with numbers?"

~

THE NEXT MORNING, Jonathan's mind swam with the image of rows of numbers.

He'd thought when he passed his accounting class in college he wouldn't have to audit someone else's books again. After a few hours trying to decipher the foundation's books and comparing them to the various grants, he agreed with Mr. Tomkin. There were more accounts than grants.

The problem was figuring out why. Was there a mistake with the bookkeeping or with the minutes? He hadn't been on the foundation long enough to know if something had been missed. Mr. Hoffmeister could have helped since he served as president two of the four years prior to Tomkin assuming the role.

Alanna had pretended to review the books as she sat next to him. If he inhaled, he could still smell her faint lilac perfume. Each time he'd looked up, she'd ducked as if he'd caught her in the middle of watching him.

It wasn't right to enjoy every moment with Alanna the way he did without addressing his relationship with Jaclyn. It wasn't fair to either woman.

Was what sparked between him and Alanna real? Or would it evaporate the moment she could leave Mackinac?

He didn't want to experience the desolation that blanketed him when she left and never looked back. It didn't matter that they jumped back to their teenage dynamics. What mattered was whether they could build a lifetime together. Anything less didn't interest him.

All morning he worked through plans for clients. When those events had up-to-date checklists, he turned to his conversation with Alanna last night.

She hadn't murdered Hoffmeister. Period.

No matter how much she'd changed in the eleven years she'd been gone, she couldn't do something like that. Especially to someone she gave every indication of liking. That left one option. He had to help her clear up what happened.

Too bad he didn't know how to start.

Jonathan closed his eyes and leaned back in his chair, praying for wisdom. While Alanna might believe Grady's death was connected to Hoffmeister's murder, Jonathan would start with the more pressing issue: proving her innocence.

Hoffmeister had kept to himself this season. Strange for a man who usually stood in the middle of every gathering sharing jokes and swapping stories. Jonathan couldn't count the number of times Hoffmeister had introduced him to one more woman, this one guaranteed to be the love of his life. The twinkle in his brown eyes had made each exchange memorable. He'd had nothing but disdain in his eyes when Jonathan introduced him to Jaclyn—she hadn't measured up. Instead, Hoffmeister had let him know she wasn't the one.

Hoffmeister had complained about Tomkin each time Jonathan ran into him that spring. Real trouble brewed between the two. So he'd start with a trip to Hoffmeister's house. See what the man had grumbled about. Alanna could go with him.

Maybe if she stood on the site and saw the past from a different perspective, she'd remember something. Now to figure out how to package the idea in a way she couldn't refuse.

## 26

The cordless phone clicked into the handset even though Alanna wanted to throw it across the room. The college gal had came in for her interview. But after the call any hopes Alanna had that the young woman would work out evaporated.

She should have known from the moment the girl stepped inside that the job would remain open.

She'd stood in the studio, a blank look on her face as she'd looked around the studio. "I really don't know anything about art. Guess this isn't for me."

"Do you want to talk about the responsibilities?"

"I guess."

Now she'd called to let Alanna know that her father had told her she didn't have to work over the summer after all. If she was going to spend time on Mackinac, she'd come as a tourist not an employee. Alanna sank onto the stool. At this rate, she would spend the summer on Mackinac.

Considering that the police wouldn't let her leave, she couldn't return to Grand Rapids anytime soon. But the idea of taking even one day off a week sounded as exotic as tea with the queen of England at Buckingham Palace.

Alanna dropped her forehead to her arms. She needed help, but where to get it? All the locals would have jobs. And she didn't have the time to find an international student like so many hotels relied on to fill the summer season employment gap. Honestly, she didn't want the headaches of helping someone find housing, even with the upstairs apartment. She didn't have time to get it ready for a resident. Time to call someone in the know.

The phone rang a couple of times before Patience picked up. "Hello?"

"Patience, this is Alanna. I need help."

"At the studio? I wondered when you'd ask."

"What?"

The woman snorted. "Who do you think gave your mom time off? Your dad hasn't worked for a while."

Why didn't Mom say anything? Alanna had no idea his health had deteriorated until he'd landed in the hospital. "Was I that out of touch?"

"*Protected* is how I'd frame it. Want me to come tomorrow? I could work after services."

"That would be great. Any ideas who might like a job?"

"I'll talk to a few people. See what I can stir up."

"Thank you." Alanna hung up. It wasn't a permanent solution, but having one day to herself sounded like a kiss from heaven. The uninterrupted time to find answers could be a gift.

When she walked out, something barreled into her. "Oof."

She glanced up and saw she'd stepped into the path of a towheaded little boy.

Jaclyn hurried up, an apology coloring her cheeks. "Dylan, get back here." She grabbed his hand and tugged the toddler closer. "I'm so sorry." She wiped her free hand on her skirt then stuck it out toward Alanna. "Nice to see you again."

Sure it was. Alanna took a breath to end that train of thought. "Dylan is a cute little guy."

"I like him. He just runs faster than I do sometimes." She eyed her strappy, three-inch-heel sandals. "I forgot to pack different shoes. I've teetered from the Grand and am ready to get out of these things." Alanna would take them off—then she looked at the road. Horses were quieter than cars but provided a waste product unknown to vehicles.

Jaclyn seemed to read Alanna's mind as she grinned. "Not the safest place to go barefoot." Dylan tugged on her hand. "Where are you headed?"

"Home. I decided to lock up a few minutes early." Start that day off now.

"Mind if we walk with you? We're headed to the fort. Jonathan's meeting us." The slightest glint reflected in her eyes, and it wasn't the sun shining off Jaclyn's cute glasses. Just when Alanna had begun to like her.

"That's fine." Alanna swallowed as the trio started down the sidewalk, Dylan tearing ahead. "Is he okay?"

"As long as I can see him."

Alanna nodded and glanced at her companion out of the corner of her eye. So this was the woman Jonathan spent time with. Jaclyn had a sparkle that would attract men even if her curves in all the right places didn't. No wonder Jonathan liked her. It shouldn't bother her, since Alanna was an independent woman, one who didn't need or want a man. Not even Jonathan. She almost choked on the thought.

"How long will you stay?"

"I'm not sure. I have to find someone for the studio before I think of leaving."

"Maybe I can help."

Sure she could. Anything to remove competition. Alanna blanched. Where had this attitude come from? Jaclyn was welcome to Jonathan. If she said it often enough, surely she'd come to mean it. Right?

It was a theory.

She pasted on a smile, feeling the strain. "I could use help. My leads have disappeared. The firm partners will call soon, and I'm stuck here. They won't like that at all."

"I'll check around. Send people your way."

"Thanks." Whatever the motivation, she needed employees. If she could find some soon, she could focus on clearing her name. She didn't even want to think what the partners would say when she had to tell them about the murder investigation. She hadn't found time to open a web browser, let alone start tracking down her classmates during the day. There'd been enough customers to keep her busy. She'd start the search tonight.

They reached the green space in front of the fort. The rows of stairs running up the steep hill exhausted Alanna each time she saw them. It didn't matter how fit she was, her calves burned each time she climbed those steps.

Dylan squealed and ran toward someone. "Jonathan!" Then his words blurred together as Jonathan knelt down to his level. In an instant, Alanna pictured him interacting with a daughter. Hers. He'd be an amazing dad, and his kids would be blessed.

"I'll call with possibilities." Jaclyn nodded toward Dylan and Jonathan. "I'd better catch up with them. Nice to see you."

"Bye." Alanna stood a moment watching the interaction between Jonathan and Jaclyn. Jonathan's response to Jaclyn seemed less enthusiastic than his intense interaction with Dylan. Instead, he smiled, gave the pretty woman a halfhearted hug, then turned back to Dylan. Could Dylan be the reason he stayed?

The insight surprised Alanna, and then she felt guilty for watching. If Jonathan wanted to be with Jaclyn, he was a grown man and could do what he liked.

See, it was easier to say this time.

It did get easier to lie to herself.

JONATHAN FOCUSED his attention on Dylan and Jaclyn, not on the beauty watching from a distance. He didn't know whether to be annoyed or flattered at her attention. Then she left without even a small wave, and he wanted to punch something.

He never should have violated his one-date policy. It was easier to avoid the thought of lifelong relationships if one never allowed things to advance past one or two dates.

Jaclyn sidled up to him and tried to grab his hand, but he slid free. "Hey, isn't Hoffmeister's home near the Grand Hotel's property?"

She shook her head a bit and looked at him with a blank look. "Hoffmeister?"

"The old guy who was murdered."

"Oh. I don't know. I suppose he lived close. Jonathan, I work in the spa. Schedule appointments. I don't know all the hotel's neighbors. You know how big the property is, right? And then there's the golf course."

"Right."

"Why the interest?"

"Curiosity."

Dylan joined them by grabbing one of each of their hands and running then swinging as he hung between them. Jaclyn tugged him to a stop then looked at Jonathan. "Just curious? Really? You expect me to believe that?"

"It's not every day a murder happens here."

"Or every day that a long-lost love returns." She stared him down. "I'm not saying this again, Jonathan. You have to choose, because you can't have both of us. It's her"—she gestured to where Alanna had stood— "or me. One or the other. Make up your mind, and let me know." She swiped at her eyes in a short, angry chop. "Come on, Dylan. We're going home."

Dylan looked over his shoulder at Jonathan, confusion twisting his face as his mom tugged him down the sidewalk.

Jonathan took the long way home. He needed every step to pray and sort through Jaclyn's challenge. Part of him wanted to push them both away. Reestablish his independence and live life without the risks and entanglements that getting close to a woman involved.

Who did he love: Jaclyn or Dylan?

It was a question he didn't want to chase to an answer. The implications bothered him. It wasn't right to maintain a relationship with Jaclyn for Dylan's sake. At the same time, he couldn't imagine facing Dylan if he did end any hope of a future with Jaclyn. Spending time with her hadn't seemed like a bad idea when dinner with her served as an attractive alternative to another long evening alone.

Still, it wasn't fair to Jaclyn if Dylan held them together.

He turned up the path to his cabin but detoured to the shed and his fishing gear. He carried his pole and tackle box to the dock. The small circles on the surface indicated fish. Maybe a couple would try his bait rather than a tasty fly. And maybe insight would hop in his mind while he waited. A guy could hope.

Jonathan settled on the edge and baited the hook. He cast to the side and watched the bobber dip up and down in the placid pond. The *chuck-chucking* call of the gray jay pulled his attention to the trees. After a minute, he spotted the white face and gray feathers of the bird. Soon an answering call echoed back.

Jonathan reached for the binoculars tucked in the box. Since nothing seemed to be happening with the fish, he'd scan the trees and see if the Kirtland's warbler hid in the trees along with the gray jays.

At the sound of steps on the dock, Jonathan swung around, the binoculars catching the midsection of someone. He lowered the device. Alanna stood a few feet away, an uncertainness in the slump of her shoulders and question in her eyes.

"May I join you?"

The fishing pole bobbed, so Jonathan dropped the glasses and tugged the pole up. She took his silence as an invitation and moved to sit next to him. Jonathan swallowed as he set the hook, her lilac perfume weaving around him.

"I'm sorry about tonight."

He turned to look at her, noting the sadness around her eyes. "What do you mean?"

"I don't mean to cause trouble for you with Jaclyn." Wistfulness softened her words.

The pole jumped, and Jonathan tugged again. He didn't want to let whatever fought on the other end get away.

"I don't do relationships well, Jonathan. I haven't since. . ."

He could fill in the thought. "Since you left." Me. "Funny, I don't do relationships either."

She pulled her knees up and wrapped her arms around them. "Guess we're a mess."

"Yeah." He gave a final tug and pulled up nothing. The hook dangled naked.

"Guess he got away again."

"Who?"

"Grandpappy." She stood and disappeared down the dock.

As he watched the dusk wrap around her, Grandpappy wasn't the only one who slipped away.

## 27

Sunday after church, Alanna returned home, grateful that Patience Matthews had been willing to work. As she settled at the small kitchen table with her laptop, Alanna knew she needed the break. Not just from the store, but to have time to investigate.

The view of the pond and her mother's gardens tried to woo her from her task of tracking down classmates. Instead, she lit a lavender candle and forced herself to focus on finding those on her list. Time passed and the distraction grew as her searches didn't lead anywhere productive. She stared at the names she'd copied from her yearbook, slowly crossing off each one as she located former classmates.

With each mark, her hope that she'd learn something spiraled. Only a handful still lived on the island. She'd already run into Ginger and Piper and knew she'd bump into the other couple eventually. Still she wrote down phone numbers. A phone call might be easier than a face-to-face interview.

When she checked the last name, she pulled the cordless in front of her and started dialing. The first several numbers had jumped to voice mail, and she dutifully left messages. If her classmates listened, she had no doubt they'd find the calls odd. After all, she hadn't contacted any in eleven years. After reaching voicemail again, she marked that she'd left a message next to a name then stood to stretch. *Guide me, Father.*

She would find the truth. She'd become tenacious to a fault for clients. Now that she could be the one landing in jail, she had even more reason to stick to this until she unraveled the tangled problem.

A knock at the door pulled her to the front room. She opened the door, uncertain whether to smile or close the door when she saw Jonathan on the other side. She hadn't come here to break up his relationship. But she couldn't deny the way her heart leapt when she saw him.

He stood a few feet back, his stance wide and hands behind him. He looked ready to tackle a day of hiking in his navy T-shirt and khaki cargo shorts. A grin tweaked only one side of his mouth, not the full-out glad-to-see-her smile she'd received even a day ago. "What do you need, Jonathan?"

"Wondered if you had time for a field trip?"

"A field trip? This is my first day off, and I've got a list of calls to make." Though she'd really wrapped those up.

"Since it's your first day, let me take you on a tour."

She studied him, uncertain what he was up to but knowing the unknown with him was more appealing than another round of messages. "I grew up here. I don't think I need a tour."

"You do today."

Alanna crossed her arms and leaned against the door frame.

"I want to ride out to Hoffmeister's house. He was having that property dispute."

"I know that."

"Let's poke around. See if we can find anything up there that might shed some light on things. At the same time, you can see the perspective he had for the accident."

A breeze ruffled her hair as if teasing her to go play. Maybe she could combine a bit of fun with investigating. She could maintain a professional distance with Jonathan. She did it all the time in Grand Rapids, though none of the men she worked with were her first love.

"Come on."

"Let me lock up." She grabbed her keys and cell phone then closed and locked the door. When she started toward the shed and her bike, Jonathan stopped her.

"I've got it covered."

"Covered?"

"You'll see. Come on."

She hesitated then followed him toward the road. Only then did she notice the tandem bike leaning against the fence. "Jonathan..."

"I'll ride in front, and this way you won't confront a scene unexpectedly again. If you still freeze, I can get you home."

She didn't know whether to be touched or furious. "I'm not that weak."

He held his hands up. "I never said you were." He straddled the bike and steadied it. "Climb on."

It seemed romantic and intimate, being that close and letting him control where they went. Still, she found herself climbing behind him and grasping the handlebars. It had been years since she'd ridden a tandem bike. She blocked the image of the romantic sunset picnic they'd shared from her mind. One stray thought that direction and she'd never recover. All the dreams she'd harbored for them would rush over her. She swallowed and closed her eyes, forcing herself to stay.

"It'll take a few minutes to find our balance." She wanted to correct him. Every time she was near him, her careful equilibrium abandoned her faster than a racehorse leaving the starting gate. He pushed off, and she gripped the handlebars. "Here we go."

The bike teetered on the verge of calamity as they bumped across the path. Alanna tried to focus on the trail but decided it was better if she looked at anything except where they were headed. Nobody wanted a backseat driver, especially on a tandem bike. But when she pinned her gaze on what was in front of her, she stared at the expanse of his shoulders. Now she didn't know where to look.

Finally, Jonathan steered them off the trail to a smoother path. Her teeth quit jarring, and she glanced around.

"Where does this path go?"

He glanced over his shoulder then turned back to the path. "I forgot it's new since you left. It's kind of a back pass as it skirts the golf course and then reaches that collection of homes where Hoffmeister lives."

"Lived."

Jonathan nodded. "It saves time from going through town to the paved street and then around the island on Lake Shore."

Only the sound of the tires against the path broke the background music of tree branches fanning and birds singing. Alanna glanced around, trying to spot some of the songbirds, surprised Jonathan didn't. "I thought you were a birder."

"I am. There's not much I haven't seen along this path though. There are only so many places to go without swimming."

Alanna laughed at the image that generated. Jonathan in full birding gear, vest stuffed with a guide in every pocket and a hat and binoculars, flailing his way to the mainland.

"So what are we hearing?"

∾

DID she really want to know? Alanna had never expressed an interest before. Instead, she'd called it odd the summer he started getting interested. Maybe she needed the distraction right now. He could humor her.

"The *beecher-beecher-beecher* comes from a Connecticut warbler. I wouldn't normally expect to hear one here. Guess the undergrowth is dense enough." He listened a moment. "The abrupt clicking comes from a black-backed woodpecker. He must not like the company." A small brown bird flew from one tree to another. "There goes the boreal chickadee."

"Where do you like to go birding?"

"The backyard. With the pond and all the trees, I really don't have to wander far to see a variety. To see any great number though, I do have to get to the mainland. Either side works, depending on my mood and how far I want to roam." As a fork in the road neared, he slowed. "I haven't gotten away for a while." He pointed down one path. "After this turn, you'll see the golf course. Watch for flying golf balls. Some of the visitors think they're better golfers than they are."

"Tell me about this neighborhood. Mr. Hoffmeister's house sat by itself. . ."

He could hear her unspoken *back then.* A lot had changed. "He broke up his piece and subdivided it. Sold the lots and made a nice penny. You'll see the homes are pretty standard. Small cottages with a Victorian flair. He sold the lot next to his house last."

"How many houses?"

"Five or six. Not too many. And most of them are occupied by weekenders. They come for a week or two at a time and rent the homes the rest of the time."

"Keep the tourists coming."

Jonathan nodded as they rounded a corner and the gated entrance to the Wawashkamo Golf Course came into view.

"Jonathan, why didn't we take Leslie Road? Why the roundabout?"

"It's your day off." Guess he should have known she'd question his path once she understood where they were.

"I think the thick trees will protect us from any misdirected golf balls." Alanna seemed to turn behind him. "You sure you should be in front?"

He pushed harder against the pedals, propelling the tandem bike across the crushed gravel. "Yep."

Quiet fell as they pedaled the rest of the way to Straits Trail. Here's where Alanna needed him. She'd keep going on Stonecliffe, never connecting to Morton Trail. That trail hadn't led much of anywhere when she lived here. Now the group of homes strung between the two.

The bike bounced across the trail. A mountain bike would have been better suited but not as much fun as having Alanna immediately behind him. He turned slightly and flicked a thumb in the other direction. "Here's the start of the homes." Alanna glanced around, and he turned back to the front. "Mr. Hoffmeister's home is up here a bit."

"He had such a great location. Secluded. Great view of Lake Huron. Relatively close to town. I wonder why he sold land."

"I heard the fudge shop had money problems. Needed the cash infusion." Could those cash-flow problems have pushed him to skim money from the foundation? He didn't seem like the type to do anything like that. He'd always seemed like an honorable man when Jonathan interacted with him.

"Hmm. I'm surprised he didn't find another way. He always valued his privacy."

"Maybe he did. Do you think he could have created the fake accounts?"

Silence followed his question. "I don't know." Alanna sighed, her breath tickling his neck. "I hate to think about him that way."

"Still, there are only a handful of people who would have access to create those accounts."

"Guess we need to figure out who else could have done it. Those accounts were created during his presidency, so it's not Tomkin."

"Could be anyone on the board."

"How easy would it be for someone on the board to do it?"

Jonathan thought a moment. "Outside the bookkeeper? It wouldn't be easy at all."

"Who was the bookkeeper then?"

"I'm not sure. I've only been on the board since Gerald came on. Here we are." Jonathan stopped the bike in front of the small Victorian cottage. On the surface it looked well maintained, but when he looked closer, Jonathan saw peeling paint and a lack of landscaping. Mr. Hoffmeister had let the details go.

Alanna slid off the bike, and the weight shifted, bumping the bike against his calves. She walked toward the side yard and around to the front. "We came here once for a barbecue. It had been a hard winter. Lots of snow and bitter cold. Even more than usual." She turned and studied the house. "Everybody was so glad to see the snow melt, and Mr. Hoffmeister invited the church over for a spring celebration. He loved the impromptu baseball game and the wild game of tag."

"He didn't do that anymore."

She glanced around and swept the area with a hand. "He couldn't after letting these other homes in. No space for baseballs to go wild."

Jonathan scanned the area, trying to imagine what it had looked like before. The homes were tucked in the trees, and he couldn't imagine a clearing large enough for baseball. "So where do we start?"

"Well. . ." Alanna frowned.

"What?"

"I don't see any crime-scene tape."

"Why would you? He was murdered in town, not down here."

"True, but if I led the investigation, I'd want people to stay back." She climbed the two stairs to the porch. She glanced around then hurried toward the front door. "That's odd."

"What?"

"Mr. Hoffmeister always had a life-size German shepherd statue right beside the door. Said since he was allergic, it was the closest he could come to a guard dog. I never thought he needed one out here by himself. He mentioned it in his note, so it should still be here." She stopped and brushed the floor. "There's still a mark where the dog sat."

Jonathan glanced around. "No dog."

"No dog." Alanna tugged at a floorboard, scooped something out, and stood.

"What are you doing?"

"Getting us into the house."

## 28

It didn't feel right, but she knew where the key was. And Mr. Hoffmeister had invited her to explore his home with the note he gave her. No, it didn't say anything about going inside his home if he were murdered, but in light of what happened, he seemed to know something was wrong. Maybe he'd left some indication in his home.

Alanna stood on the small porch, the spare key in her hand. Sometimes she wished people weren't so stuck to their habits. If the key had disappeared, then she'd leave right then. Instead, the tiny key felt like it weighed a million pounds. Go in? Stay out?

With a key, it wasn't really breaking in—she hoped.

But if she stayed outside, she'd never find answers that waited on the other side of the door. With a murderer on the loose, she had to try. The Mackinac Island police weren't any more equipped to investigate a murder than she. The difference was they thought she was a prime suspect.

She didn't kill Mr. Hoffmeister. Now she had to prove it. She glanced at the man standing next to her, arms crossed. He'd brought her here, but would he go along with searching the house?

"So?" Jonathan studied her, his chin tilted toward the house. "Are we going in or waiting for someone to call the police?"

Alanna glanced around the houses that appeared empty. It only took one nosy neighbor to compound her problems with the police.

"In we go." She slotted the key into the lock and listened for the click. The door swung open with a soft groan.

"Now what?"

Alanna let her eyes adjust to the dim light. "Let's start with a quick survey of the rooms. That shouldn't take long." The front room stood pretty empty. A dilapidated couch pushed against one wall while a row of leaning bookcases lined another. She ran a finger along the spines. "He took such pride in his collection. And this room used to have nice furniture. I wonder what happened."

Jonathan shrugged and then shoved his hands in his pockets. "Not sure. I didn't know him very well. Just friendly greetings when we bumped into each other. Maybe he had to help Ginger out when she got pregnant. She was pretty young when she became a mom."

Nothing stuck out in the quick survey of the living area, so Alanna walked to the kitchen. "Did you know Mr. Hoffmeister was something of a gourmet cook?" Jonathan shook his head. "He favored vegetarian dishes, but I liked sampling them. Usually had hints of spices my mom never touched. Made for a new experience even if I did keep a glass of water close."

"Did your family spend a lot of time here?"

"Maybe once a season. We all worked hard but liked to play when we peeled away the time." Alanna opened drawers, finding only silverware and the expected hodgepodge drawer filled with junk. At this rate, she'd never find anything valuable.

Jonathan opened a couple of cupboards but didn't seem to find anything interesting either. "Upstairs?"

"I guess." Alanna had never been upstairs. Mr. Hoffmeister had treated it as off-limits, an easy request to comply with when a wide-open expanse around the house and the hike down to the beach awaited. As soon as she got upstairs, Alanna entered the bedroom that overlooked the beach. She pulled back the curtains.

"See anything?"

She shook her head. "Why did I think this view or perspective would make a difference? I was so much closer on the beach."

"Maybe Hoffmeister saw something. Or maybe you wanted to believe this would add key data."

"Maybe." Alanna's shoulders slumped forward under the challenge of finding answers. She shifted to try a different angle. "I just want to find the truth. Even if it's not what I want, the truth is the key to bringing Trevor home. His paintings are too good not to sell with his name."

Jonathan stood next to her, his shoulder brushing hers. He stared out the window, shifting his head slightly as he scanned. "Where exactly was the party?"

Alanna scanned over the trees, trying to find the crop of rocks where they had built the bonfire. Had the trees grown that much? She couldn't find the rocks but pointed toward the left. "It should be down there."

"Should be?" The skepticism in his words pierced her.

"Things have changed." Even as she said the words, she heard her defensiveness. She couldn't help wondering what else had changed that she hadn't noticed. Alanna leaned against the windowsill, breaking contact with Jonathan. "What now?"

"We keep looking. Mr. Hoffmeister had something for you. We should at least check all the rooms. Maybe we'll find it."

Jonathan moved to the small closet and opened the door. "I don't see anything in here."

"Why would he leave it in a closet? Unless he worried someone else would come?"

"Whoever killed him would have come up here next if there was something to find."

It made sense. But it didn't answer the question what that item could be. As they moved into the other bedroom, Alanna tried to imagine what it might be.

FROM THE WAY Alanna's nose screwed up, she was deep in thought. He gave her some space to formulate her thoughts while he surveyed this last room. So far nothing had jumped out at him—other than the fact that Alanna wasn't finding anything from the view of the accident site or the elusive item Mr. Hoffmeister mentioned.

Had she imagined it?

He brushed the question aside. He didn't want to think Alanna had fabricated the situation. Yet nothing added up.

He watched her, hoping something would exonerate her and remove the cloud of suspicion. The bedroom was a clean widower's pad. If anyone came in to search the house after Hoffmeister's death, they'd been extremely careful to leave no trace of their presence. The house didn't look anything like the trashed houses he saw in movies. Instead, if anyone had come in, they'd done a thorough job of keeping their presence and identity hidden.

Alanna moved like one in a trance. Her steps faltered as she entered his bedroom. He couldn't discern what had caught her attention, since the room looked like a typical man's room. Plain bedspread in a deep navy with a couple of pillows tossed on top. A dresser with a cluttered surface. Closet door cracked.

"Why's the door open?" Alanna's whisper almost didn't reach him.

"What?"

"All the other doors have been firmly closed. Yet this one is open."

He studied it then turned to her. "I wouldn't call it open." Still, he could see her point. "Maybe it's different because this was his room."

She shook her head, her eyes wide. The door barged open, slapping the wall. A man barreled from it, gun drawn, but instead of shooting, he shoved into Alanna, knocking her to the ground. Clad in jeans, a hunting jacket, and stocking cap, the man rushed toward the stairs. Jonathan pushed after him, jumping over Alanna. She groaned but seemed okay. The man, however, would disappear if Jonathan couldn't catch him.

"Stay here," Jonathan yelled over his shoulder as he rushed after the man. The front door was flung open when he reached the main room. He raced toward it then stopped. What if the man had done that to get him to chase into the yard, leaving Alanna by herself? Then the invader could circle back upstairs and hurt her. He glanced around the room and stepped back to glance behind the couch. No one lurked there or in the kitchen, so he raced out the door and launched off the porch.

Jonathan froze, listening for any sound as he scanned the area. The bright hunting jacket disappeared into a copse of trees. Jonathan took off in that direction. The thrashing of breaking branches and leaves underfoot pulled him forward. He had to catch the man. Find out why he'd been in the house. The man left a trail as wide as an elephant, not slowing as he ran pell-mell through the trees. Jonathan huffed as he pushed to gain ground.

He pumped his arms. Willed his legs to move. For all the biking and walking the island required, he should be in good enough shape to catch the intruder. Instead, the distance spread between them.

Jonathan dug deep and pushed on with a spurt of energy. He had to catch this guy.

He tugged his cell phone from his pocket. No bars. Argh! He shoved it back in his pocket and sucked in a breath. The man stumbled, and Jonathan gained a few feet. There was something familiar about the way the man moved. Racing, Jonathan couldn't identify him from behind. The man crossed a trail, and Jonathan skidded to a stop as a group on bicycles pedaled past. By the time the straggler cleared, the man had disappeared.

Jonathan raced across the trail but couldn't see the man anywhere. Even with the bright hunting jacket, he'd disappeared. Jonathan hurried forward anyway. He had to try.

A bright blob of color caught his eye, and he sped toward it. He let out a groan when he got closer and saw the runner had hung the jacket from a branch.

He leaned over, hands on his knees, and gulped air. How could he explain this to Alanna?

ALANNA RUBBED HER SHOULDER, massaging the spot that collided with the floor. It throbbed, but she ignored the pain. She hurried downstairs. She couldn't leave Jonathan to catch the intruder alone. Yet when she made it to the porch, Jonathan and the brightly clothed stranger had disappeared.

A headache started to pound as she wandered back into the house. She'd barely settled on the saggy couch when the door banged open.

"Jonathan?"

"No, but I'd like to know what you're doing here."

She turned and froze. Detective Bull didn't look any happier to see her there than he sounded. His brows were drawn together, his stance wide like he was ready for a fight. She slowly raised her hands. "Does it help that I was getting ready to call?"

"Good thing a neighbor took care of that, complaining about a lot of activity in a dead man's house."

"I had a key. And you saw the note. He wanted me to see something."

"So you took it upon yourself to come? Without checking?" She nodded, knowing how foolish and ridiculous it sounded. And looked.

"I don't know whether to haul you immediately to jail or laugh. You're an attorney."

"Maybe, but I'm also your prime suspect." Alanna stood, refusing to let him intimidate her with his size. She thrust her hands on her hips and stepped closer. "I can't rely on you to check things like this. Not when I might go to jail."

"Am I interrupting anything?" A bedraggled Jonathan stood in the doorway, fire in his eyes.

"Just hauling this gal off to jail. You bring your girlfriend up here on that tandem bike?"

Alanna started to sputter. "We're not. . ." But she couldn't deny she wanted to be. Especially as she watched the fire in Jonathan's eyes. He looked ready to attack the detective in an effort to protect her. How she longed for that security he offered. But what about Jaclyn and Dylan? She sank back to the saggy couch. This was too complicated.

Detective Bull looked at Jonathan, eyeing the coat he carried. "Why don't you tell me what that's about?"

"After you call down to Ryan and let him know that a guy in jeans and a stocking cap is running into town. He'll be sweaty and out of breath. He was hiding in an upstairs closet when we got here. Knocked Alanna to the ground and kept running. Thought I had him, but he hung this on a tree to distract me."

Detective Bull quirked an eyebrow. "Guess it worked."

"Yeah," Jonathan growled. He looked like he regretted every moment of their time up here. This probably wasn't the time to remind him he'd gotten the tandem bike. If he hadn't come, she'd have done this alone eventually, just not today. "Do you want this thing?"

The detective nodded. "I'll have the techs look it over. I doubt it has any connection to the murder, but it's worth evaluating." He crossed his arms across his wide chest. "Let's get back to what the two of you are doing here."

## 29

The bald truth was there was no good reason.

Jonathan had a crazy idea, acted without thinking, and Alanna almost got killed. Now she sat on the couch probably headed straight to jail, do not pass go, do not collect two hundred dollars. And it was his fault.

She'd been perfectly content working through her lists and phone calls. His teasing got her on the bike and up here. It was still a good idea but would have been better if he'd cleared it with the police first.

"You can blame me."

Detective Bull studied him, skepticism tightening his already tense posture. "Really?"

"Alanna was at home working when I came up with the tandem bike. I steered us here."

Alanna looked up and started to sputter. "I would have made the trip eventually. And since that other guy was here, better now than later. At least he didn't get away with anything."

"That we know of." Jonathan shrugged. "He could have stuffed something in the jacket."

"But we have that."

Detective Bull glanced through the pockets. "Nothing clearly important."

Alanna sighed. "That would be too easy."

"Tell me everything that happened from the moment you hit this property." Bull pulled a chair over from the kitchen and took out a pen and notebook. Alanna and Jonathan tag-teamed the telling. When they were done, Bull studied Alanna. "Is there anything you aren't telling me?"

"No." She spread her hands in front of her. "That's it. We didn't see anything worth noting until that man opened the closet."

"All right." He closed his notebook and stood. "Then let's finish searching."

Jonathan couldn't believe his ears. "What?"

"I don't trust you two not to come back, so I'm staying right here while you satisfy yourselves that there's no secret code."

Alanna nodded. "I haven't seen any records from I'm Not Sharing. He was also on a couple boards, but there's no office. He had to keep those somewhere."

"Some were at his shop, but not enough to run the business. Let's start where Mystery Man waited." Bull let them precede him up the stairs. Alanna looked back as she scurried up. He had an appraising look on his face as he watched her. While it bothered her to be under his scrutiny, maybe he didn't think she'd committed a crime when she entered the house.

Now to find whatever Mr. Hoffmeister had left.

Mr. Tomkin seemed intent to point a finger at Mr. Hoffmeister, who had pointed the finger right back. They used to be good friends. Maybe it was one more thing her mind had altered with the distance and time.

As she reentered the bedroom, Alanna took in the details. Somewhere Mr. Hoffmeister had kept records. If he was like her clients, finding those documents could be key. Especially if

Gerald Tomkins allegations were valid. She turned to Detective Bull. "Have you examined Mr. Hoffmeister's finances?"

He shook his head with a barely audible snort. "I can't comment on an ongoing investigation, especially one where you're the suspect."

"It never hurts to ask."

"Why do you want to know?"

"Just curious." She couldn't tell him about Tomkins allegations. Not without more to back them up.

"Humph."

Alanna opened the closet doors and started pushing against the back wall. "Financials make short work of determining if something was wrong with his money."

Jonathan knelt by the floor and pulled up the bed skirt. "Bingo."

"What?" Detective Bull tucked his notebook in his inside jacket pocket and took a quick step in his direction.

"What guy puts one of these on his bed?" Jonathan thumped the piece of cloth with disgust. "There are file boxes under here. Maybe these have the missing office documents." Jonathan tugged the first box free.

"Maybe." Detective Bull pulled a pair of gloves from a pocket and slipped them on. "Let me."

Jonathan stepped out of the way while Alanna edged closer. She held her breath as Detective Bull eased the lid off the first box. When a stack of ledgers and array of files appeared, the man remained unflappable while Alanna wanted to grab the box and start uncovering the secrets hidden inside.

"Could be promising." Bull tapped the lid back on. "I'll take this back to the office."

Alanna bit back a sharp word—or two—at the thought of whatever the box contained disappearing off the island.

"Sure we can't glance at it here?" Jonathan spread his hands and grinned. "We've gone to a lot of trouble to find that box."

"You can drag out the other boxes. Here's a pair of gloves."

Jonathan slipped them on and knelt down again. "There's only one more."

Alanna frowned. Could two boxes be sufficient to contain all the records? Especially since the detective suggested there weren't many at the shop?

"Feel free to check for yourself." Jonathan tugged up the skirt and made a sweeping motion. "Maybe my x-ray vision missed something."

Alanna made a face at his sarcasm. "Trust me, businesses have lots of paper. No matter how small, I usually spend days wading through paper looking for one important fact."

As JONATHAN WATCHED, he knew Lanna wasn't thinking straight. She kept focusing on what she expected to see. Mr. Hoffmeister was a nice guy, but he wasn't the world's most effective business-man. If he were, he'd have a string of fudge shops like the others. Instead, he'd had one that did a good business but hadn't differ-entiated from all the other fudge on the island. It wouldn't surprise Jonathan if the two meager boxes contained everything.

If she'd decided the paperwork would save her and eventu-ally Trevor, she'd misplaced her faith. "We've got more places to poke. Maybe we'll find something there."

Detective Bull again let them precede him. That action annoyed Jonathan. Why didn't the man get in front and investi-gate? He was the detective after all.

"So how long you been with the state police?"

Bull did one of those annoying shoulder slouches that communicated he didn't care enough to really comment.

"Five years? Ten?"

"Enough."

"Like the St. Ignace office?"

Bull shrugged again. "It's fine."

"Until January?" Jonathan entered the other bedroom and checked under the bed, behind the dresser, and in the closet. Nothing.

"Snow's not bad."

"If you've got four-wheel drive and a snowmobile."

"Don't forget the cross-country skis."

Alanna studied him, a question in her eyes. He ignored it as he avoided looking at the detective. Something just wasn't right.

Jonathan stood and looked out the window. Where was the detective's bike? "How do you plan to get those boxes down to the dock?"

Alanna must have caught the warning, because she slid toward the hallway as Bull stepped to the closet. The man made a perfunctory search.

"Not too worried about it."

"Didn't think so. Still, it makes me wonder what you're doing here. Alone. Wouldn't you bring someone with you?" Jonathan stepped closer to the man, trying to block his view of Alanna as she slipped into the hallway.

"Not enough manpower." Sounded plausible, but after the way the chief shadowed him earlier, Jonathan wasn't sure.

All he knew was he had a clear signal from his gut that he didn't like the situation. He might not make a living as a detective, but something smelled. As he tried to evaluate the situation, he knew he couldn't let anything happen to Alanna. If the situation was off, he needed to do everything possible to keep her safe. She meant too much to him to pretend otherwise.

"Where'd Ms. Stone go?" The detective stepped into his space, puffing up as if to make himself look bigger.

Jonathan made a show of looking around. "She's right here."

"Nope. Out of the way."

The thought of going toe-to-toe with a second person wore Jonathan out. Still, he squared himself in front of Bull. He'd pull energy from deep resources to give Alanna time to slip away.

Bull growled. "Move now."

When Jonathan remained in place, the man shoved him against the door frame. Jonathan fought for his balance then stuck a foot out. He hoped that didn't count as assaulting an officer as Bull slammed into a wall.

"Bad choice, Covington."

As a commotion erupted downstairs, Jonathan took his place in the doorway. "It's nothing personal."

"You can tell that to the judge."

"We'll see." Fortunately, he knew a good attorney.

ALANNA RUSHED BACK up the stairs. She'd had her cell phone out, dialing 911, when she'd reached the porch and heard the distinctive crunch of horses' hooves against the trail. A small taxi had pulled up, and Police Chief Ryan climbed out followed by another man in police uniform.

"Chief Ryan." Alanna closed her phone. "How did you know to come?"

"Research."

Yes, the man used an economy of words, but that one word struck Alanna as exceptionally sparse. "Jonathan and Detective Bull are upstairs."

The young officer shook his head. "He's a maverick."

The two uniformed men moved in front of her. As the screen door eased shut, Chief Ryan looked back at her. "Stay here, Ms. Stone."

While his words sounded good, no way she'd stay in place and let whatever happened take place without helping Jonathan. She slipped off her shoes and then eased the door open. Her feet didn't make any noise as she crept through the lower rooms to the stairs.

"Bull, what are you doing? I thought we agreed to do this together." Chief Ryan's voice left no doubt he expected an immediate answer.

"Chief, I got a tip and followed it. That's what we do in the state police."

Alanna slipped around the corner and placed her foot on a stair.

It protested as if an entire marching band wanted to pass by. Chief Ryan turned with a frown. "I told you to stay put."

"Yes, sir." He hadn't been around before she left, so he wouldn't know she'd struggle to obey that instruction, but Jonathan's snort made it clear he did.

"Someone want to fill me in?" Chief Ryan looked from one to the other. "We got a call but didn't find the suspect that launched from here."

"We've got his jacket over here, but that's it." Bull shrugged. "There's no indication why he was here or how long. All we know is he didn't take anything visible with him." He tapped the boxes. "Do you have transportation?"

"Outside."

"Good, then these boxes and I can hitchhike along."

Chief Ryan turned to Jonathan. "You and Miss Stone need a ride, or do you plan to use that tandem bike?"

"We'll bike down."

"Okay, so long as you come straight to the station."

"Yes, sir."

Chief Ryan looked at Alanna.

"We'll be there." She had too many questions she wanted him, to answer.

Two hours later, she sat in the police chiefs overloaded office, feeling like she'd never get an answer since the only talking she got to do was answering his questions.

"Explain again why you thought it was a good idea to invade a murdered man's home." Chief Ryan sat on the corner of his industrial desk and knocked the top with his knuckles as he studied Alanna intently.

"We had the key." The words sounded weak, but she still believed that allowed her actions.

"But Mr. Hoffmeister hadn't given it to you, correct?"

"Yes." She rubbed at the pounding in her temples.

"I'm not charging you with breaking and entering right now, since Detective Bull vouches you didn't take anything. But if you pull a stunt like that again, I will ask the prosecutor to bring every charge against you that has a 20 percent chance of sticking. You leave the investigating to us, or it will be interfering with a police investigation."

She opened her mouth to respond then shut it. She'd only make matters worse.

Jonathan tugged at her hand. "Let's head home."

"All right." She stood then paused. "You still haven't said whether you have ideas on who the intruder was."

"The other one?" She winced at the words. "Maybe the murderer's looking for something. If that's the case, you were lucky. Don't count on being so fortunate next time."

Alanna followed Jonathan to the door but turned when Chief Ryan cleared his throat.

"Miss Stone, I've checked with friends in Grand Rapids. They say you're quite the tenacious investigator." He crossed his arms and leaned back. "Let me give you some advice. Stop. Anything you do could actually muddy things up rather than clear you. What if the crucial fact hides in one of those boxes? What if those boxes had gotten destroyed? What if you'd gone through them without Detective Bull? You could have removed anything you didn't like. Destroyed evidence. Or created the impression that could have happened. They would have sat there a long time undisturbed if you hadn't taken it upon yourselves to investigate."

"With all due respect, Chief, don't forget about the guy we chased away." Jonathan stared at him. "He was in that room and could have found them as easily as I did."

"Chances of finding him are slim to none. Officers are watching for him, but you know he's ditched the coat, cap, and anything else that IDs him."

And with that, Alanna was no closer to finding the real murderer or clearing Trevor.

## 30

J onathan had to get Alanna out of the City Hall building before she exploded. He could almost watch her mind process what they had learned and piece it together with what she already knew.

The chief studied Alanna with a hard look. "Stay out of the investigation. I know it's a challenge for you to leave things to the police. But we have it under control. You getting in the way doesn't help your case."

Alanna opened her mouth, but Jonathan raced to answer. "Thank you for your help, Chief. We'll head out now." He grabbed Alanna's hand and pulled her from the room and out of the police offices.

"What are you doing?"

"Saving you from doing or saying something that will get you in trouble."

Alanna shielded her eyes as they stepped into the sunlight.

"Let's get this bike turned back in and head home. Then we'll grab dinner, fish on the dock."

"You want to let it drop?"

"We've done enough getting in the way, don't you think?"

She shook her head, and his hope of keeping her distracted from the murder and mess evaporated. "There's too much . . . . Somehow this ties together. Grady's death. The property. Mr. Hoffmeister's murder. Even the foundation books."

Jonathan disagreed. "There's no reason to connect Grady's death and Mr. Hoffmeister. Eleven years is too long." He sighed, wishing he'd never suggested the bike ride. He'd thought it would be a quick trip and a romantic time pedaling around the island. Now he'd leave sorting everything out to the police.

Alanna sank onto a bench. Her shoulders slumped, and she looked wrung out. Worry lines crossed the bridge of her nose and forehead as she studied her hands. She seemed oblivious to the flowers and other details that would normally bring her pleasure. She didn't even seem curious to know how the Painted Stone was doing without her in its slot across the street from City Hall.

"Come on, let's head back."

She startled, as if he'd pulled her from deep thoughts. "What am I going to do, Jonathan?"

"We'll forget about this for a little while. Let the police do their job."

"What if it's so tangled they can't find the real murderer? What if I'm easier to focus on?"

"Then we'll show them you didn't do it."

"Without an alibi?" Her voice rose, and then she stopped. She glanced around then seemed to gather herself. "You're right. I can't do anything right now. It's Sunday evening." Her stomach grumbled. "Guess I am hungry."

"Let's get something to eat and go from there." He led her to one of the island's restaurants, but the meal was quiet. Alanna couldn't seem to rouse from wherever she'd disappeared. Her fears seemed to envelop her as she pushed the food around her plate.

Jonathan scooped food in his mouth as fast as was polite. Maybe she needed to get back to the house. Maybe in her home she'd find sanctuary and lose the clouds building on her face.

"Jonathan." The young voice pulled Jonathan's head up. Jonathan smiled at the grinning body torpedoing down the aisle toward him. Then he caught the resignation on Alanna's face. Before he could say anything, try to explain, the torpedo flung himself into Jonathan's arms.

Dylan.

∼

ALANNA TURNED toward the adorable boy. She might not like the way Jaclyn had claimed Jonathan, but she had to admit Dylan was the image of the little boy she'd love to have someday. The blond curls made her want to pull him into her lap for a squeeze.

"Where's your mommy?"

He grinned up at Jonathan, his tiny teeth barely filling his mouth. "She's outside talking." He climbed in Jonathan's lap, and a look swept Jonathan, a mixture of love and distance.

Jonathan wasn't hers. He belonged to Jaclyn and Dylan. Alanna swallowed against the pain and launched to her feet.

"Where are you going?" Confusion laced his words.

"I need to get home, and I know you need to spend time with this cute little guy." She forced a smile. "Thanks for your help and being a friend, Jonathan." She ducked her head and hurried from the restaurant, brushing past Jaclyn talking on her cell.

She could check on the studio, but honestly, after everything that had transpired, she didn't care if it still stood. Patience had closed, and Alanna could check sales in the morning. What she needed right now was solitude. Her life seemed to erupt more each day, losing the carefully defined shape and parameters she'd crafted around it.

It would take a long time to walk home, but the fresh air and solitude would help her sort through the latest developments.

One, her heart fully belonged to Jonathan. After everything that had happened today, and the way it had trembled when she thought he was in danger, she couldn't deny the truth. Her heart remained fully committed to Jonathan. Pressure squeezed her chest as she turned up the hill next to Fort Mackinac. Her steps slowed as she tried to catch a deep breath. Instead, it felt like the sobs would explode from her, and she couldn't let that happen. Not here.

Two, the murder investigation remained outside her grasp. Anytime she tried to do anything about it, she only mucked up the situation. She should thank God she wouldn't spend the night in the tiny Mackinac jail.

Three, she couldn't walk away from the mysteries surrounding Grady's death and the paintings. She might know Trevor had painted many of the landscapes, but she couldn't help him if she didn't understand what happened to Grady. And this was too central to her life to leave alone. She had to find the truth. For Trevor and for herself. After eleven years, she longed to walk away from the mess and somehow find peace.

Four, the day's events had reinforced that she couldn't orchestrate things on her own. In fact, when she tried, disasters happened. She needed to turn the tangled web of problems over to God. So much easier said than accomplished.

After a long hike, she finally reached the sanctuary of her parents' home. She slipped through the house, grabbing a glass of iced tea, then hurried to the back porch. As the shadows cast by the trees teased across the yard, she felt drawn to the dock. She sat at the end, letting her feet dangle off the edge, toes skimming the top of the water.

She closed her eyes and let the quiet sounds of cicadas and bullfrogs bounce around her, punctuated by the occasional birdsong. She tried to grab hold of the moment, clearing her mind of everything that happened. Maybe if she refocused, her subconscious would untangle the mess of facts and inferences.

Alanna tipped her chin up, fighting the tears that pushed against her eyelids.

She wanted Jonathan back.

And she couldn't have him.

All the ways he'd cared for her slipped through her mind. In the last two weeks, he'd continued to treat her with respect. He'd treated her like a treasure, standing beside her when she confronted her mother and pushing her to acknowledge the truth.

He'd stood beside her even as he challenged her to break free from the past. He stood separated from other men she knew in the way he put her first.

Yet he belonged to another.

She could only imagine what it would be like to be the focus of his love and attention. The tears escaped as she admitted she'd walked away from him when she abandoned Mackinac. Would life have separated them anyway? She'd never know.

All she knew for sure was he wasn't hers. She pulled her knees to her chest and lowered her head to the top.

*What now, God?*

Could she walk away from Jonathan and Mackinac?

As she considered the idea, she knew it wasn't possible. She still had to fight for Trevor so she could end the lies her family lived. And she had to untangle the allegations between Mr. Tomkin and Mr. Hoffmeister.

Then she'd leave.

∾

JACLYN HADN'T SMILED when she entered the restaurant and found Dylan on his lap. Still, Jonathan didn't apologize. It wasn't his fault the boy adored him. Frankly, it felt good to have the little man chattering on his lap, filling him in on a disjointed account of his day.

"Then I caught a frog." He spread his hands. "He was this big."

"Impressive."

"I know! Hi, Mommy."

Jaclyn smiled at her boy, but it didn't reach her eyes. "Hey, Dylan. Are you bothering Jonathan?"

"You know he's not a bother."

"I don't know anything right now." Dark circles undergirded her eyes. Had he caused her lack of sleep? "Dylan, we need to go home."

Dylan stuck out his lip and wrapped his arms around Jonathan's neck. Jonathan swallowed but slowly extricated himself from Dylan's grip. "You've got to obey your mom, Dylan."

"I want to stay with you." The lip extended even farther.

"Not today." Jonathan glanced at Jaclyn. "You okay?"

"Always am." Her jaw firmed, and she studied him. "We'll be okay regardless of what you decide. Don't take too long. I won't wait forever." She tugged Dylan free. "Time to go, bud. We'll go walk around the fort again."

Jonathan watched them leave. Earlier this afternoon he'd been absolutely certain that Alanna was the one he wanted. Then Dylan came back.

He couldn't fall in love with a two-year-old. There had to be a connection, a love for Jaclyn, or it wouldn't work. Loving one without the other wasn't fair to Jaclyn. He had to tell her. But as Jaclyn walked outside, Dylan looking behind, he didn't know how to change things.

Somehow he had to find an honorable way to let Jaclyn know where his heart lay. And then he had to tell Alanna.

He might as well walk by the office and grab a file before heading home. As he walked by I'm Not Sharing, the fudge shop remained cloaked in darkness. Someday it would reopen, but right now it was a shell. Mr. Hoffmeister had been the lifeblood of the store, especially after Ginger had decided to stop working there. Jonathan wondered if he had any succession plan or if the business would eventually peter out and close.

Too bad he didn't want a fudge shop.

Jonathan raced upstairs, grabbed the file, and headed back down. When he passed the foundation, Gerald strode out. "Covington."

"Hello, Gerald."

"Heard there was excitement up at the Hoffmeister place."

"You could say that."

"Now that he's gone, I'll get to build my house without all his noise. It's amazing how much he gummed everything up."

Jonathan picked up his pace, and Tomkin kept up. "It was his property."

"Not after he sold it to me. If he didn't want it changed, he shouldn't have subdivided. His rigid thoughts constricted any creativity." Gerald shrugged. "At least now I can do what I want within those silly Victorian restrictions. Can't say I'm fond of people telling me what to do. Any thoughts on the festival?"

"Been working on a couple other projects, but I'll have something to you soon."

"Good." Gerald slapped him on the back. "See you later."

"One question."

Gerald paused with a slight frown. "Yes."

"Have the police talked to you about Hoffmeister?"

"Of course. Especially with our dispute. Glad I had a solid alibi. After they confirmed it, they said I'm clear."

"That's good news."

"Yes." Gerald cleared his throat. "We may not have been the best of friends these last couple years, but we'd known each other a long time. There was a reason I bought that lot close to him. Thought it would be nice to be closer to a friend. Wish I'd known what a bad decision that would turn out to be. Well, see you later." He nodded at Jonathan and then strode down the sidewalk.

Jonathan watched a moment then continued toward home. Sad how a dispute over a house had effectively ended a time-tested friendship. By the time he reached his section of the woods, dusk had fallen and he was glad he hadn't waited longer.

As soon as he entered his cottage, he headed for the sink. The glass of water tasted great as it slid down his throat. Something caught his attention outside on the dock. He pressed his face against the window trying to see through the darkening sky.

The shape was too big to be a small animal or bird, and it wasn't moving.

Jonathan threw the plastic glass in the sink, where it bounced as he hurried toward the dock.

## 31

The shape didn't move. With only a few steps to go, the shape turned into a person, and he slowed down. Alanna?

His pulse spiked, from racing or concern he didn't know. Still he stopped. If she were asleep, he didn't want to surprise her, but if she was in trouble, he couldn't wait to see if she'd move on her own. "Alanna?" He slid down next to her.

Her cheek lay slack against her arm, and peace cloaked her face maybe for the first time since she returned to the island. Her chest rose on a breath, and he backed off. He could imagine the flush of color she'd hide in the darkness if she woke up to his hovering.

He sank back against the base of the dock and watched her. What would have chased her outside to fall asleep?

No one had returned to her house since they'd found the rabbit in the trap. That appeared to be a one-time, dead-end event unless she'd found something today. If she had, he doubted she'd stay in the open.

Prayers lifted as he watched. He prayed for wisdom to know how to proceed. Creativity to satisfy his clients. Clear direction to know his heart. Alanna longed for the truth to illuminate her past. He wanted the truth to display his future. The present felt fine, but he wanted more. He longed to feel the way he did when Alanna stared at him with the eyes that said he could do anything. There hadn't been many people in his life that made him feel invincible like that.

As her form shifted deeper into the shadows, he knew that's what he wanted. To become the man who could protect those dear to him. The man who could bring the smile back to her face and coax it out frequently. Ideas formed as he watched and waited. He tried to remember the details as his mind filled with ways to sort through the art problems.

He might not be an investigator, but he knew events. That night ideas for an event unlike anything Mackinac Island had seen played through his mind. He tweaked the guest list here, added art there, and by the time Alanna began to stir, Jonathan had the outlines in place. Now he just needed his phone, e-mail, and computer.

Alanna groaned. She pushed up, her head hanging, then slowly glanced around. "Jonathan?"

"Sleepyhead."

She snorted, an unladylike sound he loved. "Help me up. I've fallen asleep in places I didn't know I could."

He eased her up, and she sagged against him. She felt so right next to him. How could he convince her he wanted to come alongside her and support her the rest of her life?

His earlier plea for direction seemed answered in a crystal-clear moment. His heart hadn't played tricks on him. It knew exactly what it wanted: the woman next to him rather than the one across the island.

~

THEIR SHOULDERS BRUSHED, and Alanna fought to clear her mind. Jonathan had that effect on her, and she wished she could wash it away. Join the chorus line in *South Pacific* and wash this man right out of her hair. He had a perfectly lovely young woman already with an adorable son who worshipped Jonathan. Alanna had to get out of the way. And the only way to do that was to leave.

She was right back where she'd started. Somehow she had to clear her brother so he could take his place at the Painted Stone. He's the one who should sit there day in and day out. He could paint in the back or even in the showroom, live in the empty apartment if he wanted independence. Then sell the art he'd created. Lies replaced by transparency.

Trevor didn't have a career waiting on the mainland. Still, the thought of her law practice and her apartment didn't bring Alanna joy. She wasn't sure she wanted to leave. But she had to. Staying would hurt too much.

"Where'd you go?"

"Home." She felt her lips curve, a soft, resigned acknowledgment. It would hurt too much to stay on Mackinac—after rediscovering Jonathan only to find him taken. She needed to refocus, take control, and get back home where she belonged.

"Sure you're all right?" If the light were better, Alanna knew she'd see a row of questions in his eyes, followed by the little stutter-step he made whenever he couldn't stay put.

"Just help me get inside. I've still got a lot to do tonight."

Ten minutes later, she sat at the dining room table, the foundation's ledgers strewn around her. "The answer is in those boxes from Hoffmeister's house."

"Why do you say that?" Jonathan sat across the table, arms crossed on his chest as he watched her.

"If something funny started happening while he was the president, it might have taken him awhile to notice. But he would have eventually. I bet he'd take it on himself to find the answer because he would feel responsible. Happened on his watch kind of thing. On an island this small, you have to keep things close to make sure the word doesn't spread."

"Let me make a call." Jonathan stepped to the other room, and she heard a muffled conversation as she continued to stare at the pages. When Jonathan returned, he handed her a piece of paper. "Okay, here's the list of people who served on the board during Hoffmeister's tenure. And Gerald said Brendan was the bookkeeper with assistance from the foundation's secretary."

"Really?" Alanna rubbed her cheeks. "He hated math. Why would anyone trust him with books?"

"Not liking a subject isn't the same as being bad at it."

"True. But Brendan always sat next to Grady in math class so he could copy answers. Grady was headed to Purdue on an engineering scholarship. He might have loved basketball, but his real ticket away was his brain. Brendan. . .not so much."

Jonathan shrugged. "Just relaying what I was told."

"Someone had to help him. Or if he was pretty much allowed to do what he wanted, it would explain how everything got messed up, if not where the money went." Alanna tapped the pencil against her teeth. "Guess I need to find him and ask him about that."

"Do you want me to handle that?"

Alanna laughed as she chucked her pencil at him. "You're the numbers guy."

"Only marginally more than you." He tapped a cover. "I'd be happy to probe though."

"Thanks. I'll touch base with Laura at the foundation. See if she remembers anything." Alanna glanced at her watch. "I'll try her now." After digging up the woman's number, Alanna waited while the phone rang and Laura answered. "Hi, Laura. This is Alanna Stone. Do you have a couple minutes?"

"Sure. Just reading a novel before bed."

"I promise this will be quick. Was Brendan the bookkeeper for the foundation a couple years ago?"

"Sure. He only stopped when his dad became president."

That was odd. What happened to fathers giving their sons more work? "Did he handle the job well?"

"As well as could be expected. I'd glance at the books every once in a while, but he didn't need me. Why all the questions?"

"Just thinking about something Gerald said. Thanks for your time."

Jonathan had cleared the table and stood when she ended. "Anything?"

"Nothing other than the fact she didn't provide oversight. If he'd wanted to, Brendan could do just about anything to the books."

"Still doesn't explain why he would if he did."

"True." Alanna stood. "Thanks for your help."

"Happy to do it. I'll let you know if I learn anything from Brendan."

"Don't you love the drama I've dragged you into?"

"Absolutely. My life has been a lot more interesting since you returned." He leaned toward her, and she couldn't have backed away if she'd wanted. All her grand ideas evaporated in a moment. There'd never been another man for her. Not in all this time.

If only he cared for her. Something deeper, more real than the tension they generated without effort. She wanted someone who knew her heart, her fears, her qualms—and loved her anyway. Who chose her in spite of the hang-ups and baggage she brought to the party.

His gaze traveled from her eyes, slid down her nose, and then landed on her lips. She clung to the table, grateful for the hard barrier keeping them apart, because she knew if he slipped around the table, she wouldn't be able to push him away. She didn't want to, not anymore.

She closed her eyes, brought Jaclyn's image to mind, and then pasted on a smile.

She had to get Trevor up here now.

Tomorrow wouldn't be soon enough. Yesterday would have been better. But it was time for her to escape.

ONE MOMENT he could practically read Alanna's thoughts. The next she might as well have shipped to the Amazon. The woman could disappear without moving, and the reality left him desperate.

He couldn't convince her he loved her if she constantly pushed him away. Left.

This time he wouldn't let her leave. He'd follow her to the jungle to prove he loved her.

Alanna tapped the ledger. His gaze bounced toward it, and he started.

"You'll call Brendan?"

He cracked a smile. "Already promised."

"You won't forget?" Alanna ran her fingers through her hair, leaving it all disorganized. "Do you think Gerald could be behind Mr. Hoffmeister's death?"

"He said the police have already cleared him."

"You didn't think you should mention that?"

"Guess I forgot. You'll unravel everything. From Grady's death to the books to Mr. Hoffmeister's murder. You and I both know it all ties together."

"The last time we tried to do something, some guy blows me over. So much for Mackinac Island being a place that slows down."

"I bet you're not bored."

His words seemed to shock her. She stared at him then laughed. And kept laughing. To the point he wondered if the hysteria would stop. Tears streamed down her cheeks, and he sat watching. This was when he needed that guide, the one that explained why women behaved in such bizarre ways. The one his dad never handed down.

"Alanna..."

She held up a hand then left. A minute later he heard clunking in the kitchen, and soon she returned with glasses of water. "Here you go."

"Thanks." He studied her as he took a sip. "You all right?"

"Sure." Sadness swept over her face only to be brushed aside as she sat, and he followed suit. "I'll be back in Grand Rapids in no time. The partners expect a call tomorrow. I'll get Patience to fill in until Mom returns. Then it's back to the grindstone."

"You can't leave the island."

She looked at him then waved. "The police won't mind."

"Really? And if they don't, you're running away? Again?" He wanted to recapture the words as soon as they escaped.

"Yes. Yes, I am. That's what I do, after all. When the going gets tough, Alanna Stone is ready to leave." She guzzled the rest of her water. "Besides, you have Jaclyn and Dylan. You don't need me around, distracting you from your work and love."

"What are you talking about?"

"Don't worry. Your event will be lovely." She lurched to her feet. "If you'll excuse me, I'm going to bed." She clutched the ledgers as she moved toward the stairs. "Good night."

She swept away, leaving him in the dining room.

Jonathan gathered the glasses and put them in the kitchen sink. After turning out the lights, he locked the door behind him and hurried to his cabin. Once in the living room, he fired up his laptop. Time to flesh out the plan that had dropped in his mind.

Alanna could wade through those ledgers again if she wanted, but there was nothing there other than evidence of embezzling. He had more productive trails to follow.

As soon as his e-mail loaded, he clicked through the messages, sorting them by event and client. Edward Morris's question about the gift for Bonnie gave him pause. Rachelle hadn't called him back. Now was the perfect time to push her for an answer. And while they were talking, he'd see if he couldn't extract a few more answers at the same time.

Alanna might not get the full truth from her mom, but that didn't mean he couldn't.

———

## 32

The alarm blared for what felt like hours before Alanna bopped it off. One glance at the time told her the hours hadn't been so long after all.

She rubbed her eyes. It felt like a truck had hit her overnight — impossible considering she was on the island, but she wouldn't be surprised to reach the bathroom mirror and find tire tracks across her face. Somewhere she had to find some energy. Time was running out. When she talked to the managing partner that morning, he'd want specifics she couldn't give.

Alanna got ready as quickly as possible then headed toward the Painted Stone. She didn't have any guarantees Patience Matthews would accept the job, so she'd have to craft the best package possible. Maybe commission, maybe hourly. She only prayed Patience would agree this sounded like the perfect way to spend the summer. If not. . .well, she'd have to cooperate.

When she arrived at the studio and turned on the computer, a resume sat in her e-mail. As Alanna scanned it, she decided this woman with her art degree might fit well at a studio. She fired an e-mail back, setting up a time for a phone interview. Maybe she wouldn't need Patience after all.

The morning flew as Alanna prepped new pieces for the walls and fiddled with a display of small prints. By the time the phone rang, the Painted Stone had already welcomed several groups of tourists. Alanna stepped down the hallway with the phone and tried to shield it from the noise while keeping an eye on the art.

"Ms. Stone. Ready to leave that little island and come back to the real world?" The managing partner seemed in a good mood, but Alanna stayed on guard.

"Yes, sir. I should be ready in two or three weeks."

A whistle made Alanna pull the phone away from her ear. "That's a long time. We've already given you two."

"I asked for at least a month. After that trial, I need the time."

"Doesn't sound like a vacation from what I've heard. Bennett told us he bought art from you. Odd considering you cleaned him out in court. Now you cleaned his billfold, too."

Alanna leaned against the wall and covered her eyes. "Small world."

"Well, two weeks. That's it. A day more, and you'll need to find a new firm. We have clients waiting for you who can't wait forever. The courts have deadlines."

Alanna hung up and tried to imagine everything she loved about her job. Her stomach knotted at the thought of marching back into the office. Handling more crazy clients and their insane demands. Then walking those into court. Never knowing exactly what would happen next. Having a script that could be abandoned in an instant. She tried to conjure up her bedroom at the apartment. The peace that usually swept her at the thought of the gray room with lavender accents didn't appear.

Then the image of practicing here, with the quiet pace of the island, flowed into her mind. Maybe she could work with

Jonathan. He enjoyed event planning. She could, too. She certainly had the organizational skills to make it successful.

Reality grabbed her runaway thoughts. She couldn't stay here. Definitely not work with Jonathan.

But she didn't want to go home.

JONATHAN STARED out the window as he waited for Trevor to answer the phone before he called Brendan. He'd heard Alanna's version of events. Now it was time to get Trevors. Somewhere in the middle he'd find the truth. At least that's what he counted on.

He'd start by clearing the date for the event. Couldn't have the shindig without the guest of honor. Overnight his vision for the event had continued to emerge. It would be easy to craft another show. What the Painted Stone needed was a launch or introduction on a large scale. Something that drew folks to the island, causing them to hop on a ferry and venture across the lake for a couple of hours. That would take something compelling. Something out of the ordinary that made people talk before and after the event.

Food was a given.

Music.

But there needed to be something. . .more. Something unexpected. Something fresh and unique.

"Hello?" The groggy voice had Jonathan conjuring up the image of an artist who stayed up too late with the party scene.

"Trevor Stone. Good morning."

"Morning?" There was a pause as if the phone was pulled away.

"Do I know you?"

Jonathan chuckled. "You probably don't remember me. I'm

Jonathan Covington."

"Sure. Dude on the dock with my sister every summer. She there now?"

"Something like that. Hey, we've got a project for you." Jonathan filled him in on the art. "Alanna figured out pretty quickly your mom wasn't painting."

"Hasn't for five years." A pause, maybe a yawn, before the young man continued. "Alanna's had her head buried in the city."

"Is there a reason your mom stopped?"

"Arthritis. She can't hold the paintbrush like she used to, but they still need the income."

"Alanna's determined to get your name on your paintings."

"Don Quixote."

The image of Alanna on a horse jousting windmills settled in front of Jonathan. It fit. Too well. "You have no idea."

"So what's this got to do with me?"

"We're going to have a launch party for you. Bring you into the light."

"You haven't told Mom." His voice was flat, like he'd already disengaged from the conversation.

"Not yet. We need to make sure the date works for you." The door banged open, and Jonathan turned toward it. Alanna stepped into his office, her cheeks flooded with color and a slightly wild look about her eyes. She marched up to him and started gesturing like a mad woman. "Can you hang on one second?"

He covered the mouthpiece and queried Alanna. "What?"

"You've got to help me. Now."

He looked from the phone to her. "Can it wait a few minutes?" Her eyes turned red, and she collapsed in a chair. "I'm trapped."

"Trevor, I'll call you back."

"Whatever."

Jonathan hung up the phone, never taking his gaze off Alanna's frantic features. "Fill me in."

"The partners just threatened my job."

"Okay."

"I have to be back in two weeks or find a new job."

"We'll get you back."

Tears cascaded down her cheeks.

"Alanna, what's wrong?"

"What if I don't want to go back but I can't stay?"

"What?"

"What if I'm trapped either way? Staying or leaving?" Her shoulders shuddered, and she turned away from him. "We have two weeks to wrap it up, and then I'm gone."

"Is that what you want?"

She seemed to find something within her, because she straightened and pushed to her feet. "It doesn't matter. I knew I shouldn't have come back. Now I just have to leave. Again."

He almost didn't hear the last word. Then he wondered if he just wished it. Maybe he'd imagined everything restarting between them. He shouldn't assume she felt anything for him. But as he studied her, he couldn't discount everything that had happened. It wasn't a mistake she'd come back to Mackinac. It wasn't a mistake they'd rediscovered each other.

He wouldn't let her walk away. Not this time.

"I was on the phone with Trevor."

She spun around. "Why?"

"Because you asked me to organize his launch party. I talk to the person to capture their personality. You should have told me he still has no drive."

"What?"

"Sounded like he was still in bed, and it's after eleven."

"Not everybody's as accomplished as you are."

Her sarcasm made him snort. "I'll remember that next time I need a shot of encouragement." He shoved his hands in his back pockets. It was either that or pull her to him for a good, long kiss. Maybe then she'd stop fighting him long enough to hear what he said. He studied her, the war of fire and ice in her eyes. Maybe self-control wasn't all it was cracked up to be. Maybe they both needed to lose their hold and see what happened when they let go.

That couldn't be easy for an attorney to do. The thought scared the spit from his mouth.

"Jonathan, I think we'd better leave it all alone."

"Not happening." He stepped closer, and she edged back. "You came back against your will because your family needed you. They still do. And so does Mr. Hoffmeister. Who'll fight to the truth if you don't?"

"Police Chief Ryan. That's his job."

"And when the case goes cold? And there's another Grady kind of case? When the island decides you were involved even if it's never proven?"

"That won't happen."

"Like it didn't for Trevor?" He knew it was low, but he had to get her attention.

She stepped away, back landing against the wall with a smack as her mouth opened and shut like a fish desperate for air. "You don't mean that."

Jonathan didn't say anything, letting his gaze speak for him. The truth had to be confronted. "Come on, Alanna. Let's see this through to the end."

"Two weeks. That's all the time we have." She spun and pulled the door open. "I have to get back home."

Her feet pounded down the stairs with finality. He started after her but stopped when his phone blared to life. With a sigh, he opened it. "Jonathan Covington."

"That artist is a genius."

"Edward?"

"Of course. Her work is perfect. Bonnie will love it. Promise she'll have a piece ready."

"You know artists . . . ."

"No time for temperament. Bonnie's treatment isn't going well. The doctor isn't making any promises, so this party has to be perfect from start to finish." Edward cleared his throat. "Perfection, Jonathan."

"Yes, sir." He didn't know how, but he'd have a Rachelle Stone original painting for Bonnie Morris if he had to watch her paint each and every stroke. Mrs. Stone needed the work and encouragement as much as Mrs. Morris needed the breath of light and life. "I'm glad you like her."

"It's perfect. Bonnie finished the invitation list last night. I'll send it in an hour. We may need extra rooms, but guests can overflow in Mackinaw City if needed. Family are the key folks for the island." A phone buzzed in the background. "Got to get that. Keep me posted."

"Will do."

Jonathan moved to his desk and made a few notes before calling Brendan. The need to have a perfect event increased with each conversation. He didn't see a love as rich and deep as the Morrises often. Instead, most people seemed to manage only a cheap counterfeit. Someday he'd have to ask Edward the secret.

At this point, his love life was enough of a morass he needed to get out of relationships. Maybe after he'd squared things with Jaclyn, he could relaunch things with Alanna. If her frame of mind when she left gave any indication, he'd have a challenge persuading her to stay. She seemed intent on going back to Grand Rapids. Maybe he just hadn't made his case yet.

A guy could hope.

## 33

The grill fired up with a sputter as Alanna twisted the knob.

The chicken breast looked well marinated, and she longed for a quick bite before tackling the mysteries surrounding her. Jonathan had left a couple of messages for Brendan. Alanna doubted he'd return the calls. He seemed as self-centered as ever.

Could the mess with the foundation books be the crux of the broken relationship between Mr. Hoffmeister and Mr. Tomkin? It had to be more than house plans. Surely that wouldn't destroy a decades-long friendship.

If the problem generated on Hoffmeister's watch but while Tomkins son was bookkeeper, it would certainly make finding a resolution tricky. Could that be the real reason Mr. Tomkin had asked her to look into the problem? He knew the source but didn't know how to confront his son? Without talking to Brendan, she had no idea what would motivate him to steal from the foundation.

Maybe Detective Bull had looked through Hoffmeister's

books by now. Alanna placed the chicken on the grill then found his card and dialed the number.

"Detective Bull."

"Hi, this is Alanna Stone."

"How can I help you?" His tone was ultra-formal.

"Have you looked through Mr. Hoffmeister's books yet?"

"Why?"

"I wondered if you could confirm that they were copies of the Mackinac Island Foundation's financial records."

"Why?"

"Because someone has embezzled from the foundation, and I think Mr. Hoffmeister was looking into it. It happened when he was president, and I think he felt a need to figure out who did it and why."

"That's a lot of theorizing. Any facts?"

"The embezzlement is evident in the foundation books. I don't know why someone's been doing it. But I think Mr. Tomkins son, Brendan, at least knew about it since he was the bookkeeper at the time."

"Isn't his father president of the foundation now?"

"Yes. And I think it's interesting that Mr. Tomkin hired a new bookkeeper when he took over."

"Thanks for the information."

"Are you going to do anything with it?"

"I'll follow up on it." After the usual good nights, he hung up. Maybe it was a wasted call, but at least he could work on it now if he chose. Bet he'd have a little more luck getting Brendan to cooperate.

~

THE DOOR SLAMMED open at Jonathan's cabin. As it bounced off the hinges, a little body propelled out and flew down the dock. Alanna watched, mouth agape.

"Dylan, get back here." Jaclyn's voice sounded panicked as Dylan's little legs kept pumping. "Dylan!"

Alanna wiped her hands on a dish towel, keeping her gaze locked on the boy.

The little body flew off the edge of the dock, and Alanna tore after him as Jaclyn screamed and Jonathan hurried out his door. Alanna kicked off her shoes and jumped after Dylan. The boy thrashed and sputtered, tears and pond water streaming down his face.

"Mommy!" Hiccups choked off his words before he sank under.

Alanna grabbed him and held his head above water. "I've got you."

Jaclyn reached for Dylan as Jonathan hefted him onto the dock. Alanna treaded water a moment before gathering her energy to pull onto the dock. She coughed and rolled to her side as she watched Jaclyn clutch Dylan to her.

"Don't ever do that again, Dylan! You scared Mommy."

"Jonathan doesn't love me."

A stricken look crossed Jonathan's face at the boy's whine. "Jaclyn..."

She turned from Jonathan and struggled to her feet with the dripping boy. "What did you expect? He's two years old. You're the only father he's known." Jaclyn swiped at tears then moved down the dock with her son wrapped tightly in her arms.

Smoke poured from Alanna's grill. There went dinner. She pushed to her feet and pulled limp hair from her eyes. She started to slip past Jonathan, who stood frozen. Now wasn't the time to ask him what resolution he'd reached with Jaclyn. Yet the anguish on his face made it hard to walk away and leave him in his pain. She continued to the house and pulled the chicken off the grill.

Jonathan followed her, sank into a chair on her patio, then launched back to his feet. "I need to make sure she gets Dylan home okay."

He hurried away. Any appetite she'd had disappeared with her dry clothes. A shiver whispered through her as she sat on the steps. Fish circles blipped across the pond, forming little punctuations on the evening.

Utter stillness settled over her like a suffocating blanket as she remained on the patio. Her mind worked over the details. A twist in time had placed Mr. Tomkin next to Mr. Hoffmeister. The two didn't get along, but Mr. Tomkin had a solid alibi. Still, there had to be more to the story. More that involved the embezzling Mr. Tomkin had figured out. She needed to visit him. Give him a chance to explain.

Alanna went inside, changed, and then called Patience. The woman agreed to come in and work the following afternoon. The books still sat on the dining room table. Alanna ran a hand over the cover. She'd let Detective Bull talk to Brendan. She'd focus on Brendan's dad.

People didn't go from Friday night buddies to enemies without cause. Could it have anything to do with Grady's death? Add in Brendan and the skirmish over Mr. Tomkins house plans, and many seeds for conflict grew. She had to believe Mr. Tomkin wouldn't have bought the plot next to Mr. Hoffmeister if the rift had already existed.

She almost picked up the phone to call Jonathan and see what he thought of her approach. She shook her head. She would update him after she talked to Mr. Tomkin. He had too much to do at work, especially if he wanted to plan something for Trevor. She needed to do her part and clear her brother—and herself.

Her thoughts turned back to the graduation party. Trevor and Grady had been the first in the water but weren't the only ones stupid enough to dive into the frigid lake. She still remembered how Trevor had trembled, his skin bluish as he stumbled back onto the rocky beach. He'd mumbled something as he fell against her.

*"Something happened, Alanna. Something bad." He shivered as he collapsed to the ground. Before she could clarify, a paramedic pushed her aside and went to work on Trevor.*

*"Stupid kid. He could have died like the other one."*

*Alanna had stared then glanced down the beach where a couple of paramedics pounded frantically on Grady's chest. The compressions didn't seem to work as they kept pumping. Then the life-flight helicopter landed.*

*Two or three more teen boys huddled in a group. Brendan Tomkin had been in the group along with Randy Raeder and Chuck Matthews. Despite witnessing the event, nobody ever talked about it.*

That's what bothered Alanna. To this day, a cloak of silence dominated Grady's death. It was as if everyone had gathered together and decided to leave it alone. What was past was history. Yet they'd all decided Trevor must have done something. Was it because he'd required the paramedics? Last time she checked, that didn't make one guilty. Yet she'd never brought the issue back up with Trevor. He'd seemed traumatized, and Mom had spent the summer keeping him close, relieved to have her baby, unlike Grady's mother.

She picked up the phone. Waited for Trevor to pick up.

"You think I'll come to some event."

"Hello to you, too, Trevor."

"Alanna, I can't do that." Her brother's voice shook. "I swore I'd never go back."

"Because of Grady."

"Of course."

"What if I find out what happened? Once and for all. Then you wouldn't have to wonder what people were thinking."

"I can't do that, sis."

"Sure you can." Alanna tapped the counter. "I just need to hear what happened from your perspective."

"I was stupid. I let the older guys talk me into a race. I've never felt so cold. I really should move to Florida or Arizona cause every winter when the cold slaps me in the face, I feel like I'm back in the water."

"Who else raced?"

Trevor swallowed. "Grady, Chuck, and Brendan. May have been another kid or two. But those were the ones I tried to keep up with. Chuck rammed into me when I turned around to come back. When I got oriented, that's when I saw Grady. I tried to help him, Alanna, I really did." His voice shuddered. "I always wonder if I'd said no to that stupid race, would Grady have been okay, or would he have still jumped in?"

THE NEXT AFTERNOON, as soon as Patience arrived, Alanna headed to the foundation. Laura sat at the front desk filing a nail. "Is Mr. Tomkin in?"

"Nope. He hightailed it out of here for lunch and hasn't been back." Laura leaned forward on her desk. "If you ask me, the man isn't himself."

"Really? Any reason?"

"Not that I can tell." The woman checked her fingers then tapped them on the desk. "Guess it doesn't matter. But if you need him, I'd call his cell. He's probably up at his land. He spends all his time there. Communing with the property or some such nonsense. If you ask me, he should build already. At this rate, he'll die before he builds."

"Thanks. I'll give him a call." As she left, her phone vibrated in her pocket. Pulling it out, she clicked it on. "Hello?"

"Hey, Alanna." Jonathan sounded excited. "Are you at the studio?"

"Nope. Running around. Having Patience is a great help."

"Patience. Yeah, always your strong suit."

"Hey." She must look like an idiot standing in the street wearing a huge smile at Jonathan's teasing.

"Just calling it like I see it." He paused, and his voice sobered. "How are you doing?"

"Okay. Headed out to talk to Tomkin if I can find him."

"Want company?"

"You've already spent too much time helping me plan a brilliant event for the Morrises. I'll be okay."

"Okay, I'll try Brendan again." He paused a moment. "Meet me on the dock tonight. We can try to catch Grandpappy."

She laughed. "Still think you can catch him?"

"If you're with me."

Warmth flooded her. "Thanks. See you tonight."

Next she called Tomkin on his cell. "I wondered if I could come see you."

"Any problems?"

"Just a couple questions."

"Ask away."

She frowned. It would be better if she could watch his response as he answered. "I promise I won't take much of your time. Patience is at the studio, so I'm free to come to you."

"All right. I'm up at my property."

A minute later, she hopped on her bike and started biking up the hills toward the Grand Hotel and then behind it toward Tomkins plot of land.

When she arrived, Mr. Tomkin stood facing the lake, even though she could barely make him out through the trees as they swayed in the wind. Alanna turned up the collar of her jacket then shoved her hands deep in her pockets as she approached. She couldn't help glancing around to see if anyone in a ski mask hid in the trees. It was ridiculous, but the events of her last trip still lingered.

"Mr. Tomkin?"

He didn't turn, fixed on something only he could see.

Alanna eased toward him. "Are you okay, sir?"

"Fine and dandy. Why wouldn't I be?"

"Your friend is dead."

"That's not the worst part." He turned toward her, a haunted expression twisting his features into a shadowed mask. His shoulders hunched forward, and he looked every one of his sixty-some years, bowed by events. "Don't you see?" His voice shook. "I started studying the land. Figuring out where to get the best views of the lake." He turned a bit as if seeing the view for the first time again. "And it hit me."

Alanna studied him, a wariness churning through her. Something wasn't right, but she couldn't tell what yet.

"Don't you see?" He pinned her with a stare. "Brendan lied." His Adam's apple bobbed. "He lied."

"What do you mean?"

"He couldn't have been where he said when Grady died. He knew things he couldn't know if he'd been on the shore. He said he only went in to help Grady to shore. I believed him. And no one ever questioned." He shook his head. "I didn't. Maybe I should have, but I didn't."

Alanna tried to picture the scene. Brendan had been in the water. Why lie about that? Especially since plenty had to see him in wet clothes. "What did Brendan say?"

"He insisted Grady and Trevor raced toward the lighthouse but got knocked around by the waves from a passing boat."

"There wasn't a boat." She was almost certain. She'd remember a detail like that. "But there were more boys in the water. At least five that I remember."

"Could you see from where you were on the beach?"

She closed her eyes and pictured the beach panorama. The large cropping of rocks still clustered around in a loose interpretation of Stonehenge. But the lighthouse was around the bend of the island. That was one reason she'd thought the boys were crazy to attempt the race in the frigid water. Only a fool or a teenage boy intent on proving something would launch a dare like that. Trevor had fallen into the easily led category. Grady had been out to prove something. And Brendan? As she looked at the scene, she realized he'd stared at Grady with an intensity that smoldered when his gaze slid to Ginger Hoffmeister. The look between Grady and Brendan had been layered with meaning.

"I see you're making the connections." Mr. Tomkins shoulders slumped, and he stared across the expanse at Lake Huron lapping the shore. "I don't know why I never considered that before I came up here, determined to build a house that would shame everyone else. Then I couldn't imagine looking at that scene every day. And Hoffmeister wouldn't let me back out of the contract."

"You wanted out?" No one had mentioned that.

"I couldn't stare at this scene day after day. Yet I'm still drawn here. Blasted contract."

"You had to honor it."

"Sure. But a lifetime of friendship should have made a difference." He shrugged. "I was wrong about a lot of things."

"Did you tell Mr. Hoffmeister why you wanted out?"

"No. . .but I think he figured it out. He got real quiet and uncomfortable around me."

"I think that could have more to do with the foundation embezzling."

"You figured that out, too?" He sighed. "I knew you would bulldog just like you used to with trig problems. I hate to think that Brendan would do something like that. But I couldn't let him continue with the books until I could prove who did it."

"Maybe someone else did it. I can't figure out his motive. Yes, he took money, but why?"

"There's a lot about my son I don't understand. I tried to give him the best of everything. Maybe all I did was create a monster who believes he's entitled to do whatever he wants."

"What are you going to do?" She could tell the police chief, but it would sound stronger coming from Mr. Tomkin. He'd need to tell the man why he thought Brendan was involved in Grady's death and the embezzling. While it didn't help her with Mr. Hoffmeister's murder, it would certainly help clear Trevor's name and go a long way toward bringing him into his own on Mackinac.

"Guess I'll find Chief Ryan. Fill him in. I don't suppose the statute of limitations has expired?"

"Ten years for murder for a juvenile."

"Then he'll be okay." The stiffness evaporated from his shoulders, and he stumbled.

"More than likely." Alanna didn't have the heart to point out that if the court treated him like an adult, then there was no statute of limitations. But if they treated him like the seventeen-year-old kid he was, then Grady's death had occurred too long ago. If it was an accident, then Brendan should have admitted what happened back then. Still, the truth now was better than an ongoing feast of lies. "Maybe you can talk Brendan into telling Chief Ryan everything."

"I don't know. It's been a long time to risk opening that back up to scrutiny."

Alanna stepped toward Tomkin, intensity pounding through her. "Brendan owes Trevor the truth. He deserved it eleven long years ago, and if you don't make your son do the right thing, so help me, I will make sure he doesn't have a choice. Do not tempt me."

"I don't know."

"You have until the studio show. If Brendan doesn't tell the truth before that, I'll make sure it's announced there in a way that nobody will forget." She studied him and then felt the wave of frustration begin to recede. "Good-bye, Mr. Tomkin."

When she left, Mr. Tomkin still stood staring across the lake toward Mackinaw City. The burden of lies and fear held him in place. She prayed he could convince Brendan to come clean. The town needed the truth to be revealed. Eleven years of secrets and shadows had layered to the point she wondered how to fully clear them away.

She hurried to Jonathan's office, eager to share her news, but took her time climbing the stairs, trying to quiet her breathing. The sound of voices in hushed conversation made her pause with her hand on the knob.

## 34

No matter how he switched his perspective, Jonathan couldn't see the connection between Mr. Hoffmeister and Grady Cadieux.

Both lived on the island.

Both died.

There had to be more than those two facts connecting them. Until then, he felt stymied to clear Trevor. And without that, no matter how wonderful the event, Trevor would still paint under a cloud with the other island residents.

Guess he needed to ask Tomkin a few questions. The man knew everything about the island and the people who lived here. Maybe he could fill in pieces for Jonathan. First, he'd try Brendan again. The guy must not have his phone with him, because every time he dialed, the call went straight to voice mail. Jonathan left another message.

He dialed the foundation next, and the phone rang to the point Jonathan expected more voice mail when someone picked up. "Hello?"

"Hi, Laura. Is Gerald there?"

"Nope."

Jonathan frowned when nothing more was said. "Any way to reach him?"

"I'm sure he's on his cell somewhere. Probably back up on his land staring at the lake. He likes doing that. Boy, he's popular today."

"Okay. Well, let him know Jonathan Covington called."

Her lazy voice waited a beat. "Any reason?"

"Had a question for him about Hoffmeister. And something from a while ago."

"Grady?" The surprise couldn't be hidden.

"Yep. Thanks, Laura." Jonathan hung up. Someone needed to talk to the woman about a professional phone presence. Trevor had given him a date, so the plans for that event were started. He might as well nail down the catering details while he waited for Brendan and Gerald to return his calls. Then he needed to finalize the details for the Morrises' dinner. The night had all the hallmarks of turning unforgettable. That was exactly what he wanted to accomplish for the special couple.

Time flew as he worked through details and firmed up instructions. His door pounded open, and he glanced up.

Brendan Tomkin stood over Jonathan, a grimace pasted on his mouth. "You couldn't keep your nose out of the past."

What was the guy talking about? He didn't know why Jonathan had asked him to call. "You didn't need to come by. A call would have worked."

"No. This is better face-to-face. See, everything was going fine until you and Alanna started poking around."

"Poking where?"

"The past. You'll regret that, Covington." Brendan slipped a gun from his pocket and held it pointed at Jonathan's gut. "Amazing how everything can be fine for years. Then you and Alanna start poking around. Then Ginger decides she needs more money. Can you believe she left me alone for almost two years? Two good years after all her harassing me for more money. I finally tell her I can't pay any more, and she agrees. Then her kid needs braces. . .at ten. . .and she decides I should pay for them." He snorted as if he expected Jonathan to understand.

"So what did you do?" Jonathan studied the gun. Too bad he knew nothing about weapons, preferring a pair of binoculars or rod and pole. Brendan held it steady, with too much competence for Jonathan. It looked like he enjoyed holding it. Knew how to make it work.

"The only thing a fine, upstanding citizen can do. Tell her daddy to get her back in line. It's not like I can sneak money like I did last time. My dad's not as sloppy as hers is. My old man wouldn't even let me play at bookkeeper like Hoffmeister did."

Jonathan scrambled to make the connections. Brendan embezzled money to pay off Ginger, who was blackmailing him? But blackmailing him why? That important piece of information eluded Jonathan.

Brendan took a step closer, but a movement caught Jonathan's attention. He glanced toward the door out the corner of his eye. A shadow moved across the frosted glass. He pulled his attention back to Brendan, not wanting the man to realize someone waited.

His cell phone sat in the top drawer of his desk. So far he hadn't had an opportunity to slip it out or try anything with the computer. Brendan stood vigilant, eyes locked on Jonathan and his movements. He had to try before something happened to him or the person on the other side of the door "So what did you tell her father?"

"The typical. Get your girl to leave me alone. Had him good and intimidated until your girlfriend interrupted our little powwow." He snarled. "Then things spun out of control."

So he killed Hoffmeister. Too bad Jonathan hadn't had his

phone recording that little confession. He raised his voice as he kept his gaze locked on Brendan. "What now?"

Brendan frowned and inched closer to the desk. The gun felt like it sat mere inches from Jonathan's nose. "I'm tired of talking. You need a lesson in keeping your mouth shut."

"Did it work for Ginger's father?"

"What?"

"The lesson?"

Brendan's lips twisted into a sardonic mask. "Yeah. He won't be talking again."

"Mr. Hoffmeister."

"Who else?"

Jonathan felt a tightening in his middle as if everything coiled in preparation for one stand. He wouldn't go down without a fight. If Brendan had killed Mr. Hoffmeister, nothing would stop him from killing again. If anything happened, he wanted Alanna to know he'd done his best to spread the truth. He balled his fists and pushed from the chair. Brendan stepped back and smiled without a drip of mirth.

"I wouldn't come any closer if I were you. See, I have the gun. You...don't."

"I'm okay with that." He whistled a moment, enjoying the flummoxed look that crossed Brendan's face. "How much did you pay Ginger?"

"Doesn't matter. She won't get another dime. I made sure of that."

"Was it close to twenty-five thousand? The amount that disappeared from the foundation's books?"

Confusion flashed across Brendan's face. "How do you know?"

"Your dad sent us on a fishing expedition. Didn't expect to catch you when we started, but it didn't take long to figure out you had the access and opportunity. What I haven't figured out is why. What did she have against you anyway?" Just keep him talking. That's all he could do with that gun pointed squarely at his gut.

"Said her kid was Grady's. And if she couldn't have a daddy, I could pay the equivalent of child support since I killed her child's daddy. Crazy woman thinks I killed Grady. Can't prove it, but I can't disprove it either. Everyone knows we weren't best friends."

"Why not turn you in if she thought you killed him?"

"Can't pay from jail. She decided this was better. And it worked until I decided I was done paying. If she wants more, she has to find a new sugar daddy. This bank is closed."

The door blew open, and Brendan spun toward it. Jonathan felt a sinking sensation when Alanna stepped into the room— alone. "What are you doing?" His voice trembled, and he couldn't hide it. Didn't she know to go for help rather than come alone? At least the cops would have weapons. She must have left all her common sense at home.

"Brendan Tomkin." She didn't seem surprised to see him. "I just had the most enlightening conversation with your daddy. He's got it all figured out."

"Doesn't matter." A band of sweat appeared on his forehead.

"I don't know. The truth has a way of clearing old misunderstandings."

Brendan's posture stiffened. Jonathan watched with growing concern. How could he get Alanna out of here before the man decided she was a better target? From her steady gaze, Jonathan had the uneasy sensation she wouldn't leave. Not easily. She might make this her last stand. If only he knew what Gerald had told her. Maybe something in that would move Brendan.

"Why didn't you say anything then, when it mattered?" Alanna took another step toward Brendan, and Jonathan shifted. He had to get between them.

Brendan spun toward him. "Stay where you are." The Beretta pivoted back and forth between Alanna and Jonathan. A faint tremble shook the chunky barrel. "Nothing was supposed to happen."

"But it did." Alanna's voice held steady.

"Trevor could have changed the story but didn't."

"True. And something I'll talk to him about. But you were the upperclassman. He was a sophomore. You should have manned up."

"I planned to, but then Grady died. I was headed to college on a scholarship. Trevor still had two years of high school. I was an adult. They weren't going to do anything to Trevor."

"Other than leave him under a cloud of suspicion." Alanna crossed her arms and looked down her nose at Brendan. "And you were this big hero." She shook her head. "You had us all fooled. Somehow you got people to forget you were in the water."

"I just revised details. Instead of swimming, I dove in to save Grady. Too bad it didn't work. I thought if people forgot, I'd be clean. Funny, I never felt clean." He studied the subcompact a moment then raised it toward her head. "Guess now I never will." Jonathan stepped away from the desk. "What do you think will happen if you kill us? You disappear and no one figures it out?"

He shrugged. "It's worked so far." He waved the gun back at Jonathan. "Get behind that desk."

"I don't like you threatening a woman. Your dispute's with me."

"Funny how it's people I like who keep getting hurt. And the one person I want to hurt is off-limits." He shook his head. "I'll take care of her, too. Before she gets braces out of me." He studied Jonathan. "It's nothing personal."

Alanna caught Jonathan's gaze and tried to communicate

something. Too bad they hadn't spent more time staring into each other's eyes on the dock, around the island, and in the fudge shops over ice cream. Maybe then he could interpret her message. Instead, he couldn't decipher what she wanted as she started making small, chopping motions with her chin. His eyes followed the direction of the motion. The window? He made a slight shrug. Hopefully she caught he didn't understand.

She rolled her eyes. He'd missed that annoying, but oh-so-Alanna action.

Brendan twisted slightly as if looking for something. Maybe he wouldn't find it. Jonathan prayed he wouldn't, since he had the distinct impression time slipped away. At some point, Brendan would run out of patience.

Grady's death might have happened, but Brendan could have avoided Mr. Hoffmeister's. Maybe he didn't care anymore. After so many deaths, did another couple even register?

Jonathan didn't want to find out.

Enough waiting to see what happened. He edged another step past the desk. Brendan spun toward him. "Get back."

Jonathan shook his head. "Nope."

"I've got the gun."

"You don't want to use it." Jonathan raised his hands in front of him.

Brendan lifted his arm, and the gun steadied. "Quite a gamble." He eyed Jonathan with a hard glint. Then he pivoted to Alanna and cocked the hammer. "Want to test your theory?"

"Nope." He held up three fingers, and Alanna closed her eyes slowly. He lowered one finger, and Brendan turned toward him. He dropped his hand and tapped his side once, twice. Alanna collapsed, and Jonathan launched at Brendan. The man hit the floor.

Jonathan landed on top of him.

Felt the barrel jam his side. Twisted.

He had to move. Now. Before the gun exploded.

Alanna screamed.

"Call. Help." Jonathan bit the words out.

Brendan jammed the gun deeper. "You should have left this alone."

Jonathan made a desperate lunge. A flame of fire blazed across him as his world exploded.

Jonathan groaned, ears ringing as he slumped to the side.

Alanna.

He had to help her. Couldn't protect her if the blackness won. He fought the heaviness. It pressed harder.

## 35

T he *monster shot Jonathan.*

The thought pounded her even as her ears rang and she braced for him to shoot her. She should move but felt frozen in place, shock warring with impotence.

Clutching her cell phone wouldn't shield her from a bullet.

Yet as Brendan lunged to his feet, Alanna stared at him, the blood splatter across his shirt choking ofF her oxygen. Jonathan's blood.

Her gaze strayed to where he lay still, so pale on the floor. Then bounced back to Brendan. This man wasn't anything like the kid she remembered from school. The arrogant yet insecure kid had disappeared. In his place stood a monster. A monster with a gun. The cold steel drew her attention. She had to get out. Now.

She fidgeted with the phone as she backed toward the door.

If she left, would Brendan follow her?

She couldn't help Jonathan if she waited. The touch screen made it impossible to dial 911 without looking.

"Nowhere to run, Alanna. Not this time." Brendan's face twisted into a mask. "You should have stayed away. Left everything alone. She wouldn't have come back if you hadn't got her thinking."

Alanna reached behind her and connected with the doorknob. Just twist it and fly. Fast as she could. Down the stairs. Without tripping. That's all. Praying that someone in the real-estate office below had called the police.

"Everybody forgot Grady. Not hard to do with a loser like him."

"Loser? Really? He had big plans."

"Never would have done anything with them."

"Like you did?" Alanna twisted the knob, freezing when it squeaked.

"I've had good jobs. Made good money when I wasn't paying her off. Then I got the great idea to help myself to some money. Seemed like the perfect way to have her dad pay her off."

She had to make it across the street. Someone would be at the police station. It wasn't even a block. Her gaze tripped down to Jonathan. The red had spread across his shoulder. She couldn't let him die without trying. This time she wouldn't stand on the side watching. This time she would act.

"You know what it's like? You get a wad of cash only to have some sniveling woman come along and take it. Over. And over. And over. Each time I'd get so mad. But I'd give her the money like a fool. Well, I'm done. Thanks to you. It ends here."

"Why would you pay, Brendan? What did you do that gave her that power?"

"Somehow she saw Grady and me wrestling."

"Trevor never said anything."

"Course not. The fool kid actually believed it was a race. The competition really was for Ginger. To think I thought that girl was someone I wanted. She deceived us all—and I'd decided Grady couldn't have her anymore."

Alanna nodded. She'd seen the hate in his eyes, just hadn't understood the reason. "Wrestling isn't murder."

"It is if you hold your opponent underwater. Then I hauled him back to shore. Trevor even thought he'd help. Just made it easier to question what he'd done."

Alanna choked back her anger at his callous words. Instead, she sipped in a breath. Now or never.

She spun open the door and ducked as she raced out. Hobbled over like a turtle, she hurried down the stairs.

A roar braced the air.

*Can't stop.*

She fought the urge to turn around. The thumping above gave every indication Brendan was on his way. She had to get out of the stairway before he entered or there'd be nothing to stop the bullet he'd fire from that awful gun.

Her foot caught, and she stumbled.

She yanked against the handrail and kept moving as her ankle throbbed. Where were the people from the real-estate office? She had to move. Finally, she reached the bottom step and crashed against the door as she felt a bullet whiz past.

She ducked and slammed outside.

The light blinded her, but she kept her feet pumping. She had to get lost in the crowd. But no one seemed nearby. She raced past the darkened real-estate office below Jonathan's and across the street, sidestepping a horse-drawn taxi.

The door opened again. She glanced over her shoulder long enough to confirm Brendan followed. Gulping in oxygen, she poured on speed as she darted around a couple kids on her way up Market to the police station. It felt like she slogged through a quagmire that sucked her down. She hurried past the normally serene scene. Tourists on bikes and horses stood in front of the bright buildings lined with beautiful flower boxes oblivious to the scene she'd just left. Finally, the two-story structure came into view. Now to get up the steps and inside before Brendan broke across the street and reached her.

A few more feet.

She scrambled toward the steps. Slipped on a step. Crashed to her knees. Scurried back up and threw open the door.

"Help!" She tried to scream the word, but it barely scratched out. "Gun. He's got a gun."

The lady behind the counter jerked to attention. Ginger's eyes widened. "Gun? Here?"

"He's right behind me." Alanna searched for someplace to hide. "You've got to move."

Ginger grabbed the phone and punched a couple buttons. "Chief, Alanna Stone claims someone's after her with a gun."

"Not anyone. Brendan Tomkin."

Ginger's face drained of color so fast that Alanna wondered if she'd faint. "I've got to hide."

"Yeah. He's not happy with you."

"Then why lead him here?" Ginger's gaze darted, and she pushed from the seat.

"I focused on surviving. He's already shot Jonathan." A tremble coursed through her. Jonathan needed help. She tapped 911 on her phone. "Need the ambulance." She slid behind the counter as she relayed the information. The island's nod to modern transportation was the ambulance. No horse-drawn vehicle when lives were at stake. She'd never been more grateful.

Chief Ryan stuck his head around the corner. "What did you do now, Alanna?"

"Please hurry. Jonathan was bleeding when I escaped." She kept the phone pressed to her ear as she turned to the chief. His hand rested on his gun, but she wished he had it out and ready. Where was Brendan? "Brendan Tomkin shot Jonathan. Threatened me." She gulped air.

"Where is he?"

"Right behind me." Maybe he wasn't dumb enough to follow her into the police station with a gun and fresh gun powder residue on his hands. Would they even test for that here? "Maybe he's headed to a ferry."

"Stay put." The chief edged down the hallway. "I'll slip out back. See if I spot him."

"Don't you need someone with you?"

"Not a civilian."

Before Alanna could beg, he disappeared. She turned to Ginger. "Braces?"

A blank expression covered the woman's face.

"There are better ways to get even than making him pay for your kid's braces."

"If you had kids, you'd understand how expensive those pieces of metal are."

"Seriously? Brendan shot Jonathan. Because you demanded more money." Alanna wanted to shake her. Might as well go for the jugular. "What about your dad?"

Ginger's expression remained blank. "What about him?"

"What if Brendan killed him because of you?"

"Then he'll go to jail for a long time." Ginger glanced away. "Maybe you killed him."

Alanna snorted. "Sure you believe that."

"The police looked at you. I heard it all."

"They had to, but your dad was alive when I left." Alanna did not want to have this conversation now. Not when every fiber of her heart wanted to make sure Jonathan was still alive. She felt woozy around the edges as his red-stained shirt filled her mind. Static filtered from her phone. Sliding to the floor, Alanna pulled the cell back to her ear.

"You there, Ms. Stone?"

"Yes, yes I am." Her breath caught as if she wore a corset.

"The ambulance is at the office. They'll transport him to the Mackinac Island Medical Center."

"Is he okay?" Was there any way that facility could handle a gunshot wound?

"We'll know soon. He's got to stabilize before he's transported to the hospital in the Upper Peninsula."

"So he'll be here for a bit? Until he's stabilized?" Her throat closed as the paramedic relayed the information. Nothing sounded good. "Thank you."

Alanna stood. Waiting here wouldn't work. She had to get to Jonathan. See for herself the doctors could save him.

Ginger skidded back. "What are you doing?"

"I can't sit here." Jonathan needed her. And she needed him.

"You can't leave. The chief doesn't have Brendan."

"That we know of." Alanna brushed past Ginger and around the corner. She tried to stay aware of whether Brendan might wait, but she wanted Jonathan. She eased open the door and saw a clear hallway. She hurried to the outside door. Taking a deep breath, she opened the door and poked her head out. No Brendan.

She slipped into the flow of foot traffic down Market up the few buildings to the clinic.

Shouts caught her attention. She slid behind a bench, hoping it would provide some protection.

"Brendan, stop right there." Chief Ryan thundered across the street. Brendan Tomkin kept running, gun held in his hand but pointed down. The officer swore and took off after him.

Alanna watched a moment. Brendan ran down an alley. If she remembered, that one dead-ended at the lake. Right next to the ferry. A taxi clopped through with a bell ringing. Good thing she didn't need that one. She'd gladly leave Brendan to the police. For now she had to get to the clinic.

After running the distance to the medical center, Alanna

rushed to the receptionist. "Can you tell me where Jonathan Covington is?" The woman studied her with a professional detachment. "Are you a family member?"

"No, a good friend."

"I'm sorry, I can't help you."

Alanna leaned on the counter. "Could you tell me if he's alive? Please?"

The woman shook her head, gray curls swaying. "I'm sorry, but I can't. You're welcome to wait in the lobby."

Alanna didn't want to wait. If she couldn't see him, was there anyone who could? He didn't have family on the island. By the time she could track someone down, surely they'd transport him elsewhere. A clinic this size couldn't provide too much in the way of trauma care.

Pacing, Alanna edged closer to the door that led to the ER beds. He had to be in one of those. As soon as the receptionist turned to the side to work on her computer while answering a phone question, Alanna eased through the doors. The serenity ended abruptly as a nurse bustled past her, arms loaded with IV bags.

"Push more fluids." A woman's voice held the calm command of one who knew what needed to happen.

A young man in a paramedic jacket stood against a wall, watching the action. The way his eyes darted, he didn't miss a thing happening behind the curtain. He pushed off the wall and headed her direction. "You are?"

"Alanna Stone. I placed the 911 call."

"You shouldn't be back here."

"I have to see Jonathan."

"You'll get in the way. Look, the best thing you can do is let the doc and nurses work their magic. Once they do, we'll transport him to the ferry and across to St. Ignace where another ambulance will meet us." He gently turned her and steered her back toward the lobby. "What's your number?"

Alanna rattled it off.

"I'll call when we leave. Now go wait by the docks."

"Which ferry will you use?"

"Whichever is slated to leave next. Getting him to a trauma hospital is our number one objective." He gave her a slight push. "Let us take care of him."

She was through the door, and when she turned around, the paramedic had already returned to his post. Alanna pulled out her cell, checked the volume, then sank onto a chair in the waiting room. Guess she'd have to pray.

Her thoughts refused to form coherent streams of prayers. Instead, it felt like she groaned as she begged God to spare Jonathan. She couldn't lose him. Not like this.

## 36

The next hours passed in a blur. Waiting for the ambulance.

Hurrying to purchase a ticket on the Star Line. Praying the ferry wouldn't leave without her, while also praying it wouldn't delay. Begging the ambulance driver for a ride. She could figure out how to get back to Mackinac later. For now she wanted to make sure hers was the first face Jonathan saw.

She'd sat in the waiting room outside surgery alone. Her phone in her hand, she couldn't think of anyone to call. Certainly not anyone who could reach her while it mattered. Mom and Dad were in Grand Rapids, and she wasn't sure where Trevor lived. Her few friends lived in Grand Rapids, too, and she didn't know how to reach Jonathan's family. She didn't even know who to call to find out. She might have called Mr. Hoffmeister, and Mr. Tomkin had enough to deal with, though he and Jonathan didn't seem that close.

Then she thought of Jaclyn. Surely she would want to know. And if not, she might know how to reach his parents.

What was her last name?

Reeder? No, Raeder.

Alanna dialed 411 then paused. Wasn't there anyone else she could try? The thought that Jaclyn might come, and Jonathan might want her, pierced Alanna.

Could she handle the reality Jonathan might not choose her?

What her future would look like without him? A dismal reflection of the past?

She breathed deeply then hit CALL. Her wants didn't matter as much as getting Jonathan's family here. A minute later, the automated system connected her to Jaclyn's phone. As it rang, Alanna prayed for wisdom and peace.

"Hello?" Jaclyn's voice sounded strained.

"Jaclyn? This is Alanna Stone."

Silence lengthened. "What do you want?"

"Jonathan's been shot. I don't know how to reach his family. Do you have a number?"

"What happened?" Jaclyn's voice rose. Alanna filled her in then asked for the number again. "I might have it."

"Thank you." Alanna waited as papers rustled.

"Try this." Jaclyn listed a string of numbers. "Is he okay?"

"I don't know. They haven't let me see him since I'm not family."

"Yet."

"What?"

"Never mind." The girl cleared her throat. "Tell him we'll pray for him. Hope everything goes well."

"You won't come up?"

"Not unless he asks for me. I don't want Dylan in that kind of environment. Too much like when his father died."

She didn't know as much about Jaclyn as she'd surmised. "Thanks for the number."

A minute later, she dialed the number Jaclyn had given her and left a voice mail asking for a return call. Then she stood and walked to the window. It looked over the parking lot, gray and metallic, but all she saw was Jonathan at his dock. He shouldn't be trapped in here. Instead, he should be outside bird watching or fishing. And if not that, then planning the most wonderful events for his clients. Would he do any of that again?

Or had he sacrificed himself so she could escape?

DARKNESS WEIGHTED HIM. Tugged him back. Cloaked him.

Jonathan tried to swim against its midnight pull but sagged against the heaviness.

He wanted to open his eyes but couldn't. A knife of pain sliced through his torso. The darkness offered relief. Maybe he should succumb. Give up. Let the darkness win.

A cool hand touched his forehead. It felt good, like when his mother used to care for him.

"You may stay five minutes. Then he'll need to rest." The words sounded distant. Remote.

Why five minutes? Why rest? Would that relieve the searing pain?

Jonathan fought to crack his eyelids. The brightness blinded him, and they fell shut.

A soft hand touched his. Held it lightly. "Jonathan, you made it through surgery. The doctor says you'll be okay. Really sore but okay. Your mom and dad are on the way."

Silence settled as Alanna stroked his hand.

"I'm so glad you didn't die. There's been too much death, and I need you, Jonathan. So much. Get better."

Something soft brushed his hand. Hair? Then he felt soft skin and dampness. Her cheek? A tear? He forced his eyes to open, and as they focused, he saw Alanna leaning against his hand. He licked his lips. So dry. So very dry. Tried to speak but croaked.

She sat up, studied him with large eyes. "Jonathan?"

He croaked again.

She pressed the nurse call button then jumped up and ran to the door. "He's awake. He's awake!"

A moment later, a woman in scrubs entered the room. He tried to focus on her, but the more he tried, the less defined she was until he faded back to blackness.

ALANNA LEFT Jonathan's side only when the nurse insisted. She wanted the rights of a wife to stay next to her man. To watch each time he inhaled. To assure herself he still lived.

Instead, she waited in the lobby for the occasional gift of a few minutes to watch his chest rise and fall. Other than those moments of awareness, Jonathan lay under a blanket of unconsciousness. The kind that held him tight in its grasp.

The day melted into night, and still she waited, unwilling to leave long enough to find a car. Nor willing to go back to the island and be separated from him by so many miles. Guess she'd sleep on the uncomfortable and overly firm couch, catnapping as best she could while she waited for his parents to arrive. They should be here anytime from their homes in Naubinway, Michigan. Until then she'd stay. Surely her motives had everything to do with helping them and nothing to do with her own need to see him five minutes every hour.

Her stomach growled, but she ignored it. The doors to the wing jolted open, and she glanced toward them. Patience and Earl Matthews strode through followed by Jaclyn without her small shadow.

Alanna swallowed. "What are you doing here?"

Patience reached her and pulled her into a motherly

embrace. "We're here to make sure you take care of yourself. And give you a ride back when you need one."

Alanna let herself sink into Patience's arms. "How did you know?"

"Jaclyn, of course. Once you called her, it didn't take too much time before she found me. We had to get organized, but here we are now. Earl keeps a car in St. Ignace, and we can head back or get a hotel room here. Either works for us."

"Jaclyn came with you?"

"Someone had to make sure she got here. She wanted to see Jonathan."

Alanna had hoped she'd stay away. She'd wanted the other day to truly mark the end of Jonathan's relationship with Jaclyn. Maybe she'd deluded herself. Maybe she and Jonathan were destined for nothing more than a friendship filled with enough attraction to drive any girl to distraction.

The kind of friendship she'd have to abandon again as soon as he was okay.

Staying and watching him with someone else would hurt too much. Especially now that she'd admitted she cared deeply for him.

"I'm glad she's here then. Jonathan's parents should arrive anytime, too." Alanna tried to smile as she managed not to choke on the words. Someday she might believe herself. For now she'd try to welcome Jaclyn and support her friend as he chose the other woman. Being single wasn't so bad. She'd done it a long time. Now that she'd remembered what could exist, she couldn't imagine settling for someone less than Jonathan. Her eyes clouded at the thought. She'd learn to be content.

She had to since the alternative seemed terrible.

Patience eyed her with skepticism. "You're just going to settle back?"

"What else can I do?"

"Fight for the man. He's had several weeks to watch you side by side. At least make him choose. Don't give up."

"Then why bring her here?"

A slow smile spread across Patience's cheeks. "Because you need to decide if you're fighting. If you're not, Jonathan needs someone. She's the other contender."

That sounded crass. Jonathan wasn't a prize to fight over, yet in a way that's how it felt.

"Miss Stone?"

Alanna looked up at the nurse who'd walked into the waiting area. "Yes?"

"Would you like five minutes?"

"Thank you." Alanna shot to her feet before anyone else could say anything and followed the nurse back to Jonathan's room. "Has there been any change?"

"No, but we don't expect him to be too alert yet. He endured some major surgery on his shoulder." The nurse glanced at her, calm exuding from her steady gaze. "He'll recover barring any complications. Just talk to him. Often that pulls people from their haze."

Alanna nodded then pushed into the room. It remained antiseptic and harsh. Her shoes squeaked against the linoleum, and she collapsed in the chair next to the sterile hospital bed. All the soft wall colors and paintings couldn't change the fact he lay in a bed, IV tubes extending from his hands, and monitors strapped across him. The Jonathan she knew overflowed with vitality. This person formed a shell of that man.

She touched his fingers, trying to avoid the IV. "Hey, Jonathan. They've let me back in."

No response, not even a twitch from his fingers.

Alanna sighed and stroked his knuckles. "Jaclyn's here. Patience and Earl brought her so she could be here. Maybe I should have let her come in this time, but I'm selfish. I wanted this time with you. Depending on what happens when you wake up, I might not have more time like this." Her voice hitched, and she forced herself to go on. "I love you, Jonathan. I know you won't remember this, but I had to tell you. I won't watch if you choose Jaclyn, but I won't get in your way. I don't have that right after all this time." She looked away, blinking back the tears flooding her vision. "Coming back wasn't easy, but it reminded me how much you mean to me. I'll always wonder what would have happened if I'd stayed. . .but I didn't."

She paused. Could she go on? Did it matter? He wouldn't remember anything she said, but she'd know.

Glancing up, she startled. His green eyes locked on hers.

Maybe he'd remember everything she'd said after all.

She swallowed, unsure whether she wanted to retract the words or risk the outcome. The only way to know what the future held was to pray he'd heard and would say something, anything, in response.

The nurse knocked on the door, and Alanna saw his parents. Time to leave, but his gaze held her hostage. She liked it. Oh, how she liked it. What if he chose Jaclyn? She prayed that wouldn't happen. That, instead, he'd hold her for life.

## 37

Jonathan tried to focus on the beautiful woman sitting in front of him. Alanna's soothing voice reached him deep in the blackness. He'd fought his way to the surface, heard her words. They resonated through him.

She loved him.

He'd wanted to say the words first. Now he could feel her pulling away. Attempting to hide. He couldn't let her, not with her tendency to run. If she left, chances were she'd never return. She'd leave for good.

Did she mean what she'd said?

How could he convince her the love wasn't one-sided? He wanted to sit and meet her on even footing, but the slightest tightening of his core sent waves of fire through his shoulder. He groaned, and she bolted upright.

"Don't move, Jonathan. Do you need the nurse?"

He wanted to shake his head but didn't dare move. Instead, he licked his lips. His mouth felt squeegeed clean of any moisture.

"Here." Alanna grabbed a mug of water from his bedside

table and held it to his mouth, pointing the straw toward him. "Take a sip."

He tested the action. Then swallowed as the cool liquid hit his throat. Heaven. He tested his voice. "Alanna."

The word sounded like a croak, weak and worn.

"Hey." A soft look settled over her face, reminding him so much of the girl he'd known all those summers ago. The one he'd fallen in love with. Planned to spend his life with. "Your parents are here. I should go."

"You're here."

"Of course."

"Brendan?"

"Chief Ryan chased him last I saw. I'll let the police get him."

"This time?"

"Yeah, this time." She chuckled softly then set down the mug. "Brendan should go away for a long time."

Jonathan frowned, trying to remember all that had happened. "He murdered?"

"Yes. It looks like he murdered Mr. Hoffmeister. Everything started with Grady's death. Then Ginger Hoffmeister blackmailed him off and on all these years. He started embezzling, and both his dad and Hoffmeister knew. Then I came back and started pushing to clear Trevor. If I hadn't, she might not have blackmailed Brendan again. With her position at the police station, she knew exactly what was going on with the investigation and used that knowledge to hound Brendan."

"Why kill Hoffmeister?"

"I don't think he meant to. He just wanted Ginger to stop. Thought her dad would stop her. But he killed Mr. Hoffmeister."

"What now?"

"Miss Stone." The nurse stepped into the room then smiled as her gaze landed on Jonathan. "Mr. Covington, your parents are eager to see you. Miss Stone, time to leave so they can come in." Jonathan wanted to protest, but the nurse's no-nonsense air made him doubt he'd be successful.

"We need to check your dressing and see how your wound looks."

Alanna stood. "Should I send Jaclyn in next time?"

"No." Jonathan watched her reaction as her eyes widened and a pink climbed her neck. "I just want you."

Hope blazed to life in her eyes. He would spend the rest of his days convincing her how very much she was the one he wanted. That was a task he'd gladly add to his planner and check off multiple times a day.

HE DIDN'T WANT to see Jaclyn?

Did that mean he'd made his decision?

She wanted to believe, but at the same time she needed to use caution. For all she knew the medication could affect Jonathan's decisions.

"Rest if you can, Jonathan. I'll send your folks in." She backed from the room and hurried to the waiting room.

Patience glanced up from a Colleen Coble novel as his parents moved into the ICU. "How is he?"

"Awake." The word tasted wonderful on her tongue. "He'll be okay."

Earl turned from the baseball game on the TV and chuckled. "Of course he will. It'll take more than a bullet to the shoulder to keep him down."

"Did he ask about me?" Jaclyn stood with her back to the window, a guarded expression protecting her.

"I asked if he wanted to see you at the next opportunity." How to say this in a way that protected them both in the event

Jonathan changed his mind? "We'll have to let the nurse tell us what he wants next time."

Patience glanced at her watch. "It's already after ten. How much longer do you plan to stay? We've probably missed the last ferry." Alanna shrugged. "I'll spend the night here."

"Don't you think you should get a good night's sleep?"

"I don't want to miss a chance to see him."

Patience nodded. "I understand. But his parents are here, and you'll do him more good rested. Someone's got to be with Dylan, too."

"He's okay tonight." Jaclyn chewed her lower lip as she studied Alanna. "I'll need to get back in the morning."

Earl turned back to his game, the faint sound of the announcers and crowd noise making a soft backdrop in the quiet room. Alanna watched Jaclyn from the corner of her eye. Would it be kinder to leave and give Jaclyn a chance to see Jonathan? Or would he expect her to stay and wonder where she went? Patience thought she should leave. Maybe the older woman was right.

Everything in Alanna wanted to stay. But something told her to leave. Give Jaclyn her chance.

Alanna sank onto the couch next to Patience. "Do you think we could find a hotel room?"

"Already have a reservation just down the road. We can leave the number with the nurse so they can let us know if anything changes with Jonathan. He'll still be sleepy after surgery. You probably won't get to see him much before morning anyway."

Alanna chewed her lower lip as she considered Jaclyn. "All right. Jaclyn, do you want to stay?"

A flash of hope slid across the woman's face. "Yes."

"Then we'll be back in the morning. Tell Jonathan I'll return." Hopefully he'd still want to see her. If a few hours' absence changed the direction of his feelings, he wasn't hers anyway. Better find out now rather than later after she'd dared to hope.

The next morning, Earl dropped her off at the door. "You sure you don't want us to stay?"

"No. I'll get a ride to the ferry when it's time."

"All right. Tell Jaclyn to call by ten if she'd like a ride back."

"Thanks, Earl." Alanna slipped into the hospital, feeling good after a decent night's rest and a shower. Her clothes might be the same, but she felt clean. Her stomach fluttered as the elevator carried her to the trauma floor. How would Jonathan look this morning?

The doors opened, and the antiseptic smell slapped her in the face. Her stomach clenched in rebellion, and she swallowed to keep the bile down.

The nurse at the station looked up, a question in her expression. "Can I help you?"

"I'm here to see Jonathan Covington."

"Are you on his list?"

"I was last night."

The woman punched a few buttons on the keyboard then studied the screen. "Hmm, what did you say your name was?"

"Alanna Stone."

More punching ensued, and then the nurse turned to her. "I don't see you in his record."

"Could you buzz his room?"

"I'll walk down there. If he's sleeping, I don't want to wake him." Another nurse approached. "Would you sit here while I check a patient?"

The nurse nodded and slid in front of the bank of monitors. Alanna paced in front of the nurses' station as she waited. Finally, the first nurse returned.

"I'm sorry, but the patient is asleep. Someone else is with him and says he doesn't want to be disturbed."

Alanna nodded, her heart falling. She reached into her bag and pulled out a notebook. "Can I leave a note for him?"

"Sure."

She scribbled a quick page then folded it and gave it to the nurse. "Thank you."

A moment later, she stood in the waiting room. Should she stay? Leave? Would the note even reach Jonathan?

BY EARLY AFTERNOON, Jonathan had tired of Jaclyn's presence. She talked almost nonstop with his mother, and he missed the quiet. Anytime he asked where Alanna was, Jaclyn made some excuse for her. At one point, the nurse brought in a note, but Jaclyn took it before Jonathan could read it. The glimpse he caught made him think Alanna had written it, but Jaclyn tucked it in her purse before he could do anything.

Being tied down with all these wires and IV lines, not to mention the never-ending burning in his shoulder, was enough to drive him crazy. He wanted his small cabin and some privacy. The ability to tell people to leave sounded wonderful. Especially when Jaclyn had somehow convinced the nurses he wanted her there—all the time.

"Where's Dylan?"

She looked away from the TV where she'd clicked through channels endlessly. Didn't she get nothing was on daytime TV, no matter how many times you surfed? Nothing still equaled nothing.

"He's with a friend."

Jonathan couldn't imagine whom she'd left the boy with overnight. He was the only one who'd ever kept him other than the daycare. "And your job?"

"Someone's covering the shift."

"Hmm."

A doctor entered the room. "Let's check how you're doing today, Mr. Covington."

"Do you mind?" Jonathan glanced at Jaclyn, and color tinged her cheeks. She slid from the room.

As the doctor rewrapped his bandages, Jonathan held his breath. The pain punched him but had lost a bit of its edge. "Any chance you could keep her from coming back?"

The doctor studied him. "If that's what you want, absolutely."

"The gal I want here isn't. I'll recover faster without Jaclyn hovering."

A knowing grin crossed the doctor's face before he wiped it off. "Glad to get you some peace and quiet."

"When will I get to go home?"

"Do you have anyone to take care of you?"

"My parents or a friend."

The doctor eyed him. "Assuming you stay infection free, maybe in a couple days we can transport you home. I can confer with the doctor at the island's medical center. Make sure she feels comfortable continuing your care."

"Thanks."

As soon as the doctor left, Jonathan pulled out his cell and started dialing. He wanted out of this prison the moment it was possible. Anything was better than one extra day lying here.

He had too many events to wrap up and a woman's heart to win.

## 38

R achelle Stone should arrive any minute.

Jonathan had been surprised she agreed to pick him up, but he couldn't thank her enough for freeing him from the prison of his hospital room. His parents had planned to get him settled at home when his uncle had a stroke. They'd left only when he'd insisted his uncle needed more help than he did. All he wanted was his cabin and being left alone. He'd considered calling Alanna but decided not to. He didn't want to see her again until he was at home in real clothes. The nurses and physical therapists delighted in torturing him. He tried to mask the pain. Reality remained that his shoulder felt like someone routinely speared him.

Now after three days inside the four walls of this room, he wanted his cabin. At least there he could sit on his deck, fire up his computer for a few minutes, and make sure the details of the Morrises' event still held together.

And now that Brendan had been arrested for involuntary manslaughter, murder, and attempted murder, he could throw his efforts into finalizing Trevor's official debut at the studio.

Rachelle sailed into the room, a Kentucky Derby-worthy hat

resting on her sophisticated bob. He smiled at the image of Alanna looking like her in twenty years.

Now to convince Alanna he meant forever.

That was the next item on his agenda. Two successful events and one heart won. Not necessarily in that order.

"You don't look too much worse for wear."

"You haven't seen my stitches."

Rachelle held up a hand. "That's all right. I appreciate the way you protected Alanna. More than you know. But I don't need to see the evidence of your bravery."

Jonathan wished he had some dark corner to hide as heat flooded his face. Maybe he could blame the closed air in the room.

"So where are your things?"

"Don't have any. It didn't cross my mind before Mom and Dad had to leave."

"Why didn't you say anything?" She sighed with a motherly expression. "I'll get you some clothes." After writing down his sizes, she left.

Jonathan barely had time to wonder if Alanna would be glad to see her before Rachelle returned with a bag of undergarments, button-up shirts, and jeans.

"I figured you wouldn't want anything that pulled over your head."

"Thanks." Ten minutes later, he'd changed and finished checking out.

The drive to St. Ignace and the ferry passed in silence, only the strains of some classical symphony filling the car. Then Rachelle followed him onto the ferry.

"Pushing things a bit." There was no question in her statement.

"I'll be good as soon as I'm home."

"Sure you will."

Silence settled again as the ferry pulled away from the dock and picked up speed. The lake spray threatened to soak him as the ferry worked across the water. As soon as they reached the dock on Mackinac Island, Rachelle edged him to a bench and forced him down. "I'll find a taxi. No way you're walking or biking home."

The island felt the same—abuzz with summer activity, even as he saw it tinged with tragedy. No one had mentioned Ginger yet. Would she pay for her part in the crime spree?

Rachelle came back and dragged him to the taxi. Then she got him settled in his cabin. "I'll go check on Alanna. Send her here."

"You don't need to do that."

She gave him a knowing smile. "I'm not the Stone you want babysitting you. Besides, I need to work at the studio. I have a painting to finish for your client."

"So you took the commission? Is your arthritis allowing you to paint?"

"The doctor has me on a medicine that's helping. I figured after the ways I let you and Alanna down, the least I could do was help him." She fiddled with her purse strap. "I have a few things to do for this party you've planned for Trevor, too." She turned to the door then back. "Thank you for all you're doing for him. It'll be nice to see his name on his paintings."

Before he could say anything, she disappeared through the door. It was a start. The woman might not admit what she'd done by putting her name on Trevor's paintings was wrong. But she could start fresh now with the painting for Bonnie.

He couldn't wait to see what she created. Somehow he knew she would craft the perfect image.

Now he just needed to do the same for Lanna.

It was past time for that.

ALANNA DUSTED THE CANVASES. She couldn't see a speck of dust, not surprising since she'd circled the studio at least twice a day since Jonathan was shot. Her body refused to sit still, and she had nothing left to investigate. The only details to wrap up related to Trevor's debut. She didn't know enough about what was left to do without consulting Jonathan, and she couldn't do that while he remained in the hospital.

Everything seemed squared away. Trevor would move up for the balance of the summer with Patience helping him. Mom had indicated she could slip up here a couple of times a month now that Dad seemed on the mend.

They didn't need her. She needed to decide if she could handle a return to her old life in Grand Rapids. The thought sapped her energy; yet if nothing changed with Jonathan, she had no reason to stay. She didn't want to leave, but she couldn't remain, not like this.

The feathers tickled another canvas, and she finished.

Now what? The studio sparkled. Everything was ready for next Saturday's event.

The bell sounded, and Alanna turned. "Mom? What are you doing here?"

"Just deposited Jonathan at his cabin."

The words struck her like a blow. Jonathan hadn't called her, but had asked her mom for help? Ouch. "Are you staying long?"

"Through Trevor's party. Your aunt Mary is staying with your father. She'll bring him up for the party if he's well enough. So I'm here to paint and send you to the house. Jonathan didn't want me babysitting him. I have a feeling you're much more what he had in mind."

"Or Jaclyn."

"Who?" Mom wrinkled her nose. "That woman? I don't

think so. Go gather your things and scoot. The day's still young. And I have lots of painting to do." Mom made a shooing motion with her hands, and Alanna obeyed.

Jonathan was at his cabin. That must be good.

She hurried home but stalled when she saw a bike outside his door. Who could that be?

A woman stepped out of the cabin. "I'll be back tomorrow. But all looks good for now. Don't push too hard, and get some help. You may be home, but if you're not careful, we'll have to transport you right back to the hospital."

"Thanks." Jonathan's voice reached her, though she couldn't see him.

The woman hopped on the bike and pedaled past Alanna without a wave. She'd have to ask Jonathan, but right now she just wanted to see him. Alanna hiked to Jonathan's door and dismounted. After leaning the bike against the wall, she knocked and entered. "Jonathan?"

He lay on the couch, a pillow shoved beneath his head and another at his side. "Lanna."

"Are you okay?"

"I will be. Glad to be home. Your mom sent you?"

"She thought you'd rather have me."

He grinned, which only emphasized the purple bruises under his eyes. "She's pretty insightful."

His laptop beeped, and she frowned at him. "What are you doing?"

"Shooting out a few e-mails about Trevor's event and the Morrises' party."

"Aren't you supposed to rest?"

"Sure, but this is resting. Anyway, if I didn't do it, I'd lay here and worry. That wouldn't help me heal." He patted the couch next to him. "Come here."

She edged toward him but decided the couch was too

narrow for two. Especially when one had a wound. She grabbed the kitchen chair and set it next to him. "What can I do?"

"Tell me why you didn't come see me again at the hospital."

She looked away. Would he understand? "I wasn't sure where things stood, so I came back to the island. I knew I'd see you. But I had to figure us out."

"Did you?" He studied her, his intensity almost knocking her from the chair. "Did you figure us out?"

"Not really." She sucked in a breath and studied her hands. "That's not true." She risked looking in his eyes again. "Jonathan, I can't imagine my life without you."

"That's what I remembered."

"What?" Did he somehow remember what she'd said? She'd die of embarrassment.

"I heard words I've wanted to tell you." He reached up to stroke her cheek, and she leaned closer, tugged by the electricity of his touch. "I love you, Alanna. I've loved you since all those times out there on that dock. I loved you when you disappeared, but this time I won't let you leave. Not without a promise to come back. Again. And again. And again."

"Jonathan."

He pressed a finger against her mouth, stilling further words. "Alanna, I've told Jaclyn several times we aren't going anywhere. I'm sorry she keeps getting in the way, but since you came back, I've realized she's not the woman for me. Not when the only woman I've really loved is sitting in front of me."

Alanna swallowed hard. It felt like a golf ball had lodged in her throat. He'd just said the words she longed to hear. They felt like a balm to her heart and soothed her questions.

"What about Dylan?"

A frown crept across Jonathan's handsome features. "I'll miss him. But I couldn't stay with Jaclyn just for him. It's not fair to either of them." He took her hand and tugged her close. "Tell me you feel the same way."

She braced against the couch, trying not to jar him as he tugged her closer still. She felt his breath against her cheek, closed her eyes, and inhaled.

In that moment, she could imagine a future with him. A future that involved the island and building a life together. Moisture flooded her eyes at the realization that she could give up everything in Grand Rapids without a second thought. Nothing there mattered—not in the light of his love.

"Say something... You're making me nervous."

She swiped at her eyes and then laughed, a watery sound. "I love you, too, Jonathan. Always have."

His face lit from the inside, and he grinned. "Come here, Lanna." His lips settled on hers in the perfect kiss.

## 39

The next Saturday morning, Alanna woke early, started running, and didn't stop even as people gathered at the Painted Stone. Excitement thrummed through her, though it was lined with an edge of tension. Would people respond to Trevor? Would all the pain be worth the end result?

Jonathan had insisted on coming, but she'd made Mom promise not to collect him until the last possible moment. His shoulder didn't seem to bother him much. Still she worried even though he deserved to see the fruits of his labor.

She touched her lips, still warm from the kiss they'd shared last night. In the days since Jonathan returned to Mackinac, their relationship had accelerated from a reborn friendship to dreams of what the future held. Tomorrow she could bask in that. Today she would celebrate Trevor and his art.

The studio looked amazing. She'd accented his largest paintings with spotlights and cards explaining the setting and story behind each painting. Jonathan had postcards made of Trevor's best work and grouped them in packets for the guests who attended. She'd spent two nights at his cabin wrapping the packets in raffia. Now that she'd collected them in baskets, the overall effect made the time worth it.

One of Jonathan's contacts had made the hors d'oeuvres. A long banquet table stood on each side of the room, sheathed in creamy white tablecloths and loaded with tiers of finger foods. Quiche, cocktail shrimp, and things she couldn't name filled one table, while the other had all kinds of sweets. She couldn't wait to try a pint-sized fruit tart, popping one in her mouth as she walked past.

A crystal punch bowl sat on a round table in one corner, rows of punch cups surrounding the bowl. The peach liquid looked great and smelled even better.

Everything looked ready. She just needed the guest of honor. Trevor had assured her he'd arrive at least an hour early. Alanna glanced at her watch again. If he walked through the door that instant, he'd only arrive ten minutes early. She pulled out her phone and dialed his number. It went straight to voice mail. It would take all her restraint not to throttle him the moment she saw him.

She fought the urge to chew her fingernails for the first time since middle school.

Patience sailed toward her, an elegant dress sheathing her body. "Where's your mom?"

"Collecting Jonathan."

"And Trevor?" Patience looked around. "I haven't missed him, have I?"

"No. My brother is delinquent."

Patience clucked. "He can't control everything."

"He can be on time." Alanna glanced toward the door as another group entered. Jonathan brought up the rear. He looked so good in khakis and a button-down shirt, his left arm resting in a sling. She didn't fight the smile as he worked toward her.

"Quite a crowd you've got here, young lady."

She nodded. "Someone amazing organized this event."

Patience chuckled. "You two act like you're back in school. I'll leave you to make eyes at each other."

Jonathan grinned then leaned down to brush her lips with a kiss. She leaned gently into him, thanking God for bringing them together. Even the frustrating moments didn't seem so daunting with Jonathan next to her.

Reluctantly, Alanna stepped back. "I've got a chair tucked behind the counter for you."

"Putting me to work?"

"Of course." She grinned up at him then sobered. "Thank you, Jonathan. This could be an amazing event—especially if Trevor graces us with his presence."

"He will." Mom slid an arm around Alanna's shoulder. "He called an hour ago to say he was on his way but running late." Mom straightened the pink silk scarf at her throat. "You kids have done quite a job. Thank you."

Alanna cleared her throat, trying to push words around the sudden lump. "You're welcome."

"And if you ever try something as stupid as chasing down a murderer again, I may kill you myself. The gray hairs I have thanks to you."

Alanna rolled her eyes then caught Jonathan's gaze. His snicker pulled an answering one from her. She raised her hand as if on the stand. "I swear I will never do anything like that again. Once was more than enough."

"I would certainly hope so." Mom turned to Jonathan. "Jonathan?"

"I can't promise I'll never do it. If anything similar happens, I won't back down."

It was Mom's turn to roll her eyes. And she wondered why Alanna did it. "Well, I'm going to check on my painting then mingle with all these people you've drawn. Maybe even sell some art."

Alanna smiled as another group came in. Even if Trevor bailed, she could sell his art. Only the island's long-term residents cared, and now they knew the truth. Truth had come at a cost, and she prayed Trevor would accept his freedom and steward it.

An arm slipped around her waist, and she startled and spun around. "Trevor Stone!"

"Hey, sis. So all of this is for little ole me?"

"Yes, though I'm ready to strangle you. Where have you been?"

"Getting Dad." Trevor pointed toward the hall where a wheelchair sat. "It took longer to check him out of the rehabilitation hospital than I planned."

"Dad." The word whispered from her.

"Go tell him hi." Trevor glanced around the room. "Guess I'd better say hello to everyone."

"Yep. And sell lots of paintings. We need to sell another three or four this month."

He saluted. "Yes, ma'am."

Alanna watched Trevor as he moved around the room, stopping to say a word to each group. He could make this work. He seemed to have found a natural ease as he talked to everybody.

Jonathan nodded toward the hall. "I know your dad is eager to make sure you're okay."

Alanna eased down the hallway then knelt beside the wheelchair. "Hi, Daddy."

"Lanna." A slow grin spread across his face. "You're okay."

"Yes, sir. God kept me safe through everything."

"You shouldn't tempt Him."

"I didn't mean to. Things kind of spiraled."

"How's Jonathan?" The change in topic caught her, but one

look into her daddy's eyes confirmed he wanted the honest answer.

"Good, I think." She sighed. "I'm not sure I can go back to Grand Rapids. The thought of separating kills me."

"Long distance can work."

"But I don't want it to. Not sure I can live here though."

"You'll figure it out." His assurance settled over her, and she breathed it in. "Get me into the studio. I want to see Trevor's moment."

"He's doing well, Daddy."

"Of course. He's a Stone, isn't he?"

Soon the regulars greeted her father like a returning hero. In some ways he was, even as his road to full recovery still had many steps.

Servers in their white shirts and black pants flowed seamlessly among the guests, refilling the hors d'oeuvres and punch. Alanna ended up sitting next to Jonathan at the cash register ringing up sales while Jonathan handed out postcards. Her family members took care of welcoming one and all.

Hours later the last guest left, and she studied Jonathan. He'd held up well, but she didn't want to push him too much. "Ready to head home?"

"Sure." He watched the waitstaff tear down the tables. "We did it."

"Yes, we did." Satisfaction filled her. "Thank you."

He took her hand, rubbing his thumb over her knuckles. "You're welcome. Now on to the other event that matters."

TWO WEEKS LATER, THE MORRISES' guests started arriving by ferry and settling into their rooms at a couple of bed-and-breakfasts. Jonathan felt almost completely recovered, and it was a good thing. He'd already made numerous trips between the sites to make sure everything was ready for the guests.

Nothing would mar this event. Not if he had anything to do with it.

Bonnie looked thin but serene as Edward pushed her wheelchair up the hill toward the fort. Edward grunted and pushed harder. "Why did I pick this location? Remind me."

Jonathan laughed. "Because Bonnie loved the view. Next time let the taxi bring you around the backside of Fort Mackinac. It's easier from there."

"Next time."

A large tent sat in the open field to the side of the fort. Rows of tables and chairs filled the tent, and he'd arranged for a multitude of games to be brought from the fort for the younger guests to play. Already he could see some playing with the wooden hoops and sticks and others with the horseshoes.

The aroma of barbecue filtered from the pit the caterer had installed. The spicy scent made Jonathan's stomach rumble in anticipation. He couldn't wait to have a couple of sandwiches once everyone had been served.

This was exactly the type of event Edward had ordered. And based on the delighted grins on his and his wife's faces, they planned to make wonderful memories with their family and friends as they celebrated a lifetime of love.

Maybe it really was possible to have a love of a lifetime. One laced with both joy and pain. One only had to look at the Morrises to believe it just might happen.

Edward whistled. "Lookie there."

Jonathan turned to follow his gaze. His heart stuttered in his chest as Alanna approached. She looked amazing in a flowing sundress that revealed narrow ankles and athletic calves. The sweater knotted around her shoulders was the only nod to the bite in the breeze on an end-of-June day on the island. The bright flowers on the gauzy material were perfect against the blue sky. He couldn't tear his gaze from her as she approached.

She took Bonnie's hand. "Thanks so much for inviting me."

Bonnie smiled. "Delighted to have you. The more the merrier in my opinion."

"That's my girl." Edward frowned though his voice was filled with affection. "She always said the only good party is one overflowing with friends and acquaintances."

"It's a great way to live." Alanna turned to Jonathan. "I'm sure you're busy. . ."

Bonnie made a shooing motion. "Not at the moment. Edward will call if we need anything. Enjoy all your hard work."

Jonathan met Edward's gaze. They paid him too much to have him disappear as the events got under way. Edward shrugged and patted his pocket. "I'll call."

"Yes, sir."

Alanna slipped her hand into his, and they strolled toward the fort. When they reached a bench, he tugged her down. It felt so right to have her hand nestled in his, like an empty piece of him had found its home.

Children ran in wild circles while adults worked through the food line. Edward and Bonnie waited at the head of the line, welcoming everyone as if they stood in a receiving line at the wedding. The legacy of their lifetime together was clear from the simple touches and unspoken communication to the number of people who had come to the island to celebrate them.

That's what he wanted. A life well lived in forty years. One lived with the woman on the bench next to him.

"What are you thinking?"

Her quiet words pulled him to her. Did he dare say? He took in her smooth skin, direct gaze, and the slight upturn of her lips. He'd never been more certain of anything in his life.

He might be certain, but when he opened his mouth, nothing escaped. It was like a block existed between his thoughts and his vocal cords.

"Must be serious." She teased.

"Alanna, I want to spend the rest of my life with you." The words came out in a rush, blurted from a full heart.

"Jonathan . . . " Caution replaced the teasing light.

"Listen. . . When you returned this summer, everything that existed between us erupted to life. I know it took a few weeks for me to sort through everything with Jaclyn, but I've never loved anyone like I love you, Alanna. You make my days complete. You make me complete, a better person than I ever was without you. I love you, Alanna. For always."

He stopped as she started biting her lower lip. Tears leaked from her eyes, and panic spiked through him. "Don't cry, Alanna. This was supposed to make you happy."

"I am." The words were choked. Then a smile crested on her face, like the sun breaking through the clouds after the long Mackinac Island winter. "I love you, too, Jonathan."

# EPILOGUE

*our weeks later*

Alanna fidgeted in front of the mirror in her bedroom. The white gown was simple, its A-line design skimming her waist to balloon over her hips before it settled mid-calf. She wore a hat rather than a veil. After everything they'd endured, she didn't want anything coming between her and Jonathan.

They'd waited eleven long years to find each other and rediscover their love. Now that they had, she'd insisted on a quick wedding. She was ready to begin life as Mrs. Jonathan Covington.

Mom bustled into the room, Patience Matthews entering behind her. Mom stilled and placed a hand on her chest. "Alanna, you look beautiful."

"Thanks, Mom." The rising tide of excitement crested over her. It wouldn't be much longer now. Soon. . .soon.

Patience extended the small bouquet she held. "I had quite the time finding lilacs but got them shipped in. Too bad you couldn't get married during the lilac festival. That would have made things simpler."

Alanna laughed, remembering how uncertain everything had been at the beginning of the season when the lilac festival had flooded the island with color. "These are perfect." The heady aroma of lilacs, a mix of white and lavender blooms, was better than any perfume she could wear.

Everything was perfect. Trevor had settled back into life on Mackinac. He'd even offered art lessons on various Saturdays. So far the classes were small, but the idea seemed to catch on. By next summer, people would have to sign up in advance to get guidance from the great Trevor Stone. He'd started painting a couple days a week in front of the studio. It drew a crowd and pulled interested buyers into the store.

Dad was on the mend. He and Mom planned to move back to the island in time for the winter. Why they'd want to do that she wasn't sure, but he insisted nothing could happen the medical center on the island couldn't handle. Based on what she'd seen when Brendan shot Jonathan, he was right.

Her future wasn't quite so settled. She'd returned to Grand Rapids long enough to move her things to storage and reclaim Midnight. The cat seemed to enjoy sitting on the porch and stalking birds, but Alanna needed more than that. Maybe she'd open a small practice or work with Jonathan, but for now she continued to run the studio while she prayed about what God wanted her to do.

"Come on, Alanna. Dad's downstairs."

Alanna nodded. Her future plans could wait. Right now she wanted to become Mrs. Covington as quickly as possible.

She took one more glance in the mirror, excitement meeting her gaze.

Patience and Mom each grabbed an arm and eased her toward the door. She took a last glance around the room. Tonight she'd move into Jonathan's cabin next door. Even if it was small, that's where they decided to begin their lives together. It would be a great place to start their married life together. When they reached the downstairs, Dad sat in his wheelchair. Trevor stood behind him wearing a suit, ready to push Dad.

The pastor and Jonathan already stood outside on the dock.

A small group of close friends and family waited in chairs. In a twist, Jonathan had planned the event, pulling together the perfect ceremony from his web of contacts.

"Are you ready?" Dad smiled up at her.

"Yes. Yes, I am."

"Good. It's time you married this man."

"Dad!"

He chuckled, but a serious look settled in his gaze. "I have no doubt he's the man for you. You'll have a good life, though nobody guarantees easy."

"Amen to that," Mom stage-whispered.

Patience chuckled then scooted around the group. "I'm off to claim my seat." She kissed Alanna. "Best wishes, dear."

"Thank you."

Mom kissed her cheek next. "I'll let that anxious groom of yours know it's almost time. Love you."

"Love you, too." Alanna loved the way God was rebuilding their relationship. He was so good to her.

Alanna sucked in a steadying breath as her daddy reached up. "Ready?"

"Yes, sir."

Trevor slowly pushed the wheelchair down the temporary path workers had installed. Alanna stalled when her gaze collided with Jonathan's. There might be rows of chairs between them, but at the arbor at the end of the dock, he was locked on her. She couldn't tear her gaze from his even if she wanted to.

In that moment, she thanked God for bringing her home.

For showing her it was time to stop running from the truth, and for saving this man for her.

She had all she wanted and more for a lifetime of love.

# DEADLY EXPOSURE

*Chapter One*

Dani Richards barely noticed where the usher pointed as she turned to take Aunt Jayne's arm but groped emptiness. Dani spun in a circle, searching for her. "Aunt Jayne?"

"She went that way, ma'am."

Dani nodded at the usher and hurried across the plush red carpet toward the boxes. She slipped into their box, but it remained empty. Then she heard a raised voice from the adjoining box. She darted to it, parted the curtain and pushed through. Aunt Jayne relaxed next to a young woman whose stiff back and chin pointed high made it clear she was trying to avoid eye contact. "There you are. You scared me to death, Aunt Jayne."

"No need to worry. I looked for our seats and found this lovely young lady instead."

"You don't belong here." The woman looked from Dani to her aunt, emerald eyes flashing. Her regal bearing sagged with a hint of disappointment. She glanced beyond Dani into the emptying foyer.

Aunt Jayne patted her hand. "Don't worry. Your young man will join you. You're too lovely to miss."

Dani examined the woman more closely, wondering why she seemed so familiar. In her job as a reporter, she worked with too many people to count in an average week, but this woman tugged at her memory. "Have we met before?"

"Please leave." With a quick twist of her wrist the woman glanced at her watch.

"Sorry for the interruption. Come on, Aunt Jayne. *Cats* starts any minute." Together they reentered the foyer and slipped up the stairs to the right box. Dani released a deep breath, determined to enjoy every moment of the evening. After the latest trial she'd covered on her crime beat for Channel 17, she'd earned the reprieve. Her aunt deserved her full attention on a night when the cloud of Alzheimer's had slipped away, even fleetingly.

Aunt Jayne sank into her seat and smiled. "Thank you for bringing me, dear. It's so nice to have you in town again."

Dani settled beside her in a maroon seat as the orchestra crescendoed into the opening notes of the musical, prepared to relish each moment. She'd spent the five years since graduation working her way through the ranks of broadcast journalism, moving from Cheyenne to Des Moines to St. Louis. She'd given it all up to move to Lincoln for Aunt Jayne. Her mom believed she'd lost her mind, and her dad tried to convince her to take a job at his station in Chicago each time they talked.

Lincoln had been lonely, especially when Aunt Jayne's bad days outnumbered the good. She'd wanted to dance when she reached Peaceful Estates and found Aunt Jayne alert and excited. A sliver remained of the woman Dani remembered from summers spent in Lincoln. If only she reappeared more often.

The curtain rose, and Dani leaned into the railing. She glanced at the neighboring box, but couldn't see more than outlines in the darkness. The opening song began, and her attention focused completely on the stage covered by a large set that resembled a junkyard. The actors stretched and danced as they mimicked cats and sang. The scenes flew by, and too soon the curtain sank for intermission.

Dani shifted against the seat and straightened. Renee Thomas. That was the woman's name. She'd interviewed the grad student for a story on promising research at the university. Though Renee had been formal and distant tonight, she'd been much friendlier and relaxed during the interview. Odd, since people tended to freeze in that setting. She'd practically glowed as she discussed the research, something about protecting the food supply from terrorist attacks. Dani had worked with her to describe the research in layman's terms.

Aunt Jayne tapped Dani's arm lightly. Dani smiled. "Are you okay? Need a break from sitting?"

"Maybe we should hunt for the story. Surely it's hiding somewhere." Aunt Jayne looked at her, amusement glowing in her eyes.

"There's a loose plot, keep watch." Dani stretched in her seat and her gaze slid into the box to her right. Renee sat motionless. She studied the woman, remembering the edge of worry that marred her expression. Renee had remained alone after all. "Let's stretch our legs a bit."

They stepped into the wide hallway. Dani looked around, hoping tonight wouldn't be the time she ran into the only person she'd allowed to break her heart. Caleb Jamison. The thought of him made her emotions spiral into a tornado of anger and hurt. She looked over her shoulder, afraid he'd appear like some horror-movie ghoul. Wished she could wipe her memory of him.

"Aunt Jayne, let's step up here. I interviewed your new friend last week. Maybe she'd like to join us."

Dani approached the neighboring box. She knocked on the doorframe, parted the curtain and entered the woman's box. A spicy fragrance tinged the air.

"Renee?" Dani waited a moment. The woman never turned. The seconds ticked by. "Are you enjoying the show? Andrew Lloyd Webber is a genius."

Renee remained silent. Dani stepped closer. One part of her mind began to insist she leave. Now.

Dani tapped Renee on the shoulder. Her skin felt cool. With quick steps she circled the seat and stood in front of Renee. Dani looked down, looking for a flash of recognition. Instead, Renee's gaze remained fixed, a horrible grimace pasted to her face. The emerald scarf wound tight around her neck in contrast to the way it floated earlier.

She sucked in a breath and willed herself to remain calm. Between the tightness of the scarf and the bruise lying under the woman's jaw, Dani's instinct jumped to murder. Bile rose in her throat. She put a hand over her mouth and swallowed.

This couldn't be happening again. Images of her college roommate's distorted features floated in front of Renee's. She'd been too late then. She couldn't be now. Dani rushed into the hall, fumbled for the cell phone in her evening bag and dialed 911. No service. She thrust the phone back into her purse. "Somebody call 911. There's a medical emergency. Does anyone know CPR?"

She didn't wait for an answer but ran back into the box. She sensed someone behind her and turned to find Aunt Jayne. She pulled her attention back to Renee, and tried to ease her to the floor, struggling under the leaden weight.

*Please don't let it be too late.*

Concerned faces peered into Dani's from around the curtain. A well-dressed gentleman slipped into the box. He eased Renee the rest of the way to the floor, then loosened the scarf. He checked the woman's neck for a pulse. Dani watched him silently tick the seconds off his watch for an eternal moment. He shook his head and glanced at her. "It's too late."

Dani shuddered. She rose to her feet and took Aunt Jayne by the arm. "Let's get you back to our seats where you can be comfortable." A couple minutes later, Dani stood in the foyer. She took a step toward Renee's box, then turned back to her own. Aunt Jayne seemed fine, but Dani hesitated.

The news director would expect a complete report. She'd found the body, so she'd own the story from this moment. Somehow she'd balance that with caring for Aunt Jayne until she was back in her suite at Peaceful Estates. Interview questions ran through her mind. Someone had to have seen something.

"Ma'am, you have to stay until the police arrive." A tenor voice tickled her ear.

Dani jumped back against the wall. She turned toward the sound. An usher had invaded her space and her gaze met a fishy stare.

"You're a reporter with Channel 17, right?" He slid a half step back and licked his lips. "They...the police, I mean, should be here soon. They'll want to talk to you. You found the body."

She stepped to the side, unable to bear his proximity. "I promise I won't leave before the police arrive."

"Maybe I should clear the box." His gaze darted around the small area.

"It's a little late for that. Quite a few people have moved in and out already."

"Still, there must be something. They never told us what to do in a situation like this." Beads of sweat pooled on his brow as he twisted the top button of his shirt open. Angry uncertainty flashed across his face.

Dani leaned farther into the wall. "Are you okay? I'd be happy to get help."

"I'm fine." With a parting glare and tug at his collar, he turned on his heel and headed down the hall.

Dani watched him disappear, and then turned to the box. A security guard huffed up the stairs. A couple followed him. The man, tall and trim with a long stride, caught her eye. The woman held his arm and managed to keep up without looking rushed. Every brown piece of hair was in place, and her blue cocktail dress perfectly fit her athletic form. The man looked at her. Dani froze. One look in Caleb Jamison's face, and she reverted to the teenager head over heels for the star football player. The teenager who couldn't say no. The teenager who ached when he stopped seeing her. Stopped calling. Stopped caring.

The ice disappeared in a flash of anger. Her hands trembled. Her stomach clenched at the thought of his smug, self-satisfied face. She couldn't go back there. The echo of their baby's cries as she was given to others jarred Dani's mind. Caleb had abandoned her long before the birth. Yet here he was, cocky smile and all. He took a step toward her, and Dani escaped into the box.

*Intrigued? Want to read the rest of Dani's story in* Deadly Exposure? *Then go here for links to your favorite bookstore or online retailer to purchase it.*

# BEYOND JUSTICE EXCERPT

## PROLOGUE

**JANUARY**

If he didn't find that flash drive now, he would have to disappear.

Immediately.

Some place el jefe couldn't find him. It was that or die.

"Where is it, Miguel? What have you done with the information you stole?"

The young man shuddered as he choked on a breath. Blood poured from his nose, broken in the first punch, the horror of it fresh. Blood dribbled out his mouth. Blood dripped off his chin. Still he refused to speak.

Rafael drew back his fist, ready to strike again, then held his arm back as if against a powerful force. This was not who he was. It was not who Miguel was. All of this was so broken. Somehow he had landed on the wrong side of the great family his own had served for three generations.

How was he now opposing the young man he loved like a brother? He scanned the bare room. Four bunk beds lined a wall. A urinal in the corner. A barren sink with a square mirror. A single light bulb hanging well above his head. Where could Miguel have hidden anything in this desolate place?

The stench of urine and sweat, of bodies crammed into a space designed for half as many, mixed with the coppery aroma of fresh blood.

Limp sunlight pushed back the shadows from a barred window high on the wall. Sunlight that reminded him of the times Miguel had tagged along when Rafael did odd chores at the estate. Sunlight that reminded him how wrong it was for Miguel to be here. He was the son of a lord, not someone who should be locked up.

"Where is it, Miguel? I can't ask again." He flipped open the blade of the knife he held and slid it under Miguel's chin. "Give it to me, or I have no choice but to kill you."

Miguel flinched. "We always have a choice." The youth lifted his chin and met Rafael's gaze with pain-filled eyes. "We are brothers, Rafael."

"We were. If you don't give me that flash drive, we are both dead."

"I don't know what you're talking about."

"Liar! El jefe knows you were in his computer. He told me himself. He sent me."

"You kill me, and my father will hunt you like a rabid mongrel." False bravado flashed in Miguel's eyes.

"Your father told me to kill you, amigo."

The spoken words resounded in the narrow space between them. He looked at señor's precious son. His heir. Could he somehow take Miguel with him and disappear? No. Would Miguel give him the list? The boy raised dark eyes to meet his gaze, defiance hardening them. Somehow Rafael had imagined he could avoid killing while serving the family even as he'd crept up its structure. But now he had no choice.

Retrieve the information for el jefe before it falls into the wrong hands or be killed.

Heat flooded him and red clouded his vision.

"I'm sorry, Miguel . . ." He stepped forward, knife clasped in his fist.

~

## CHAPTER ONE

### THURSDAY, MARCH 30

The euphoria of winning a hard case vied in her thoughts with wondering what came next as Hayden McCarthy left the Alexandria courthouse. A colorful dance of tulips lined a flower box of the town house across the street, and the faint aroma of some hidden blossom scented the air. It was over.

Her client had needed her absolute best. Hayden had delivered it and obtained justice. She shifted her purse and readjusted her briefcase as she started down the street. Continue straight on King Street, and in a block she'd be at the office. Turn, and in four blocks she'd be home. Her town house's proximity both to work and the heart of Old Town Alexandria was why she loved the space she shared with a friend from law school.

So . . . which way to go? The thought of going back to her office and confronting the waiting pile of work held no appeal. She would spend one night savoring success . . . and recovering from the adrenaline pace of a roller-coaster trial and jury.

She'd make a salad and cup of tea, maybe pick up a novel. If that didn't hold her attention, she'd dig into her trial notes. Analyze what had worked and how the risk of requesting a new foreman after deliberations had begun had paid off.

Each step closer to home, her conservative navy pumps

tapped the refrain. She. Had. Won. She let a smile spread across her face.

She left King Street and headed north on St. Asaph. Some of the buildings she passed housed businesses, but with each block the area became more residential. In one condo a senator lived. In another a congressman, next to him a chief of staff and other people with powerful political positions. When Hayden first moved to the city from small-town Nebraska, her head had turned at how easy it was to rub elbows with those who controlled destinies. Now it was only scandals or surprise retirements that caught her attention.

The evening was so pleasant she detoured and walked the couple blocks to Christ Church. The wrought iron fence around the church grounds beckoned her to settle in the shade of the stately trees. She opened the gate, then walked until she reached a bench. Settling on it, she breathed deeply and closed her eyes.

*Father, thank You. It went well today.* She pushed against her eyes, daring relieved tears to fall. There was no one else around, and Hayden sat quietly, waiting . . . for something. Here within the shelter of a church more than two hundred years old, shouldn't she feel God's presence?

Yet there was . . . nothing.

Not even a rustle of a breeze through the leaves that she could pretend was the Spirit moving.

*I need You.*

Still nothing. Then slowly she sensed His smile as warmth spread through her.

A couple came around the corner then, strolling along the garden path arm in arm, smiling at one another. They looked at ease and in tune as their strides matched.

What would it feel like to be that comfortable and safe with someone? To know you could trust another person with your most hidden parts? Hayden shook her head. Her life was full to the brim—no room for a relationship. She stood and walked the rest of the way home at a brisk pace.

When she reached her town house, she crossed the courtyard and dug her keys loose from the pit of her purse. The Wonder Woman keyring, a gift from a grateful client after she won what he called the unwinnable case, jiggled as she unlocked the door.

The moment she walked inside, Hayden kicked off her heels and set her bag on the chair next to the glass table by the door. Soft classical music flowed from the kitchen, and the aroma of something spicy filled the small space.

"Emilie?" Hayden leaned down to rub one of her arches, then straightened and moved toward the kitchen.

"Down here." Emilie Wesley's bubbly voice came from the stairway leading to the basement. "Can you check the oven for me?"

"Sure. What are you making?" Hayden moved around the granite countertop and turned on the oven light. Emilie was a wonderful cook, but she often got distracted. "Mmm, lasagna. Looks great. It's bubbling around the edges, and the cheese looks perfect. You expecting company?"

Hayden opened the fridge and pulled out salad ingredients. A salad plus a glass of sweet tea and she could disappear into her room . . .though the pasta looked wonderful. If she was lucky, Emilie would save her some for lunch tomorrow.

Hayden was dicing a red pepper when two sets of footsteps echoed up the stairs.

"Look who stopped by, Hayden."

"Hmm?" Hayden looked up and into clear blue eyes that matched the Potomac as it moved into the bay. His pressed khakis and Oxford with pullover sweater portrayed an understated GQ elegance that screamed old money and matched the clean haircut and polite smile that revealed teeth so perfect they might be caps. Andrew Wesley, her roommate's cousin. She hadn't seen him in years.

The knife slipped, and she felt a sharp pain in her finger. She turned on the tap and stuck her finger beneath the flow of cold water.

"Andrew, do you remember my roommate, Hayden McCarthy? Hayden, this is my cousin Andrew. It's been a while, but I'm pretty sure y'all have met before." Emilie's eyes danced as she tugged the man into the room. His mouth curved into a relaxed grin, the look as familiar and practiced as Hayden's in court.

The years had been good to Andrew Wesley. He'd been handsome when they'd first met, but now he was something more. He had the build of someone who worked out and took care of himself. Compact, muscular, and distractingly good-looking. Hayden pasted a smile into place.

"Hayden?" The deep voice was thick as the richest chocolate. "It's nice to officially meet you—again." He gave her a devastating smile.

"Emilie is always talking about you."

"Good things, I hope." She grabbed a paper towel and turned off the water.

"What else would I say?" Emilie's eyes widened as she saw blood seeping through the paper towel. "Ooh, do you need a Band-Aid?"

"I'll be all right." Hayden took a deep breath and met Andrew's gaze.

"Any friend—or cousin—of Emilie's is welcome here." With her good hand she scooped up the diced pepper and sprinkled it on top of the salad. "I'll leave you two to enjoy your dinner. It looks good, Em."

"You don't need to leave, Hayden." Emilie leaned closer, not hard to do in the galley space that felt even smaller with

Andrew's presence, and handed Hayden a fresh paper towel. "We're working on plans for a spring festival. Think inflatables, fair food, and fun. It's a community event for his non-profit." She grabbed a purple grape from a bowl next to the sink and popped it into her mouth. "You can help us."

His cousin's roommate wrapped the paper towel tighter around her finger, then turned to the refrigerator, shielding her face from his view.

Had they really met before? He had a vague recollection of an awkward girl visiting his cousin during a law school break, but his memory didn't match this attractive woman with the black hair and . . . stocking feet.

As Hayden put away the vegetables she'd used for her salad, Andrew looked for something to break the uncomfortable silence.

"I like the idea of a festival, Em, but I'm not sure we can pull it off."

"Oh? You already have the location." Emilie claimed the pot holders and opened the oven. "We can do this because we're the dynamic duo. Besides, you've got a staff and board of directors to help. We'll create the framework, and they can do the rest."

Andrew shook his head. "You haven't worked much with a board. And don't forget, I'm not the senior guy in the office."

Emilie slid the pan from the oven and set it on top of the stove. "You're a Wesley. Everyone takes one look at you and snaps to attention. Your dad is too powerful to tick off." She softened the words with a smile. "You might as well embrace it."

That was something that hadn't happened yet in his thirty years. Being Scott Wesley's son was like wearing a coat made for someone else.

He leaned against the counter and redirected the conversation—a skill he'd picked up from his father. "I've heard about Emilie's day, Hayden. Tell me about yours."

Hayden paused, salad dressing in hand. "I won a case today."

"Oh?" He studied her face, but she didn't give anything away. Not much of a talker?

She shrugged. "I kept an innocent man out of jail. So it was a great day for my client and his wife."

"For you too." Emilie stepped next to Hayden and squeezed her shoulder. "This woman worked a lot of late nights on that case and is on the fast track to becoming a partner." Hayden started to protest, but Emilie kept on. "She'll never brag about herself, but she's good. Nobody will be surprised when she becomes the youngest partner in Elliott & Johnson history."

Soft color tinted the woman's cheeks, and she glanced at Andrew. "I'm not any better than a hundred other attorneys in town."

Only a hundred, huh? In a city overwhelmed with attorneys, she'd ranked herself fairly high. Well, the last thing he wanted to do was spend free time with an attorney. He'd spent too much time in their presence growing up to be wowed by their brilliance or awed by their stories.

She held up her salad bowl and fork. "I know y'all have plans to make, so I'll slip upstairs and not interrupt. It was nice to see you again, Andrew."

Andrew put a hand on her arm before she could disappear. "You really want to walk away from Emilie's lasagna for that?" He crinkled his nose and pointed at the bowl of greens.

Emilie grabbed an extra plate. "There's plenty, Hayden."

Andrew grinned. "Always is. She forgets there's only two of us."

He said it as though these evenings were frequent, but they weren't.

Emilie was as busy as anyone in town, so he'd pounced on her invitation. When they all sat down at the island a few minutes later, he watched Hayden. She looked tired. A good trial would do that, his dad always said. He and Emilie kept a quiet conversation going, with Hayden interjecting now and then.

She'd made it through law school, and he admired anyone who did that. He'd quit after a semester—but that had more to do with wanting to become his own man rather than an ever-lengthening part of his father's shadow.

A phone beeped, and Hayden glanced at hers and frowned. "Sorry, but I need to prepare for a meeting in the morning. Nice to see you, Andrew." She stood and brushed past him with a small smile.

He watched her cross the living space and head toward the stairs. As she climbed from view he reminded himself that he didn't have time to feel attracted to anyone right now. Not when Congressman Wesley was gunning for a title change. Anyone he was seen with would end up plastered across the social pages of the Post the next day. Who would willingly sign up for that?

He turned back to the kitchen and found Emilie smirking at him.

"I'm not sure you're her type, Andrew." Her smile widened until her dimples showed.

He made a face at her. "Don't think I don't see right through you. I know why you had me meet you here." He was just surprised it had taken this long. "It doesn't matter. I'm too busy to get involved right now."

*Intrigued? Want to read the rest of Hayden's story in* Beyond Justice? *Then go here to find links to your favorite bookstore or online retailer to purchase it.*

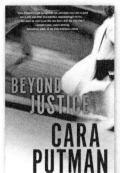
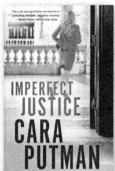

# DISCUSSION QUESTIONS

1. To help her family, Alanna Stone goes back to a place she swore she'd leave behind. Have you ever done something like that?

2. Family plays a pivotal role in this book. In what way do you agree with how Alanna prioritizes her family? Or do you disagree with how she handles them? Why?

3. Everybody has secrets, but when Alanna uncovers some of her family's secrets, she's not sure how to react. Have you ever faced a similar situation? How did you handle it?

4. The truth can set us free, but the process of finding it can be scary. Have you ever had to take a risk to find the truth? What helped you in the process?

5. If the truth is supposed to set us free, why do you think God makes the truth so challenging to identify sometimes?

6. How has God brought truth into your life? Was the process easy, or was it more like a painstaking journey?

7. Jonathan Covington has waited a long time for the woman of his dreams. Then suddenly he has to choose between two. Does he make the right choice? Why or why not?

8. Have you ever had a relationship that is clouded by events in the past like Alanna's and Jonathan's? If so, did you stay in the past, or were you able to break free? What advice would you give to people like Alanna and Jonathan?

9. Alanna returns to Mackinac Island after years away. What changes does she find? Have you ever made a similar journey? Was it easy to spot changes in others?

10. What advice would you have for Alanna or someone in a similar position of walking away from the comfort of their routines and launching into a new adventure?

# ABOUT THE AUTHOR

Cara C. Putman lives in Indiana with her husband and four children. When she's not writing, Cara lectures at a Big Ten University in law and communications. She has loved reading and writing from a young age and now realizes it was all training for writing books. An honors graduate of the University of Nebraska, George Mason University School of Law, and Krannert School of Management at Purdue, Cara loves bringing stories to life. Learn more about Cara and her writing at cara-putman.com.

# ALSO BY CARA PUTMAN

WWII Historical Romances

Canteen Dreams

Captive Dreams

A Promise Forged

A Promise Born

A Promise Kept

Cornhusker Dreams

Buckeye Promises

WWII Romantic Mysteries

Shadowed by Grace

Stars in the Night

Legal Thrillers

Beyond Justice

Imperfect Justice

Delayed Justice

Flight Risk

Lethal Intent

Romantic Suspense

Deadly Secrets on Mackinac Island

Dying for Love, novella prequel to *Beyond Justice*

Hidden Love, novella

Deadly Exposure, book 1 in Hometown Heroes